THE
NEVER
TILTING WORLD

RIN CHUPECO

☾

THE
NEVER
TILTING
WORLD

☀

HARPER TEEN

An Imprint of HarperCollinsPublishers

HarperTeen is an imprint of HarperCollins Publishers.

The Never Tilting World
Copyright © 2019 by HarperCollins Publishers
www.epicreads.com

Library of Congress Cataloging-in-Publication Data

Names: Chupeco, Rin, author.
Title: The never tilting world / Rin Chupeco.
Description: First edition. | New York, NY : HarperTeen, [2019] | Series: Never
tilting world ; 1 | Summary: "After an ancient prophecy is betrayed, a world ruled
by a long line of goddesses is split in two—one half in perpetual day, and the other
in an endless night—and two young twin goddesses set out on separate and equally
dangerous journeys to the Breach that divides them, hoping to save their broken
world"— Provided by publisher.
Identifiers: LCCN 2019021103 | ISBN 978-0-06-282179-9
(hardback)
Subjects: | CYAC: Goddesses—Fiction. | Twins—Fiction. |
Sisters—Fiction. | Prophecies—Fiction. | Voyages and
travels—Fiction. | Fantasy.
Classification: LCC PZ7.C4594 Nev 2019 | DDC [Fic]—dc23
LC record available at https://lccn.loc.gov/2019021103

Typography by Molly Fehr
Map illustration by Virginia Allyn
19 20 21 22 23 PC/LSCH 10 9 8 7 6 5 4 3 2 1

First Edition

For all the best doggos who drag their leashes over to my part of the sidewalk, because I give the best pats. Good doggos.

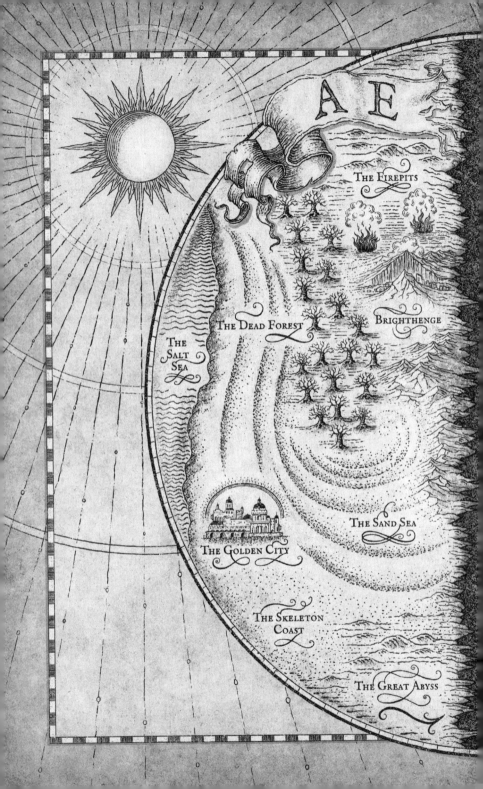

A demoness

Is what men call

A goddess they cannot control

—fragment of Inanna's Song

Chapter One

TIANLAN OF THE CATSEYE

— ☾ —

IT WAS CLEARLY HIS FAULT I'd punched him in the face.

It was still the man's fault when I did it again, and when I did it a third time, and when I did it the next twenty-one times. I lost count after that—his fault too, because I'm the kind of woman who keeps score.

It was his fault I'd kicked in his ribs, heard that satisfying crack the instant my steel-toed boot hit vulnerable flesh. It was his fault I'd broken his fingers when he wouldn't drop the knife. His fault I'm painting the sides of the broken street with his filth.

Strangers passed us, looked away. People minded their own business in Aranth; ignorance was a strength here, inattention a survival trait. The passersby were smarter than my current victim. Their eyes took stock of the heavy robe I wore, the blacker-than-black piping lining the edges of my cowl. If not that, the enormous blade strapped to my back would have at least suggested to the average intelligence what my job required.

It was one thing to intervene while a man was being beaten, but it was another thing entirely to intervene in Catseye business.

Especially with a Catseye who'd just been stood up by her date.

I flexed my fingers, hauled the man up by his collar. His face was an abstract mess of blood. It reminded me of those Lichtbachter paintings squirreled away in rich old Vanlersmit's attic, where he thought no one would find them: people with faces dribbling down canvases like liquid, drawn ugly, surrounded by objects painted square when they ought to be round, by cats with beaks and fish with legs in putrid patches of color. Never understood how those hideous things sold quickly and for large amounts of cash, even after the Breaking—not that I was complaining. I wished I could package his face up and sell it like I had those old Lichtbachters, because then my day wouldn't have gone to waste.

Or rather, night. No such thing as day anymore. Not in Aranth.

"Had enough?"

A low groan was my answer.

"Was it worth it?" I waved the book in front of his face. It was a first-edition volume of classic mythology dating back to the Golden Age, mint condition. Or it *was* mint condition when I bought it, before this carrion feeder tried to knife me during the brief lull between storms.

He opened his eyes. I could see at first glance that he was one of those rare Acidsmiths, although an inept one; the patterns of Water around him were nearly nonexistent, and the fire-gates in his eyes were faint—the thin rings of color around his irises were redder than what his apparent alcoholism allowed for, but not enough to show he could use his skill. Most people were born with the capacity to see patterns and manifest gates, albeit at varying strengths, but fire-gate users were never strong enough in Aranth to do much of anything; that, plus his lack of sobriety, meant he could barely spit dirty water in my direction. He was certainly inept enough that he'd chosen a knife as his weapon of choice instead of channeling poison.

Neither would have worked on me.

His gaze fell on mine and widened in horror. My eyes glowed like shining glass despite the heavy gloom, one as golden as an idol and the other a pale silver. "B-bright Lady," he stuttered.

I grinned. "Not a lady," I said, and let the aether-gates within my eyes flare.

He recoiled, whimpering at the back of his throat. I knew what he was seeing, what he was thinking. I could siphon off his life, reduced him to nothing more than a skeleton and sagging flesh. I could introduce festers and sores on his body, accelerate them so that his last few days would be spent in untold agony. Assaulting a Catseye, even unsuccessfully, was punishable by death, the sanction to be carried out at our discretion.

Instead, I healed him. I felt the bones under his skin knit quickly, the muscles firming. There was a click as his rib cage re-formed and the joints in his fingers reattached. The painful gashes on his face and arms thinned out and closed at my touch. Aether patterns seeped into his insides, finding the familiar contours of spleen, heart, and the last stages of liver decay. Corrosion at that stage required at least a good month to treat, but I scoured and cleaned the wreckage as best I could. Then I washed away his insobriety, but not the hangover he'd be suffering tomorrow, because where's the fun in that?

"Take some milk thistle for the next three weeks when you can find it, and for the Good Mother's sake, find other means than ale to drown your sorrows." I let him go.

He scampered away on his hands and knees without another look back, until the night swallowed him up.

I had little faith that he would take my advice, but I could hope my tough love had ensured that he would at *least* think twice next time. Because there was no doubt there would *be* a next time, and the Good Mother help him if another Catseye— or Starmaker Gracea, if he was that unlucky—became his target. People tend to hold fast to their baser natures. These days, they were the only things they had left.

I examined my book and sighed. There was a long gash across the leather cover, slicing through the first few pages. I'd paid thirty crowns for this and three other books—penny romances I wouldn't have been caught dead with, had Ame not enjoyed them.

"She never even showed up, you idiot," I grumbled aloud, still raw from the rejection, and tucked a lock of hair behind

4

my ear, careful not to remove the colored-feather pin Mistress Daliah had given me. The fight hadn't even dislodged it.

I resumed my trek toward the tower. Somewhere in the city, bells began to toll, signaling the final Hour of Waking. I cursed the lateness; the goddess's daughter would be fast asleep by now, if she and her mother weren't still waiting up. Not a good impression for what was my first night on the job.

Above me, houses huddled together, little sign of life within save for occasional sparks of light; glowing Air-and-Fire-patterned rushlights for those who could afford the luxury, and tiny stubs of candlelight for the less fortunate. The majority of the population were either Stormbringers, Windshifters, or Icewrights—redundant talents when you live in a storm-swept city surrounded by ever-expanding ice. Water was abundant, but food was scarce, limited to what we could catch in the seas and what little vegetation could thrive in the absence of sun.

I quickened my pace, aiming to reach the Spire before the next storm broke in—I scanned the sky—twenty minutes, as swift as the furies and as predictable as clockwork.

When I passed through the gates that separated the Spire from the rest of the city, I was met at the entrance by a couple of Icewrights, encased in the heavy Water-patterned armor they were expected to maintain until their shifts were over. I had argued against such idiocy; they would be weak and depleted by the end of their rounds, ripe for attack. Starmaker Gracea, however, had remained adamant—it would do good for morale, she insisted, and it would be an excellent exercise in endurance.

But Starmaker Gracea wasn't in the tower tonight. "Stand down," I ordered the guards, to their obvious relief.

The bright blue rings in their eyes faded as their water-gates closed, and their sleet-enchanted armor disappeared to reveal simple chain mail. "Thank you, Bright Lady," one voiced his gratitude, taking in a deep breath of cold wind.

Not a lady, I kept myself from saying, and grunted instead. "Stay alert." I reached out to grasp them both by the arms. Patterns of aether swirled, and I focused my gate on their minor aches, cleansing them of both exhaustion and cold. "The Banishing takes place tomorrow, and nothing must be allowed to disturb the goddesses' rest."

"Understood, Catseye Tianlan." One of the men looked uncertain. "But Lady Gracea won't be happy about this."

"Lady Gracea manages the Spire for Her Holiness, but *I'll* be guarding the goddesses from now on. Tell the Starmaker she is free to take the matter up with me at her next visit." I knew Gracea wouldn't like it, but had I a habit of admitting truths to myself, I would say the opportunity to tweak her nose was partly why I did it. Instructions given, I began my climb up the spiraling tower just as the rains began.

From my vantage point, I had a good view of the chaotic sea that the city overlooked. Wind-tossed waves the size of small ships fought one another for supremacy, while lightning flashed somewhere in the distance, accompanied by the rolling of thunder. The seas were wine-dark, the color of bitter dregs lingering at the bottom of a tavern keg. They surrounded Aranth on three of its four sides, whipping higher with every passing month. Had we settled farther east, nearer to the Great Abyss, the city would be vulnerable to the strange unearthly creatures corrupted by the breach; farther west, and no one would have survived the freezing temperatures. There was no escape from the endless cycle of night.

Directly below us were the man-made ice floes surrounding the city; waves frozen in motion, a glacial ice wall that stopped seawater from flooding in. The constant tsunamis crashed uselessly against these walls, kept successfully at bay. But already I could see faint cracks in the glittering ice as water trickled through.

Winter had traveled closer this year than it had the previous one; I could make out the glittering caps of ice on the horizon, creeping toward the city. *The goddesses will have a harder time of it tomorrow, completing the Banishing.* Past the ice was a mantle of impenetrable darkness that leached away all illumination, held at bay—barely—by the city's meager lights. Nobody knew what lay in wait beyond it, and nobody wanted to find out.

For a brief moment, in the spaces between the howling wind and the unending downpour, I thought I saw a shadow rise. It was a deeper color than even the darkest of Aranth's nights, and taller than even the Spire.

No. No no no no no no . . .

I drew my sword and pointed its tip at the darkness, unable to steady it. I was shaking.

It was *here*.

I stood rooted to the spot, petrified, *remembering*. The screaming. The dying. Catseye Madi, ripped apart by clawed beings that crept out from the bowels of the world, summoned by that terrible shadow. Stormbringer Cecily, drowning in a pool of her own blood. And Nuala. Good Mother, *Nuala*. My team, lost in that swirl of death and darkness.

How could something so massive get past the perimeter, past the guards—

Choose your sacrifice, Catseye.

No!

I blinked again, and it was gone.

Not real. It's not real, Lan. Just like the other dozen times you've imagined this. Stop thinking. Stop thinking about—

Nuala's screaming face, her terrified gaze locked onto mine as misshapen hands snatched her away—

Stop thinking about it! My skin broke out in a cold sweat, and my hands shook. *Stop thinking, Lan!*

Catseye Sumiko had done her best to stopper my recollections of that ill-fated excursion into the wildlands, but the mind was trickier to cure than the body, and they bubbled back up to the surface at unexpected times.

She wanted me to talk about it. Dedicated sessions would help me come to terms with my trauma, my shock—my guilt. Everything I'd managed to suppress since returning.

I refused.

I was better off forgetting.

My sanity demanded it.

We were the first team to enter those wildlands, tasked with finding the Abyss.

I wanted us to be the last.

Asteria had reassigned me to guard duty soon after. Which brought me here to the Spire.

You're alive, aren't you? Be grateful and keep moving. You can't stay weak when you're supposed to be protecting them.

I meditated briefly, focusing on the sea before me. I imagined myself rolling with the waves until I felt myself relaxing, until I remembered not to worry about the things beyond my control. I inhaled and exhaled noisily until the anxiety passed, until my legs started working again and my breathing didn't sound like a panic attack. *All good,* I thought, feeling my heartbeat return to its normal pace. I sheathed my sword, ignoring my clammy palms. *All good.*

All good.

The inside of the tower was spacious, warmer than it looked on the outside, and by then I had left most of my panic at the door. Noelle was waiting for me with a mug of tea in one hand and a dry towel in the other, because Noe was better at her job than I ever was at mine.

"Are they still up?" I peeled off my cowl and discarded my cloak, pretending everything was fine, like I hadn't been hallucinating monsters on the way here. Noe took them, hung the dripping garments where they wouldn't cause a mess. I rubbed my hands and breathed noisily against them, willing heat back into my chilled fingers.

"I'm afraid so." There was a note of disapproval in her voice.

I sighed. "Not my fault I'm late. Someone tried to skewer me near Wisham's."

"Most imprudent timing, milady. Her Serene Highness will not be pleased."

"It isn't *my* fault someone wanted to knife me."

"Two weeks ago, you said Lord Selk was too dirty to even be spat on, and he—"

"It isn't my fault someone wanted to knife me *this time*. And have you *smelled* Selk? Water drowning us on all sides and he can't spare a bath before meeting his liege? Why do you always think everything's my fault?"

"Stabbings have never slowed you down before."

"You're a cruel woman, Noe. No consideration at all for my well-being." I accepted the tea and gulped it down noisily, warmth blooming down my insides.

"As you say, milady. Shall I let Her Holiness know you've arrived?"

"I've kept them waiting long enough. And stop calling me milady. You don't call me that on your days off."

"This is not my day off, milady."

I had to grin at that. "I missed you too, Noe. It's been a while."

"Three months, to be more precise." Noelle's expression was deadpan as always, but the warmth in her tone told me everything else. "Try not to stay away for too long next time, milady."

I winced. "They're not mad I'm late, are they?" Asteria

wasn't draconian about punctuality, but she's not the type of person you want to keep waiting. And Blessed Mother, I hadn't even *met* the daughter yet. Not exactly the best start to a relationship.

"I'm sure you'll find a good explanation for them. You'd best be going, milady." Noelle was the tower's redheaded steward, a no-nonsense woman with clear blue eyes unringed by gates, making her rise all the more extraordinary. She occasionally condescended to have a drink with me in one of the chintzy tea shops that passed for culture in the city; Noelle's mother had once been a genteel woman of sorts, a lady attendant to some powerful noblewoman back when the world still sanely spun, and the teahouses reminded us of better days.

Noelle's job was to be a glorified domestic, which I found hilarious at first because she was fond of spiders. But we'd fought off gangs and run cons back when we were street rats without a future, and I knew she would have no qualms about doing some stabbing herself if needed—would probably know the appropriate dinner knife to use, too.

"Thanks for the vote of confidence," I said with a groan, but took her advice. Toweling vigorously at my face, I proceeded up another flight of stairs. There was little I could do to stop looking a mess, but I combed fingers through my hair anyway, tried to wipe off as much rain and grime as I could. You're not supposed to keep Aranth's most important people waiting past the final Hour of Waking, and I'd already taken far too long with the drunkard and the books.

Asteria waited for me at the next landing, and she was beautiful. If real daylight ever found its way into Aranth, the kind that was as golden as butter and warm like a mother, and wrapped itself up all graceful and purposeful like a woman, it might resemble the goddess.

"I was beginning to wonder if you'd changed your mind," she said in a voice as soft as sympathy, her color-shifting hair floating around her despite the absence of wind. I watched as the strands changed from a soft purple to honey orange to star-yellow.

"Changed it right back." This wasn't a demotion, she had said. Protecting her daughter was just as important as patrolling Aranth's borders, if not even more so. I needed rest, was all. And Asteria was right—I'd been away from the city for far too long. "My apologies. It won't happen again."

The goddess studied me carefully, and I forced back a twinge of anger. I hadn't traveled all the way here, relinquishing both my position and what bits of my pride had survived with me, for misplaced commiseration. I hadn't ended the day dumped by a pretty girl and nearly shanked by a drunken prick, only to endure her pity.

"Attend to Odessa first," she finally said. "For now, you are to officially take up lodgings at the Spire. We can talk more later."

"As you wish, Your Holiness." Odessa, the mysterious child of the Spire. I knew Asteria's daughter had a strange disease, one that none of the other Catseyes could heal. I was told she'd never left the tower her whole life, that the only time the other Devoted saw her was during the Banishing. Even then, I heard, she kept her distance, like her illness was contagious.

"Odessa is a sweet, compassionate girl. She's enthusiastic about books, and she'll likely talk your ear off over those. I hope you're well-read."

"I've opened books a time or two in my life."

It sounded just this shade of impertinent, but Asteria laughed. "I think you'll get along." She moved down the hallway, stopping before the closest of two doors. "Odessa," she called, knocking lightly on the wood. "Tianlan, your new Catseye, is here."

The hinges creaked, and a girl stormed out. "I don't need another guardian, Mother. Catseye Lenida was dull as dirt, and nothing she did ever cured my—" She stopped abruptly and gaped at me.

I gaped back.

Her name was Ame. She had gorgeous gray eyes and a gently rounded face, but it was her hair, coal black and wind-wild, that had drawn me in that first time. It hung down her waist, curled and loose against some unseen breeze. From behind a pile of books she had glanced up at me, her smile curious and sweet, and I was lost.

Later, I'd gone to sleep without nightmares for the first time since returning to the city.

The tiny bookshop was right beside the orphanage, and she was often there, browsing, when I visited the latter. I had come to look forward to those weekly trips, to watch her eyes light up as she chattered on about history, or romance novels, or any other book that struck her fancy. It took weeks to work up the courage to ask her out; weeks to believe, day by passing day, that a sabbatical from ranging wasn't so bad after all.

She tasted sweet; a soft, eager mouth beneath mine, her arms laced around my neck as I tipped her nearly into the bookcase, as greedy as I always was.

But she'd never shown up for dinner earlier tonight.

And why should she? Her name wasn't Ame; her name was Odessa, and her hair was an infuriating mess of colors like her mother's instead of the lovely midnight black I knew, and apparently she'd never even been out of the damned tower, so the girl at the bookstore must have been my goddess-damned *imagination* this whole time.

I'd propositioned the goddess's daughter.

I'd propositioned the goddess's *daughter*.

Ame—no, *Odessa*—was turning pale.

"I have some matters to finish," Asteria continued serenely, unaware of the tension. "Tianlan, see me in my study later. Odessa, please don't give your new Catseye any more headaches like you gave the last one."

Her daughter nodded wordlessly. Asteria left, and I followed Ame—no, Odessa—to her room, where she sat down hard on the bed and stared at her feet.

"So," I said after a while, really, *really* wanting to break the silence with something spiteful, but also all too aware that she was my liege. I didn't want to be fired on my first day. "This was why you stood me up."

"I didn't mean to," she whispered; still not looking up, face a fiery red. "You said your name was Lan."

"It's short for Tianlan. Never liked how formal it sounded." And because I couldn't completely bottle up my anger, I added, "Unlike you, I was being completely truthful."

"I"—she twiddled her thumbs—"I'm not"—she looked out the window—"I really wasn't planning on"—her gaze drifted everywhere but at me. "I'm sorry. I thought I could sneak out, but—"

"You thought you could sneak out?" It was difficult to keep the disbelief out of my voice, and the sense of betrayal. "The point is you weren't who I thought you were." Everything she had told me was a lie. She wasn't the shy daughter of a strict fruit seller, she was Asteria's daughter and a *goddess* in her own right. "Was that the only reason you never showed up, *Ame*?"

She looked away, and my throat closed up.

"I guess that's my answer, then."

A low, hurt sound escaped her, and it killed me that even after all her falsehoods, she could still get to me. It no longer mattered what her reasons were. The dynamics of our situation had altered the instant she became my charge.

"It's fine," I said roughly, though it felt anything but. "You don't have to explain yourself to me. I'm just the new Catseye, here to see to your health. I don't know how you used to sneak out of the Spire, but that ends on my watch. Understand?"

She nodded meekly. "But I want to explain why I—" She broke off abruptly, caught up in a fit of coughing.

I was by her side immediately. Whatever we were before, whether or not she'd lied to me, I should have taken her condition into account.

"Lie on the bed."

Aether-gate healing is a magic made of sensations rather than sight. I could pinpoint wounds and illnesses based on an innate sixth sense that not even I could fully explain. Just as with the drunkard, the patterns of Aether gathered in areas where she required healing, guiding my actions accordingly.

There was nothing visibly wrong with her. She was at the peak of health, more so than the other denizens of Aranth below us. And yet the shadows gathered at a spot above her heart, pulsing with some unknown ichor. There was no reason for her to be coughing, no reason for her to be tired or even exhausted. Nothing within her explained these symptoms.

Asteria had said that her illness drained Ame's—*Odessa's*—strength daily, no matter how long she rested. And despite my attempts, I couldn't purge it completely from her body. If it was left untreated, I knew it would eventually consume her whole.

It frustrated me that I was helpless here. I was supposed to be the best; the one the patterns favored the most, the one with the brightest, most powerful aether-gate. In my arrogance, I assumed I'd be different from the rest of her healers.

I shrank the shadow until it was no more than the size of a pea, but I couldn't eradicate that final spot. And I knew that the next night would find it grown again, nearly as large.

"How long have you had this?"

"All my life. Mother and the Devoted try to keep it a secret. Wouldn't be good for morale."

"I'll heal you," I said, before I could stop myself. It didn't condone her lies, but I understood now why she might have wanted to pretend. "I swear it. I'll find a way."

Her face brightened as she looked up at me, her beautiful hair swirling into hues of pink and lavender, and I was momentarily struck dumb all over again. But then her smile faded. "Thank you," she mumbled. "Are you—are you going to tell Mother?"

I sighed. "No. Not if you don't want me to."

"I—" Her hands pressed down against her sternum, and she took a long, shuddering breath. "Okay."

"Get some rest. I'll be right next door. If there's anything you require, don't hesitate to call for me, even if it's in the middle of the night."

"Okay." She rolled to her side, facing away.

I hated sounding so formal, so aloof. I used to talk about everything with Ame. In the several weeks I'd known her, I'd told her bits about my work as a ranger, even touching lightly on the reasons for my enforced leave. The smatterings of education Asteria had forced on me actually stuck, and I remembered enough to discuss classics like de la Croix's *Histories of the Known World* or Merchaud's *Letters of a Devoted* with her—there was no awkwardness between us then.

"I got something for you."

She looked back at me, and her eyes lit up when she saw the

books I held out to her. Her fingers ran through the first two covers, then halted at the third. "It's a first-edition print of the *Creation Divine*," she breathed, looking like I'd just spun straw into gold.

"You mentioned you'd never read it. Old Wallof found a copy. I badgered him not to tell you until I could buy it from him." Ancient legends of past goddesses—the irony was not knowing she was one when I'd bought it. "Nothing about your mother, but it's got a few illustrations. Some look a bit like you—"

That wasn't entirely accurate. The book had poorly drawn pictures of drab women staring mournfully out at me with bulging eyes, bull noses, and perplexed expressions. There wasn't much information either, save the usual vague yarn about generations of twin goddesses protecting the world since time immemorial. Everyone knew that.

But that was before the Breaking. Before Asteria's twin tried to kill her, and her daughter. Before Asteria's twin had killed *Odessa's* own twin.

The only features the women in these illustrations had in common with Ame—*Odessa*—was their long multitoned hair, which ended in a flame-like trail behind them. They couldn't capture vividness and beauty like that in books. We didn't have color in Aranth the way Odessa wore colors in her hair.

She'd spotted the tear in the leather, her eyes widening. "What happened?"

"Just a small mishap, Your Holiness."

She flinched from that. "I—don't call me 'Your Holiness.'"

"It wouldn't be proper, *Your Holiness*." I knew I was a hypocrite, but a line had to be drawn before I could be tempted to step over it. "Good night. I'll see you in the morning."

When I left the room, she was still staring after me, her arms wrapped tightly around the book and a look of pure misery on her face. The desire to step back in and comfort her was overwhelming.

I pushed the ache aside. She was unreachable now. It didn't matter how I felt about it.

Asteria looked up as I entered her study, pausing in the act of brushing her own long, impossibly colored hair. I placed my sword on her table, still in its sheath. "Is Odessa asleep?" she asked. "I noticed you brought a history book for her."

"The *Creation Divine*—a first edition."

"I remember reading that. I was quite young then," she sighed, though did not explain further. The past was a painful subject, I knew, a place she was reluctant to visit. She set the brush down. "How did you know what books she'd like?"

"Research," I said shortly, not eager to elaborate and betray myself.

"Not stolen, I would hope?"

"Of course not." I'm not a woman of many principles, but I learned early on in life that you don't need logical reasons for wanting to do things. And I wasn't going to insult Ame— *Odessa*, my mind snarled—by giving her stolen presents.

"Lan, you tried to pick my pocket at our first meeting. You

had no idea I was the goddess of the very city you lived in. You've gotten better at following the law over the years, but old habits die hard."

"I've been behaving."

"You palmed one of the Windshifters' brooches last week." Nothing gets past Asteria. "Filia can afford the loss."

"What did you do with the money?"

I shifted uneasily. "I don't see why that's important."

"You lived in Mistress Daliah's orphanage for a time, did you not? I pay you enough coin to live comfortably on, and any vices of yours—those I know of, at least—require little extravagance. You come here with a book and a feather behind your ear. Mistress Daliah was ever fond of giving away those feather pins."

I gave in. "I bought the book with my own money. As for the rest . . . Filia's a vain little hen. Losing brooches will only improve her character. She is constantly misplacing her trinkets and blaming the servants for it. So I said I'd start taking her jewelry so she wouldn't have anything to accuse them of stealing." She dared me to. I could never resist a challenge. "Besides, the orphans could stand to have a few more supplies this month."

She actually laughed. "I can't say I disapprove."

"You've been giving the Devoted freer rein than usual. I had to try and balance it out in other ways, Your Holiness."

"I want to know how far they'll push when they think I'm not watching. Perhaps I should favor the Catseyes tomorrow instead of the Starmaker."

"Rather you didn't." I'd never really liked being part of the Devoted and rarely interacted with the others. I was always more at ease with my fellow rangers—

No. Don't think about that *now*.

"I know you hate politics, but that's how the game is played. Pitting them against each other means they'll be too busy to plot against me."

"They wouldn't dare." How could anyone think to go against the goddess who was literally keeping their city afloat?

"You'd be surprised." She unsheathed the sword and touched the blade, running a finger lightly along the edge. The metal glowed; something about a goddess's touch helped fight off most of the creatures that plagued the area; all weapons in the Devoted's arsenal had been blessed in this manner. Asteria's voice grew softer, sadder. "What is your diagnosis?"

I kept my voice level. "I'll need more time. . . ."

"I cannot lose her, Lan." A new note entered her voice; anger, determination, more than a trace of arrogance. Some people still spoke in hushed whispers about how she had broken the world to save it from her mad twin. So many had died that few were old enough to remember the Breaking, and they spoke of Asteria's terrible majesty. The Asteria I served now was gentler, soft-spoken and quiet, but behind that kind exterior lay a mind of steel.

I knew about her previous Devoted. I knew none of them save Gracea had survived the Breaking. I knew she'd fled here to protect what was left of her people and had founded Aranth.

Her desire to see everyone safe was something I'd always admired in Asteria. I respected and trusted her—but sometimes, even I wondered if those old stories about her were true.

"We're the only ones of our kind left. In time, she will marry and have children of her own. It would break my heart to see them afflicted with her sickness."

The thought broke my heart too, but in a different way. Of course she'd marry someone. Aranth would need more goddesses. "I'll figure it out."

"I'll save her even if I have to break the seas open again—" She broke off with a loud gasp, rising to her feet.

"Your Holiness?" I grabbed her arm—

The pain hit me on all sides. The tower, the room, Asteria— they all disappeared, and in their place I found myself staring up at *a great emptiness, rising from the bowels of an endless abyss. It was nothing I could describe, because that's what it was—a great and abhorrent nothing; a loathsome void.*

I saw Aranth ravaged by floods and ice, the storms sweeping mercilessly through until the screaming had tapered off and there was only silence. A large wave loomed, and the city disappeared underneath its swell.

The shapeless thing lifted its maw toward the heavens and screeched. And then it turned its eyeless gaze on something beyond mine.

My child, it whispered.

The vision faded. The goddess had sunk back down into her seat, and I was sprawled on the floor.

"What was that?" I croaked. I knew that Asteria had visions sometimes—of the future or of an immediate present, I was never sure—but I'd never had the opportunity to use my Cats-eye abilities to gain access to what she saw. It wasn't something I was willing to ever do again.

"I saw a creature," she whispered, no longer calm, but harsh as the storms waging war outside, "made from hollowed stars, rising from the breach. It is coming this way. It is searching for me, and it is searching for Odessa."

Chapter Two

ARJUN, SON OF CLAN ORYX

———————— ☼ ————————

THE ROYAL SUN GODDESS, Heiress to the Realms of Light, Blessed of the Sun, Second of the Blood, and enemy of my people, was a blithering idiot.

She sat atop the beast's cadaver and wept, paying no attention to my approach. The Salt Sea had receded again, the third time in the last month alone, leaving nothing but acrid black sand, several more miles of useless territory on the Skeleton Coast—ironic, because this hadn't been a coast in decades—and this gruesome offering in its wake. The corpse was easily two hundred tons and a hundred feet long and had perished long before the waters gave it up to dry land.

Her hands pressed down against the heavy spines along the creature's back, and I saw patterns of Light gathering around the goddess, sparking and hissing like she was a flint from which life could spring forth. She pushed, and the ridges underneath her rippled in response to her frantic movements. But for all her efforts, the beast remained inert, and silent, and dead.

She was alone. You'd expect an armed escort with someone of her importance, so my assumption of idiocy obviously held. I wore armor forged by Stonebreaker craftsmen, a necessity to survive the heat out in the desert and the near-lethal rays of the sun, but she wore none that I could see.

An idiot, even for a goddess. When the fires flickered low and the silence in the caves went on for too long, the elders would tell us how the Sun Goddess Latona had ripped the sky in two and feasted on her twin sister's heart, dooming us to a lifetime of wasteland because she could not stop craving the light. That *this* goddess, Latona's daughter, was just as cruel. We were born hating them. We had every reason to.

I would never have this chance again. This was my opportunity to kill one of the women responsible for sending the world to shit.

This was justice. That was all. But I wavered, lowering the Howler, and with my hesitation the chance for a preemptive strike was lost.

"It's an aspidochelone," she sniffled without quite looking at me, still pushing down.

"A what?"

"An *aspidochelone*. It's a great whale, one of the largest known. People used to mistake them for islands. They'd land with their ships and take refuge on the creatures' backs, only to realize too late they were standing on living animals."

From behind the beast's torpedolike head, she paused in her attempts at resuscitation to glance down at me. Only the Sun Goddesses had multicolored hair; hers was cut a few inches above the shoulders, and it floated around her head like it had a mind of its own. But her eyes were magnificent, and I drew in a sharp, quick breath at the sight: the sunlight glittered against bright, pale irises shining with tears.

Mother Salla had told us about the Sun Goddesses' atrocities, but she'd never mentioned this.

"It's dead," I said, not sure what else I was supposed to say.

You're a moron too, Arjun. You really think you can take on a goddess alone when armies couldn't? If she were anything like her mother, you'd be a smoking pile of ashes by now.

But she isn't her mother, is she?

"I have a theory," she said softly. "I've looked through the old histories. I've learned the names of creatures long dead, researched places that didn't survive the Breaking. It wasn't the healthiest pastime, Mother used to say. There was no point in mourning what couldn't be brought back. But one of my ancestors, a goddess named Nyx, did the impossible and resurrected a dead bird. She wrote her process down. We must channel all the gates at once, she said, for the Gate of Life to open. I don't really know what that means—to channel them all at once is impossible. But I thought . . . if she could do it, then maybe *I* could. . . ."

I didn't know what she was babbling on about, or why she was treating me like I wasn't a danger to her, but that was one more factor to my advantage while she was vulnerable on the aspi-*whocares*. I was within cannon's sight, closer than anyone from the Oryx clan had ever been to a Sun Goddess. But the Howler felt heavier on my stump than usual, the weight dragging my arm down.

She was crying over a damned whale. How the hell was I supposed to shoot a girl crying over a sand-damn-rocked *whale*?

She sniffled again and wiped her eyes. "You're very polite, for someone who wants to kill me."

I paused. "And you're very frank."

She nodded at the barrel strapped to my limb. "I try to be. How long were you tracking me?"

"I wasn't. I was following the water." The Salt Sea was a deceptive name—it was a toxic dump posing as seawater, more gray than blue, three parts corrosion to one part brine. It took four hours for any of the Mudforgers to squeeze drinkable water from it, and the portions grew smaller with every passing week. It'd been six weeks since we'd found any fish safe to eat, and two years since we'd found anything bigger than a mackerel. It was a miracle anything of this size had survived this long. "You can't bring it back from the dead. No one can."

"I can. I just need time. But you won't give me that either, will you?"

She hadn't planned things through. Even if she could summon the beast back to life, unless she could whip up an ocean of water to go along with it, it'd suffocate in the air and die all over again. I'd rather harvest it for parts—blubber for candles

27

and wax, whalebone for weapons and utilities, everything else that wasn't rotting for meat—and also probably get around to shooting her before I started.

"No," I admitted quietly. "I won't."

I watched those magnificent eyes change color, the silver of her irises switching to green terra-gates as Earth sparked about her, replacing the patterns of Light. "Do you still plan on killing me?"

Sky and land, ripped in two. The heart of a goddess's twin, eaten. A lifetime of wasteland.

"Sorry," I said, and raised the Howler. My own patterns of Fire blazed into being around me, and I funneled them through the barrel, hearing them multiplying and ricocheting off each other inside the steel chamber until I'd worked them up into an explosive, furious heat. I pulled the trigger, and my fire-gates flared.

She threw herself to one side, and the shot screamed past, missing her completely. Her fingers dug into the whale's rubbery hide, and I lost my footing as the ground rocked underneath me. I was a Firesmoker down to my bones, and as a Firesmoker I'd die. But Sun Goddesses could change their incanta, could shift from Mistshaper to Shardwielder to Earthshaker as easily as the rest of us changed clothes. Whichever way you looked at it, it was cheating.

But the small, short-lived earthquake was meant to knock me off-balance, not kill. She wasn't taking me seriously.

I ripped off another shot before the ground broke my fall,

and she leaped. The blast brushed against the dead whale's side and missed her by a few inches. It was at least a fifteen-foot plunge, but she hit the ground rolling with an ease that suggested practice, and scrambled to her feet just as I did. I lifted my gun again, and the fire-gates in her own eyes flared. Hissing streams of Water spewed forth from her fingers—aimed not at me, but at my Howler. I felt the faint sizzle of acid striking the barrel, and with a grunt I jerked it back out of her reach.

My eyes flicked to the dead whale, saw her hand still braced against its side. An Acidsmith incanta—she'd drawn out patterns of *Water* through her fire-gate instead of the usual Fire, and the result was poison instead of flames. There was nothing in the dry, heated air for her to pull fluid out from, but the liquid pollutants still swimming around inside the decomposing aspidochelone were a creative alternative, albeit a disgusting one. I was wrong—she was smart. She was resourceful with her incanta. It was a good enough reason to want her dead.

"I don't die easily," she snapped, panting. The toxin had melted the Howler's tip and part of its iron sights, which meant anything I fired out of it now would be sans accuracy. She could have just as easily flung the acid in my face; I'd be dead at the worst, and incapacitated at the least. She glared at me, reading the unspoken question in my eyes. "I don't kill easily, either," she bit out.

"You've already killed us."

She shook her head. "You don't understand."

"There's nothing to understand. We're chasing a dying sea

under an endless sun that kills us with a thousand little cuts every day. There'll be nothing left soon. Nothing but sand and bone." I jerked my stump, white and mottled from old burns and worse, toward the whale. "Your kind killed us the day your mother decided her revenge meant more than our lives, and you'll both kill more of us before you're done."

She brought her hand down on the beast's hide again, the angry slap echoing across the sand. "You *don't* understand! If something as enormous as an aspidochelone could live this long, then what's to say there aren't more of them? That maybe there's more of everything else? That studying *how* could mean a chance for the rest of us, too? I know we can't bring things back to the way they were before the Breaking, but what if there was some other way to save the world?"

"And how do you propose to save Aeon? Create more water? Purify the toxins in the Salt Sea? Not even your mother could do that. Bring every creature back to life?" I looked up at the hulking carcass and sneered. "Yeah, I can tell you've done a fine job there, woman."

She stared at me, at a loss for words. I gripped my damaged Howler and took a step forward. A few more, and I'd be close enough to touch her if I wanted to, wouldn't have to worry about missing the shot. Of course, she could have cracked the barrel badly enough that the gun could potentially explode in my hand—not like I *had* a hand there to worry about. . . .

A new sound tore my attention away from her—a low, harsh moan. We turned to look out at the desert, where a figure dressed in black was staggering toward us.

He wore no armor, nothing heavier than a warm cloak and breeches, sewn in a style unfamiliar to me. He wore a cowl too thick for the weather, blue vertical strips lining either side of it. The closest thing to identification that I could see was a silver brooch—a star, from the looks of it—pinned to his chest. He carried no supplies and stumbled as he walked. Out here alone, he should already have been dead. I'd seen enough remains of kinsmen who hadn't survived solar burns to know he could not have traveled any great length through the barren lands and still be walking. He was either an extremely lucky man, or . . .

The Sun Goddess took a step forward, no doubt intending to help.

"He's not human," I rasped.

She looked puzzled for a moment, before her eyes widened. "A mirage?"

"Looks like it." Mirages were more than illusions. Mother Salla believed they were souls unable to pass over, doomed to wander until the world was either healed or utterly destroyed. They were dangerous more often than not; they attracted patterns in the same way steel attracted lightning, and they left natural disasters in their wake.

The being was pale, its arms outstretched. As it drew closer, I saw that I was right. Mirages had no eyes; empty sockets stared back at us, and the goddess cried out in horror.

Its jaw worked, the skin so thin that I could see the flesh tearing while it spoke, the voice loud in the stillness. **A twin,** it croaked, and I had the strangest sensation that although its mouth was moving, the words were coming from somewhere else. Already I could see Earth patterns dancing around it, working themselves into a frenzy. **A twin. Many-haired twin. Haidee.**

Crap. Mother Salla never said mirages could talk.

The goddess stiffened. "It knows my name."

I raised the Howler.

"No," the girl blurted out. "I want to hear what else it has to say."

"I don't answer to you." But I lowered the gun all the same.

Aranth, it croaked, I felt, directly into my brain. **Heal the breach at the heart of the world. The Cruel Kingdom hungers. Sacrifice overthrows chaos. Sacrifice heals the Breaking. Help us. Help us. Help us**—his voice rose into a near screech, almost painful to hear—**Help us help us HELP US HELP US HELP**—

I fired. The shot went wide before I remembered the Howler's precision was down to shit, and I swore.

And then I saw a rapid swirl of dirt-whipped wind behind him, bearing down on us, and the mirage promptly became the least of our worries.

My stomach clenched. The air was always motionless in the dunes, but sandstorms were a different story, sweeping in from the west ever since the world split, fueled by pockets of wild magic that had nowhere else to go. They came without warning, always seemingly out of nowhere, and the sharp, corrosive dust swirling within could cut you from the inside out, if you didn't suffocate first. There was nowhere to take cover except beside the beached whale—and there was no way in a thousand infernos that the Sun Goddess would allow me near that. Few people could outrun these storms, but I cursed and turned, prepared to try anyway.

A hand closed over my arm; with surprising strength for someone barely half my size, the Sun Goddess dragged me toward the aspidochelone and shoved me against a cushion of blubber, up against the corpse's massive jaw. I was stunned enough to let her. "Don't move!" she snapped.

Already the storm was bearing down on us both. I gritted my teeth and curled up as much as I could, trying to fit into as small a space as my body could physically allow for. **Arjun,** the mirage wailed, a horrifying sound—and then it was gone, swallowed up by the approaching chaos.

When the dust storm hit, it felt like a punch to every exposed part of my body all at once, strong enough for the dead whale to rock on its base. The Sun Goddess shoved her hands into the soil, and the winds parted before her, just wide enough that they flowed swiftly to either side of us. She'd diverted the gale, but it wasn't enough to prevent wayward slices of sand from nicking us, biting into flesh and leaving bloody cuts in their wake. My armor wasn't made for sandstorms, but I had better protection than the girl beside me, who was making soft, choked sounds as the wind scraped against her unprotected skin.

I didn't want to. No way, no hell. I'd no obligation to help her, not even when she . . .

I growled and yanked her into my arms, pressing her face

against my chest while I buried my nose against her hair, pinning her between me and the whale. To her credit, she kept up the barrier, her whole form trembling from the exertion.

It took mere minutes for the center of the maelstrom to hit us, several more before we were out of the danger zone. The storm spun away, leaving us gasping for breath and up to our knees in stones and grit.

Everywhere itched. I could feel sand down the back of my neck, pooling around my waist, running down the backs of my legs. I groaned, trying to shift into a more comfortable position. A pair of hands pressed against my shoulders, and I looked down to see the girl staring back at me, wide-eyed.

"You didn't need to do that." She sounded exhausted. Up close, her eyes were even prettier; no longer flashing with an incanta gate, they were almost colorless. She was smudged in grime like I was, but her short hair continued to move independently of any gust of wind, running the gamut of colors from yellow to brown to even green. "I thought you wanted to kill me."

Furious—at myself, mostly—I pushed her away. "Let's not make any assumptions just 'cause I didn't, woman." More sand had gotten into the Howler, making it useless for anything until I'd scrubbed it out and repaired the metal, both of which would take hours of work. I stared at it as my mind worked frantically, trying to figure out what to say—*I don't owe you a goddamn thing despite this*, maybe, or *I was trying to murder you, so why spare my life?* or even just *What the fuck is going on?*—but in the end, I opted for the simplest choice. "Why did you save *me*?"

She studied me, some of those wayward locks falling over her eyes. Even at the height of the storm, even when the sand had been at its thickest, her hair had smelled fresh, scented with a fragrance I couldn't identify. "I don't kill," she said again, simply. Her gaze wandered back to the bloated whale-corpse. "The man. Where did he go?"

"I'm guessing when the sandstorm formed, it took the rest of the specter's energies along with it."

"He talked of a twin. A sister, and an Aranth. I—" Her voice shook. "But I don't have a sister. Did he mean Mother? She had a twin before. . . ."

"Before your mother up and killed her, you mean."

Her face flamed, her anger evident. "No! My mother had to kill her. Her sister broke the world, not us. But why would a mirage know anything about—why would it know my *name*—unless—" Her fists clenched, unclenched. "Why am I explaining this to you? You won't believe me, anyway."

She was right; I didn't.

A new sound met our ears—this time it was a rumbling, ominous noise, and it sounded like it was coming from somewhere inside the hulking cadaver two feet away.

We moved on instinct, reaching the same conclusion at the same time. We tore across the desert at high speed, trying desperately to put as much distance as we could between us and the whale. The sibilating sounds rose to near-deafening intensity, like steam rattling out of a kettle spout. A very large, two-hundred-ton, hundred-foot-long kettle.

We managed about twenty yards before everything exploded.

I threw myself forward. The goddess did the same, and we lay unmoving in the dirt with our hands over our heads. I smelled more than felt the viscera raining down around us, the *splat splat splat* of entrails hitting dirt until there was one final *goosh* that trailed off into silence.

Once the worst was over, I snuck a quick glance back at the aspidochelone—or what was left of it. The blowout took most of its stomach, but the head and parts of its tail remained intact. If it had been quietly decomposing the last couple of days, then the gases inside must have built up to alarming levels. The sandstorm had only hastened the inevitable outcome. If the girl planned on resurrecting the monster still, she was going to have to work doubly hard after this.

The goddess in question was a mess. Blood was caked down one side of her. Giblets and some pieces of innards hung around her neck—hell if I wanted to know what they were. She looked ridiculous. I could only imagine that I looked the same, from the way she was gaping back at me.

And then, irrationally, she began to giggle. The bits of blubber clumped in her hair slid down her face, and for some reason that triggered my own quick burst of laughter—like we hadn't been trying to kill each other five minutes before. The comedy of it all, knowing we'd come out of both storm and whale intact, was a temporary relief.

It didn't last long.

An invisible wind knocked me off my feet, sending me sprawling onto my back. I was up on my knees in an instant with the Howler inches from her face. The barrel was hot against my skin, a clear sign it was damaged. What happened after pulling the trigger would be unexplored territory, potentially of the fiery kind. My other hand twitched toward a knife I kept hidden in my boot, slow enough so as not to attract her attention to it.

To her credit, she showed no signs of fear despite the combustible cylinder planted against her cheekbone. "It's broken."

"Won't know for sure until I test it out."

She looked me right in the face, daring me with those beautiful silver eyes shining brighter than platinum, and I found myself staring again—maybe it was the ice water flowing through her veins that kept the sun's heat out. "Do it, then."

I pulled. The trigger clicked uselessly against metal. My other hand moved.

A whip of air and I was down again, the knife spinning away. "I'm leaving." She wiped off what sludge she could from herself, looking royally pissed that I'd dared to fire. "Please don't follow me."

"Like hell I won't." Even as I said the words, I knew them to be bluster. I had no weapon and no backup. For all I knew, the mirage was still hiding nearby, and I didn't want to stick around for it to say hello again. "You owe me a gun."

She smiled. "Send me a bill, then."

Air patterns kicked up the soil, briefly obscuring her from view. When the dust settled, I was face-first in sand again with a mouthful of gravel.

Spitting out pebbles and cursing, I scrambled up, but she was gone.

"Arghh!" I snarled at the sky, frustrated and embarrassed that I'd been bested by a little slip of a girl, goddess be damned. Salla would probably yell at me if she knew I'd let her live.

If she knew, I reminded myself, returning to the whale remains. I was angry, and humiliated—and relieved, when I thought about it. If she'd really wanted me dead, I'd have been just as gutted as that whale.

Besides, I had almost-fresh meat, so it wasn't like I'd be returning empty-handed. Despite the explosion, this whale alone could last the whole clan many weeks.

I remembered the eyeless mirage, the way it sounded out *twins* and *breach* and *heal us* without ever using a tongue. Its words sounded far too similar to the Sun Goddess's claims that she could bring things back to life.

Not possible. The world's too broken to repair. And they don't get points for wanting to revive something they destroyed in the first place.

I could think of reasons why it knew the Sun Goddess's name.

But how in the sand-encrusted hells—and this'd be the catalyst for all the bad dreams I'd be having in the coming days, that much I was sure of—had it known *mine*?

Hell and sandrock.

I retrieved my knife, rubbed off the worst of the blood against the side of the aspidochelone, and, grimly, set to work.

Chapter Three

ODESSA, BREAKER OF STORMS

———————— ☾ ————————

I WAS GOING TO TELL Lan I was in love with her at that dinner.

I still am.

If I tried to make it up to her, would she accept? Would she even forgive me? I'd only ever been courageous that first time we met, when I had looked up from the pages of *The Queen and Her Hunter* and found her staring at me the way Erik the huntsman might have looked when he'd glimpsed Queen Rahne for the very first time. That had been two and a half months ago, not long after I'd started sneaking out.

That first time had been such a rush. I remembered how my hands shook, how I'd been convinced I was going to be caught. But I always timed it well; easy enough to put the guards to sleep for a couple of minutes or so, as they were already exhausted from overusing their Stonebreaker armor. Easy enough to disguise my hair, to locate the lone city bookshop where I'd occupied myself before Lan had sauntered in and changed my life.

Easy enough to hide my condition; I was never gone from the Spire for long. I actually felt better in the city than back in the tower—time spent with Lan gave me the energy that the other Catseyes' healing couldn't—which only stiffened my resolve to keep playing truant.

And then the kiss. Sweet Mother, I'd been dreaming of the kiss every night since it happened; the way the book spines dug into my back, the mortifying noises I made, the look of pure lust on Lan's face as she stumbled back, unwilling to scandalize Mr. Wallof any further, long enough to ask me out.

Have dinner with me, Ame, she'd whispered, still as formal as a graveyard despite my swollen lips, like she hadn't been the reason for them. *Stay the night.*

I was thrilled.

I was frightened.

But Mother just *had* to decide another Banishing was imminent on the morrow and placed me under heavier guard. I was to have a new Catseye, she told me, one of the best in Aranth—except every Catseye unlucky enough to be assigned to me was the "best in Aranth" until they couldn't heal me, so I had little faith in her assertions.

I was going to miss Lenida. Catseyes could heal everyone but themselves, and Catseye Lenida had both horrible eyesight and a narcolepsy problem, so it was easy for me to sneak out while she snored for three hours. A new Catseye was going to make playing truant harder.

The new Catseye had wound up being the very date I'd stood up.

It would have been the best-case scenario for my situation, actually, if it wasn't for all the lying I'd done beforehand.

Was that the real reason you never showed up? she'd asked me in that quiet voice.

I don't know, Lan. I don't know if I was going to show up at dinner even if Mother hadn't posted more guards. Because I couldn't promise you forever. Because it was only a matter of time before you learned that I lied, and you'd despise me for it. And I was right.

But I wanted to make things right now. Now, after realizing that I could actually *lose* her—

A wave of exhaustion passed over me. *Don't get too worked up or you'll get sick again,* I told myself, rolling over till I was facedown, groaning into my pillow. My intended apology/confession had wound up strangling itself in my throat instead, at the look of genuine hurt on her face. I had a lot to make up for before she'd trust me again.

I knew it was ridiculous. I had *literally* battered down seas, dispelled storms. Surely coming clean about my feelings was an easier task.

That's because you wouldn't care if the seas rejected your affections, Odessa. You didn't lie to the storms about not being a goddess of Aranth.

Confessing was not as spontaneous or easy as I thought it would be. The girls in the romances I'd read never seemed to go about planning their love admissions like they were strategizing for a bloody war. More common for them to blurt it out in the heat of the moment, like the words would burst out of them eventually anyway.

I'd been trying to work out a plan to apologize: complete the Banishing, set up a lovely candlelit dinner afterward to make up for the one I didn't get to, then confess as honestly as I could. Beg her to give me a second chance. Tell her yes, I wanted to spend the night. Eventually. One day. But I needed more time to process everything she meant by that, once I stopped dissolving into a heady mess of dirty thoughts and mentally flailing every time I let my mind slide in that direction.

I mean, she was right next door now! I could sneak over in the middle of the night and—

You know you haven't the guts, Odessa!

But first things first.

Twenty minutes later, once the dizziness had passed, I sat on the bed, wearing my best defeat-the-Banishing dress—a blue silk affair that flattered my too-skinny figure and flared around my hips, with sleeves that ended at my elbows so I didn't have to keep pushing them back from my wrists. And there was lace involved—by the Mother, so much lace. I had no idea what Lan's preferences in clothes were, so when dressing for seduction, I'd opted for the tried and true.

I crossed my legs and tried to push my chest out, but it was not the most comfortable position. I considered lying down on one side while propping myself up on a forearm, but that didn't feel right, either. Upright and stiff-backed, like a queen?

Leaning back on my elbows, all come-hither-like? Should I tug the garment down to expose a shoulder? All I had to go by were the raunchy covers of my romances, and it occurred to me now how extremely uncomfortable all those women had to be to pose for those paintings.

A knock sounded and I scrambled for position, pushing the cloth down to let a collarbone show. The door opened and Lan peered warily in. She didn't look as angry as she had the night before. She hadn't quit, either. That was a good sign, wasn't it?

"Good morning, Your Holiness. The rain's let up. I'll let the others know—" She paused, staring at me. Her face was expressionless. Did she like what she saw? Or was the come-hithering not working?

"Is your leg bothering you?" she finally asked.

"No-o-o." I swung both feet to the side of the bed, beet red. Miss Merrilyn from *Capturing the Prince* made it look so easy. "I'm okay! It was a—there's nothing wrong with my—I'm okay!"

"Your mother's waiting. The Devoted have gathered, and I don't think we should prolong this any more than necessary. It's not good weather to stay out in."

It was never good weather to stay out in for me. "Lan. I . . ."

"Yes?"

Tell her. Tell her. *Tell her.*

"I'm ready," I whispered.

"Good. Best not to keep your mother waiting, Your Holiness."

I rearranged my skirts and hopped out of bed. If she'd

noticed that I was wearing flower pins in my hair, or a goodly amount of rouge on my cheeks despite my limited supply, she made no comment. I felt quietly disappointed as I followed her out of the room.

As always, Mother was the epitome of elegance, in a serene white dress with no adornments. I felt overdressed standing beside her. "You're looking very lovely this nightspan," she pronounced, beaming. "Isn't she, Tianlan?"

Lan shrugged. I saw the faint dark circles, the slight redness in her gold-and-silver eyes. She didn't look like she'd slept at all, and I felt ashamed of my selfishness, horrified I hadn't seen it sooner. Was there something they weren't telling me? "The water's rising fast, Asteria," she said. "Janella thinks the floods will come within the next three hours."

Mother smiled. "This is your first time witnessing the Banishing this close, isn't it? Just follow our lead; Odessa is quite good at it."

We performed the Banishing whenever necessary, which used to be once a year, twice if needed. Now we do it every three months. Aranth was built atop the only strip of land under habitable weather, close to bordering the large ocean that extended eastward into nowhere. But both water and ice were encroaching on our small patch of territory, clamoring to break through our frozen dyke.

I was not averse to performing the Banishing. Knowing that the sea and sky would stop at my command was a potent feeling, one of the few times in my life when I didn't feel so helpless in my sickly, fragile body. But there was also another, more selfish reason I looked forward to the rite: the Banishing was the only time I was ever allowed out of the tower. I always felt guilty about it, but the days I looked forward to were also the most dangerous times for the rest of Aranth.

For all they said about goddesses who could do anything, I knew there were limits. I couldn't use aether-gates like the Catseye to make others better. But I could inflict other curses instead—poison, lethargy, a host of other ailments—and sometimes I wondered if my ability to curse rather than heal was a character flaw, some defect I had beyond the physical. But my mother, I knew, had the same shortcomings.

All the other elements were mine to command, and I could use them with ease where others struggled. There weren't a lot of things in life that I was good at, but I knew I was *good* at this.

Mother squared her shoulders, as Lan wrapped a thick cloak around me. I shivered when I felt her warm hands brush against my neck, oblivious to the cold. "Let's begin, before we have to deal with floods along with everything else," Mother said.

The Spire was built on a cliff that faced the worst of the endless waves. It was a visual reminder for the citizens below that we goddesses were the city's bulwark, the one thing standing between them and utter destruction.

We walked down the steps hammered into the stone, a path that led to the base of the ice wall that encircled most of the city limits. Torches showed us the way; the night was just as dark in the Third Hour of Waking as it was in the Thirteenth. The area was closed off to the rest of the citizens; any careless van-dalism could cause the walls to disintegrate and water to flood the city within minutes. I stumbled a little; try as I might, I always found myself winded and out of breath despite the short descent. But this time I had Lan's hand on my arm, gently steer-ing me, and I clung to her gratefully.

A cluster of Devoted waited, along with several of their assis-tants. Gracea was the first to step forward, the first to curtsy. As Aranth's only Starmaker and leader of my mother's Devoted, she took her role seriously. I'd had little interaction with the rest of Mother's council, but Gracea had always struck me as a little too smug for her own good. "Your Holiness," she murmured calmly, though the constant tugging at her gold-piping-edged hood revealed her nerves. Like her, the other Devoted wore their official robes, colors marking their cowls to indicate their respective abilities—blue for Icewrights, yellow for Windshift-ers, and so on. "We are ready."

I stared out into the endless sea. I'd felt restless since leav-ing the tower, an uneasiness that I'd never experienced during previous rituals. Why did I feel like there was something out there, hidden within the wind-tossed waters, watching me? I shuddered at the thought.

The other Devoted appeared to share my unease. Seasinger Graham always had a kind smile for me and a friendly word, but it was clear he was more worried than usual. Windshifter Filia kept glaring at Lan for some reason. Several Icewrights were monitoring the floes before us, exchanging hushed opinions, and a half dozen Stormbringers were already channeling their gates, attempting to appease the rain by lessening its impact around us. Only Mistshaper Gareen seemed relaxed, flirting with one of the other Devoted women—today it was Miel— like nothing was wrong.

Mother looked out at the raging sea, her prismatic hair flying around her. "Janella, how fast is the wind today?"

Gracea's assistant, a girl with doe eyes standing at the back of the group, spoke up. Like many other citizens, she had been born with muted gates, the red tinge around her irises marking her as a dormant Firesmoker. Only Mother and I could channel Fire nowadays, but even for us it was difficult—there weren't enough of the patterns in Aranth for the average user. "Nearing forty knots, Your Holiness."

"A dozen knots too many for my taste." She extended a hand toward me. I accepted it, felt her strength flow through my fingers and bolster my own. "It's your turn this time, Odessa."

Mother usually helmed these summonings, but she'd been encouraging me to take the lead of late. I took a deep breath, snuck a quick glance back at Lan, who looked worried but also strangely expectant.

I turned back to the angry sea, and my air-gate glowed. I pulled in every pattern I could muster from the waters and channeled them into the frozen ice walls, and soon felt Mother's own magic adding to mine.

Water was easy enough to draw from; it was everywhere. Mother and I forced the temperatures around the ice barrier lower, far beyond its normal freezing point until the ice stopped expanding when it solidified and began *contracting* instead. The result was an extremely dense, nigh-impenetrable, glacier-like dike that could weather most of what the sea could throw at us.

For the time being, anyway; our creation required constant vigilance. We'd had to contend with large chunks of permafrost drifting closer to the city, where a collision with the dike could prove fatal for Aranth. Sea creatures, too, were a danger, and their increasing presence over the years meant we had to replenish and reinforce the dike with greater frequency. Some of the Devoted spent most of each nightspan monitoring the dike's status, marking down places that needed further buttressing. Mother relied on their reports to decide when to perform the next Banishing. But the seas had been getting worse, the permafrost drawing ever closer, and the time between Banishings was growing shorter.

Breath left my mouth in faint puffs, turning into icicles halfway out. I didn't feel the cold, even as a thin sliver of ice formed up against my skin like brittle armor. The Devoted rattled off the list of chinks they'd detected in the barrier.

"A vertical cut along column five, five inches in length and an inch in diameter—"

"—three crisscross marks on column twenty-three, water trickling through—"

"—gouge in column sixty-five, five feet in diameter, ice crumbling—"

I closed my eyes and let instinct take over, patterns of Water flowing through and manifesting as hard crystallized ice along the dike's borders, letting the Devoted's calls direct my aim.

I'd done this exactly thirty-six times since the night I turned eight and my gates opened for the first time. It was exhausting work, but reinforcing the dike was half of what made up the Banishing. The hard part came right after.

"All clear," Seasinger Graham said. He turned to his assistant, Merika. "Inform the others," he barked, tapping her on the shoulder. She flinched, eyes wide as she glanced back at him, then nodded briefly before dashing off. The other Devoted had seen the Banishing unfold many times before, but they sighed their relief each time like it was the first.

"Are you okay, Your Holiness?" Graham asked me gently.

I nodded. I wasn't tired; it was strange to have a disease growing inside me, yet feel stronger with every pattern I wove for the Banishing despite it. I looked back at Lan; she was smiling. "Well done, Your Holiness," she said, and my heart soared.

I was going to tell her tonight.

"Odessa." Mother gestured. Obediently, I followed her and the others back to higher ground, back to the Spire. The city was protected for now, but that alone was no longer enough.

It was a balancing act. Even the sturdiest walls would buckle from colliding with permafrost that stretched on as far as the horizon allowed. But melting too much of it would bring more tsunamis and floods, damaging the wall more quickly. Too little, and the thaw could release strange diseases that had been hidden within the ice for millennia, to ravage the city. The trick was to burn the ice hot enough to dissolve immediately, without giving it a chance to add to the sea and before any airborne sicknesses could be introduced into the wind.

Noelle had come prepared, the dry driftwood lying at our feet. "Lan," Mother said, but my Catseye already had her flint ready. One spark, two, and the driftwood began to burn. Seasinger Graham was already drawing in his own Water patterns, the water-gate in his eyes a bright, shining blue while he sapped the moisture from the air around the small fire, letting it burn longer than it should have.

I abandoned Water for Fire, grabbed eagerly at the heat. It took a good five minutes for the patterns to burn their way through my body, filling me up with the energy I needed to disintegrate great big chunks of the permafrost. At the same time, Mother amplified what she needed from the flames, then funneled them my way. I focused on the closest of the heavy glaciers marring the landscape.

My first volley of fire hit one heavy block squarely in the middle, evaporating it completely. Steam hissed briefly, but I was already concentrating on my next target. Again and again I fired, and each volley found its mark, carving off blocks of ice until I'd destroyed a respectable portion of the floating threat.

I directed my energy at a particularly large lump, the tip of a giant iceberg. It broke apart just as easily as the others.

And then I halted, staring, as tentacles wrapped around the smaller floes and a hideous creature rose from the waters. It had a large, bulbous head and was a sickly purple in color, with yellow bulging eyes. I knew somewhere within the frothing mass of feelers was a large beak-like mouth capable of snapping a man in half. This monster was no stranger to Aranth's port, nor to the books that made up Mother's library. The dwindling life in the ocean meant a lesser food supply for creatures of its size, and sometimes they drifted close to our shores, desperate enough to hunt human flesh as a replacement.

"Kraken!" Graham roared. We'd conducted enough drills in Aranth for people to know what to do. Already the ice wall, its favorite point of attack, was rapidly being evacuated while the army started forming up along the lower cliffs, some of the Devoted in command. The kraken's tentacles had a long reach, but the upper landings of the Spire would escape its touch.

But the kraken wasn't the only demon rising from the water. I saw an arm as tall as my entire body reach out from the dark depths of the sea, pulling itself up onto an ice floe to reveal a creature made of night. It was a moving shadow, a lean, emaciated figure so black that I could not make out any features save for strange blue stones that glittered along the underside of its chin, like a caricature of a beard. Heavy onyx horns hung on either side of its head.

But it had no face. It was a moving, humanoid blackness devoid of life.

I had never seen it before. And yet I knew what it was almost immediately.

No more than two hundred feet separated us, far enough yet still horrifyingly close, but somehow I knew it had teeth. I could *feel* its teeth, could almost taste the *scrape* of them unseen against my back. I could feel its eyeless eyes on me, and a peculiar sense of recognition slammed into my gut.

"What is that?" Gracea gasped.

There was a muffled thump; the flint had slipped out of Lan's fingers—her *shaking* fingers. "It found us," she whispered.

We'd known our share of monsters. Krakens and their stranglers. Devil whales and their ragged mouths dripping with diseased blood, their hollow gullets. Serpentlike cetea with teeth and arms in place of fins. These were some of the creatures born from the Great Abyss, where the Breaking of the World occurred; a personification of poxes cursed into Aeon—or so it was said. But never before had we encountered this twisted amalgamation of shadow.

"What do we—" Gracea backed away, and the others followed her. "Your Holiness! What are we—"

Mother's voice was inhumanly level, absent of all emotion, but her eyes glittered strangely as she took in the shadow. "Gracea, your priority is to ensure that the dike does not break. Graham, take Pieter and Miel and assist her. The rest of you focus on the kraken. I'd rather not fight it at close quarters, and we'll all have better success attacking from higher ground. I'll handle the other. Janella and Emil, bring everyone in the city to the shelters, to await my next orders. *Move!*"

Lan was still shaking but pulled herself together quickly and took my hand. "We have to leave, Am—Your Holiness."

I shook my head, my eyes trained on the monster. I couldn't

leave Mother here all alone to face the shadow-creature.

That would be irresponsible, when it was me it was searching for.

The kraken had disappeared underwater, to resurface with frightening speed along the borders of the ice wall. Tentacles slithered across the top, sliding down to the other side of the barrier—and jerked back when dozens of arrows made of pure ice struck each in turn. The strategy was always to keep our distance—as bulky as those appendages looked, we'd learned in the past, very unfortunately, that they were surprisingly quick. The wall still held, but I knew the kraken's weight wasn't doing it any favors. I saw the waters shifting to accommodate the behemoth, saw a rising crest of waves speeding toward us.

"Tsunami!" Gracea screamed. "Get away!"

"Odessa!" Lan tugged harder, then dropped her hand with a gasp. Her fingers were tinged blue, close to frostbite from my touch. Icicles now covered my skin at a rapid rate, but I didn't feel the cold.

I felt like I was burning.

I could feel patterns flaring from Mother, saw more steam hissing up as she burned her way through the worst of the waves before they could hit the barriers. Whips of it blazed into the kraken's scales, and the giant octopus shuddered and retreated back over the wall.

The shadow-monster, too, dove down into the depths. It resurfaced thirty feet away from its original spot and appeared to be *walking* across the water, though it must have been hundreds of feet deep. It was tall enough that it could reach me from where I stood along the cliffs. Lan tugged at me again, but I refused to budge.

"Odessa—"

"It won't hurt me. It won't."

Dark fingerlike tendrils grasped for me.

My aether-gates opened.

And then I was standing over an abyss, staring into its depths. Lan, Mother, the Devoted—everyone was gone. There was only the shadow and the unending darkness and the bottomless gorge before me, where one more step promised unending death.

Images passed through my head—misshapen forms twisting in the darkness, shadows writhing from someplace where no light had ever entered. I saw Aranth dying, the city swept under by a rogue wave, never to resurface. I saw bodies.

"No," I wept. Mother had visions, sometimes. But I was too young for them, too young to expect so terrifying a power so soon.

Be satisfied, something whispered. *A divine power of the underworld has been fulfilled. You must not open your mouth against the rites of the underworld.*

I knew what this ritual meant. I knew what the shadow wanted. I'd read enough of Mother's books to know.

"You're the galla of clarity, aren't you?"

It said nothing, but I knew I was right.

I reached out toward the creature with the blue beard, with the cruelly curved horns.

For one horrifying, glorious, mind-numbing moment I felt time slow, spiraling out into infinity. We stared at each other; a girl cloaked in a skin of ice, facing down the shadow of a great and terrible beauty. For the briefest second we were the only two beings in the world, human and monster. For the briefest second I was uncertain which of us was which.

Its not-a-mouth shifted, and uttered a word—

And then the world slammed back into focus, throwing me onto my back, until I was staring up at the crying skies and threatening clouds. A faint ache echoed from somewhere in the back of my head. I couldn't feel my arms, my legs.

A hand settled in my hair, shifting down to my shoulders, the small of my back; nudging me up until I was encircled by strong arms—Lan. The cold drained from my body, life returning to my limbs; surrounded by her presence, I felt warm.

"Odessa!"

I blinked slowly up at her. "Is it gone?" A heavy weight was pressing down on my mind, making it harder to think. How much energy had I expended, to leave me feeling so weak?

She nodded, pale. "It vanished into thin air, just like that. Did you—?" She broke off, ran fingers up my cheek. "You're burning up," she said instead, and her eyes glowed.

More heat stole into me, washing the rest of the chill away. I sighed, my eyes fluttering.

Another hand on my forehead, cooler than Lan's. "My poor child," Mother murmured. "How is she?"

"She's all right. Just had the wind knocked out of her, I

think. What in the hell was that? Wasn't that the same thing you saw in your vision?"

Vision?

"No. It was made of shadows too, but the other had a different shape. And this had a—a different kind of hunger. Was it . . ." Mother gentled her voice, aware she was treading on unstable ground. "You reacted like it was something familiar to you, Tianlan. Did you perhaps see it during your journey to . . ."

Lan stiffened, said nothing for several seconds before swallowing audibly. "I . . . I don't remember. But I think there were . . . things that attacked my team then, that were of a similar shape. But none with those horns. Or those blue stones. I—" She stopped again, breathing unevenly. *"I don't remember."*

"Stop. Tianlan, relax. Don't think about them. They can't hurt you anymore. Close your eyes, and stay with me."

The Catseye nodded, her face twisted in pain. "Asteria, there's something wrong with Odessa."

"What?"

"There's a—the sickness—the shadows inside her are bigger again." Lan's voice shook. "But I can't shrink them back to what they were before."

"Get her back to the Spire, immediately! I'll handle everything else here." I was looking up at Mother then and saw a strange, fleeting smile cross her face as she stood. "Inanna's Song," she murmured, turning away. "So it's not too late, after all. . . ."

Already I could hear the shouts of the others above the worsening storm, interlaced with Mother's own commands to secure the area, to search the city and—

It was getting harder to think.

"Odessa, you wonderful fool," Lan whispered softly, her voice as gentle as she ever let it be. "You're going to be the death of me one day."

I love you. How do I get you back? I closed my eyes instead. "It called me 'daughter,'" I whispered.

"What? Why—"

But the rest of her words were lost to the winds, for I was already asleep.

Chapter Four

HAIDEE OF THE GOLDEN CITY

THE MIRAGE STARED UP AT me from the pages of the *Bestiary of the Dead*. Or someone who resembled him, anyway. But I recognized the clothes immediately: the same peculiar style, the same cloak so thick he would have sweated out his own weight in water traveling through the desert.

The illustration showed him offering a cornucopia of odd-looking fruit to a beautiful woman with colorful hair not unlike my own. The lady was too busy thrusting a sword through a shadowy titan to pay him notice. There was an inscription written underneath, and it said *A Devoted priest attending to Inanna, the Heavenly Queen, as she slays a galla.*

I paused in my reading to gate some patterns of Air and allow a few breezes through the room, light enough so as not to dislodge the rest of my research. It was inordinately hot today—warmer than even our typical fire-scorching weather—and here in the engineering rooms, tucked within the bowels of the Golden City with steam rising from the nearby vents, the heat was especially cloying.

I sat back, thinking. Inanna was a direct ancestor of mine, the first of us. Aeon had always been ruled by a sovereign goddess, her title passed down from mother to daughter, but to all the goddesses Inanna was our Great Mother: the epitome of what a true ruler should be. Like her, my mother had her own selected coterie of Devoted, though their influence on the Golden City's throne was restricted to military rather than political matters—my mother knew her own mind and rarely conferred with others.

But her Devoted's clothes were light and flowing, and their armors were made of Earth, relying on Stonebreaker incanta more than solid metal for their defenses. None of them wore the strange archaic clothes the mirage did.

I drew out the silver brooch, stared at it. I had picked it up in the sandstorm's aftermath. Unlike the mirage, it had not disappeared once the dust had settled. I'd been rather sly about it, certain the boy had not seen me—

I grunted, irritated every time I thought of my would-be executioner. A desert forager from one of those clans that lived underground, past the ergs and along the beginnings of the stone plateaus, where sand was minimal and the rock solid enough for tunnels. His skin was dark, and he wore a *hezabi* head scarf on his head, popular among the original Qedarites that had roamed these lands before the Breaking, so I presumed he was an offshoot of one of their tribes.

He was obviously a Firesmoker, and they were always the ones to suffer the worst accidents. I understood his hostility, but I had saved his life. He had protected *me* from the winds. Surely both actions had meant something.

But he had tried to repay my kindness by—

Didn't matter. I'd left him eating sand, and he wasn't worth another thought. Ass.

I focused on the brooch again. It was an unfinished star with a point missing, and a crooked line slashed through its center. Some books said it was an emblem the Devoted of old once wore. And his clothes told me he was from some colder climate—an astonishing revelation, since there was *no* colder climate, except . . .

I stared at the etching. Had the mirage crossed over from the other side of the breach? Had it accomplished what no other person living could?

Few people had survived to describe the Great Abyss—the breach, the center of a great cataclysm that had cost the world a spine, with an outburst of magic so strong the world had stopped spinning, dooming us to an unrelenting sun. Three-quarters of the world perished when that breach was formed.

Mother had sent scouting expeditions to the Great Abyss in the past. Promised them wealth and power beyond their imaginings when they returned.

No one ever came back from those campaigns.

There was no known way to cross that deadly gap—not alive.

How did the mirage bridge the chasm? As pure energy? Impossible; this brooch couldn't have been carried over by something that was completely incorporeal.

There was no way to bring someone back from the dead. Yet my ancestor, Nyx, had done just that. It was possible, definitely, that she was lying—but why? She had told none of her contemporaries, and the diary detailing her attempts had lain hidden and unread for years until I'd stumbled upon it in Mother's athenaeum. Very few journals penned by my foremothers had survived the Breaking.

I took out Nyx's treatise again, skimming through.

It was not a complete resurrection, I fear, a fault of my inexperience, no doubt—some miscalculation I made performing the Gate of Life. It was alive by observation, but not in the manner that science proves. It possessed no heartbeat, exhibited few mannerisms of the average fowl, and its skin had a waxed cast to it, like new life had given it transparency. It neither ate nor slept, but was content to watch me most days and nights. Even now, it watches me still.

But it is a gentle bird, silent but sweet. I think I shall call her Hemera. . . .

What had gone wrong? Nyx recounted channeling every conceivable pattern—Fire, Air, Water, Earth, Aether—into the bird's corpse, but strangely enough, she had neglected to mention what gate she had used for the experiment. I gated Air when I had conducted my experiment on Betsy the aspidochelone— perhaps that was my error?

And then there was the mirage.

"Cruel Kingdom," I said aloud to myself, frowning. Where had I heard that before?

I would have loved to study mirage anatomy as well, but wherever they went, sandstorms followed. I suspected that the Golden City's air-dome would do little to protect us, even if I found a way to bring a mirage inside the—

A loud cranking noise and metallic screeching jerked me out of my thoughts, before a peculiar hissing filled the air. It sounded like something was about to boil over.

I leaped out my chair. "Rodge! Jes!" I yelled as I tore past their rooms, not stopping as I bolted toward the North Tower, where the ominous noises had emanated from. Inside, I ran past the mazelike troughs and tubes, years of experience allowing me to dodge past whirring gears and interlocking pipes without thinking. Yeong-ho was already at its center, struggling to raise one of the many levers that opened and closed the tower's intricate steam pathways and tunnels. Charley was there as well, the gates in her eyes shining white as she tried to divert some of the steam pouring out of nearby vents away from us.

"The chain drive's loose in valve twenty-six!" Yeong-ho shouted, and I changed course, barreling past a startled Jes to head deeper into the mechanical labyrinth, nearly tripping over an exposed spigot before reaching the valve in question.

As I'd feared, the metal had worn down so thin on one of the transmissions that its gear had lost two teeth from the resulting pressure. That had slowed it down enough to affect the speed of the other cogs, sending some screeching to a halt and increasing friction a hundredfold. If it lost one more tooth, the resulting chain reaction could scrape off the whole left wall of the North Tower and cause everything to collapse, with us inside.

And should that fall, the city would be out half its water supply. Here in the desert, that would mean we were as good as dead.

"What can I do?" Rodge had appeared, red-faced and panting, Jes already unscrewing the bolts that kept the cog in place. Behind me I could dimly hear Yeong-ho bellowing more orders at Charley. I realized then that I was still clutching the *Bestiary of the Dead* and promptly tossed it onto a nearby wooden bench.

"Find me a replacement!" I hollered, pointing at the wheel. "Ten-inch diameter, Y-spoke!" I gated more Air, funneling and honing it until the tip was as sharp as a knife, and then shoved it in between the cogs. That would have to hold. Without a substitute on hand, removing the gear now would make things worse.

Rodge paled. "Haidee, not even you can hold up a whole—"

"*Ten inches diameter, Y-spoke,* Rodge!"

He dashed away, and I focused all my concentration on that broken wheel, willing it not to move, not to send everything else crashing down around us. The gear struggled, still turning slowly despite my best efforts, so I gated another knife of Air, and then another, and then another, frantically jamming as many as I could fit into that enclosed hole, and then using the air itself to shove against the wheel with all my might. The strain was unbelievable—I was fighting a twelve-foot-tall, ten-ton machine, and my feet skidded across the floor as I struggled against the recoil. Jes tried pushing at the wheel in an attempt to aid me, but I shook my head. "No use losing your hands on top of everything else!"

"Well, with Rodge taking his sweet damn time, I ain't gonna stand back and—"

"I'm not!" Rodge was back, snatching away the broken gear and slamming a new one in its place. With quick, deft fingers Jes screwed the metal back into place as I let go and sank to the ground, gasping. There were fainter creaks as the new cog settled into place before the whole arrangement regained momentum, soon turning at the same speed as the rest.

"That was close," Rodge panted. There was not as much steam billowing out from Yeong-ho's last position, and since the burly man had ceased yelling, I assumed they had defused the situation there, too. Soon enough, he reappeared with Charley in tow, both exhausted but relieved.

Like the others, I was caked in both sweat and grease, my face red from the exertion. "Everything good?" I managed to ask, still unwilling to move from my position on the floor.

Charley wiped at her forehead, leaving a long smudge against her temple. "Barely. We nearly lost the—" She let out a loud, hacking cough.

Immediately, Yeong-ho moved toward her. "A mandatory checkup with Catseye Franck," he said sternly.

"But—"

"No buts. You've taken in a lungful of steam. Best make sure it isn't quicksilver."

We called the towers "sweat rooms" for good reason, but these hydraulic-powered engines were what gave the Golden City life. With them, we could manufacture clothes using large quilling wheels overlaid with incanta to shield us from the worst the relentless daylight could offer. We relied on them to pump up groundwater from ancient aquifers a thousand feet beneath the city—our only source of water. We used them to power the air-gated dome of the metropolis, which was our main defense against solar rays and roving nomadic tribes, and also against the heat. The hydraulic machinery required water to work the gears—water we could not spare.

But some of the mines under our territory contained quicksilver, and converting that into the steam needed to power the machines worked well enough—as long as the poisonous gases didn't escape from the engines and into the public vents. Jes and Rodge looked concerned, but Charley grinned and shrugged. Accidentally ingesting quicksilver was a risk every mechanika took.

"We're running out of materials to repair the engines." Yeong-ho, like his father before him, served as the Golden City's architect, our head mechanika. He'd taught me everything I knew. "Her Majesty will need to send out more troops soon."

"How—how much do we need?" We controlled the mines east of the city, but they were often susceptible to raids by desert clans. We had better weapons, but our wagons were sluggish. And since the nomads had no mining equipment themselves, they often chose to target the caravans on their return instead.

I knew what I would do in my mother's place. I would send out forty or fifty Silverguards armed to the teeth with fire-lances and stack the caravans high with cannons and glowfire. Any desert tribe seeing all that firepower on display would, I hoped, be smart enough to avoid carrying out what would be a suicide mission.

Yeong-ho sighed, running a hand through his dark hair. "Fifty tons, at least. I can manage with fifteen or so to guarantee nothing else falls apart in the next three weeks, but beyond that—" He left the words hanging.

A sonorous, mournful bell sounded from the direction of the Citadel, the highest tower in the city where Mother and I resided—twice, thrice, *four* times—proof I was in trouble. The Chimes were meant to warn the city of impending dangers or to issue proclamations, but Mother had been using them lately to announce when she wanted me in her chambers. She'd done it enough times that the others were familiar with the routine; Charley shot me a sympathetic look while Rodge helped me up. "Is something happening?" Charley asked.

"Knowing Mother, it's probably another lecture on why I spend more time here than at the Citadel." I bent over and retrieved the *Bestiary*. Mother had always disapproved of my decision to be a mechanika; I had deferred to her wisdom in almost everything else but that.

Rodge grunted. "Probably about that fandangled ball doo-hickey you've gots to go to in a couple of days."

I cringed. Mother had made it clear that I was to find a

66

potential consort among the many suitors expected to attend. It had never been a requirement for me to attend any of the previous balls she'd thrown, and I'd used her leniency to skip them altogether. This was different. This ball was to be thrown in *my* honor. I'd been dreading it.

"You can hide it out here with us," Charley volunteered. None of them had been invited. "Just sneak out when no one's—" She broke off into another coughing fit.

"To Franck you go," Yeong-ho commanded. "And stop telling Her Royal Highness to disobey her mother."

I flexed my fingers. "I'll go see what she wants. She'll need to know about this, anyway."

Jes grinned, a strangely innocent expression that belied his usual demeanor. "Come back in one piece," he said, and Charley guffawed, still choking.

Her Royal Holiness Latona sat on a jeweled chair that was just as opulent as the rest of the throne room. Despite the city's name, gold was a useless metal in these parts, and nonessentials were forged with it to conserve the iron and steel needed for weapons and machinery. In this part of the city—the wealthier side—the dome was tinted and shuttered to keep most of the sun's glare out, though Mother and I were practically immune to it. There had been some vague promises to do the same for the other districts, but the materials, for some odd reason, kept getting earmarked for other, higher priority projects.

Mother was clad in a simple white gown, braids carefully

coiled behind her back, but as of late I'd been noticing the faint shadows under her eyes, the languid way she moved that suggested a lack of sleep.

She wasn't alone; a cluster of nobles stood nearby, a few talking quietly among themselves. They were all old men in their fifties with perfectly manicured hair and expensive tailors on retainer, save one boy my age who was sitting quietly to one side with his nose in a book.

"You're late." Mother eyed my grime-smeared face and dirty work clothes with disdain. "And you've been to the towers."

"With good reason, Mother. The structural integrity of some of the gears is failing, and we'll need more ores soon to ensure that the irrigation system—"

"There are other pressing matters to discuss. Including your unannounced departure from the Citadel yesterday."

I froze. Sometimes I underestimated my mother's cleverness, and caught in her bright pale gaze, I couldn't help but squirm. "It was just for a little while."

"That makes no difference when it was without my permission!" Her voice rose, sharp in the sudden silence. "You'll rule here after me, child. There are responsibilities to remember, and you cannot choose to gallivant out in the wasteland any time you choose."

I'd had this argument with her many times before, and it wasn't one I wanted to get back into, especially with an audience. So I maintained a sullen silence.

Mother sighed. "Lord Arrenley?" she asked, and a gray-haired man stepped forward. "Tell my daughter how Commander Evander and his men fare."

"I sent them to the mines three days ago to harvest more ore, my liege. They should be back in time for the gala."

I looked up, surprised and annoyed. Mother always demanded that I tell her everything—but then turned around and withheld important information of her own, leaving me in the dark.

Mother smiled grimly. "There isn't much going on in this city that I don't know about, Haidee. In time, you'll learn how. Besides, I've heard Yeong-ho complain enough times to make a guess."

"Shouldn't I be told these things, too?"

"If you'd poked your head out of the towers every now and then, I might have. Return that book to my library, and take up the treatise Counselor Seathorn sent regarding his thoughts on court customs. Perhaps that will keep all other foolish stories out of your head."

"If it came from the counselor, then that isn't likely," I grumbled.

That earned me a rare laugh from her, and a few more from the other nobles. "There is more to ruling than slumming as a mechanika, Haidee. I trust you'll find Vella's latest creation more suitable to wear for the party?"

She was quick to spot the look on my face. "No protests. This is for your own good." Mother's gaze softened; for a minute she looked almost sad. "This is for the good of the city, too."

"I know. I just . . . it makes me uncomfortable."

"You'll get used to it in time. I did. You need not marry immediately, Haidee. But it would do the citizens good to know that we are thinking of their future."

"My liege?" one of the nobles asked. "Shall we start?"

I waited. I didn't want to have to *ask* to join their meeting. Asking came from a position of weakness.

Mother turned away. "Seamstress Valla will be along shortly for your final dress fitting. I trust you'll stay long enough for that."

She and the other noblemen disappeared into another room, and I quietly fumed.

"I take it you're having as bad a day as I am," someone murmured by my elbow.

It was the boy with the book—the young lord hadn't followed the rest into my mother's inner sanctum. He was dressed exactly how I expected the children of the Golden City's wealthy to dress: in an embroidered shirt and trousers underneath a heavy frock coat, ridiculous given the weather. But he looked genuinely friendly, and a friendly face was something I sorely needed at that moment.

"Thank you . . . I didn't catch your name."

"Lord Vanya Arrenley, Your Holiness."

Of course. Of course he had to be a scion of the richest noble in the city, the lord who controlled the quicksilver mines to the west. The Arrenleys also oversaw the biggest of the gambling houses that had sprung up to meet the demand for entertainment.

He caught the change in my expression. "If you would much rather be alone . . ."

"I wouldn't, but I'm not sure what a noble's son is doing here."

He shrugged. "Playing errand boy for my father. I'm the third son, so not as important in the greater scheme of things."

"Not training to be a politician like he is?"

He made a face. "Not as well as Father wants me to be. I'm certainly not important enough to be in there with the others."

That made two of us. "What are you reading?"

"History, mainly." He held up his book, *The Ages of Aeon* stamped neatly across its pristine leather cover. Mother didn't have that in her study. "Perhaps you'd like a look?"

I was surprised, pleased, suspicious. "Why?"

"This is the only copy known to have survived the Breaking. Father guards this book so zealously, I doubt Her Holiness is even aware that it exists. I thought you might like a look. After all, I live to serve the goddesses."

I made a face at him, but his grin told me he'd said that in jest. I was still convinced he had some motive—nothing came for free in the Golden City. "Mother banned books that talk about the Breaking. She insisted that nothing but anger would come out of people forced to relive their trauma, even if just in pages. Are you telling me you own contraband?" That the nobles had access to more books than we did didn't sound fair to me at all!

"Nothing so scandalous, unfortunately."

I hid my disappointment. "It's a work of fiction, then?"

"It's a collection of poetry and hymns allegedly written by one of Inanna's Devoted—or the collected writings of some anonymous madman, depending on which historian you believe. Some of the poems are mild enough, but a few border on the fantastic."

"I see." This wasn't quite my field of interest.

"Father normally has no patience for balladry, but he's quite partial to this book. Strange rituals, guardian statues, the Cruel Kingdom—"

"What?"

"Strange rituals? Guardian statues? Your Holiness, what—"
Seamstress Valla chose that moment to bustle in, wrestling with several armloads of lace and satin, but I was already making for Mother's study instead of the private dressing room where I was to be measured. "I'm sorry," I called over my shoulder. "But there's something I need to do first."

Mother's study didn't have many books—and I remembered now where I'd heard that phrase before. . . .

There! A volume older than most of the others, untitled. I flipped the pages and found what I was looking for:

Where the darkest hour and the brightest light meet
the Hellmouth shall be crossed
by she strengthened under the gift of day,
by she liberated with the gift of night.

But the Cruel Kingdom hungers for a sacrifice.
Sacrifice overthrows chaos.
Sacrifice is necessary
for what was two to become one.

This was it! Unfortunately, the strange poem was still as puzzling to me as when I had first read it months ago. What did a Cruel Kingdom have to do with the Breaking, and why did the mirage consider this so important?

A faint rustling noise. I looked down; two folded pieces of paper had slipped out from the pages. They hadn't been there before.

I picked one up, absently tucking the other into my pocket to read next. I thought it would hold more explanations about the strange writings, perhaps even Mother's thoughts on the matter, but—

Latona, my love, it read. *Three days is far too long not to see you. Farthengrove is a beautiful place, but it does not have you and our children in it.*

My face turned red. A love letter!

Mother never spoke of my father, never mentioned if he was a noble or not. For all I knew, I'd been hatched from an egg she'd nurtured.

The letter was unsigned.

Children, he had written.

I should put this back. I shouldn't be reading this. This was a personal, intensely private letter. About my father.

Potentially my father.

Potentially my father, and *children.*

I continued to read.

I am worried about Asteria. I am not a Devoted, nor have I ever been an important person in the realm of Aeon, but I beg you:

do not leave without healing the rift between you two. She took the gifts in your stead because she knows you have no desire to rule Aeon. We can remain here in Farthengrove and live the rest of our lives in peace now. Forgive her for not telling you of her plans beforehand. She may be ambitious, but I know that she did it for us as well.

You know they cannot be trusted; that they separated you two at birth is all the proof you need that they have raised you to be deceived. Surely there must be a compromise. Think of our children. Sweet Haidee and gentle Odessa would not—

"Haidee."

I spun, my heart pounding. Mother stood in the doorway, eyes glittering with an unnatural light. The paper slipped from my hand, and she watched it float to the floor.

"I'm sorry," I stammered. "I didn't mean to look—"

Mother crossed the room, stooped to pick up the letter. She examined it carefully. Something sparked in her eyes—grief? Sadness? "You've always been too curious for your own good, Daughter."

"Was that my father? Did I have a sister?" I was shaking. How could Mother have said nothing all these years about something so important? "Where are they? What happened to them? Mother, surely I deserve to know who my—"

Fire-gates opened without warning, and a burst of flame reduced the letter into soot and ash. Smoke curled, but the fire left no marks on her palm.

"The gala starts in the seventeenth hour, two days hence," Mother said, every word a threat. "Do not be late."

~

It was later, imprisoned in my room with guards posted at my doors, that I allowed myself to feel anger.

How could she? How *dare* she?

I had family! How could she treat them like they were inconsequential—like my right to know who they were was unimportant? Were they dead? She wouldn't have kept that a secret from me for sentimental reasons.

But what did I really know about my mother? What else was she hiding from me? Because if she could go so far as to hide the fact that I had a sister . . .

I thought about the boy from the desert, so convinced that Mother had caused the Breaking. . . .

It was then that I read the second letter.

> *My love,*
>
> *I ride with all the speed I can muster, but I pray this letter reaches you long before I do.*
>
> *They betrayed us! Refuse the rituals they ask! Destroy the tablets! Flee Brighthenge! The magic that place wields can destroy the world as easily as it can revive it. Remember how you laughed when you said your customs were older than time itself, that Brighthenge spells were meant not for destruction, but for life? That you would have refused if she had foretold the destruction of our children as I'd feared?*
>
> *I was not amused then, and I am not laughing now. They do not intend to kill Asteria for the ritual—they intend to kill you!*

Chapter Five

LAN OF THE TWO LIVES

—————————— ☾ ——————————

"SHE'S TIRED," I SAID, stroking Odessa's hair, exhausted myself. "She should be awake before long. She's in no danger from anything else."

Anything else besides the black spot above her heart—once as small as a penny, and now as large as a fist. For hours I had poured every ounce of magic I had into her, but nothing I did could shrink it back down.

Asteria sighed, leaning back to close her eyes. "You need some rest yourself, Lan," she murmured. "There's nothing else you can do."

She was dealing with this a lot better than I was. Order had been restored now that the danger had passed and the shadowed creature was gone, but I'd spent the aftermath tucked against Odessa's bedside, unwilling to leave her while she slept.

"There has to be another way." What if those shadows inside her grew big enough to swallow her whole?

Asteria hesitated. She turned to Noelle, who, ever the dedicated servant, was hovering by her elbow. "I would like to talk to Lan in private. Ensure that no one else visits Odessa while we're away, and don't leave her side until we return."

"As you command, Your Holiness."

Puzzled, I rose and took one last look at Odessa. Reassured by her deep, peaceful breathing, I left the room and followed the goddess to her private chambers, settling down on a nearby chair. Asteria stared out her window, at the rain and the fog blanketing Aranth while it tried to settle back into some semblance of normalcy, if there ever was such a thing. "You're certain this wasn't the shadow you encountered?" she asked.

My memories were still fractured, but some things I could recall, if vaguely. I wanted to help Odessa, but even those brief glimpses of recollection sent faint tremors through me, like my mind was warning me from remembering too much. "I'm not sure. It felt different. I think the one we encountered *spoke*. We all heard it speak. I think . . . I . . . ."

Nuala. Madi. Cecily. Merritt.

Choose your sacrifice, Catseye.

My shaking redoubled.

"No more," Asteria said sharply. "Don't push yourself, Lan."

"But if there's something I can remember that connects this to Odessa's—"

"Not at the cost of your sanity." The goddess stared off into the distance. A strange smile touched her face.

"How much do you know about Inanna?"

I was surprised by the change of subject. "I didn't even know

77

that goddesses existed until ten years ago, when you rescued me from the city sewers . . . so not much."

"The Great Mother. All goddesses sprang from her line. There was a time when the sun and the moon took their turns in the sky, granting us both the brightness of day and the comfort of night. Nature was bountiful. Inanna fashioned men from the earth and made us in her likeness. But she knew she could not grow attached to any of the world's creatures, lest her partiality sway her mind and make them flawed."

"Let me guess. She grew attached, anyway."

"She fell in love, yes." Sorrow laced the goddess's voice. "With a man she had made, perfect in form and figure. For him she left her other duties incomplete, allowing war and sickness to plague the lands instead of cleansing them. In due time he too died and was sent to the kingdom of death. She followed him there but realized that not even she could defeat mortality. And so, as the legend goes, she split herself in two—one to rule the heavens above, and another, shadowed self to rule the lands below, dooming the world to lie forever in between. And that is why every generation of goddesses bears twins; a sign of her dual nature."

I nodded, still not understanding where she was going with all this.

"When Inanna first descended into the underworld, dark creatures not of her making already thrived there. Shadowed forms of teeth and tusks, demonic entities that hunted for souls to deliver unto their realms. But seven high galla, in particular, served as guardians of that realm. Keepers of the underworld mysteries, distinguished from the others by great horns on their heads. It was they who granted her entry, they who ensured that she could return to the land of the living."

"And one of these galla visited Aranth? Why didn't you mention this before we left for—when I—" I cleared my throat, suddenly hoarse. Galla. Those were the shadows that had killed my team.

"I could not be sure. So many illusions plague the lands outside Aranth."

"What does this have to do with Odessa?"

"I believe the shadow at the port was a high galla. There may be a connection between them and her sickness."

"But why choose her?"

Why not target you? was my unspoken question, but she knew me well enough to answer.

"I don't know. Perhaps it's because she's younger, more impressionable. Perhaps I am not as easy to take. I once had a choice, Lan, like every goddess before me had to make. I . . . chose wrong. But I had no idea how great the ramifications of that decision would be. Had I known that the price for my life and for Odessa's would be a world unmade . . ." She gave a quick, almost nonchalant shrug. "I had a sister, once. We were raised in seclusion, unknown to the people. It was easy for them to forget we were twins."

Much like Odessa growing up lonely in the Spire. Asteria might not have been conscious of it, but she had inflicted on her daughter the same isolation she had suffered. "And what was the choice you were supposed to make?"

"It doesn't matter," she said heavily. "My twin paid for hers with her life. Fortunately, Odessa will no longer be forced to choose, as we had. The high galla will not harm her, that much I know. Regardless"—she drew in a long breath, like she was bracing herself for a forthcoming battle—"you must return to the breach."

"No!" The chair overturned in my haste, but I didn't care. All I could see were the bodies strewn around, the horrifying shadows looming over me with their fanged teeth and their bloody absence of eyes. I could feel the sharp of the dark scraping against my cheek again, a voice that was not truly a voice echoing in my head.

Choose. Choose.

I couldn't go back. I couldn't go back there.

"Lan." Asteria had shifted so that my hands were wrapped in hers, her pale eyes bright. I tried to pull back, but her grip was a vise. "You never told me what happened."

I knew that, and I knew that she had every right to ask. That she hadn't said much about her concern for my sanity. But now it was Odessa's life at stake. I swallowed, licked suddenly dry lips. "I told you about those demons. About how they wiped out the rest of my team."

"Yes," Asteria said quietly. "But you never told me why they spared you."

She'd praised my courage then, my skills. How strong I'd been. How I'd done my damnedest not to let my team all be torn to the winds and served up as meat, a celebratory feast to whatever other ravening creatures made that darkness their home. Everyone had looked at me with awe, like I was someone better than what I knew I was. *Tianlan of the Two Lives.*

I'd said nothing to dispel their assumptions. In my old life as a street rat fleecing the good people of Aranth, I'd stolen and lied to survive. I was still that same fraud, and a black-piped hood and better lodgings couldn't change that.

She leaned closer and released my hands. Hers crept up my face, her touch cool and soothing. "You never told me," she said, "how you were able to travel all the way back from the breach."

"I don't remember." I had no recollection of the passage of time once the slaughter was over, once the shadows had turned away, and I was left with the dead. I had no memories of dragging Nuala back to Aranth until they'd found me beside her corpse a mile from the city, close to dying myself. Our journey to the breach had taken three months of travel, past the Lunar Lakes and then the Spirit Lands to reach the borders of the Great Abyss. I had made it back from there to Aranth in less than a day, with nothing to show but a lover's dead body and nightmares that festered beyond my healing.

"The map you made for us. Was it accurate?"

I gripped her wrists. "You can't let Odessa go to the Abyss. That's suicide. She could die from the journey alone."

"I have no intention of doing that." Asteria turned away, weary. "I thought that Brighthenge, once my temple, had been taken over by the Abyss. But the high galla have a pact with

Brighthenge. The appearance of this one tells me some aspect of my temple has survived, that some magic may still remain there. There are healing springs, powerful magic within its sanctum. The magic that ripped the world apart—it can also cure my daughter. For as long as Odessa's disease could be contained, I thought I could spare her Brighthenge. That is no longer the case."

She looked at me. "I will not force anyone to join unless they volunteer. The mission is the same: find a secure path into the breach. But now it is imperative that we reach Brighthenge as well, and assess its current condition. I would travel to the breach myself if there was anyone who could take my place defending Aranth. Can you say the same? Would you risk returning to the breach again, for her?"

I froze, feeling exposed—like she could read every thought I'd ever had of Odessa, pure and otherwise. "I—I can't go back there—"

"I would ask Catseye Sumiko to accompany the mission as well, if she is willing—"

"I don't need any help!" I roared.

"You're a brilliant ranger, Lan. And in the wildlands, which we still know so little of, you flourish. But you cannot do this on your own."

"'Flourish' is not the word I would use."

"Not even for Odessa?" she asked again, and I *knew*. She wouldn't force me to volunteer, but she'd frame it in a way that I couldn't refuse. "I have eyes, Lan. I see how you look at her.

82

I know of her forays out of the tower, though I suspect you didn't."

"I've done nothing but treat her with respect," I said through gritted teeth. How dare she? How dare she use my affection for Odessa to twist this against me. Had she done this deliberately? Had she selected me for Odessa's new Catseye not because she felt sorry for me, but to keep us both in line?

"Understand, Lan, there's nothing I won't do to protect my daughter. You're the only one left who knows the way back to the breach. What would you have done in my place? If you were her mother and I your subordinate, what would you have done differently? You are of the Liangzhu; *Tianlan* in your people's tongue means 'azure sky.' A bold decision by your mother, I've always thought, to name you for something most people would never see again. It might not appear that way now, but there is no one else I would trust on this journey than you. Will you?"

She knew what I was going to say. If there was anything I feared more than those horrible shadows, it was Odessa's death. "I'll go," I spat out, balling my hands into fists. "Damn you, *I'll go.*"

Asteria rose to her feet, her worry framing her face in lovely lines. "I am sorry, Lan. Show me a better alternative, and I will take it up in a heartbeat."

"It's an excellent plan, Mother." Odessa stepped into the room, Noelle trailing in after her and looking slightly apologetic. "But it would be so much better if I could accompany the next expedition into the breach, with Lan."

I spun around, my face pale, wondering how much she'd overheard. Asteria rose from her chair. "I won't allow that, Odessa."

"Your Holinesses," Noe said, and cleared her throat.

"You don't know." The young goddess had been crying, her cheeks streaked with tears. "You don't know what I know. I know what it wants. It's not going to stop until it finds me, and every day I stay here puts you all at risk."

The creature called her *daughter*, she had said.

"Odessa," I said gently, and she stumbled into my arms, burying her face against my chest. "Did it say something else to you?"

"It didn't need to." Her words were muffled. "As soon as I saw it, I realized what it wanted. I'm the reason it's here in the city. If you're going to that terrible place again, Lan, then let me go with you."

"You've never even been outside the city. And with your condition—" This wasn't how I wanted to protect her. She should be safe in the Spire. What was the point of risking my life if not for that?

She gripped my arms tighter. "Not going outside the city didn't stop the spread of my sickness, did it? I can die just as quickly here as in some other part of the world."

"Your Holinesses," Noe repeated.

"No, you won't," Asteria said sharply. "You'll be safe in Aranth. Our defenses will be enough. We'll fight every monster that comes to these shores."

"You don't understand." Odessa lifted her face from me, her eyes distant. "That creature—it wasn't attacking us. It was *warning* us. Aranth won't survive the year, Mother. The waters are rising too fast, the ice coming in too quickly. In months the city will be gone."

Asteria's vision swept to the forefront of my mind. Aranth, disappearing under the waves. Odessa must have seen it, too.

"Still," I muttered. "We can't—I can't let you just—"

"I will not permit this, Odessa!" Asteria's face was strained. "It's too risky. You can die of worse things out there."

"You knew!" Odessa snarled, turning on her. "You knew this was going to happen! You told me it wouldn't! You saw the galla yourself! I have to do this, Mother!"

"This isn't some game—"

"It was you who told me about the ritual, about Inanna's Song! About what it means to us as goddesses! What difference does it make if I die here or out there?"

"It does make a difference!" Asteria roared, surprising us. The goddess never lost her composure. "Aeon is a dangerous world. You can barely stand on your own two feet for more than an hour, and you still think you can survive the most dangerous place in it? I forbid you to set foot out of Aranth! If I have to chain you up for the rest of your days, there will be no compromise on this! And don't think I won't carry out that threat!"

"You're not serious!"

"Try me!"

Mother and daughter stared at each other; angry, stubborn, neither willing to relinquish her position.

In that sudden, unexpected silence Noe cleared her throat again. "Your Holinesses, we have visitors."

"This is not the time, Noe," I hissed.

"They span the whole coast."

"What?" I made for the window and looked out—and swore.

The galla surrounded us. Titans made of shadows, flickering in and out of vision, yet staying perfectly still. They blocked out the horizon with their vaguely human shapes and towering height, waist-deep in the waters surrounding the ice floes that continued their inexorable journey toward us. They could have attacked long before we were made aware of their presence, yet they—didn't. They watched us silently like colossi, without sound or movement, but the potential for violence hung thick in the air.

Asteria had joined me by the window, but Odessa remained where she was. "They're warning us," the younger goddess whispered. "The world is dying, and they know it."

"But why would they go out of their way to do that?" I demanded. "We're far from allies."

"Aeon's their world, too." Odessa shivered. "If it dies, then maybe so do they."

It was hard to imagine them capable of dying, given how horrific they were. "Are they trying to *intimidate* us?" And was it working?

"They won't hurt us. Not tonight."

"How can you be so sure?"

Odessa stared serenely at the horrifying figures. "I just am."

I stewed. "Noe, I want the city on alert. Find Janella and tell her to—"

"Done."

"Send word to Gracea. Keep everyone away from the shores—"

"Done."

I sighed. "I did tell you not to leave Odessa's side, didn't I?"

"Technically, milady, I am still by her side. The guards keeping watch below have sharp ears. I communicated to them everything I thought necessary through an open window."

"Thanks. Though I would have appreciated earlier notice."

"That was not for lack of trying, milady."

I could feel the patterns swirling around Asteria, glittering with the potential of a small tornado. "I won't permit it," she snapped, her eyes trained on one of the creatures. It moved its head in our direction.

"Mother," Odessa began again, but Asteria made a sharp gesture with her hand. "Thank you for volunteering, Lan." Her voice was too steady, too imperturbable to be natural. "I will take a day with my Devoted to put together another team, and you shall make for the breach the day after that. The journey, at least, should be smoother than the last. Whatever those demons intend, it appears that we have their blessings. Should that change, I am confident that I can hold off any attempt they make to take this city."

"Surely you're not serious," Odessa said, disbelieving. "Lan, tell her you're not going without me."

Breathe. In and out, in and out. "I am going without you." I tried to sound stern, hoped the faint wobble in my voice wouldn't give me away. "I agree with your mother. Whatever happens, this is still the safest place for—"

She turned away from me, her hair shifting to a sudden fiery red.

"I swear that I'll return, Ame—*Odessa*—"

She was out of the room before I could finish. I heard the sound of a door slamming shut.

Asteria leaned out the window. I could hear the crackle of patterns manifesting around her, bathing her in brilliant lights. The winds howled and the rain continued to pour, but her words traveled far, reeking of both fury and desperation. "You have what you want. Leave!"

I didn't know if it heard her, but the monster turned away all the same, and the rest of its terrifying brethren followed.

I stepped away from Asteria, prepared to give her privacy now that our conversation was at an end. But as I glanced back at her one last time, I could have sworn that there was a faint smile on the goddess's lips as she watched the demons wade back into the frothing waters, the waves closing over their heads until they were lost underneath the storm-swept seas.

Chapter Six

ARJUN, LUCKY SON OF A BITCH

———————————— ☼ ————————————

"I GOTTA ADMIT," KADMOS TOLD me, already up to his elbows in innards and fat, "you've always been a lucky son of a bitch. Of course in all the acres of emptiness out here you'd be the one to find a damned whale ripe for the picking." He tossed a wrapped bundle to Derra, who grinned and stacked it up alongside the others.

We'd spent nearly a day harvesting what we could from the dead beast, the Mudforgers doing their best to slow down the inevitable rot with water-based incanta and packing the carcass with good ol' desert salt. Our two wagons groaned as we stacked as many portable chunks of meat as we could onto them; the wheels weren't used to this much bounty at any one time, and they squeaked in protest. I estimated we were about four-fifths of the way done with the salvaging, despite five hours of nonstop work and over half of the clan pitching in. This was the biggest catch we'd had in a long while, and Mother Salla wanted to make the most of it.

"Yeah, Kad, I'm coming up roses everywhere." I tucked my newly refitted Howler under one arm as I scanned the area, frowning. The aspidochelone remains were located at least twenty miles away from our underground home, and the threat of more sandstorms and mirages, not to mention possible ambushes by other nomadic brigades roaming the desert, made our task a nervous one. My hand drifted to the glowfire grenades strung around my hips like a makeshift belt, and I felt reassured by their presence.

I'd been on edge for hours. When I'd gone out on patrol at the end of yesterday's cycle, I could have sworn I'd seen another one of those mirages wandering the dunes.

It had stood there, with no indication that it wanted a fight. It was far enough away that I couldn't see its face, but I *knew* it was watching me, and the watching was what unnerved me most of all. And then it turned away without attacking, disappearing behind another sand mound.

I spent the rest of my shift waiting for an attack that never happened. Faraji, who'd taken over after me, reported nothing out of the ordinary on his watch, but it took me a few hours into the next day cycle to finally fall asleep.

Now, perched on top of the beast's corpse, I scanned the wasteland again, but all I saw was endless dust.

"This will tide us over for months." Mother Salla inspected the strips of blubber we'd lined up, looking pleased. "It is fortunate you stumbled on it before the insects and the heat could render the meat inedible, Arjun."

It was Mother Salla who taught us how to boil those tissues for oil, how to fashion whalebone into durable bows and Howler pieces. She could tan skin into leather, could stretch out food rations to keep us all fed, could hit a bull's-eye at a hundred and fifty yards with an adequate gun and nearly double that with a good rifle. It was she who'd found the underground network of caves that saved our lives, she who'd reared us like she was our trueborn mother. She must have already been old around the time of the Breaking; it was hard to tell what she might have looked like young, though she'd joked once that she'd stopped counting when she hit fifty. Most of us were orphans when she'd taken us into the Oryx clan, and for many she was the only parent we'd ever known.

I cleared my throat. My clan knew nothing about my run-in with the Sun Goddess, and I intended it to remain that way. "Yeah. All that matters is that we're making the most out of it now, right?"

She tilted her face up to mine. "You're rubbing your wrist again."

I looked down, saw that I was worrying at my stump, and let my hand drop. "Sorry. Itching."

"I raised you from infancy, Arjun. I know your tells. You have a habit of doing that when you're keeping something from me." There was no accusation in Mother Salla's gaze, but there was curiosity.

My mind flailed, trying to find the middle ground between telling the truth and continuing the lie. "There was a mirage. I barely managed to dig myself out of the sandstorm it brought in."

Mother's brows knitted together. "I'm glad you're all right, but this is not your first encounter with one. What happened to make you so worried?"

"It knew my name." That had shaken me far more than I was willing to admit. "I didn't even know they could talk."

Mother Salla stared out into the desert, and I saw her jaws clench. "It knew your name," she echoed, so quietly that I very nearly didn't hear her. "They've always been mute before. Something has changed to make them stronger."

"Stronger?"

"The magic spiraling at us from the west—it's been gaining energy. The dead are finding voices. Derra and Salome reported finding one attempting to speak a few weeks back, but they assumed the words were nothing beyond death rattles. Perhaps some are even regaining memories of their past lives, no longer the mindless wraiths they were doomed to become." It was almost like she was talking to herself instead of to me. "Perhaps they have even found some new purpose now. Ah, Asteria. You foresaw this, didn't you?"

"So you're saying there's some new magic making them remember things?"

"I know enough about the patterns to know what's possible. Something might have triggered a surge, enough to motivate new mirages to crawl out of their purgatories and . . ." Mother Salla paused. "And do what? I have no answers, either."

It occurred to me that none of us knew much about Mother Salla's life before the Breaking. We knew she was the best fighter among us, that she could survive almost anything the sands could throw at her, but I never thought about whether she'd learned all that long before the world burned, or if she'd had to in the months after. It hadn't seemed important. "How do you know this?"

She didn't answer, her eyes trained on the horizon. "We have company. Have we gotten all that we can, Mannix?"

"We could harvest more if we've got the time to."

"We don't." She raised her voice. "We're leaving!" she shouted, and everyone dropped whatever they were salvaging and began hoisting themselves up on one of the two wagons, Mannix and Faraji taking the drivers' seats.

I saw clouds of dust rising up from some distance, caught a quick gleam of sunlight catching on silver, and swore. "Hurry!" I yelled down at the rest. Then I planted my foot firmly against the whale's head and adjust my Howler, my sights trained on the first of the rigs coming into view. Nine hundred paces. Eight hundred. Seven. "Come on," I muttered. "Come on, come on, *come on. . . .*"

"Get down from there, you lunatic!" Kad roared from below. "We'd hate to leave you!"

At four hundred paces I could make out the symbol they'd splattered on the side of their fire rigs: rings of flames licking up the sides, surrounding a grinning yellow skull. The Hellmaker tribe: violent, sadistic, psychopathic. Fire patterns sprang up around me, and I let them whip themselves into a frenzy, adding double the spark that was needed. The Skeleton Coast was a vast tract of dry land, but the Hellmakers thought they owned the whole lot, with everyone in it their livestock.

Because the Hellmaker tribe were also goddess-damned cannibals.

"Arjun!" Mother Salla screamed at me.

I pulled the trigger.

The resulting blue fireball sent the first rig careening straight up into the air, breaking apart quickly as it fell back down. A few screaming figures were buffeted up by the momentum, most of them on fire. Already I was reloading and training my barrel at the next rig, sending off another shot before I turned and leaped off the whale, landing with a grunt on a pile of blubber as Faraji gunned the engine. We took off after the other wagon, and I craned my head to see, hopefully, whether the Hellmakers had abandoned the chase after seeing what had befallen their comrades. No such luck.

"I think you just made them angry," Faraji said.

"I'm more concerned about how hungry they are." The Hellmakers didn't have as many incanta casters in their tribe as we did, so their armor was rougher, their spells not as fully formed. They wore black greasepaint under their eyes to limit the sun's glare, and their clothes were cobbled together from what they could salvage in the desert and from the people they'd eaten. It was not a comforting thought. Already the rig taking the lead was firing off shots of its own, missing widely.

But our wagons were heavier than theirs, and no matter how

many incanta Faraji could work into the engines, they were getting closer.

I didn't have time to build up another explosive shot, and my next attempt glanced harmlessly off the side of the Hell-makers' ride. I adjusted my aim; the driver caught one right in the chest, and I knew he was dead long before he'd tumbled off into the sand, his partner frantically trying to regain control of the wheel. A well-placed shot from Mother Salla took him out too, and the vehicle reeled listlessly to one side before crashing against a dune. Two down, four to go.

I popped the cap off one of the grenades and tossed it in the sands just as another vehicle neared. It promptly took out the passenger, leaving a bloody mess on the seat, but the driver continued his pursuit despite being covered in his companion's grisly remains. My second grenade was more successful, exploding right under the rig's engine and turning the machine and the two cannibals on it into a blazing inferno. Three down.

The next closest rig had already pulled up and was worrying our side. Our first wagon had a better head start, which meant they were likely to make it out; ours wasn't looking as lucky. One of the Hellmakers keened, leaping from their vehicle onto ours, but all it took was one swipe of Air from Mother Salla, and the body was falling lifeless onto the ground. When another tried, I shot him point-blank in the face.

"A little more speed would be appreciated, Faraji," Mother Salla suggested through gritted teeth.

"Not for want of trying, Mother, but—aaah!" Faraji clutched

his suddenly bloody shoulder, but managed to keep our wagon steady. I took out the Hellmaker's wheel, and then the Hellmaker, as he fought for control. "You okay?"

"Yeah," Faraji panted. "Just keep racking up the body count on their end and not on ours, aight?"

I looked back to gauge how close the nearest Hellmaker vehicle was, and Mother Salla let out a queer, choked gasp. "What is that?"

I turned to where she pointed. Up ahead, a figure clad in black was walking toward us, unmindful of the ongoing chase. It wore clothes similar to those on the mirage I'd encountered before. It was hooded, but from the curve of its body and the way it walked, I thought it might be a woman. "Well, shit," I hissed.

"Do I run it over?" Faraji shouted, panicked. "Do I run it over?"

Salla, the mirage murmured.

"Mother Goddess," Mother Salla whispered. *"Jesmyn."*

"Go around it!" I yelled, hefting the Howler up so I could fire at the Hellmakers again.

But as we watched, telltale winds began to whip around the mirage, and I saw the swirl of dust and grit that was becoming far more familiar than I wanted it to.

"Sandstorm!" Mother Salla screamed. "Everyone down! Faraji, keep it steady!" Already she was grabbing some of the bigger pieces of whale meat and piling what she could over Faraji and then herself, and I hurriedly followed suit.

At the speed we were going, there was no way to reverse course and retreat. The mirage waited placidly as we tore toward it, close enough for me to hear it whisper **Arjun** once again before it was soon lost within the storm bearing down on us. We cowered as best as we could in our seats, the stink of brine and entrails mixed in with the hot, arid taste of sand. I closed my eyes and tried to ride it out, but there was a sudden burst of pain on my arm, a heavy blow that knocked me into the air, and I landed hard on the ground, grunting.

The wagon was gone, and Faraji and Mother Salla along with it, but the wind continued to howl, and there was nothing else I could do but huddle up and hope none of the Hellmakers ran me over.

When everything died down, I cautiously poked my head out. The wagons had escaped, that much I was grateful for. I struggled to stand, but a heavy boot landed on my spine and I flopped back into the sand.

"Hello, meat." The heel dug painfully into my back and I stopped moving, hoping desperately that I hadn't broken a second Howler in only two days. Hands grabbed me, turned me over, and pinned me into place. I looked up at a grinning Hellmaker with wild blue eyes and a scar running down the side of his face. There was a knife in his hand.

From what I could see, one of the rigs had survived the sandstorm, and the wreckage around us told me there were no casualties for the Oryx clan. Except, potentially, me.

"Thought you could get away?"

"Technically," I said, because they were idiotic enough not to deprive me of my gun while I was down and therefore, hopefully, also idiotic enough not to notice me quietly feeding more patterns into it while I bought myself more time. "Most of us got away."

He stooped down, and a line of spittle dropped from the side of his mouth, dangerously close to my head. He shifted his foot, and I bit back a cry when he kicked my injured arm. "A lot of difference that makes to you, meat. You'll keep us fed and fat for the next couple of weeks, and we'll hang your skin out like a painting over my tent."

"That's not really as flattering a tribute to my looks as you think it is." Something was wrong. The winds had picked up again—without the mirage nearby, the desert should be as still as stone. I shifted my head and caught sight of a black figure out of the corner of my eye.

Bereft of witty rejoinders, the Hellmaker simply snarled and raised his knife.

And was slammed away by a sudden gust of wind that spiraled out from nowhere. Almost at the same time, I fired my Howler, catching one of the Hellmakers who'd been holding me down, turning him into a red streak on the ground in two seconds. My next volley was weaker, using enough patterns to sting in favor of speed, but a second Hellmaker still hit the sands, wailing and clawing at his eye.

Now on my feet, I tossed another grenade at the group and ran toward the lone vehicle. I could hear sounds of pursuit behind me, then a burst of fire that came dangerously close to my ear before the shooter's snarl was cut off abruptly. The sandstorm was back, but this time concentrated solely on the Hellmakers while I stood, unharmed, scant feet away. The mirage had not dissipated when the sandstorm had passed. Instead, it remained where it was, watching me—like it had when I'd been on patrol the previous day.

I leaped into the rig and, after a few seconds of fumbling, found the trigger to start the engine. The mirage was protecting me. The idea terrified me more the longer I dwelled on it. Why the hell was it protecting me?

The Hellmakers were still up to their eyebrows in grit and tornadoes, too busy to notice when I tore out of the place, wheels screaming. I turned back to look one last time. The mirage did nothing, only watched me leave, and from underneath its cowl I saw a mouth form words that weren't words. **Inanna awaits you and the goddess**, it whispered, and I fled.

Mother Salla clung to me, nearly weeping in her relief, after I'd stumbled wearily into the entrance of our caves. "We thought they'd gotten you," Millie said, sobbing outright, clinging to my hand.

"I know you've made it your personal mission to kill off every one of those damned cannibals," Mannix said, a relieved grin on his face, "but did you have to make us worry, too?"

"Couldn't leave till I got my hand on one of their sweet

rides," I bullshitted, grinning and hoping my legs wouldn't buckle underneath me now that the adrenaline had passed. "Can someone see to my other hand? I think I'm running out of them."

An hour later, I was tucked into my cot with my injuries bandaged, a good stiff drink of codrum already down my throat, burning my insides in the most pleasurable way. My brothers and sisters surrounded me, needling and begging me for more information.

I hammed it up, of course. Skipped the part where I was facedown in the dirt with a knife trained on my head, and the part where the mirage came swirling in to save my butt. So I bragged about nabbing the rig while fighting off cannibals, and they ate up every word.

Except Imogen, the brat. "So you're really going to claim that you faced off ten of those buggers with nothing but a Howler and got off scot-free."

I waved my injured hand in her direction. "Not completely free of the scot, as you can see."

"Are you sure there weren't twenty of them? A hundred? Ten million?"

"Immie!" I protested. The others broke into laughter.

"Be nice to him," Kadmos chided, slinging an arm over her shoulder. "He brought you a new ride to tinker with."

Imogen rolled her eyes. "Not if I have to hear some ridiculous story about Mr. Perfect Warrior over here."

"I believe him," Millie said sincerely.

"That's because you're *too* nice, luv," Kadmos chortled.

"Hey, Arjun wasn't the only one who got injured, you know," Faraji complained, his own shoulder dressed and treated.

"I agree," Mother Salla said firmly, shooing the others away. "Faraji, go back to your own bed so you can heal properly. Kadmos, see to the rig. Scrape off that foolish insignia on the side and give it a good scrubbing." They had already pushed the vehicle down into the camouflaged crevice where we kept all our other wheels, preventing anyone from realizing the area was inhabited.

"Are you sure you're okay?" Millie asked worriedly.

I laughed. "I'm fine, Mil. Go see what you can do about my gift. You're the best mechanika around here. Kad'll only muck it up."

"Thanks," Kadmos said dryly, and Faraji chuckled.

"How did you get away?" Mother Salla asked the instant everyone was gone.

I straightened up. "Getting to the point so soon?"

"While I don't deny your skills as both a fighter and a sharp-shooter, there were far too many Hellmakers out there for you to make it back with nothing worse than a bloodied arm."

There were no windows in the caves, so I focused instead on the small fireplace, where some sort of stew was bubbling over. Tarika could do wonders with salt and the herbs she'd managed to grow underground, surrounding them with soft patterns of light and what little water we could spare, and it smelled like she could make even rotting whale meat palatable.

"The mirage saved me," I admitted slowly. "When the sand-storm hit, it didn't dissolve like the others. The Hellmakers were about ready to cut me up if it hadn't intervened. I nipped out of there while they were busy." My turn to ask a question. "When we first saw it, before we got hit—you said something."

Mother Goddess, she had said. It was blasphemy, for one of us to offer up any sort of prayer to Latona, and she had said it without thinking. And she had mentioned a name, as well.

She nodded. "Jesmyn. A Devoted I was particularly close to. I . . . recognized her voice."

"What?" I sat up. "Devoted? Like the Sun Goddess's Devoted? You were *friends* with one?"

"No. The Devoted of a different goddess."

"You told us they were *all* evil. You said that they destroyed the world, that they should be never be shown mercy."

"The *surviving* goddess and her Devoted, yes. Latona killed my liege." Her voice was pained, not a sound I was not accustomed to hearing from someone as strong as Mother. "They killed Asteria, the goddess I served, and they killed Jesmyn, my dearest friend and the strongest of us all."

"But why?"

"Only one of the goddesses was supposed to rule Aeon. Asteria had been chosen, but Latona—Latona yearned for the privilege." Her voice hardened. "I swore that she would pay. That I would avenge Asteria upon the Sun Goddess's body."

Things clicked into place. "You were a Devoted. Not the Sun Goddess's Devoted, but her sister's?" She nodded. "And the mirage . . ."

"Jesmyn." Mother Salla stared into the fire. "This is not the first time I've seen her spirit wandering, but this is the first I've ever heard her speak."

She'd *seen* her before? "I didn't know."

"I always thought it was my punishment, to be haunted by the friends I couldn't save. I would have known her anywhere. The dark robes we were required to wear, the silver brooch she wore that was much like my own. I had lost mine years ago, but she had always been the more careful of us. She was as punctilious in death as she was in life."

"The other mirage knew my name. It—this Jesmyn—knew my name as well. Why?"

Mother Salla gazed steadily at me. "Your mother was a Devoted."

I would have fallen, had I not already been sitting up. "What?"

"Devika. She was a beautiful woman. She led Asteria's Devoted. Jesmyn and I served her. She died at the Breaking." Her eyes flicked past the fire, into some memory I couldn't see. "I swore to protect you, to keep you safe. You were the first child I took in, the most precious to me. Even in death, it appears Jesmyn and the others seek to keep the vows they swore both to Devika and to Asteria."

"Why didn't you tell me all this before?" I choked.

"What use would it have been for you to know? They are dead. The world lies in ruins."

"They might be dead, but they've come back all the same."

Mother nodded. "It was my decision to say nothing. Your

mother would have wanted you to live without being encumbered by the sins of our past. But if some of these mirages have started to regain sentience, then there is something they want us to know. Jesmyn studied the goddess's prophecies, believed the daughters would prove more vital to the world's survival than their mother. I was more skeptical—such auguries were always cast in riddles—but perhaps she might have been onto something. One of the daughters is dead now, but one still remains."

Haidee. "So what do I do?" I asked. "Head out into the desert and look for your friend? Ask her what she wants to tell me? Not that I think she'll be in any mood to talk."

"You are not as angry as I would have expected you to be."

I shrugged. "I would have been meat on a hook in the Hellmakers' camp if she hadn't intervened. But I want to know more. The mirage mentioned that Inanna was waiting for me."

She froze. "That means she wants you at the Great Abyss, Arjun. But why?"

The Sun Goddess's face slid through my mind, and I shoved it back out. "I don't know."

"You're rubbing your wrist again."

I jerked my hand away. "I . . . met someone yesterday."

"The goddess's daughter?"

I made a sound of disgust. "You knew all along?"

"I wasn't completely sure until just now. Jesmyn always believed Haidee and her twin could save us. But with the young Odessa dead, we thought it was impossible." She smiled at my stricken expression. "I'm not mad, though a little put out you didn't trust me enough."

"I do trust you," I muttered, flushing. "It's just—I didn't exactly—hell, I was going to kill her, and she spared my life!"

"Latona would have hunted us down had Haidee told her of you. She would have sent out armies by now."

"You've seen her about too, haven't you?" I accused. "Why didn't *you* kill her?"

It was her turn to pause.

"You told me the goddesses gave us all the evils in this world," I persisted.

"I said that Latona should be destroyed, yes. But as for Haidee . . ." Mother Salla smiled sadly. "She was a delightful baby. I used to watch over her. I've seen her exploring the desert on her own during the last two years. I've raised my gun more than a few times and aimed it her way."

"But you never shot at her."

She heaved a sigh. "No. It's one thing to shoot Latona, and another to shoot a seventeen-year-old girl who I doubt had much say in her mother's atrocities."

Mother Salla didn't have a lot of flaws, but a soft spot for kids appeared to be one of them. My brothers and sisters and I were proof of that.

"You said we had to take them all down," I argued, but with less heat than I knew I should have. "You said they won't hesitate to kill any of us."

"Didn't you say that she spared your life?"

I scowled, not having an answer to that.

"She cares, this girl. She is not to blame for Latona's sins. Her own history is . . . complicated, one I doubt that she is even aware of. She would be more likely to agree to a cease-fire. Even an alliance."

"These are a lot of assumptions based on the words of mirages, Mother."

"'When the dead find words, the goddess and the Devoted son will meet atop a fish not a fish, on a sea not a sea. It is she who travels to the endless Abyss, and it is he who guides her.'"

A chill took over me. "What the hell?"

"One of the prophecies Jesmyn was fond of quoting—nearly eighteen years ago. A prophecy tied to Haidee and her sister when they were born. It was an enigma then, but I can tell," she added, gazing at my face, "that you know what it means."

I nodded, still speechless.

"Death would not have changed Jesmyn's goals. If she has reason to see you both to the breach, then I believe her."

"How many times have you seen her out there?"

"Enough times to accept what she tells you. I taught you everything I know, Arjun, and you've always been my best student. If there's anyone capable of surviving the desert, it would be you. But you must understand all the risks involved. As good as you are . . . the desert can take even the best of us."

I stared at my hand. "Do you know what that mirage wants us to *do* there?"

"As far as we know, the world died at the Great Abyss. Brighthenge, the hallmark of the goddesses' power, was destroyed. But that temple held the answers to life and death, to mysteries so complex they puzzled even the cleverest Devoted.

106

Perhaps there are answers waiting there that can save us. Perhaps Jesmyn's specter knows this. I believe Haidee has an important part to play there, and it would do all of us well to see her alive to accomplish this. I agree with Jesmyn—if anyone can protect her, it would be you. Any possibility that the world can be healed is one worth making the attempt for."

"Now you sound like—" and I cursed quietly, bit my lip.

"Who?"

"Nothing. No one." I straightened. "Are you saying you're giving me permission to—leave?"

"I permit nothing. I've always instilled in you all a sense of independence, that you are beholden to no one, that you must make your own choices. We have no reason to return to the surface. We have enough food here to tide us over for months, enough materials to keep us occupied until then. If you believe that this is the right course for you, then I will not stop you. All I ask is that you return home in one piece. Unless you have need of reinforcements—"

"No. Nothing's been proven yet. I'd rather—I'll do this on my own." Silently, I cursed Haidee. All this crap about saving the world and healing the breach—I didn't want her to be right. "Kad spotted the army leaving the Golden City days ago, off to the mines. Our stocks might be replenished, but we could always do with a little silver." The goddess's army was always ripe for ambush, if one knew how to strategize. "And my arm'll be good by the time they return."

She laughed at my eagerness. "You're right. We could use

more resources for our metalwork. What are you suggesting?"

The mirage wanted me at the butt end of the world, with the whale-loving goddess. To do what?

I wasn't angry that Mother Salla had never told me about my past. But Haidee—if she was right—

And it was better than some mirage chasing after me forever, hounding me to get to the Abyss before the next group of cannibals found me in between sandstorms.

"We still have those Silverguard uniforms from our last outing." That had been fun, waylaying the soldiers manning a Golden City caravan that had lagged behind due to the sandstorms that frequently plagued that route. We'd stolen a good share of the silver and left the men butt-naked for their superiors to find. "They're due tomorrow at the city if their schedule holds, and I'm feeling lucky. One last good haul before I have to leave and find the mirage."

"Is that true?" We both turned around to find the rest of my siblings peering in at us from the doorway, having obviously heard enough of the conversation, because Millie looked about ready to cry. "Are you going to leave, Arjun?"

"We're going with you," Imogen said immediately.

I scowled. "No, you're not."

"You're going to head off to hunt down some weird mirage on your own?" She snapped. "Are you *trying* to die?"

"No, but you're not abandoning your own responsibilities just so you can come with me to test out a theory." I knew very well that it wasn't just a theory, but they didn't need to know that. Every instinct I had told me that I was going to find myself at the Great Abyss whether I wanted to or not. And there was no way I was going to drag my brothers and sisters into that.

I didn't want to be right, but I've never been *that* lucky.

"Are you really going to let him go?" Faraji asked Mother.

"I believe Arjun's doing the right thing."

"Besides," I added, "I shot down ten million cannibals, remember? I'll be fine."

Imogen looked faintly envious, but Mother Salla's blessing had clinched it for the others. Kadmos clapped me on the back. "I still have no idea what's going on . . . but damn, man, you better get back soon, or I'm gonna claim full ownership of that rig you just brought back."

I grinned. "Well, once Millie finishes working her magic on it, I'll bring you back to the spot where the Hellmakers abandoned a couple more. You'll need a replacement, because I'll be taking this one with me."

Besides—the damn goddess *still* owed me for destroying my Howler.

Chapter Seven

MALEEYAH, FORMERLY ODESSA

———————— ☾ ————————

"TELL ME AGAIN WHY YOU'RE coming with us," Lan asked, while I curled up on her chair and watched them pack.

Noelle shrugged. "You'll need someone to look after your belongings for the journey."

"You do know what happened on my last expedition, right?"

Noe shrugged again. "Only that I wasn't there to take care of you, milady."

They'd been at it for hours, and I would have laughed at their ridiculousness if I wasn't also sulking. I was all too aware that I was trespassing despite my anger, but as Lan had said nothing about kicking me out, I saw no reason to leave.

Instead, I let my gaze drift around her room. For a self-professed former thief, Lan had significantly little in the way of possessions. The room was almost spartan—I remembered her joking once that she only stole luxury items but never kept them. A small wardrobe contained what little there was of her clothes, and the dresser was practically empty of creams and lotions, save for a tube of ointment that protected against windburn. The closest she had to paintings were a row of ranger badges lined up neatly on the wall.

"Having my clothes folded properly is not a major requirement for this campaign, Noe," Lan was saying. "And not to be offensive about it, but you don't exactly know any magic to fall back on."

"Several other members of the detachment have no proficiency in spells, either." Noelle had always been unfailingly polite, but from my experience, that didn't mean she didn't get her way when she dug in her heels deeply enough. "And I believe that what I lack in magic I will more than make up for in other areas should a fight arise."

"Nobody faces off against twenty-foot shadows armed with just a cudgel, Noe."

"We must agree to disagree, milady. If you will excuse me, I have my own supplies to pack."

"This isn't over, Noe! There is no way I can in good conscience send you out to—she's not listening to me," Lan sighed, as Noelle glided out of the room before the ultimatum was finished. "And why are *you* smiling?"

"You two are very close, aren't you?" I asked softly.

"We grew up in the same orphanage. She was two years older than me. Her mother was a proper chambermaid, but her father was a general and taught her how to defend herself. She's the best fighter I know, saved my ass more times than I can count. I'm still not entirely sure why she took up this position when Asteria offered. She was always looking after the spiders that the orphanage accumulated, and I'm surprised she wasn't keeping any as pets at the Spire." Lan lowered her voice. "Are you still mad at me?"

The corners of my mouth turned down. "Are you still mad at *me* for not telling you who I was?"

"I said it no longer mattered. Odessa, you know I'm the last person here who'd want to return to the breach. But if the choice is between me risking my life and losing you, I'd choose the first."

On some other occasion, I would have felt giddy at the confession. "And I'm saying that losing *you* isn't worth it. Let me go with you."

Lan shook her head. "On the off chance I don't make it back—" I scowled at her, and she quickly amended, "On the remotest possibility that I don't . . . well, as much as you don't want to hear it, Aranth will go on without me. I can't say the same if we lose you."

But the strange galla *wanted* me on the journey. They wanted me to reach the Great Abyss. They wanted to protect me. Lan knew nothing about the rituals, but I did. Even now, when I closed my eyes, I felt a strong pull east, past the seas that bordered Aranth and into the wildlands.

The galla with the blue jewels had given me the first of their gifts, and this newfound feeling was part of it, I was sure.

But Lan's and Mother's minds were made up, and I knew nothing I said would change them.

"What are these?" I asked instead, touching one of the badges. There were names inscribed on every one. *Merritt, Wricken, Derel, Aoba, Cecily, Madi, Yarrow . . .*

Lan paused. Her words came out in short bursts. "Former comrades."

My hand dropped as I realized what that meant. "I'm sorry."

"It's a ranger custom. It's the least we can do to honor them."

Lan wasn't wearing her own badge, either. It was up on the wall a slight distance away from the others, together with another name. I touched it, reading the name off its shiny engraving. "Nuala?"

"Nuala," Lan said, her voice so very strange, and I felt jealousy well up, tamped down immediately by shame.

A chorus of bells rang out, a signal for the group to gather at the dock. Lan slung her bag over her shoulder. "Odessa." Her voice was almost pleading. "I don't want to leave with you angry."

"If I promise not to be angry, would you stay?"

"I can't."

"I guess we both can't have everything we want, then." I walked out of her room without another look back, my eyes brimming with tears that I quickly dashed away. It was no good crying now. Not when I had to act fast.

Maleeyah was waiting for me in my room; unsurprising, because I had summoned her there. "Is there anything I can do for you, Your Holiness?" she asked nervously, shifting from one foot to the other. "Your mother is expecting me at the pier soon."

"It will only take a minute," I said gently, and in this at least I was honest. I opened my aether-gates, channeling every kernel of magic I had straight into the other girl.

She made no sound when she toppled over, unconscious, and I caught her easily, laying her out on my bed. Mindful of the time, I started stripping her of her clothes, then shimmying out of my own. Maleeyah and I were almost the same size, which was why I'd chosen her. I used Air patterns to lift her slowly into the air, letting the currents ease her into my dress.

I flexed my fingers and summoned Light this time, and watched as Maleeyah's hair changed from black to a multicolored array similar to my own, though her hair didn't quite float the way mine did. I shifted her onto her side so that her back faced the door. Mother would assume I was still mad; whenever we argued, she would often leave me to my own devices afterward, checking in again after supper. By the time she discovered this ruse, I hoped to be long gone.

Then I turned the patterns on myself, checking my progress in the mirror as my hair grew darker, the same shade of black that Lan had found so appealing when we first met. The memory sent another shot of guilt through me that I quickly elbowed aside. No use in dwelling on that now.

"I'm really going to go through with this, aren't I?" I asked my reflection. A small, traitorous part of me wanted to remain in the Spire. I'd never done anything like this before.

But I had to go. I knew what those galla were. The blue jewels gave away their identities.

Once upon a time, Mother had sat me down and told me about Inanna's Song. It was a ritual every pair of twin goddesses undertook; a pact Inanna had made with the Cruel Kingdom to keep these demons from escaping into Aeon. But when their turn had come, Mother's twin had made a mistake and caused the Breaking. Mother never told me what that error was, only that I would not need to go through the ritual like they had.

The galla's appearance proved her wrong.

I combed what locks I could down my face to obscure my features, pulled a cowl over my head, and grabbed the bag I had packed several hours ago. I had to do this. If it meant I could save the world somehow, or reverse the effects of the Breaking . . .

"I'm sorry," I told the sleeping Maleeyah. It would be ten hours or so before the lethargy I'd introduced into her system dissipated. She'd be the perfect decoy.

The others were already gathered by the small pier. Above our heads the *Brevity* loomed—our largest and fastest ship. I'd watched them careen it two days ago, cleaning it from top to bottom as best they could despite the thunderstorms and lightning lancing across the sky. It was Mother who had christened it, joking that she hoped we would use the ship that way— briefly and only when necessary. So much for that.

They were loading cannons and armaments up the gangplank, numerous weapons of war I didn't even know we had. At least *Brevity* and its crew would not leave unarmed.

The Devoted were carting various trunks bearing equipment, clothes, and enough food to last us months. Half had volunteered for the journey, with the other half expected to man the fort while the rest were away.

"We'll fish for what we can and save some of the nonperishables for later," I heard Gracea tell Mother. I adjusted my hood and walked calmly past them and onto the ship, despite my wildly beating heart. "The riverwinds near the city have been mapped out well enough, at least. Once we reach the Lunar Lakes, we'll disembark and figure out the best next step."

"Take good care of the people under your charge, Gracea," Mother replied. "I want you to lead this expedition, but I will not accept any more deaths."

The Starmaker shrugged. "The alternative is Odessa's ill health and the destruction of Aranth, Your Holiness. We shall be most careful. The first expedition's mistake was to divide into smaller groups in an attempt to cover more ground. In their haste, they put themselves in danger, without regard for their own—and at great cost. By keeping together we shall increase our chances, however strong those shadowed creatures are. My skills will be enough to repel their darkness."

It was clear that she was delivering snippy criticism at Lan, and I very much wanted to slap the smile out of the Starmaker on her behalf. The Catseye herself was already on the ship, surveying the seas with grim determination, and I made sure to stay away from her. Of all the people on this expedition, it was

Lan who could recognize me despite all my attempts at camouflage.

Noelle strolled up the gangplank, carrying multiple weapons of different sizes with considerable ease. Lan's mouth fell open. "Where did you get those?" she sputtered.

"Her Holiness has a small armory, milady. She gave me permission to select as many weapons as I required."

"You must have cleaned out her inventory, then," Lan said, as Noelle handed her a halberd. "Do you even know how to use these?"

"I believe I am more than proficient. And Her Holiness has blessed them all with Light, which makes them just as deadly."

"Are you, perhaps, planning on using them all at once?"

"I thought you might be interested in a few, milady."

"At least now I know how you've been amusing yourself in the Spire while I was away." Lan gave the halberd a few practice swings, testing its weight. She sighed. "I'd still rather you stayed with Odessa, Noe."

"I could say the same for you. But we are here, and by the looks of it, we are about to depart. Have you said your goodbyes to her?"

Lan looked down. "We didn't leave under the best circumstances. I wish I could have . . ." She stared back out at the city, then turned away. I hid my face from view, blinking back tears.

A loud crash made me look up; a clerk had stumbled, tipping over a Devoted's trunk and sending clothes spilling out.

"You incompetent degenerate!" Holsett came striding forward, face red with fury. He raised his stick, and the clerk cowered back.

But Lan was there, staring down the older man. "Let it go, Seasinger," she said, her voice calm. "It was an accident."

"She's right," Seasinger Graham said, coming up behind the man. "There'll be worse days ahead. Learn to control your anger now while we're still on dry land."

Holsett stared hard at Lan before moving away, muttering.

"My apologies, Lady Tianlan," Graham said. "Tension is high today, but that's no excuse for this kind of disrespect."

"Not a lady. Thank you for speaking up as well, Seasinger." As Graham left, Lan extended a hand to the clerk. He scrambled to his feet, shooting her a grateful look before bowing quickly and scurrying off.

"Is it always like this?" the Catseye asked, staring after the retreating young man.

"I've been told that Holsett has a temper at times," Noelle suggested.

"No. What I meant was—" Lan paused, sighed. "Never mind. Graham seems all right, but I'm not sure I can say the same about some of these Devoted."

Neither could I. I had limited contact with most of Mother's subordinates, but I always thought them hard taskmasters. This seemed a little extreme, though, even for them; the expedition no doubt had everyone on edge.

A horn sounded from somewhere below, and the planks

were raised. I watched the sails unfurl, heard commands being issued by Gracea, who stood behind the wheel.

Lan snorted. "Might not like that old git, but she was once a shipman's daughter. I suppose she knows what she's doing."

"You have little experience with ships, milady?" Janella was idling by her side, looking nervous and fiddling with the strings of her hood. Like the other clerks, she had on a muted gray cloak, though she wore a scarlet robe underneath it.

"I like to do all my thinking on dry land," Lan said sourly. "I'm surprised to find you here, Jan."

The other girl smiled nervously, and her fingers brushed back a small lock of her dark hair. "I might not wield any magic, milady, but I am well-versed in the histories of Aeon, even in the lands after the Breaking. The history of Brighthenge is my specialty. I believe my knowledge will be of some use to the crew."

"I hope so, for all our sakes. It didn't go so well for me the first time." The anchors had finally been hoisted, and I could feel Air patterns holding steady behind the sails, maintained by one of the Windshifters as the ship began to inch its way out of the harbor. I risked a peek back and saw Mother gazing out after the ship, a satisfied expression on her face as we left the dubious safety of Aranth's port and began our journey into the wildlands.

Don't sound the alarm. Don't sound the alarm. Don't sound the alarm. It was only, finally, after the city slipped from view that I exhaled my relief, surprised to find my knees shaking. Mother had always seemed omniscient to me. I never thought I would be able to outmaneuver her, or get away with this. . . .

How would she react after discovering me missing?

How angry would she be?

Would she come after me? That thought horrified me most of all.

But the fear soon passed, replaced by the dizzying realization that I was *out of Aranth*. I leaned over the railing, bracing myself against the wind, and I couldn't stop the laughter rising out of my mouth. I was out of the Spire! I was no longer trapped! For the first time I was *free*, and it was hard to contain the sudden elation that bubbled up from my chest.

And then all too quickly that jubilation faded, and I was doubled over, coughing weakly against the bars. Damn this weakness.

A few puzzled glances were being directed my way, so I abandoned the fresh air and scuttled toward the cabins, still giddy. A mumbled question led me to the room Maleeyah was supposed to be occupying, and I sat down heavily on the small cot. The high wore off soon enough, and was replaced by trepidation.

I'd always—almost always, I amended—obeyed Mother. What *would* she do when she discovered me gone? Send out another group after me? Once we reached the riverwinds, that would be practically impossible.

I opened my pack and drew out a thick volume. It wasn't mine; I'd stolen it from Mother's collection earlier that morning. I turned it to a page I'd read so many times before I could repeat the text from memory.

When they approach with lapis lazuli,
accept their offering of clarity.
When they approach with the blue turban of the open country,
accept their offering of courage.
When they approach with the twin-egg beads,
accept their offering of abundance.
When they approach with the lapis brooch,
accept their offering of life.
When they approach with the jeweled measuring rod,
accept their offering of beginnings and endings.
When they approach with the sapphire ring,
accept their offering of rulership.
When they approach with the glittering eyes,
accept their offering of a mother's love.
For every gift, a terror.
For every radiance, a sacrifice.

Inanna's Song. The ritual that mimicked her descent into the underworld. All the goddesses had performed this rite, and now it was my turn.

This strange text was all I knew about what to expect—Mother had been keen about not telling me the specifics, much to my frustration. It said nothing about what came after accepting the gifts, only that it guaranteed peace in Aeon.

And that, once upon a time, Mother's twin had made a mistake that disrupted the ritual and broke the world. A catastrophic mistake whose details Mother had refused to tell me about. In hindsight, I wished I'd insisted on knowing more. . . .

I thought about the strange horned shadow, its beard of blue jewels. An offering of clarity. I'd seen my first vision in that encounter, of Aranth dying—was that my gift? For every radiance, a sacrifice. What sacrifice then would it demand from me?

"You were wrong, Mother," I said softly. "World's end doesn't mean rituals do. It's my turn now."

Still—was I right? Was I interpreting these rituals the correct way? I had little idea of how they'd been accomplished in the past to make a comparison. What if this was all a trick?

Had I even interpreted my *vision* correctly? Was the destruction of Aranth something that would happen in my lifetime, or a warning for a time still far in the future? I had been so sure it would take place within a year's time, but . . .

I closed my eyes, trying to assess myself. Save for the earlier bout of dizziness, I hadn't suffered from exhaustion since leaving Aranth, despite all the excitement. I felt better out here than I'd ever had in Aranth. Strange, since the shadow in my heart had grown since. Was this another of the galla's gifts?

I didn't know what the ritual's endgame is. But surely, if this was the common practice done with every goddess that lived before me, it would be to everyone's benefit for me to finish it? If this could save Aranth, maybe even permanently counter the effects of the Breaking, then why not?

I'd just have to push through, I decided. I had nothing else to look forward to but a lifetime of isolation back in Aranth. I'd rather take my chances with Brighthenge.

There was something written along the margins of that page—a scrawled offhand comment that had not been part of the original text. It was not in Mother's handwriting.

A demoness is what men call a goddess they cannot control.

That line haunted me for years. It didn't seem to have anything to do with the rites, so why had someone written it down here?

The ship reeled, and I nearly slid off my cot. The waves out here were capable of capsizing larger ships than the *Brevity*; without the Windshifters, we probably would have sunk long before we reached any of the riverspouts.

My head spinning, I grabbed onto a post for support and waited until the dizziness passed, then shoved the book back in my bag. Perhaps the open air would help me breathe easier, though I would have to make doubly sure no one saw through my disguise.

The first person I saw was Lan, retching noisily over the side of the ship, Noe placidly standing beside her and holding her long hair up. "I hate this," the Catseye groaned into the seas below. "I *hate* this. This was why we went through the damn wildlands on foot instead of taking a ship."

"Quit slacking off, Maleeyah." I turned, surprised, and a sack of potatoes and a paring knife were shoved into my hands. "We're gonna need our strength," Windshifter Gareen said gruffly. "Peel these and make sure they're ready for supper later."

"Why aren't *you* peeling the—" I began, then remembered who I was supposed to be.

The man grinned cheekily. "Because I'm a Devoted and

you're not. I'd find Merika, but Graham's still . . ." He paused, then grinned. "Anyway, get on with it, or Gracea'll be pissed when there's no supper to be had." He darted off to where Windshifter Halida was waiting for him, rosy-cheeked and giggly. I rolled my eyes.

I couldn't exactly refuse without blowing my cover, so I scurried off to a quiet area so I could get this over with.

But there lay the question: How did you peel potatoes, exactly?

I'd never had to peel any kind of food in my life. It was something I'd always taken for granted, and no one had thought to teach me. I stared at the knife. It ought to be simple enough, somehow. Scrape the sharp edge along the skin and it should slide right off. Right?

It worked better in theory than in practice, and an hour later found me having nicked myself twice for every successful swipe I made, with five badly peeled potatoes for my efforts. At this rate, I was certain I would faint from the loss of blood, and the ship's crew would wind up either starving or poisoned.

Another call sounded from above, and I glanced up to see Holsett gesturing frantically. "Riverwind ahead!" I heard him shout, and the deck exploded into a fresh flurry of activity, people lashing the sails or pushing some of the heavier cargo to one side or just bracing themselves for impact. I looked ahead and gasped aloud.

The riverwind would be a thing of beauty if we weren't heading straight for it. It was composed of visible currents of air flowing the way a river or stream would, except they did so several inches above the waves. My past history lessons told me this was easily one of the largest patterns of Air independently existing, and how it was able to flow on its own without any outside influence, human or otherwise, was still a mystery to our scholars.

"Angle us toward its mouth!" Gracea shouted, and I saw a small spinning entrance resembling a large waterspout, serving as a bridge between the sea and the riverwind.

I swallowed hard. We were going to make the crossing through that?

Gracea yelled out several more commands, and I felt a sudden lurch as we sailed within range of the spout. With a heavy shudder, the whole ship lifted up from the water, spinning slightly despite its heavy bulk. I clung to part of the railing, potatoes tumbling everywhere.

I cast a panicked glance around and found Lan and Noelle together, both clinging to the rails as I was and also to each other; Noelle still quite stolid and nonchalant, and Lan the closest thing to horrified I had ever seen her.

It took a minute for us to bridge the gap; the ship righted itself quickly enough, but instead of sailing across the seas, we were now literally sailing *over* them through the long tunnels of air above the waters. Despite the heavy winds around us, we felt none of the gusts; Lan sank down to the deck with a relieved groan, her head in her hands.

Faint laughter echoed all around, and the others returned to their duties now that the initial danger had passed. I scrambled to pick up the potatoes that had gotten loose, wincing when I accidentally nudged one of my cuts.

A flash of red caught my eye. Another sack landed by my feet, and Janella grabbed a small stool, sitting down on it. She took out her own knife. "What's taking you so long, Malee?" she asked impatiently. "Where's the hot water? It's not like you to dawdle. I know you're a bit nervous, but Gracea made it clear these were supposed to be ready by the time we found the spout and there's not many peeled—" She came to a stop, staring hard at me.

In my initial surprise, I'd forgotten to cover my face. Anyone on the ship who knew Maleeyah well enough would not have been fooled by now, but I had been hoping to draw out the facade for as long as I could.

"Hold out your hand," Janella finally said. I did, and she placed my knife on it, angling it into a different position than I'd previously been holding it. "You'll need to peel the skins like this, Your Holiness," she said quietly. "But first, you'll need to pour some of the hot water from this kettle I brought into this pot. Let the potatoes steep for a few minutes before you start peeling. The heat helps slide the skin off faster, you see, and it would prevent a lot of those cuts you've been accumulating."

I gulped. "Why are you not sounding the alarm, Janella?"

"Way I see it, Your Holiness, there's no point. We've just entered the first of the riverwinds, and from what I know of the map Starmaker Gracea had out earlier, it would be impossible to return to Aranth until we've drawn closer to the Lunar Lakes. I'm in no position to be doling out the scoldings, so I suppose I should leave that to my betters. In the meantime, though, Catseye Tianlan would yell at me for allowing you to be hurt like this." She smiled kindly. "I suppose you were worried about us, too. I heard that you wanted to come, but Her Holiness Asteria forbade it."

"You're not going to tell on me?"

"Did you really think you could stay on this ship and never get caught?"

I shook my head, sheepish. "I was hoping to hide until returning was deemed impossible."

"I reckon you'd met your goal." Janella looked concerned. "I trust Maleeyah isn't too out of sorts?"

"She's fast asleep on my bed at the Spire," I confessed. "She'll be drowsy when she wakes, but that's it."

"I can *try* to keep up with the pretense if you want to drag it out, but I can't guarantee much." Janella glanced to her side, where Lan was bent over and throwing up again. I ducked back down. "Count your lucky stars that Lady Tianlan is too busy being sick to observe much, Your Holiness."

"What is this river?" I whispered. "I've never seen anything like it."

Janella brightened. "Beautiful, isn't it? The theory goes that when the world broke, the flow of magic in nature was disrupted as well. Trees bursting into flame of their own accord, acid rainfall leaving the ground barren, the creation of river-winds like these that are strong enough to bear ships—with the world no longer turning, the patterns became imbalanced. All our understanding of the laws of nature has been thrown out the window."

"Creature ahead!" someone screamed.

Janella started. I whirled, just in time to catch the silhouette of a large tail, barely visible against the hurricanes around us, before it disappeared into the changing winds.

"Hell." Lan wiped at her mouth. "I want a report, any of you who saw it. Is it one of the shadow creatures?"

"I—I can't be certain, milady." Gareen spoke up. "It seemed solid to me."

"Mereen, Graham, Miel—I want you off to starboard. Holsett, Aleron, Tamerlin—divide the port side among yourselves. I'll take the helm. Noe, take the back."

"Stern," Noelle corrected.

"Whatever the hell it's supposed to be called, you're over there. If you see anything, yell out. The rest of you, prepare to attack on my mark. Air knives and ice blades only. Let's not summon up stronger wind while we're being tunneled in from all sides." Gracea might know how to maneuver a ship, but Lan knew how to fight. The others scattered to obey.

I couldn't keep my eyes off Lan. It was stunning to see her in her element like this. Despite the danger, I could feel my breath catching. Even Captain Lazar from *The Pirate and the Princess* had nothing on her.

Janella let out a small shriek, clapping a hand to her mouth. I barely managed to repress one of my own; for a second, the winds behind us had parted, and we saw an eye half the size of the ship, staring down at us. And then the currents closed over it again, and it was gone.

"Starboard!" I heard Cathei yell out, but almost immediately something slammed hard into the hull, sending most of us tumbling to one side. A few volleys of ice shards flew through the air, but I wasn't sure if any of them made a hit before the creature swam back out of sight.

"Everyone, hold on to something that's bolted down! Gracea, find someone else to take the helm!" Lan screamed at the Starmaker. "I want as much illumination as you can give me!"

The older woman paused. "You can't give me orders—"

Another hard slam, this time at port. "Unless you want this ship to shake off every bolt and screw it has, you're going to do what I say and like it!" Lan all but snarled.

But the second hard impact had already convinced Gracea. Blinding light ripped down both sides of the ship, and there was a loud wheezing scream that almost deafened me. Once our eyes adjusted, we saw a large creature with a round bloated body and overly large pupils, blinking back from the sudden glare. It turned its bright black eyes at us and shrieked again.

"Ice!" Lan roared, and the next volley of icicles hit their mark. The monster thrashed frantically, rocking against the side of the ship.

"Your Holiness," Janella croaked, but I'd already hopped up

and dashed toward the railing. With the steady buffet of winds, I knew it was hard for the others to form the ice they needed for their projectiles. I peered down into the churning waters underneath us, farther away now that the riverwind was slowly ascending, with us along for the ride. I reached out with my hand, concentrating, willing the unruly seas to obey my unspoken command. The waters were an inky, putrid black, almost indiscernible from the night sky surrounding us. I could feel their patterns leaching out toward me, slow-moving and slack, and I struggled to amass as much as I could from them.

But I couldn't. I was too weak to spin the patterns like I wanted, too weak against the size of the ship and the winds tugging us into all directions.

I saw it, then: towering on the other side of the ship was another massive galla, its dark head wrapped in a turban made of gleaming sapphires, from which a pair of horns sprouted. It was large enough for it to bend its head down toward me from where it stood, and no one else seemed to notice. It was a sooty, looming shape against the gray clouds overhead; without its jewels it could have disappeared into the sky behind it, camouflaged against the lightless night.

The first galla had gifted me with clarity. Was this second for courage?

It extended something that passed for a hand, and I realized it was waiting.

I had accepted that first galla on impulse, but to accept the second now was a conscious decision, and with it meant accepting every consequence thereafter. I wavered, for a moment unsure. Could I really do this? *Should* I do this?

But the screams of the others soon shook me out of my stupor, and I reached out to secure its grip.

Be satisfied. A divine power of the underworld has been fulfilled. You must not open your mouth against the rites of the underworld.

And then it was gone.

The monster was back, circling around us so quickly that I knew we wouldn't have time to react before the next strike. But the magic now bubbled around me, thick and hungry where it had previously been enfeebled and out of bounds. I was almost there. A little bit more, a little bit more . . .

The large creature retreated slightly, then surged forward again, mouth opening to reveal rows of jagged black teeth, but Noe, who had scampered partway up the stern, took careful aim. The monster wailed and reeled away, one eye slamming shut as my steward's javelin found its mark. It rolled over, still somehow buoyed up by the winds, trying to shake the hurt away. Though injured, it drew closer, angrier now, ready to try again.

My water-gates opened.

The corpulent beast slammed hard against a sudden wall of ice that separated it from the ship, with enough force that I was certain the loud crack that resonated through the riverwind was not the sound of ice breaking apart, but the sound of an inhuman head being split open.

With one last scream, the creature tore away, leaving us

blessedly alone. "The galla of courage it is, then," I murmured. It was an apt title. I felt . . . strong. Stronger than before I'd gone onboard the *Brevity*. Channeling that much power through my gates should have made me pass out. But now—

The lights sparked and dimmed, and Gracea braced herself against the wheel, breathing hard. Lan managed a long, throaty laugh. "Damn, Noe. I'm not even sure if wounding it was a good or bad thing for us, but that was some throw."

"It was a good javelin," Noelle said mournfully, staring down at the depths.

The others were picking themselves up from the floor, nervous laughter interspersed with faint cheers. Lan straightened up, then marched in our direction. I whirled around frantically, trying to find some means of escape, to no avail.

Grimly, Lan tugged my hood down. "Your Holiness," she said, and my heart plummeted. "You're right. We both really can't have everything we want."

Chapter Eight

HAIDEE THE DEBUTANTE

——————— ☼ ———————

THE CACOPHONY OF SOUND THAT accompanied my entrance threatened to rupture my eardrums.

Mother had these parties twice a month to keep the Devoted and the rest of the bourgeoisie occupied in these times of peace. To most, the celebrations were a break from the monotony occasionally interrupted by nomad attacks and sandstorms, neither of which had ever been successful when pitted against the resolute strength of the Golden City's air-domes.

I don't blame the people for wanting a distraction. And only Mother could find jugglers, bards, dancers, and other talents to cultivate in the middle of this desert, to curry enough demand to make such performances a thriving industry on its own. An orchestra composed mainly of trumpets was not the standard at these grand functions, but this was my first official debut into society as an eligible bachelorette, and Mother had pulled out all the stops to celebrate.

Seamstresses, too, flourished in their trade, and I was wearing one of Vella's best fashion creations—a flowing white gown that made me feel pretty despite my slightly ungainly movements caused by the thick, stiff brocade. Typically, a dress like this came with a handmaiden to follow behind me and carry the end of the train, but I had waved her away earlier in the evening, deciding to risk people stumbling over it at inopportune moments for the chance at some privacy.

Mother and I hadn't talked since that incident in her private chambers, and I couldn't blame her. I had broken her trust but felt she had done the same to me. Didn't I have the right to know who my father was? And as her heir, shouldn't I have access to more information about the Breaking and everything that had happened there?

And then there was the discovery that I had a sister. What kind of person would she have been? Would she have loved tinkering with gears like I did, or would she take more after Mother, organized and clever? Knowing about her sooner would have made life a little less lonely—but Mother had decided otherwise.

And also, the letter: *Flee Brighthenge! The magic that place wields can destroy the world as easily as it can revive it—*

It seemed likely that my father and my sister were both dead, judging from Mother's reaction—but had they died at the Breaking?

I was just as stubborn as Mother was. When I snuck into her chambers again the following day, she had cleared her study of

134

books, and empty shelves met my eyes. I was determined, however; if I had to run back out into the desert and get my answers
out of the mirage instead, I would.

Mother was chatting pleasantly with Lord Leron and some
of her Devoted on the other side of the room. I shifted nervously, resisted the urge to scratch at the back of my neck and
the faint itching there. Like many of the guests today, Lord
Leron had arrived with several sons in tow, hoping I would
select one that would suit my fancy, as if they were nothing
but properly turned-out petticoats. This was a custom every
goddess endured—we could select our own mates from a pool
of suitors, with the subsequent engagement announced later
that night, and the wedding four months after. Mother's idea
of a compromise had been to delay any engagements for a year
until I was sure of my decision, while holding more galas in the
meantime.

Most of the sons in question didn't appear to be offended
at being subjected to this selection process, as if they were
slabs of meat rated for quality—I suppose the benefits far out-
weighed the possible insult. But I had no intentions of getting
affianced today or in the immediate future. It felt like another
millstone around my neck, tying me down to the duties of a
goddess-queen, preventing me from venturing out into the desert on my own, as I wanted.

"The belle of the hour," Mother said lightly as I approached
her and her circle of Devoted. Most I already knew by face,
but I dutifully made my introductions like I was meeting them

for the first time. "Stay with us for a while," Mother encouraged. "Lord Kellivore here has something to say about the Sun Towers."

"You do highly commendable work there, Your Holiness," the man complimented me. "I admit I have little knowledge of gears and cogwheels. How they power the Golden City may as well be magic to me!"

"Thank you, milord," I murmured. "With better resources, I warrant we could do even more."

"I don't see how much more you can improve barring better access to rainwater," Lord Manderey pointed out. "Given our limited supply of silver and ores, Her Holiness and her daughter are working miracles."

"Speak for yourself, Harold," Lord Ackers retorted. "I wouldn't mind expanding the dome to have more land for gambling houses!" Laughter met that comment.

"If we had more supplies," I said, before I could stop myself, "we could do even more than that."

"How so, Your Holiness?"

"We could build controlled shelters outside the dome for the other people living in the desert. With them, we could house a small community with ease, milord," I said, growing excited by the idea. "We'd only need rudimentary construction materials, but we'd beef them up with quicksilver and the same mechanisms we employ up at the towers at an affordable cost. The greenhouses we use here can be employed on a smaller scale even out in the desert, as we have the right tools to keep them sustainable. I have a plan to tap into the aqueducts for . . ."

I trailed off. Half the lords were staring at me like I'd lost my mind; the other half looked on pityingly.

"And why, pray tell," Lord Ackers said, "should we care about those violent nomads?"

"It's . . . well, I assume that if we helped them, they wouldn't be violent any longer."

"I don't see the point," Lord Ledermene said. "They would see that as a sign of weakness and demand more from us. They're a temporary threat, anyway. They'll die out soon enough."

"If you'll excuse me, gentlemen," Mother murmured, laying a hand on my arm. "There are a few things I wish to discuss with my daughter."

We moved away, to a small veranda. Most of the city was asleep, and the dome's reflective sheets had been activated, lowering at least 40 percent of the sun's glare. Beyond our territory there was nothing else but sand as far as the eye could see. The Golden City had been built close to the Salt Sea, but that was before the waters had ebbed further, and we had to rely on the construction of aqueducts that drew water from underground to meet the city's needs.

"You've always been too passionate, Haidee." Mother said nothing about out earlier fight; we rarely talked about our spats in their aftermath, pretended like things were back to normal between us without ever voicing our concerns again.

"I don't like them treating me like I don't know any better," I said stiffly.

"They're men. It's in their blood. But they're right about one thing: our subjects take priority. I know that it pains you to think about those suffering outside the dome, but there is very little we can do about it at the moment."

"Why not? Why can't we help? If we're the rulers of Aeon, then surely we can do more than just rule a city! Just because so few people remember the world before the Abyss doesn't mean we should give up figuring out how to set things right!"

"I've been at this longer than you have. It's not something you can fix with a snap of your fingers. You can't save everyone, Haidee."

"I know." I stared out into the horizon, wondering how many people were still out there, starving and struggling and hating us like the nomad boy had. "I just feel like it doesn't have to be a choice between us and them."

She adjusted the straps on my dress. "But it is a choice, my dear one. It's one we have to make, however unpleasant. Vella did marvelous work on your gown today."

"I feel like I'm wrapped up in the world's most expensive bandages."

She chuckled. "When I was your age, the dress I wore for my own party had a longer train. It was easily three yards' worth, and I was sure everyone present had stepped on it at least twice. Someone finally had the temerity to take a knife and put an end to my misery by cutting it away."

"Somebody destroyed your dress?"

"I was furious about it, until I realized what he was doing. And then I . . ." She stopped, a small smile on her lips, before recalling herself. "Lord Alphonse is waiting for you, my dear. It's best you make your rounds."

I groaned but obeyed. Some unspoken rule had me switching admirers every half an hour or so, probably to provide a wider sampling of beaus, so to speak.

In the hours that followed, I found my worst fears confirmed. Lord Alphonse talked about nothing but sandracing, Sir Emmett was obsessed with pedigree as much as his family was, and I had caused a minor scandal earlier by throwing my drink at Sir Leopold's face when he intimated I should focus on gowns and primping while he ruled the city on my behalf. Sir Belledier, my latest suitor, was nice enough, but he also had the personality of a mushroom, and small talk was the extent of his conversation.

At least the desert nomad had been honest about his opinion of me.

Annoyed by the thought, I'd asked for punch, seeking any excuse to send Belledier away, and he complied, trotting off obediently. I leaned back against a nearby wall, watching a few jugglers tossing knives at each other while an appreciative audience clapped.

"You look like you bear the whole world on your shoulders," a voice commented, and I turned to see Lord Vanya offering me a glass of sweetwine.

I was glad to see him. "Well, it *is* a challenge to walk in this outfit."

"I could see that, though it's a rather picturesque look. It's the kind of dress that forces you to stay put whether you like it or not. One could say it was an impractical choice, but I'd say it was a deliberate move on Her Holiness's part. No offense meant to Her Holiness."

I glanced sharply at him. "You seem to be very familiar with my mother's inclinations."

"I would say we all have a significant motive in gaining your mother's approval, Your Holiness. I was worried when you left abruptly the other day."

"I apologize for that. Personal business. I see you come as the lone suitor of the Arrenley family?"

He shrugged. "Ivan has already been suitably married off, and Misha, while unattached, is too busy pursuing a military career to make courtship a priority. I am afraid you're stuck with me for company, if you can stomach me long enough not to throw a drink in my face like you did with poor Leopold."

"Do you intend to rule in my place, since my poor little head is 'too beautiful to comprehend the complexities of running a city'?"

"Ah, so that's what that cad said? You should have chucked the whole punch bowl."

I laughed, and he grinned. "Make no mistake, Your Holiness. My father would like to cement an alliance with Her Holiness by marrying our house with yours. And I'd like to believe that I'm quite capable of managing the Golden City *with* you instead of *against* you. And at the risk of offending every asinine chauvinist in this room, I would even go so far as to say that I'd step back and watch you take the lead in most matters, shut my mouth wherever I have the least experience, including incanta and gates. I know quite frankly that my main role in this affair is to beget your mother another heir, but I hope I could offer something more than that."

My cheeks were red. "Not a lot of people would admit all this so openly, milord."

"I'm blunt, if I must be honest about it, but I'm also well read, moderately intelligent, and passably attractive. I can string words together without sounding like a fool most of the time, and I'm told I'm not too much of a boor. I would also add that had I not been attracted to you and thought that we would make a formidable team together, I would have told my father to go gird his own loins and woo Her Majesty himself if he wanted to marry into her family—but that sounds a bit too calculating after I listed all my favorable assets and fluffed myself up, doesn't it?"

"You're incorrigible." Given all the double standards that had gone into planning this gala, his honesty was appealing. There was, of course, always the chance that he was a magnificent liar gifted with a devil's tongue, but I was willing to overlook that for now. "But I'm not even certain I want to get married yet."

"Neither am I. Just say the word, tell me you're not even remotely interested in me, and I'll leave with my metaphorical tail tucked between my legs. But if you would like to at least be friends, then perhaps you can honor me with a dance so my father thinks I've seduced you just a little?"

I laughed louder this time, offering my hand to him, which he quickly accepted. "Sir Belledier was supposed to fetch me a drink," I remembered, just as we reached the dance floor.

Vanya settled a hand on my waist and lifted the other with my own. "Boring as he is," he said dryly, "I thought I'd rescue you from more platitudes about the hot weather and sandfishing. I told him you wanted to see his collection of sandworm tackle. The poor fool probably rushed home to retrieve it."

"And you were quick to swoop in to take his place." Mother looked approving as we swept past the throne.

"If you would rather view his collection instead, I can step aside."

"What I know about sandworms would fill a thimble, and my interest in them even less." Vanya was an excellent dancer, expertly weaving his way around my ungainly dress and keeping his steps slow and deliberate so I wouldn't have to struggle to follow. "And what do you do in your spare time beyond getting rid of potential rivals?"

"You make me sound like a criminal, Your Holiness—"

"Just Haidee. 'Your Holiness' makes me sound old."

"Well, there's history, as I mentioned before. And poetry."

"Well versed in the Cruel Kingdom, as you've also mentioned?" I began on a sudden impulse, hoping I sounded like I knew what I was talking about. I regretted not taking a look at *The Ages of Aeon* when he'd offered. Mother's untimely arrival had lost me that opportunity.

He took the bait. "Your family has never been light reading, milady. But Ivan was old enough to remember the Cruel Kingdom being taught in his lessons—he was thirteen then, long before anyone thought the Breaking was possible." He snorted.

142

"He claimed there used to be vast oceans—more than one!—where people could swim to their hearts' content. How ridiculous is that?"

"And the Cruel Kingdom?" I persisted.

"He was a lazy student, but he did tell me stories of Inanna descending to the Cruel Kingdom for her lost love."

Inanna! I knew that legend, but I hadn't known what they had called that bleak underground world she had entered. "So Brighthenge was where the Breaking took place?"

"Well, Brighthenge was allegedly built atop the Cruel Kingdom's entrance. The previous goddesses created some sacred barrier to prevent monsters from escaping, or so the books imply."

"Has anyone in your family ever seen this Brighthenge?"

"My father has never been. Few people were allowed entry—only the Devoted, I believe. My apologies, Your Holi—uh, Haidee, but while everyone knows about the goddesses of Aeon, there's very little documentation about their personal lives or the mysterious customs that surround them. Her Holiness dislikes talking about it—Father's seen her demote or exile others from her court just for asking. He'd never even seen your mother until after the Breaking, when she emerged from the Great Abyss and proclaimed herself the sole surviving goddess."

"And that's all you know?"

"As much as anyone here does. There's a limit to what even my father can collect." He looked puzzled. "But surely you knew that?"

"What else do you do when not reading up on my family history, then?" I changed the subject, not wanting to arouse his suspicion. More than enough time to broach the topic again later, once his guard was back down.

"I've fiddled a time or two with gears. I've been endeavoring to build a water clock at my father's manor as an experiment to determine a more accurate way of telling time, but it's been a long process. I've figured out a way to substitute most of the gears we do use with those constructed from silver alloys and a mercury-zinc compound."

My eyes widened. I wouldn't have put it past him to have done his due research on me and discovered my interest in all things mechanika. It was also possible that he was a genuine tinkerer like I was. "I've never had enough silver on hand to experiment on that scale. You'll have to show me one day."

"Is that an offer to visit?" Lord Vanya asked archly.

I wrinkled my nose at him. "Yes, you rascal, you've gotten me interested." And maybe I'd find another chance to read his book, too.

"I would've thought you'd have built water clocks up and down the borders of the city by now."

"Water clocks are considered nonessential architecture. And with the towers breaking down or losing a gear every other week, it's hard to muster enough energy for other things—"

A commotion had risen by the throne, where Mother was already on her feet. A swift gesture put a stop to the orchestra, and the music trailed off into silence. "I've just been informed

144

that the Silverguards are marching for our city gates," she announced. "The drawbridge shall be lowered in five minutes. Redguards, form up by the entrance and prepare for potential hostilities." She gestured at me, then turned toward the stairs.

This was not how we welcomed the returning army from the mines. "Excuse me," I said, shaking myself free of Vanya's hand, then stumbled up the stairs toward the roof deck, which offered a full view of the sands outside the Golden City for miles around.

From there I could see the Silverguards marching home, their steps several beats quicker than usual. My eyes flicked to the borders.

The dust storm coming our way was terrifying to behold. It stretched the whole sandscape as far as the eye could see. The army should be able to outrun it, but there could be no room for error.

"What's going on?" Vanya had followed me up; he too stared at the approaching disaster with mounting horror.

"I need to go higher," I blurted out, pointing to another set of stairs that would lead to the highest point in the city. "Stay here."

Vanya hadn't been lying when he said he would defer to me in all things magic; he nodded briefly and stepped back. "Good luck, Lady Haidee," he said fervently, casting another worried eye outside.

Mother was already consulting with Yeong-ho when I arrived. Above us was a perfect view of the blazing sun, unmarred by clouds. A clear sheet of curved glass, which was nonetheless dense and as durable as steel, separated us from the deadly glare. The dome had always protected us from sandstorms in the past, but I'd never seen one of this intensity before.

"We don't have much time, Haidee," Mother said sharply. "Focus. As soon as the army makes it inside, we'll begin."

We'd done this enough times together, although the size of the winds raging toward us made me nervous. I could see that the incanta encompassing the dome's shield had already been lowered by the city entrance. The army was no longer marching in step; they were racing to the gates, the heavier caravans following behind them.

The sandstorm was nearly upon them. "Come on," I whispered, "Come on guys, come on. . . ."

"Open the roof," Mother instructed. "Close the gates."

Yeong-ho hesitated. "Not all the Silverguards have made it in, Your Holiness. And the caravans—"

"There is no time, Yeong-ho. Do it!"

The man bit his lip, pushed down the lever. The shield of air above our heads flickered and began to dissipate, leaving just enough space for us to rise above the dome's protection. Mother's eyes glowed a light blue, and a smaller roof of air covered us again, offering just enough defense from the sun's heat while still enabling us to direct our incanta out of the city, without the dome's stronger barrier in the way.

I followed Mother's lead and gated Air, watching as the storm shifted closer and closer. "A few seconds more," Mother

146

whispered, voice strained from the weight of all the wind she was stopping herself from unleashing.

Most of the Silverguards had found sanctuary past the gates, leaving half a dozen still without protection. One of the soldiers stumbled and fell. Another man sprang into action, dragging his fallen comrade away. For all his bravery, I knew neither had any hope of making it through.

I ignored my mother's startled shout and directed my energy in their direction, prematurely releasing my incanta. Winds surged past me, with enough force to prevent the sands from slicing through the duo. I saw the second man force the first back onto the ground before flinging himself down, and both were lost in the resulting dust.

"Haidee!" Mother yelled, and I hastily whipped up another round of air just as the gates to the Golden City closed completely, and the bridge was swiftly brought up again. A fresh layer of Air flickered into view as the dome materialized over the entrance, once more airtight. The sandstorm hammered against the barrier, but it held secure.

And then, to my horror, the whirling sands began to *burrow* into the ground, attempting to bypass the dome by going *underneath* it.

I heard the cries of horror coming from below, from those who had remained behind to watch. I could hear Yeong-ho yelling out frantic commands into the receiver at Jes, ordering him to expand the shield several yards down into the sand to block the attempt.

Mother sent a spinning counter-wind straight into the center of the storm, and I followed suit. We both hit the eye, repelling some of the force and mitigating its strength. We fired again and again, weakening it further; after the twentieth or so attack the sands finally settled, until not so much as a breeze remained.

Mother turned to me; still breathing hard, still angry. "You acted before I gave the order to."

"They were going to die!" I saw the two soldiers picking themselves up. One lifted his right arm, and I saw that he had a stump instead of a hand. My heartbeat quickened.

Mother had fallen silent too, her eyes not on the soldiers, but on a speck in the distance that was rapidly drawing closer. "Mirage," she seethed, voice dripping with venom.

This specter looked similar to the one from a few days before. It wore the same robes in the same style, with a similar cowl drawn up over its face. A silver brooch gleamed out at us from the center of its chest; it was too far away for me to know for certain, but I was convinced it would have the same half-finished star insignia. It explained the dust storm's unusual activity—it had been a direct, controlled attack.

I couldn't see its face, but I knew it was looking up at us.

Mother's hands flickered with energy, and a ball of fire appeared in her hands, growing larger with every passing second. With a snarl, she lobbed it at the silent creature, and the ground around it exploded. I gasped, and Yeong-ho slid down, hands protectively over his head.

The mirage stood, unhurt, while the sands around it burned. It made no other attack.

"Why didn't it disappear?" I whispered. "When we destroyed the sandstorm, it should have . . ."

"It wears the robes of my sister's Devoted," came a hiss from Mother. "Sometimes the dead find it difficult to die." Mother threw lightning this time. It sizzled the ground around the mirage, but undaunted, it refused to move. One lightning bolt hit it directly; a fission of energy ran through its body, but even then it made no sound, showed no emotion, and remained upright.

"Die!" Mother cried. "Why won't you die?"

It ignored her; instead, it looked right at me. **Haidee**.

Mother turned away. "Yeong-ho, I want the whole city on lockdown," she ordered.

"Mother," I quavered, "it said my name."

"No one is to enter or leave without my express order. There will be no rest until that *thing* is nothing but a smear on the ground. Tell Captain Irrada to prepare our glowfires, all that we can spare and then some more. Ah, Lord Vanya." My suitor had crept up the stairs, looking alarmed. "Regrettably, the ball is canceled until further notice. Inform General Alistair that all residents are to return to their homes to await further instruction. I will be imposing martial law on the city today and setting a curfew. No nonessential personnel are to be wandering the streets or the punishment will be severe."

The boy nodded, flashed me a rueful smile. "Perhaps another

time on the water clock, Lady Haidee."

"I'm happy that you've found at least one boy to interest you," Mother said, "but you are to wait inside your room until I summon you again."

"But why?" I protested. "You know I can help. Mother, *it knew my name*. And if that mirage is harder to kill, then you'll need everyone capable of incanta—"

"Do not question my orders again, Haidee!" There was anger in my mother's eyes, but also fear. "Do as I say!"

I stared back at her. "You know, don't you?" I said slowly. "You know that it's looking for me."

"Don't be ridiculous."

"You don't want me anywhere near it. On any other occasion, you would tell me to stay by your side, to add to your spells and attack it alongside you. There's something about the mirage that you're not telling me."

"Haidee, return to your room."

"Not until you tell me!"

"No excuses, Haidee!"

"Why won't you help me? If there's a chance to return everything back to what it once was, then why not pursue it? We could help everyone here in the city and even beyond—"

"Because I don't intend to!" Mother shouted. "Inanna took everything from me with the Breaking! This will change nothing!"

"There are people dying out there! We can't just pick and choose who we should save! They deserve sanctuary, too!" The

150

next words fell out of my mouth before I could stop myself. I knew I should have shut my mouth, given Mother's previous reaction, but her refusal to tell me still hurt. "And I deserve to know about how my father and my sis—"

The slap stunned me; for all the ferocity of our arguments, Mother had never raised her hand against me before. She was in just as much shock as I was; she stared at her hand, lowered it.

"I won't say it again, Haidee." Her words were slow and eerily calm, but every syllable was a warning not to be crossed. "Return. To. Your. Room. Lord Vanya, see to it that she does, then report back to me."

"I'm sorry," Vanya whispered, as we left the throne room, looking shaken. "I don't know what's gotten into Her Holiness."

"You don't need to explain her to me," I interrupted bitterly.

"Is there anything I can do?"

"I suppose disobeying her would be out of the question?"

He hesitated, clearly conflicted.

I had to smile; he really was trying, wasn't he? I leaned over and gave him a friendly peck on the cheek. "My apologies. I didn't intend to put you in a situation where you had to choose between my mother and me. Have a good day, Vanya."

"Haidee," the boy began, troubled.

I curtsied to him and entered my room, made a point of bolting the door so Vanya could hear the lock being turned, and wrestled my way out of my ungainly costume so I could slip into my mechanika garments. Once I was certain he had left,

I grabbed the bag I had spent the better part of two days packing, and then unpacking, and then repacking, grunting slightly under the weight. I'd designed it myself and had affixed three small wheels at the bottom—two in front and one behind—for better mobility.

Mother had burned the letter for no other reason than to prevent me from reading it. If I couldn't get answers from her, then I'd have to find information through some other source. I knew there was little to find out in the desert, and that the mirage could still be hostile, but Mother's actions had all but cemented my decision.

There would be guards stationed at my door before long. Mother had already posted sentries just to make sure I went to her stupid party.

I had no intention of using the door, though.

I dragged a trunk out from underneath my bed and fished out a bolt of silk that I'd carefully measured and cut into a conical shape. After strapping the cloth to my back with a secure harness and with my bag in tow, I climbed out my window.

My room was a couple of stories below Mother's, but as our tower was the tallest in the city it was still a fatal drop at over a hundred feet. Balanced precariously on the small sill, I glanced down at the unforgiving ground below me and gulped.

Theoretically, it *should* work. I'd used a dummy for an initial experiment, to great success—but knowing the math was sound was one thing, and using a living, breathing person to test it out was another thing entirely.

I gripped my harness grimly like it was a lifeline—technically, it *was*. *This better work,* I growled to myself, and jumped.

My room faced away from the city, toward the dunes, which made it less likely for anyone to pay attention to my free fall. I hoped my screams would be lost to the winds as I plummeted down, so much faster than I had imagined. If I pulled the sails too soon, I could slam hard into the tower walls. Too late, and I'd be a lifeless stain on the ground.

Now! I tugged hard and the makeshift canopy billowed up above me, halting my rapid descent. Almost at the same time I channeled Air, the currents pushing up against the silk to help stabilize my steering and further slow down my descent. But I'd miscalculated a little, opening the chute a second past when I was supposed to, and wound up tumbling ungracefully across the ground.

Reassured that nothing was broken, I sprang up, checking whether anyone had seen me. There was no outcry. No one had spotted my flailing attempt at flight.

Jes and Charley were manning the gates; they gaped at me as I arrived. "Where are you going?" Jes demanded, staring at my bag; I'd brought a good amount of equipment I was certain I would need for the trip, but I'd never thought to make it light-weight. The wheels helped, but it was still an ungainly load.

"You have to let me outside, Jes," I pleaded.

He hesitated. "I . . . Haidee . . ."

"Is it because of the mirage?" Charley asked. "Or was the ball really that bad?"

"It's important, Charley. I swear, I might know a way to stop these sandstorms once and for all, but I need to go outside." I felt bad about stretching the truth, but I was desperate.

"It looks like you're not coming back for a while."

"I'll return, I promise. You both just have to trust me."

Both hesitated and glanced at each other. It was Jes who made the decision, flinging the lever across. "I do, Your Holiness."

I hugged them both. "Thank you."

No one noticed the gates opening, or closing once I'd made it across. I scrambled behind one of the abandoned wagons and paused for breath, pleased that I had gotten away so easily.

It took me a moment to realize, though, that the caravan was empty of goods. Where had all the silver gone?

A hand landed on my shoulder, holding me in place while an arm wound across my throat, cutting off my breath. An arm, I realized, that ended in a stub where a hand ought to be.

"You dimwit," a voice rasped against my ear.

Chapter Nine

LAN THE HUNTER

——————— ☾ ———————

"THERE IS NO DIRECT ROUTE back to Aranth at this point," Seasinger Graham said, scanning the seas of air like an answer lay tucked in between the currents streaming on either side of the *Brevity*, waiting to be found.

"Then *make* a way," I fumed. The cause of my ire sat beside Janella, looking both apologetic and unrepentant at the same time.

Graham spread his hands. "You ask the impossible, Catseye. According to the maps you yourself supplied, there is no return path back to the city until we reach the entrance leading into the Lunar Lakes, and that will require at least two more night-spans."

Gracea scowled, not liking this new revelation one bit. For once, we were in agreement. "This will delay our trip considerably, but we have no choice. As soon as we reach the fork in the river that dips back north, we'll make the return journey to bring Her Holiness back, and then start out again."

"You can't!" Odessa blurted out, starting to her feet. "I need to be here!"

"No, you don't." I had never felt more furious at her. "You're going back to Aranth. There is no bargaining to be had here, Your Holiness."

She flinched. "I have to be here. That creature could have capsized the ship!"

"That's beside the point."

"No, it isn't! You know I can be useful. At least give me the chance to prove myself again!"

"You're still sick—"

"Not anymore. I feel stronger now than I ever have back at the Spire!"

Already I could see the others wavering, more inclined to agree with her than not. The monster had come upon us unexpectedly, and there were too many nerves still frayed and shaken from that encounter.

"Your mother doesn't think the same, my dear," Gracea said. "And she shall surely have our hides if we don't bring you back."

Odessa glared at her. "I'll wreck this ship," she threatened.

"Your Holiness . . . !" The Starmaker gasped.

"I'll wreck it, I swear. And then I'll destroy every ship in the harbor. It'll be months before you can build a new one. Not even Mother can fix that. Don't think I won't do it!"

"Your Holiness, why are you being so stubborn about this?"

"Because they're *calling* me, Starmaker. There is something at the breach that only I can do, and I *know* you will all fail without me. Either I come along, or no one gets to leave." Odessa turned to me, her eyes pleading. "Lan, you know me. Please, *please* trust me."

I sighed and placed my hand on her shoulder. "You know that I trust you, Odessa," I said quietly, gently brushing a wayward lock of red-shifting-into-green hair from her eyes. A soft blush stole over her cheeks. "But this is not my call to make."

My aether-gates opened.

Odessa let out a muffled, outraged sound. And then her eyes rolled up into her head. I caught her before she could fall, gently gathering her in my arms and turning her over to Noe.

"What did you do?" Gracea squawked.

"Put her to sleep, ironically enough." I hated it. I didn't want to have to resort to using my magic against her, but I believed her threats, and I knew I had no other choice. An Odessa mad at me forever was infinitely better than a dead Odessa.

Gracea sighed noisily. "I suppose it's better this way." Before anyone could stop her, she turned to poor Janella and hit her hard across the face, the blow as loud as a crack of thunder. The young girl hit the deck; stunned, blood trickling out her nose.

"Gracea!" I barked.

"This is a far more merciful punishment than what I'd planned. You should be flogged for not alerting us immediately of her presence on this ship. Once we return to Aranth, I'm half-tempted to carry that out myself." The Starmaker raised

157

her hand again, and I stepped in, caught it before she could land another hit.

"Gracea," I managed through gritted teeth, disgusted. "There will be no more disciplinary actions of this sort on the *Brevity*."

"This is my ship, and I'm in charge."

"I. Don't. Care. Lay a hand on her—or on anyone else—and you'll answer to me."

I could see shining patterns crackling around Gracea, the air-gates in her eyes simmering with Light. I hadn't closed my own gates after putting Odessa to sleep, and I allowed them to flare brighter in response. The Starmaker could quite easily choose to strike me with lightning if she really was that much of a fool, but she wasn't impervious to her own bolts, and I wasn't releasing her wrist just yet.

Her gates faded and she grunted. I let go. "Odessa was your charge," Gracea said. "Perhaps if you were better at your job, we would not be in such a predicament." I said nothing, unwilling to rise to the bait. She turned away. "Holsett! Stay the course!"

"Thank you," Janella whispered, as the others slowly dispersed.

"I'm not happy you didn't tell us either, Janella, but that doesn't warrant Gracea's stupidity." I offered her a small napkin, which she accepted, dabbing at her nose. "Finish up the meal preparations, and alert me as soon as anyone spots any other creatures within the riverwinds. Send for Noelle. I'm not letting my ward out of my sight until we see Aranth's docks."

"Catseye Tianlan." Sumiko drifted closer. "Would you require any help? It's been quite a while since I last—"

"No," I growled. "I don't need it, Sumiko."

"I think it would be good if you would at least submit to a—"

"*No*, Sumiko." Did I sound too defensive?

The woman bowed, her long black hair falling across her face, just as Noe arrived. "Very well. You know where to find me should you change your mind."

Noe and I had initially planned to share a cabin, but Odessa's presence meant a change of plans. Noe was to occupy the smaller room next door instead. Noe had placed the still-sleeping Odessa on one of the beds. "She's right, you know," my friend said.

"What?"

"The young mistress is right. She's a better asset to us here than back in the city."

I exhaled. "Not you too, Noe."

"An observation, nothing more. I'll move my things out."

Once she'd left, I curled up on the bed beside Odessa and took her hand. It didn't take me long to cleanse her again, as I'd done every night before, but the fist-size black hole inside her remained—now slightly bigger than before.

I hated that she was here, hated that she thought she had to be here.

The *Brevity* was to take us through the eastern path along the Lunar Lakes, which led into the Spirit Lands, instead of the westbound route my team and I had undertaken. Asteria was expecting the strong acid rains that frequently blanketed the eastern region of the Spirit Lands to have finished their season by the time we arrived, and we expected to travel into that barren but uninhabited region unmolested. It was a small reprieve; we would be approaching the Great Abyss from a different point than I had months earlier. Much better than going through the Spirit Lands, where ghouls and strange creatures warped by the Abyss thrived.

I closed my eyes. I remembered, faintly, the dead bodies surrounding me, and remembered cradling Nuala's body in my arms, certain that I would be next to be torn limb from limb like the others.

But they'd spared my life.

I was a coward, but I couldn't go down that same path again. I couldn't face their ghosts.

And there was something else. Something else I couldn't remember. A . . . mountain. A pair of stones, glowing so brightly . . .

The pain in my head sharpened, and I gave up, closing my eyes. "I'm so sorry, Nuala," I whispered, fighting not to dissolve into tears. Whatever Odessa claimed about these shadows, I knew she could not be certain about their motivations. And if they wanted her here only to kill her once we'd arrived at the Abyss, then I knew that I would brave as many terrors as there were in all of Aeon to ensure she did not meet the same fate as the rest of my poor team.

I woke a scant hour later to tugging at my hand. Odessa was awake, too weak to muster up any magic against me still, but she had resorted to carefully freeing herself from my grasp in the hopes I wouldn't wake.

"I wouldn't do that if I were you," I said, my eyes still closed. For as long as I was holding her, she wasn't going anywhere.

"Let me go," she hissed.

"Never."

"I'm not going back!"

"You're outnumbered and outvoted."

"You're going to die!"

My grip tightened around her hand, even as I fought to ignore how soft it felt against mine, or that not too long ago I could do more than just hold her. "And how do you know that?"

"You're going to die. I saw it." It came out as a loud sob. "If I'm not with you, you're all going to die. Noelle, Janella, Graham, Gracea—all of you. None of you will make it."

"How do you know that?" I repeated.

"I—I dreamt it. Just now."

Odessa was too young to be having visions like Asteria did. Those manifested in the goddesses' early twenties, and never before. "They're not real. One dream isn't proof."

"Ever since that first galla made contact—that's all I've been seeing. Destruction, and death." Odessa's other hand wrapped around mine, squeezing. "You say it's not real, but how can you know for sure? How can you know that the visions my mother sees aren't figments of her imagination, or if they'll ever come true?"

"Asteria's predictions have come to fruition before. She built Aranth on the strength of them. And your mother's foretelling only happens when she's awake, little goddess. That's how we know that they're more than dreams." Asteria had also said that the galla wouldn't harm Odessa, and the goddess was never one to say such things lightly.

But not all the monsters in the wildlands were galla.

"Lan—"

"Does your 'vision' tell you that we'll survive if you join us?"

Odessa was silent, helpless.

"We're going back to Aranth. This is not up for discussion."

"I hate you," she whispered, and rolled away.

I exhaled loudly again, staring up at the ceiling. *Hate me if you must, but at least you'll still be* alive *to hate me.*

Our meal arrived shortly, Noelle pushing the cart in. Odessa ate poorly, refusing the rest after a few bites.

Noelle had also brought along a map, which I soon spread across our lone table.

"From what I could garner from Nebly," Noe said, studying the contents intently, "we're due to hit the maximum speed in roughly fifteen hours. We can't go much faster, or the force of the wind would break the masts off within ten minutes. It would definitely destroy the riggings."

"Hopefully we don't encounter that devil beast again at our next pass." I snuck another glance at Odessa. She had curled up on the bed again, mostly hidden under the blankets, and was refusing to look at either of us. "Any more sightings?"

"The beast's put the caution back in Gracea, at least. She's sending off light every half hour or so to make sure nothing's lurking to ambush us. The winds are whipping fast around us, and the riggers have their hands full maintaining tension for the mast, but so far we've been very fortunate." Noe, too, glanced at the huddled figure on the bed. "I've sent for enough hot water, milady. You could both use a bath."

Odessa said nothing when the buckets of water were lugged in and poured into the small tub at the farthest corner of the room, said nothing when Noe and the others left. She looked up briefly when I loomed over her, still looking cross. "What?" she snapped.

"I know you're mad, Your Holiness, but it would do you good to freshen up."

"So you can bring me back to Mother all scrubbed up in ribbons. No."

"If you're not going to bathe, then I will."

Silence. I shrugged and opened the closet and found the small divider, dragging it in between the bed and the tub.

"Wh-what are you doing?"

"I need some scrubbing myself." I've never been shy about nudity. The orphanage didn't have the funds for separate baths, so Noe, the other children, and I had splashed in common washrooms together for years. There'd even been a time or two, when we were young enough and the rains weren't always as fierce, that we would dance naked along the streets and get in a free soak that way.

It occurred to me that Odessa wasn't used to such luxuries.

I hung up my cloak, looked over my shoulder to see that Odessa had escaped the confines of the covers, and was staring at me with wide eyes. "I'd much rather you bathed first," I offered, hoping her desire to be clean would override her current anger.

She glanced down at herself, at her stained dress. "I suppose," she said, trying not to sound too eager. She stepped behind the screen, blocking my view of her and the tub. I moved toward the bed, stripping it quickly of its sheets.

"Are—" Odessa's voice rose from behind the barrier, a strange, tilting sound to her voice. I could hear clothes rustling. "What are you doing?"

"Neither of us were clean when we lay down here, Your Holiness. Best to change the sheets."

"But—I was hoping—" I could practically see her embarrassment through the screen.

"I'll finish up here and step out to give you some privacy if that's what you want, Your Holiness."

"No, I didn't mean that!" A pause. A low sigh. "Never mind."

I was folding the blankets when I heard the sloshing of water, a soft breathy sound as Odessa slid into the tub, and I froze. I'd been too busy focusing on mitigating her ire, too concentrated on remembering that I'd bathed with Noe and so many others that I'd almost forgotten *she* was different, that *she* was *naked*. In the room. With me.

A soft purring moan wafted from behind the screen.

I nearly ripped the sheets in two from gripping it too hard. "I'll be back once you're finished," I called back to her, wincing at how high my voice sounded. "Knock on the door to let me know when you're done."

"W-wait!" More sloshing. Odessa had risen from the tub. "Why are—"

I yanked the door open and raced outside, slamming it harder than I should. Then I leaned my back against it and stared out into the never-ending winds, at the black-hued sky above us. The cold bit into me hard because I'd forgotten to grab my cloak when I left, but hell if I was going back inside in either of our states.

We must have traveled hundreds of miles east on the river-wind by now, but it was as dark as I'd always known it. I stared up at the sky overhead, hoping for a glimpse of stars now that we'd traveled beyond the impossible swirl of clouds that hung over Aranth, but to no avail. All I could see were small sparks of rushlights that Gracea was creating to light the ship's path.

"She's your charge, you besotted fool," I muttered out into the darkness, ashamed of myself. *Mother Goddess, you haven't even seen her naked, to be acting like this!* "You damn pervert. Get the filth out of your head and do the job you're paid to do. *You can't have her,* Tianlan."

But that's the problem, isn't it? It was serious enough for you to proposition her. Asteria mustn't have known that detail or she'd have your head.

Noe poked her head out from the other room. "I heard noises. Is there something wrong, milady? You look a little—"

"Go away, Noelle."

"As you wish, milady." The door closed again.

I couldn't get Odessa back to Aranth soon enough.

It felt like I'd been standing there forever before I heard the soft knock behind me. To my relief, Odessa had already changed into fresh clothes and was rooting around in her bag. A few of its contents had tumbled onto the bed.

The time spent outside had done wonders in tamping down the more ardent of my thoughts, fortunately. "Books again?"

She looked down at the romance novels that had spilled out. *Capturing the Prince. Untamed Wildness.* "I thought I might get bored."

I snorted. "And you brought your ointments, I see."

"What's wrong with that?"

"Nothing." She was a cloistered girl, sheltered from every bad possibility life threw at her. She didn't belong here, on this ship heading into hell-knows-what.

"It doesn't work, you know," Odessa said.

"What doesn't work?"

"Romance. It's not like the stories. Life's more complicated than a book, I guess." She looked away, brushing her hair.

"Mother dislikes romance books. It's why I've had to get mine outside."

My mouth twitched. "You risked getting discovered for that?"

"Mother's volumes were depressing. I needed something cheerful. There was one book in particular, about rituals, that gave me nightmares."

"Rituals?"

"Things goddesses had to do in the past, to ensure prosperity and good fortune for all. Including rituals that deal with galla. That's why I wanted to be on this expedition. I know how to deal with them."

"I still don't think that's worth risking your life."

She looked away. "I'm still mad at you," she said softly.

"I know."

"It's going to be a long while before I forgive you."

"I know. You were very brave when that creature attacked the ship."

She couldn't stop her blush. "Really?"

"I've never seen anyone use so much of their gates as you did then." She couldn't have possibly channeled so much in her weakened state. The ferocity of the attack had stunned me.

She paused, and I knew she was being evasive about something. "Like I said, I could help. And I'll forgive you, too, if you'll let me stay."

I leaned toward her and pressed a chaste kiss against her temple. She didn't move. "Go to sleep, Your Holiness."

Later, when she was doing just that, I stepped into the tub. The water was cold by now, but I took a deep, shuddering breath, and dunked my head down, and tried to forget about how warm her forehead had been against my mouth.

I came awake almost immediately when the knock sounded at the door. "We have a situation, milady." Noe spoke from the other side, voice slightly muffled. "It would be best if you were outside to hear about it."

I snatched a quick look at Odessa on the other bed, but she appeared fast asleep. I donned my cloak hurriedly and joined the others on deck, where Gracea was standing, tight-lipped, with Grenny, her helmsman, and the other Devoted.

"What do you mean we're lost?" the Starmaker hissed.

Grenny, who'd been on hand to witness what Gracea had done to Janella, was already stuttering and trembling. "It's just that this is no longer the course we originally set out on, though we have faithfully followed the maps, milady. There were no miscalculations on my part. It is simply that the geography, so to speak, is no longer what it once was. The map is no longer accurate."

"Is that possible?" Graham demanded. "Are the riverwinds capable of changing courses on their own?"

"We rarely have occasion to travel this far out into them, Seasinger," Janella volunteered. "Perhaps the terrain has evolved without our knowledge."

"The reason I allowed you on this journey was because

you've studied the maps longer and better than any of us," Gracea snapped. "What has changed?"

The brunette flinched. There was a faint cut on her upper lip, and the bruise on her right cheek was darkening. "The only logical explanation I can think of is that the seascape itself is warping, milady."

"Warping?"

"There have been documented cases where strong bursts of magic warp the patterns around these riverwinds, forcing them to change directions, create new paths. It is similar to how a river on land can wear away at the rocks underneath it, or how erosion can alter the shape of how one flows. But while the corrosion can take decades, even centuries, the patterns here tend to be more volatile. Something might have triggered the riverwinds to shift away from their original channels in only a matter of months. Weeks, even."

"Like what?"

"An . . . an explosion, maybe. A sudden burst of energy from somewhere, big enough to disrupt the magic."

"What caused this one?"

"I . . . we don't have any pertinent data to answer that, milady."

Gracea scowled. "Are you telling me that we have no choice but to follow this path without any guide whatsoever and *hope* it doesn't lead us off a cliff?"

Nobody said anything.

Gracea chewed at her bottom lip. "Watch the sails. Keep

the wind low at the bow. Windshifters, I want pairs of you on watch at all hours; channel as many patterns against the current as you can. That should slow us down enough to keep an eye out for any dangers ahead and act accordingly." She paused to glare at me like this was somehow also my fault. "I trust that Her Holiness is still inside the cabin?" she asked icily.

"Fast asleep. She's had a busy day."

"Perhaps you should check up on her all the same. She has such a talent for squirming out from under your nose, after all."

I pushed myself off the wall. "All right. You've been on my case ever since I stepped foot on the *Brevity*. Spit it out. Are you planning to go ahead and say everything you'd like to say to my face, or would you prefer a good ol' round of fisticuffs instead?"

"Lady Tianlan!" Graham gasped.

Gracea reared back at the mention of violence, her eyes narrowing. "You were responsible for Odessa's safety. That she escaped onto this ship with you none the wiser is evidence of a lapse in your judgment. I told Her Holiness it would be foolish to let you join this expedition, especially given your failure from the last time. You yourself were adamant about not taking part. Your reluctance to be here will prove more hindrance than asset to us."

I took a step forward and balled my fists, but Grenny and Noe hastily placed themselves in between us before I could reach her nauseatingly smug face. "I made no secret of my distaste for this mission," I snapped. "But you have no experience facing off against these creatures—neither in Aranth nor on this boat. If you'd like to go and get yourself killed, then by all means go on without me. I bet I'd find Brighthenge before you do. Let's see how long you'll last on your own."

"It surely will not be any worse than the last mission you led," Gracea purred.

I stepped past Grenny, but it was Noe who laid a hand on my arm. "She's not worth it, milady," she murmured.

"Definitely *not* a lady. And I'll decide who's worth what, because she's not in any—"

I stumbled; so did everyone else. The current had picked up, faster than I'd anticipated, quicker than I knew it should, and fear gripped my chest. I recognized the signs.

I knew next to nothing about ships, but I did know a lot about spotting danger a mile off.

"Milady?" It was Noelle again, shaking me gently by the shoulder. The others were looking at me with a mixture of surprise and worry; I must have blanked out in midsentence, staring at nothing. I swallowed hard and closed my eyes. Breathe in, breathe out. All good.

"Where are we now?" I opened my eyes and made for the ship's bow, clambering up to get a better view of the rivers up ahead. The rushlights showed me a fork in the wind some ways up ahead—a calmer stream on the left, but riptide-like flows on the right. "Has anyone been plotting these new routes for us?"

"I—yes," Nebly warbled. "Grenny and I have been drawing new maps as we travel—"

"Keep to the left."

"Pardon?"

"Keep to the left. And you better be damn sure you do, because the right leads to our deaths." I heard his sharp intake of breath. "Raise the rigging and unfurl the sails, or whatever it is you're supposed to do to keep us from straying to the right! And get me a spyglass!"

Nebly scurried off, squeaking out my orders.

"I am the captain!" Gracea sounded outraged. "I will not have you assume command of my ship like some—"

"For once in your life, Gracea, shut up with the squawking! And make some light!"

"I will not—"

"Make some light, Gracea, or I swear by every Good Mother before Asteria that I will in this instant sic five kinds of herpes on you!"

Gracea shut her mouth. Orbs of light wafted up before my face before they were tossed out ahead of the ship's bow, and I could see the looming divide before us more clearly.

I could now also see the sheer drop on the right, a waterfall of air leading down into darkness. Gasps rose from the others as they, too, saw the danger.

"This makes it harder to steer the ship left." Fear crept into Gracea's voice as she finally understood. She dashed up the stairs without so much as a thank-you and took command of the wheel. "Graham, Miel! Fire up your gates and keep those counter-winds coming starboard. Channel them as hard as you both can manage! Jeenia and Holsett, assist! We'll need to tack hard and fast long before we hit that fork. Ensure that you all keep the ship's prow at forty degrees, or we're as good as sunk!"

I dashed back toward the cabin and found Odessa sitting up on the bed, awake and puzzled by the shouts from outside. "What's happening?" she quavered.

"Stay here. Gracea's about to do something to the ship, and I actually want her to succeed this time."

She scowled. "No. I'm going outside."

"Your Holiness—"

"There's nowhere for me to run, Lan! And if anything happens to the ship, it won't matter whether I'm in here or out there!"

I needed to keep an eye on the riverwind flow outside, and I knew Odessa was going to disobey as soon as my back was turned, anyway. "Keep close to either me or Noelle."

At her nod, I ushered her onto the deck, and she gaped at the twin rivers up ahead. "Are we going to make it?" she breathed. "Can I do anything?"

About to say no, I paused. The others were doing a good job firing off gates on the ship's right side, but the closer we got to the forks, the more restless the currents began to look. "I want you to find something secure to hold on to. Here at the center mast—not over the railing, you hear? The ship's about to do an abrupt left soon, and I don't want you pitching over. Is there a way to slow down the currents up ahead, so Gracea can maneuver easier?"

She thought for a moment. "I could try to stopper the

direction of the wind for the moment, build a sort of air-dam so the ship won't rock as much when she makes the turn?"

That sounded good to me. "And can you do all that without having to move from this spot?"

She nodded.

"Good. Noe, keep her safe."

A sudden crash against the side of the ship sent us tumbling to one side, the force lifting the starboard almost straight up into the air and nearly capsizing us. I saw barrels flying, tumbling past us to plummet down into the swirling waters below. Odessa shrieked as she slid sideways, but I grabbed her by the waist and anchored her firmly against me, my other arm straining from our combined weight. Noe had latched on to another mast, but there were cries of pain as others were not as fortunate. "Creature at port!" Nebly screamed.

I dashed to the railings to have a look myself and saw a familiar gargantuan eye glaring back at me before swimming out of view. "Devil beast's back!" I shouted over to the rest, biting back a fresh string of curses. With it worrying us from the left, we'd never escape the deadly river on the right. Another shudder ripped through the ship, though the force was considerably weaker.

"We won't make it!" Graham shouted down to us. "The beast's blocking our path!"

"We need to get rid of it, then!" I grabbed a rope ladder hanging down the side of the ship. It would take all of us just to summon enough gale force needed to push the whale away, and that was firepower we didn't have. Not when everyone else had their hands full trying to steer the ship left.

"What are you doing?" Gracea gasped.

"What are you doing?" Odessa echoed behind me, voice rising to a shriek.

"What does it look like? Still thinking of leaving me back in Aranth?"

I waited for the devil beast to draw close enough again and swung out.

My hand slapped against the beast's rough hide. It sensed my touch and tried to shy away but I doggedly pressed on, my palm firmly against its skin as I forced patterns through the point of contact, locating its heart and sending every debilitating sickness I could think of straight into its core.

The beast screamed, and it was a most awful sound. It veered away almost immediately, struggling, and its tail punched hard against the side of the ship one final time.

The rope slipped from my fingers. I scrabbled desperately at the side of the ship, managing only to rip out a fingernail as I plunged straight down into the inky swirl of—

I stopped, hovering soundlessly in the air. I looked up.

Odessa's hands were stretched toward me, her face panicked as she yanked me up with Air. How had she gotten this strong?

"Milady!" Another rope ladder whipped down beside me, and Noe's face appeared beside the goddess's.

"You're both lifesavers," I panted, grabbing on and hoisting myself up, inch by painful inch, until I lay sprawled on the deck once more, Odessa hugging me tightly. "I thought you were really going to fall," she sobbed.

"I *was* going to fall," I corrected her, coughing a little. "And I didn't, thanks to you."

"Still thinking of leaving me back in Aranth?"

I looked up at her grinning face. How had she done that? "I don't think we have much choice in that anymore," I said, as the triumphant shouts of the rest of the crew told me that we'd veered into the left river and were now speedily sailing away from the endless deep, and into more territories unknown. I staggered to my feet. "Keep it steady," I continued. "We should be at the lakes before long."

And then I turned back to the railing, and threw up again.

I hate ships.

Chapter Ten

ARJUN THE SANDPILOT

———————— ☼ ————————

"WHAT KIND OF CONTRAPTION IS this?!"

Her Holiness had been at it ever since we'd left her city and started hightailing it after the mirage, who'd been leading us on at a breakneck pace, tough to match despite the rig's own impressive speed. I stepped harder on the pedal in response. No matter how fast I drove, we couldn't pull up alongside the mirage; it felt like we were doomed to forever follow the specter rather than catch it.

I was hoping to run it over, preferably. The goddess was convinced it was leading us to the breach, but I'd much rather have gotten it stationary long enough to demand more answers.

"The coils are barely working as it is, and these other cylinders don't seem to be doing anything much beyond providing some ugly aesthetics, which is a *terrible* waste of good metal! The whole instrument panel is a haphazard mockery of good design! Half the switches on this side don't even work, and the other half make *no* sense—"

"Will you," I said, through gritted teeth. "Shut. Your. Damn. Rathole. For just a second."

It was her turn to glare. "Rude," she muttered, fiddling with the controls.

"Will you *please* shut your damn rathole for just a second, *princess*. And stop messing with the switches. I don't want you accidentally blowing us up."

"It's Haidee, not *princess*. And I don't even know *your* name."

I scowled, but it was obvious she wasn't going to let up until she got what she wanted. "Arjun."

"Well, Arjun, do you even know what these switches do?"

"I didn't make this, I only stole it."

"Oh well, *gee*. That explains everything, then." She slouched backward, folded her arms across her chest, and transferred her baleful stare to the endless sands before us, at the speck of black that was the mirage, still somehow outrunning us. I continued to drive.

The peaceful bliss lasted a good five minutes.

"I thought you wanted to kill me," she grumbled. "Why are you even coming along?"

"Coming along with *you*? *You're* coming along with *me*." Balancing my wrist against the wheel, I jerked a thumb behind me, where an enormous sack lay stashed against the back seat. Hell and sandrock, it even had *wheels* underneath it. "How the hell were you expecting to lug all that through the desert chasing after a mirage, without a ride?"

"I would have found a way."

"You never think things through. You want to bring some whale back to life, but you don't have enough water on hand to stop it from suffocating if you succeed. And now you wanna hike your way through the dunes, with no mount or vehicle to your name."

It was her turn to bristle. "Oh? So you know everything about me now?"

Damn right I did. She was the enemy. That was all I needed to remember.

But that wasn't even true anymore, was it? Mother Salla's vengeance had been directed solely at Haidee's mother. There was a reason she'd chosen not to attack the younger goddess, despite all the times she'd seen her out in the desert. Something about her own encounters with the mirage had made her think that Latona's daughter was worth saving.

That didn't stop the goddess from being a huge pain in my ass, though.

"You don't want to know," I said roughly, "what the rest of us think of you."

We drove for another five minutes before she responded, more quietly, "But I don't know what it is you think about me."

I glanced at her out of the corner of my eye. She was watching the drifts sweep past us.

"I wasn't even a year old when the world broke," she continued. "After that, being alive was all the reason they needed to hate me. I don't know what hand Mother played in all this. She banned all talk of the Breaking in the Golden City, distracted everyone with merrymaking and revelry in exchange for their silence. Their tacit approval. But I don't just want to protect the people under our rule. I want to help everyone outside the dome, too, and I don't know if I will ever be successful at that.

"But I have to try. And it's hard when your own mother's against you. When it feels like your mother's happy to have the world broken as it is." She finally turned to me. "If you hate me so much, then why bring me along?"

My turn to say nothing. She waited expectantly for a few minutes before giving up, looking away with another sigh.

"Did you ever do it?" I finally offered. "Bring something back from the dead?"

She looked startled. "No. It's a complicated process. I'll need to wield all patterns like they were one, but I also have to figure out the right gate to use. I've tried Air so far, but that didn't work. And without pure Water to draw from, it's nearly impossible. I . . . I think I'll have to travel farther west for that."

"But you tried it on the whale, anyway."

"Yeah." She sounded bitter. "Maybe I really just don't think things through, like you said."

"Your mother's gonna be searching for you."

"I don't care."

"It's unusual to have someone used to the good life in the city come out here just because a mirage said so."

"Are you saying I'm spoiled? Because I'm a damn good mechanika, which is the furthest thing from being spoiled."

"Sure."

"I have friends there, you know. All mechanika. They treat me better than any of the nobles did. They'd never betray me."

"Mother Salla—my clan leader—doesn't completely hate you. She said she knew you as a baby."

"She was one of my Mother's Devoted?"

"No. Your aunt's."

"Oh." She shifted uneasily, looking at me like I'd sprouted another head. "Is that why—is that why you tried to kill me? If this is some trick—"

Even I had to wince at that. "If this was a trick, I would have brought more people, and you know it. My mother doesn't want you dead, surprisingly enough. And neither do I." Not anymore, anyway.

"I never knew my aunt Asteria. Only that she tried to kill Mother, and tried to destroy the world in the attempt."

"*My* mother thinks your mother was responsible."

"That's not true!" she snapped.

"Mother Salla was there at the Breaking!"

"In case you didn't notice, so was mine!"

"Latona wanted to rule Aeon in Asteria's place!"

"That's a lie! Mother was going to save her!"

"Says who?"

"My father wrote about it in a letter!"

"Yeah, because fathers are always impartial. Look, maybe we'll just flag down the mirage and ask it." I stuck my head out the window briefly. "If it ever lets us catch up!" I shouted after the fleeing ghost, but that didn't slow it down, either.

She sighed. "Did your mother ever tell you about some of the prophecies?"

"Yeah. One." She was gonna know it sooner or later, anyway. "'When the dead find words, the goddess and the Devoted son will meet atop a fish not a fish, on a sea not a sea. It is she who travels to the endless Abyss, and it is he who guides her.'"

She blinked. "But that's us."

"Us and the damn whale, yeah."

"So we're destined to meet? To travel to the Great Abyss together?" She smiled suddenly, her eyes awash in silver. "Was that why you came to the city? To look for me?"

"Stop trying to make me your friend," I growled, not liking how easily she threw the word *destined* about. "We knew your soldiers were returning with metal from the mines, and we wanted to see how much we could steal without anyone noticing. We pilfered a few of your guards' outfits and snuck in at the back of the regiment. The sandstorm was an unexpected bonus. *And* a setback." My clan had stolen all the silver from the wagons and escaped detection. I had stayed behind, overriding their protests.

Because I *was* looking for her. I figured I'd spend a few days casing the city exits until she ventured out again, but the mirage had saved me the effort.

Not like I was gonna admit any of that.

She beamed at me. "I saved you."

"What?"

She beamed harder. "I was watching from atop the dome. I

182

redirected the winds away from you and your friend, just like before."

Great. "Yeah, well. Thanks."

"It was very bad of you," she continued severely, "to be stealing from my city."

"Equally bad of you to be hoarding city resources, or we wouldn't have to resort to stealing."

"Ah." She reflected. "That's true. So was larceny the only reason you were there?"

"I—no. Like I said, we think there's something to what the mirage—"

"So you *didn't* want to find me?" She sounded disappointed.

I gave up. If she wanted me to pretend to like her, then so be it. "I found you anyway, so what's the point?"

And then I slammed on the brakes, hard.

Haidee lurched forward, but I got an arm out between her and the dashboard. "It stopped," I said tersely.

The mirage was immobile, staring out into the border that lay between the Skeleton Coast we occupied and the vastness of the Sand Sea: flatlands made of preternaturally even sand that shifted and ebbed almost like water. No one in the Oryx clan had ever traveled into that dust trap, and for good reason.

"No way in hell are we making it through that in one piece." I turned to the mirage standing a few feet away. "Do you hear me? We're NOT crossing this hellscape! The rig can't cross this! We may as well attempt to cross an actual ocean! Can't you conjure up some new wind or magic or whatever to get us across? Or better yet—an actual route we can *drive* through?"

It watched me from underneath its cowl. I had the sickening sensation that if it raised its hood, there would not be much flesh remaining to see.

"Why can't we cross this?" Haidee asked.

I pointed at a spot nearby; something rippled beneath the earth, the sands flowing aside to briefly reveal a large, dark shape winnowing through the fine dust like it was swimming through water, and then disappearing again from view. "That's why. There are monsters the size of towers hiding within those depths. May as well serve ourselves up as fodder."

She stared down at the deceptively smooth ground before us, left eyebrow twitching like mad. "I've read about the Sand Sea, but I've never seen it with my own eyes. Do you know how many miles this spans?"

"No. Never known anyone to actually make it across."

She was already dragging her sack out of the vehicle, pawing through its contents. "The coils and metalworks on the dashboard—they're only there for show. If I'm careful, they'll be more than enough to construct a roof above us, and I could weave enough incanta on its surface to keep any monster's teeth and claws out. I should terraproof the tires while I'm at it, too, though we won't be needing that."

"You're not seriously considering—"

But the goddess was in a world of her own. "I'll need to make this airtight enough to prevent sand from getting in, but also ensure there's enough circulation I could funnel from outside to give us fresh air to breathe. . . . I could work one of these exhaust pipes into ventilation."

"Are you listening to me?"

"Of course. It shouldn't take more than three hours—"

"Three hours?" I shouted. "And then you want us to ride this rig through a Sand Sea full of monsters?"

She shrugged. "Do you want to turn around, then? You go back to Mother Salla, and me to my city?"

I didn't want that, either. Not empty-handed. "I agreed to hunt down the mirage," I groused, even though that wasn't entirely the truth. "Not run all the way to the center of the world."

Her voice dropped, suddenly sly. "I'd never pegged you as someone who'd give up so easily. But if you're having second thoughts, we can double back. I can drop you off with your clan and pay what you think is a fair price for this sand buggy. I'll go on and—"

I didn't hate Haidee exactly, but that didn't stop me from wanting to throttle her for having no sense of self-preservation.

"I'll come with you," I snapped. "You're going to get us killed, and we're both gonna wind up at the bottom of some demon's stomach, but I'll come with."

"Thank you." It annoyed me how genuine she sounded. "Like I said, it shouldn't take more than three hours to build what we need."

"Three hours," I grumbled, watching the mirage warily. It hadn't moved from its spot, eyeballing us back. It understood,

I realized, and that was a frightening thought. "And what can you do with this wreck in three hours, exactly?"

A lot, apparently.

Haidee, as it turned out, really was a mechanika, and an even better one than Millie. Being able to command multiple incanta was a definite advantage, but I grudgingly admitted that the goddess would have been a master at it even without them. In half an hour she had chopped off the metal cylinders she had scathingly referred to earlier as *ugly aesthetics*, and reshaped them into a metal roof over the rig using a mobile alternator that funneled her own fire incanta through her welding device as she worked. "It'll keep us impermeable to sand and grit," she explained with a shrug, like this was all just child's play.

In another hour she had reengineered one of the exhaust pipes into a purifier, allowing air to circulate through the vehicle while trapping any dust particles before they found a way in. She had crawled underneath the buggy and remained there for close to fifteen minutes, fusing holes and fissures shut to keep us sealed. The creatures making the Sand Sea their home would find it difficult to attack while we drove our way through, she was certain. "Most of them, anyway," she added.

"*Most* of them?" I had contributed nothing to the work; she had shooed me away whenever I drew near. I spent my time trying to approach the mirage instead, but it kept vanishing and reappearing some distance away, keeping me from drawing closer.

"I can't guarantee what manner of beasts we might find out there, but at least I've upped our chances. Even taking into account any arsenic in the rocks that might leach into the sand, I doubt it's of a high enough concentration to corrode the metal. There may be animals inhabiting the area possessing toxins, but the roof and the incanta I'll be adding there will make it harder for them to get to us. It should work in the same way our dome protects the Golden City, albeit cruder. I would have whipped up something better had I more time, but—why are you looking at me like that?"

I worked at picking my jaw off the ground. All I'd brought were a few changes of clothes and my armor, my Howler, a bushel of glowfire grenades, and food rations. "No reason," I heard myself say faintly. "Did you bring the whole mechanika facility with you?"

She grinned. "I wasn't dragging my bag along just to suffer the weight."

"What else did you bring?" I reached into the sack and pulled out a Howler—except it had a longer barrel and better sights, and was superior in every way to the one I was toting.

Her Howlers had been retrofitted with an extra clasp and trigger, much like mine was. She'd modified her guns so I could use them.

She'd been expecting to find me.

Hell and sandrock.

"I brought three." She sounded almost embarrassed. "I *did* mess up your gun. Wasn't sure you had a replacement."

"You were planning on looking for me?" I'd been trying so damned hard not to admit that finding her was the main reason I was even near the Golden City in the first place, and it turned out she'd been preparing for the same thing.

I must have looked far too incredulous. Haidee's back stiffened. "I wasn't deliberately seeking you out. I just like to be prepared for any eventualities."

I let that slide, too busy running my fingers down the symmetrical grooves of the barrel walls. "Thanks." I was truly grateful. Howlers were hard to come by, and on the Skeleton Coast they were our main line of defense against both the elements and enemy groups. It was a clearly expensive gift; despite having more abundant resources, the city dwellers were notoriously frugal with their metalworks. "For this, and . . . for the whale."

"The whale?"

"We took it apart. Salvaged it for meat. I know you hoped for the opposite, but . . ."

"You ate Betsy?"

"We had to—wait. You named that damned whale Betsy?" She blushed.

I threw up my hands. "No, it's all right. Name her Betsy. Betsy kept us from starving. Name the buggy Dandelion if you want, I'm not going to argue." In the space of three hours she had converted the war rig into some kind of sand-submersible, and if she wanted to name *me* Betsy, I'd let her if it gave us a fighting chance of living through this. I snuck a glance at the mirage. "Now what?"

"Well, I'll need to test it out first." But rather than get into the new custom jeep, she turned toward the Sand Sea. She neared the edge where the ground ended and the dust-ocean began, and took a deliberate step forward before I realized what she was doing.

"Wait!" I leaped for her and knocked her down, sending us both sprawling away from the border. Her footprint dissolved as a shadow swirled in the exact place she had set her boot down, a small whirlpool spiraling around and distorting the ground briefly before resuming its facade of a placid surface.

"Oh." Haidee inclined her head, trying to get a closer look despite nearly having had her blasted foot eaten. "They move pretty fast."

"That's all you can say?" I choked out. Did this girl have no understanding of actual danger? Forget about any of the other nomads out here trying to kill her; she could accidentally kill herself all on her own, given enough time. How was she even alive that first time I saw her on her damned Betsy? How had nothing gotten to her before that point? Why was she the one of the two of us with all her limbs intact? "It could have bitten your leg off!"

"I wanted to ascertain the density of the sand and how they could swim through something so—"

"Listen. If you're expecting to tag along, then here are a few ground rules to keep in mind. One: don't bloody put your foot down in places where I've just told you there are monsters swimming underneath. Two: you walk where I walk, spit where I spit, hide where I hide, and step nowhere else. Three:

you're running every plan you make with me first, *before* you go ahead and do it, which means you're going to listen to me and do as I say—"

A brief cloud of smoke caught my attention, unfurling like a plume about ten miles away in a straight line behind us. I knew what that meant.

"And four—you sure you didn't leave anything important out when you were making this buggy sand-friendly?"

"I—I'm pretty sure I've done everything I need to—"

"Good, because four: we're both getting into your new rig and testing it this instant, because as I said in rule number three, you're going to listen to me."

"But I don't—" Haidee twisted her head to watch as vehicles poured out from behind a small ridge, and her eyes grew round. "Oh. *Oh.*" When I yelled at her to get in, she didn't even protest, just scrambled into the buggy after me and bolted the doors shut.

I revved the engine. "Any surprises you've added in here that you should tell me about before we start?"

"I had some spare spark plugs that I swapped in for the old ones that came with the vehicle, so the buggy should run faster than it used to." Haidee rattled on, so quickly I could barely keep up, "I've also repaired all the cracks I could find. This rig runs on fire-and-air-melted sand, so we can always just shovel more in if we run out."

"Swell." I hit the gas and the rig all but flew forward, straight into the Sand Sea. "Hang on," I shouted, a part of my mind screaming at me and my willingness to believe in ridiculous mechanika goddesses without so much as a test drive, and the rest of me screaming to keep moving because I'd just gotten a closer look at the buggies coming our way, and it turned out they were the Hellmakers come to collect.

"What do they want?" Haidee cried.

"They're cannibals."

"What? Is that why they're after us?"

"Remember when I said I stole this rig?"

"You *stole* from cannibals?! Why would you steal anything from *cannibals*?!"

"I had a really, *really* good reason, all right?"

We plunged straight into the Sand Sea—but instead of sinking completely, we wound up floating along its surface, half-submerged. I increased our speed, and we started swimming along at a reasonably quick pace, faster than I thought we would. I still had a good view of our surroundings above the sand, and whatever creatures that had been wriggling in its depths were leaving us alone. So far.

And then I saw why. Some of the Hellmakers had plunged in just like we had, but without the benefit of a roof or engines that actually worked, which meant they were now up to their elbows in fine grit. They flailed around, abandoning their rigs to struggle back to shore—and I heard one of them scream, so loud I could hear him from inside our sealed compartment.

Something unseen sucked him into the sand without warning, and the Hellmaker disappeared from sight. Panicked, one of the other men floundered wildly for the shore, and something scaled and coarse, with a huge bulging throat, jerked out of the sand and swallowed him whole. Stunned, Haidee and I both watched as the creature dove quickly back under the surface, leaving no other evidence in its wake.

"Yeah," I said shakily, "I *really* didn't want to cross this shitty ocean."

Most of the Hellmakers had stopped short at the boundary, hopping out to stare after us. I recognized one of them—the asshole with the scar over one eye who'd tried to skin me the last time. His mouth was moving, and I could tell what he was saying wasn't very nice. Grinning, I drove us farther on, leaving them bereft of supper.

"It's gone," Haidee said unexpectedly. "The mirage's gone."

I cast a look around, swore. She was right.

"What do we do now?" she whispered.

I gritted my teeth. Too late to back out or turn around. The Hellmakers would track us down again. "We head straight on, and hope it's waiting for us at the other end."

"And what's at the other end?"

Hell if I knew, either.

We drove west, anyway.

Chapter Eleven

ODESSA OF THE WILDLANDS

———————————— ☾ ————————————

THE LUNAR LAKES WERE BEAUTIFUL—in a particularly ethereal, horrific way.

Under Gracea's rushlights they bloomed below us like glittering eyes. Individually, each was like a bright mirror whose surface occasionally rippled, the waters as pure as any I had ever seen before—a bright silver-blue sheen that the seas around Aranth had never had in all my life spent in the city, watching from my tower window.

But collectively, they were an asymmetrical mass, an irregular cluster of holes in the ground that disquieted the eyes. When viewed all at once, they inspired not awe, but an outright sense of revulsion at the sight. Their repugnant geometry resembled to me an open wound that bled silver against the world's surface, an amorphous beehive like I'd seen in old textbooks, one that dispensed unseen danger instead of honey.

"They used to be one giant lake," Merika breathed, nearly halfway over the rails in her eagerness. "But after the Breaking it splintered into dozens—hundreds, even. Not even the rangers have explored them in their entirety yet, but the original was measured at thousands of feet deep at certain places. It used to be teeming with aquatic life, but the influence of the Abyss has reached even here. They say whatever survived has been warped into monsters."

"What a comforting thought," Noelle murmured.

"My father used to tell me stories about the sun," the young clerk continued sadly. "His grandparents would bring us to their vineyard, and we would pick fruit. He climbed trees to pick out these large red berries. I—I think I remember that, dimly. There were no monsters then. I don't remember all the details, but I remember feeling—happy."

"Stop loitering, Merika!" Graham called from behind us. "I have more errands for you to finish before we land."

The clerk drew back, her eyes suddenly fearful. Lan touched her elbow, about to say something comforting, but then blinked and drew back in surprise.

"I have to go," Merika mumbled to us, then scuttled away.

"Is something wrong, Lan?" I asked, puzzled by Merika's abrupt change in attitude.

"No. It's nothing." She glanced back down at the lakes. "That looks grotesque," she said with a long shudder.

"This isn't your first time at the lakes," Noelle pointed out.

"Yes, but I've never had to see them from above like this

before." And then she swore.

"What's wrong?" I asked.

"See that?" She pointed at the horizon, where a gathering of gray storm clouds huddled. "Acidfall," she growled.

"But Mother said the rains should have stopped by this time."

"Nothing's set in stone in the wildlands. We can't travel that route for as long as the acid continues to fall. We—" Her hands shook. "We have no choice. We have to avoid the area. Gracea," she yelled up at the other woman. A strained cease-fire had existed between the two ever since our last encounter with the devil beast, but it made for a tense crew. "Tell the others to prepare for our descent!"

"And *where*, pray tell, shall we be doing that?"

Lan leaned slightly over the rails again and let her hand float along the wayward breezes flowing beside us, her eyes falling shut. "The riverwind's end lies at the mouth of one of those lakes. I don't know how steep the embankment is, but we can beach the ship and plan our next move, or anchor there and scout around. I—" Her voice broke, and so did my heart, from the pain in that sound. "The shadows I encountered last time were on the other end, toward the Spirit Lands. I can't guarantee what might be lurking around this side."

Gracea nodded curtly. "Let me know once the lookouts find the spout connecting the riverwind down. From this height, it shouldn't take half an hour to hit ground."

I couldn't stand looking at the lakes anymore, and pushed myself away from the railing. Since we'd started sailing down the left riverwind path, no one had said anything about my returning to Aranth. There didn't look to be *any* visible routes back; the unexpected change in the riverwinds' course had affected all pathways, it seemed.

The rest of the crew were nice at least, and were soon introducing themselves to me, giddy at the presence of a goddess in their group: Andre, Cathei, old Slyp, Lorila, Salleemae, among many others.

"Is there anything I can do to help?" I stammered, trying not to recall my utter insipidity from a few days ago. Attempting to entice Lan with a bathtub seduction was a stupid idea, but my inhibitions had been stripped away the instant my clothes had. Was there something in the wildland air? Lan hadn't even noticed!

In hindsight, *The King and the Courtesan* probably shouldn't have been my main guide to romance.

Lan nodded. "Stay with Noelle. However skilled Gracea and her crew are, this will be a bumpy ride."

It wasn't long before one of the Devoted stationed at the prow called out, signaling that the spout lay in sight, and I scurried back to the stairs leading belowdecks, to get out of everyone else's way. I'd gotten what I wanted—for now—and I didn't want anyone changing their minds.

"Noelle," I said, "do you know how far we've traveled?"

The other girl pursed her lips. "Not in any specifics, Your Holiness. But I do know that the Lunar Lakes are located nearly three thousand miles from Aranth."

I gasped. "But we've been sailing the riverwinds for two nightspans!"

"Air currents carry us more swiftly than the speed that one normally travels when at sea. Catseye Tianlan opted for the land route with the last expedition, a journey that took them close to three months before they reached this place. The currents are considered far more dangerous than traveling by ground, but they are far quicker and we are somewhat pressed for time. We can stay inside the cabins in the meantime, Your Holiness."

"No. I'd like to see the ship descending, if I can. I don't think I'll ever be in the position to view this again, as Mother is quite certain to ground me for the rest of my life after this."

"Some might say seventeen years in a tower is already a punishment of sorts, Your Holiness."

Noelle's face was a careful mask, but I smiled at her wryness. "My mother is a creative sort. I'm sure she'll come up with something even more confining."

"Sails down!" The cry rang out, and the ship tilted ever so slightly forward; we had reached the riverspout. I wrapped myself firmly around one of the smaller masts, Noelle bracing against another post as the ship started its descent into the lake. My stomach plummeted from the sharp angle; there was no way to slow the ship at this point, and all we could do was rely on the crew's skill to keep the *Brevity* from breaking apart.

"Mother of Rot." Lan was turning green again, fist pressed against her mouth. Her eyes sought mine out, relaxing when she saw where I'd anchored myself, and then she promptly gave up all pride to reach for an empty bucket.

We had not thought about securing some of our provisions, however. I saw barrels and crates flying past, one nearly beaning Nebly on the head before it tumbled out into the swirling waters.

With a loud splash, the ship landed right at the center of the lake, thankfully intact. The winds shifted and died down, an unnatural calm taking over. I was so used to the howling wind battering the *Brevity* the last few days that I wasn't sure what to make of the sudden, eerie quiet.

"Are we alive?" Lan asked weakly, righting herself.

"I'm afraid so," muttered Janella, who looked even worse off than the Catseye.

"Thank the goddess." Lan wavered slightly, looking surprised that the deck wasn't rolling, and loped toward Gracea with the unsteady gait of one no longer used to walking on land. "I'd like some of the Seasingers to monitor the waters around us and see if there are any other creatures lurking in wait. Don't let the silence here mislead you. There are more things hiding here than what you think you see."

Gracea frowned. "Graham, are there any sandbars nearby to beach the *Brevity*?"

The man concentrated, bright blue eyes searching into the distance. The lake was large enough that we couldn't quite see the opposite end, but that wasn't a problem for Seasingers. "No," he said presently. "I would suggest dropping anchor a little ways off from the spout instead. I do not believe the lakes are interconnected, and we may need to return to the ship in a hurry if there are other demons wandering the land."

"Focus on gathering what we can to start a fire," Gracea ordered, "and scour the immediate area for any vegetation that we can study and possibly harvest. Seasingers, continue watching the lake for any irregularities. Again, none of you are to stray far from the ship."

"You'll need a scout," Lan said, as the rest of the ship's crew began lowering the gangplank in anticipation of our disembarking.

"Absolutely not," Gracea said angrily. "It's too dangerous for us to split up."

"I'm not volunteering anyone besides myself, Starmaker."

"I'll go with you," Noelle said immediately.

"No," I said, almost at the same time.

Lan glowered. "I'm not asking you for permission, Odessa. I know the lay of this land better than anyone on board."

"That's not saying much, all things considered. And anyway, *I'm* technically the highest-ranking member of this ship."

"That means nothing if *you snuck on board.*"

She didn't understand. None of them did. I *had* to be here. My presence was going to change everything, and they were too ungrateful to see it!

And then my vision shifted.

I saw Lan, bone-weary, gripping a silver brooch in one hand. Janella was draped over her shoulder—dead or passed out, I couldn't tell. All too quickly the image faded again. What was that?

"Odessa?" Lan asked, noting my pause.

"Do whatever you want," I shot back, frustrated and fed up. I could predict every single incident in this journey, but it still felt like no one would ever believe me. "And I'll do what I want. That's the only thing we can seem to agree on."

"I would advise you not to leave the *Brevity*, Your Holiness," Gracea snapped.

Some of the crew were already moving off the ship, so that command had clearly been made from spite more than anything else. "I would hate to disobey a direct order, Starmaker."

Her gaze was hard. "Do not think that I am as lenient as Tianlan when it comes to your protection, Your Holiness. As long as this ship is under my command, you will do as I say."

"Yes, Starmaker. I have heard of the discipline you enforced at your punishment of Janella." She reeled back like I'd struck a blow. "But I answer only to my mother, and I will respectfully decline your suggestion." Where had this newfound courage come from? The Odessa of the Spire would never have talked back to a Devoted with such brashness. The Odessa of the Spire would never have disobeyed.

But the Odessa of the wildlands didn't care.

I loved it.

"Come back, Your Holiness!"

But I was already fleeing down the gangplank, startled faces looking on as I marched toward solid ground, with Noelle and Lan at my heels. "That might not have been the smartest move, Your Holiness," the latter said quietly.

"I'm already in trouble either way, so I wanted to tweak her nose while I was at it." Maybe I was a new Odessa now. It was exhilarating, to feel like I was my own person without needing to answer to anyone else. The galla of clarity, and now the galla of courage. Perhaps the underworld was actually doing me favors. "She's not chasing after me. Is she too scared to step on land herself?"

"The ship is where she rules sovereign, Your Holiness," Noelle explained. "She's all too aware that Lan holds the respect of much of the crew. She knows the lay of the land better, and Gracea resents that."

"You're pretty good at getting to the heart of the problem," I said with a smile.

"The politics within the Devoted are one reason I prefer to be the Spire's steward instead, Your Holiness."

"Be that as it may," Lan said, "it won't do much good to antagonize her."

"Does that mean we're okay?" I didn't want to keep fighting with Lan. I wanted to *kiss* Lan. She looked flawless as usual, with her perfect hair tied back in her long, perfect braids and her gorgeous bow mouth and the way she kept looking back at me when she didn't think I saw. But there were faint shadows around her dark eyes and she was paler than usual, and obviously this was the furthest thing from her mind. I was also all too aware that everything we did from this point on would be watched.

She sighed. "For now. But I want you to stay close to me, at least. So many things can happen out here."

I switched to fire-gates and summoned more Air. Then I whipped out my own rushlights, just to remind everyone else that Gracea was expendable if I wanted her to be. It was only as the sparks drifted out over the ground that I realized how dark it was out here. Though there weren't as many clouds shielding the sky as in Aranth, there were no stars out, either; just an endless view of black, shapeless night.

I wandered as far away from the ship as I dared, just within the outside boundary of the swirl of Light Gracea had sent down after the group. Unsurprisingly, Lan stuck close. Catseye Sumiko hovered nearby, not quite intruding, but near enough to make her presence apparent.

A sudden cry rose from the *Brevity*; I could hear Gracea swearing. "What's the matter with her this time?" I asked, annoyed.

"Your Holiness." It was Slyp. "There's been some damage to the ship. Even if we find a way into the other lakes, or get up another riverwind, we won't be moving until the damage has been repaired."

"Did this happen during our descent?"

The old man lifted his hands. "Could be. The bowsprit is cracked something fierce, and the yards aren't looking good, either. We'll be beached for a while, whether we like it or not."

I knew practically nothing about running a ship, but if Gracea was pitching a tantrum, I assumed it was bad. "It will keep her from killing anyone else, at least."

I turned to my Catseye and stopped short when I saw how

pale she'd become. I reached for her hands, and found them cold and clammy. "Lan—"

"The ship's damaged," she echoed. "And we can't travel through the east because of the acidfall. We'll have to—we'll need to—"

Journey through the western border of the Spirit Lands. Lan would have to travel the same route that had seen her team killed. I wanted to tell her it was going to be all right but didn't know how to make her believe that—I hated feeling so helpless. "Surely there must be another way we could—"

"I can't!" The words came out her in violent bursts. "I'm not going back there! I won't!"

"Lan—"

But she'd already turned away, her breathing ragged and eyes unfocused, back toward the ship and to Gracea. I moved to follow.

"Stay here, Odessa."

"I'm not going to let you—"

"*Stay here*, Odessa!" She'd never raised her voice to me like that before, with all the panic and the grief and the anger so very evident, and any rebuttal I was about to make froze in my throat.

Catseye Sumiko looked back at me, silently asking for permission. I somehow managed a nod, and she scuttled immediately after Lan.

"You have to allow Lan to process this, Your Holiness." Noelle's voice was just as soft. "She keeps it bottled up, but I worry that returning to this place will bring those memories back."

"But I want to help."

"Sumiko has experience in these matters. Give her the necessary space to try."

I acknowledged the wisdom of her words. What else could I do?

Still, I kept glancing back up at the ship, wondering.

"We may have to careen the *Brevity* if Gracea wishes to transfer us to another lake, but I shudder at the effort grounding the ship would take," Noelle said.

"Are you saying we're stranded out here?" Merika squeaked. "We can't return to Aranth?"

"Of course not. It will take months to complete the journey back to the city on land, but Catseye Tianlan will at least know the way."

"Does she, really?" Cathei inched closer, lowering her voice. "They said that it took her a day to travel back from here to Aranth when the journey out took a dozen weeks. Not even she knows how she found her way back, or so they said. Did a monster carry her off and set her down near Aranth? They say she gave up her soul for safety, watched as everyone else around her was slaughtered—"

"I will not tolerate such talk, Cathei," I said sharply. "And I will appreciate it if you let the rest of the crew know my distaste for it."

The woman looked abashed. "I'm sorry, Your Holiness. We don't believe that, I swear. It's just that there's talk."

"But as there's *talk*, you'll no doubt ensure they keep their mouths shut in favor of keeping their tongues."

"Your Holiness," Noelle said, admonishing.

"People don't think much about the truth when the lies sound more interesting, Your Holiness," Slyp grunted. "Few people believe me when I talk about life before the Breaking, for instance. Things were different before, that I'm old enough to remember. Trees as far as the eye can see. Birds of all kinds, and squirrels and butterflies and badgers every spring."

Nebly let out a derisive laugh. "Butter what?"

"What is spring?" I asked.

"It used to be when flowers bloomed all over the land, Your Holiness. Lovely to see. You only appreciate things like those when they're gone."

"Sounds like an old wives' tale," Nebly said, not without envy.

Goddess.

I almost hadn't noticed it; it was so dark that it blended well with the shadows, even with the light of Gracea's patterns floating around us. It was an elongated body with limbs too thin to be natural, creeping so close to the ground I could have easily disregarded it as some strange mist, or an untethered silhouette. On my knees, I froze, waiting as it approached me.

"Your Holiness?" Noelle asked uncertainly. They couldn't see it. "Is something wrong?"

"Don't move. All of you." I knew it wouldn't hurt me—they'd never harmed the goddesses that came before. But I didn't know how they would react to outside interference.

It had horns just like the last two, but on its head were a pair of glittering beads, made of the same blue stones.

Like the others, it waited.

It knew I had to be willing.

"Yes," I whispered. The first galla gave me visions, and the second greater strength in the gates, but *for every gift, a terror; for every radiance, a sacrifice*, and I had no idea what they had taken from me in return. What abilities would this one offer me? And what would it demand in exchange?

"Your Holiness?" Cathei quavered, staring past the creature she couldn't see.

It shifted closer without moving, and I felt the faint brush of fingers against mine.

Color poured into my vision; herbs and plants of malachite hues, more vibrant than the sad-looking vegetation we tried to cultivate in Aranth. Threads of patterns danced around me; I'd channeled terra patterns before, but these were different. For a moment, I saw the wildlands the way they were before the Breaking: lush and vibrant, filled to bursting with flora of every shade of green.

But then my arms broke out into poison; brown filth stole up my wrists, clung to my shoulders. I cried out, trying to fling the toxins away from me, but in another second they had disappeared, and my hands were clean again.

Be satisfied. A divine power of the underworld has been fulfilled. You must not open your mouth against the rites of the underworld.

And then it vanished into nothing.

New energy thrummed inside me, eager to find release. I stared at my hands and thought I could actually see them crackling a bright, verdant hue.

"What's going on?" I heard Gracea call out, but I ignored her and placed my hands on the soil. Back in Aranth, where floods were common enough that dry streets were a rarity, the ground was too wet for farming or ploughing, and we kept our meager plants potted aboveground. But here? The ground was neither too dry nor too wet, and while I knew nothing about tilling the soil, there was something curled up inside of me saying that that didn't matter.

I reached out for those strange new patterns, let them wind themselves around my core. When I pushed all those energies outward, I felt a new gate flare behind my eyes—one I'd always known I had, but had never used before—not blue like water or clear as air or even the gold-and-silver of an aether-gate, but a soft, bright green.

The ground underneath me broke apart between my knees and *sprouted*. A slender vine poked its way out from the soil, lazily wound past my thighs, and reached for the dark skies above. More joined their sister, curling up and around, hungry for the clouds. Some of the crew cried out and stepped back as the earth beneath us blushed green, the brown, broken soil soon overrun by what I knew was grass while more plants burst into life, swelled heavy with flowers and fruit, and opened.

"What are those?" One of the devoted, Miel, gasped.

"Trees," Noelle whispered in disbelief as one bounty-heavy plant trembled and yawned before her gaze, revealing round, plump berries that swayed tantalizingly in the still air while my rushlights danced around them, casting them in an unearthly glow.

Gates and patterns, I knew, were utterly dependent on the environment around them. People who were born Firesmokers, for example, could not wield such abilities in a city made from sea and storms.

But we were no longer in Aranth. We were much farther east in the world, where even Water and Ice were not so violent in their composition as we were used to, where life that we could never nurture in the city could find a way.

The plant that had woven itself around me broke away but continued to grow, higher and higher until it became a magnificent tree, like those I had only ever seen in drawings, in books of ages long past. I watched the leaves climb over its branches, immersing them in a cloak of emerald.

The crew of the *Brevity* stared at the tree, and then at me. There was a disturbance in the back of the crowd; Gracea had finally worked up the nerve to leave the ship, and at the edge of the gangplank, she gaped at me as well. With her was Lan, whose mouth fell open as she took in the miracle I'd performed.

"Spring," Nebly whispered.

"They're not poisonous," I murmured, proved it by plucking

one ripe berry from a flourishing bush. It tasted sweet in my mouth. I reveled in the crew's awe. I could sense a spike of fear among the others as well—I reveled in that, too.

An odd buzzing had settled behind my ears, but I ignored it. I was Odessa of the wildlands now.

Chapter Twelve

HAIDEE OF THE DOLUGONGS

———————————— ☀ ————————————

I THOUGHT I'D PLANNED FOR all conceivable contingencies while I was refurbishing Arjun's driving rig as a decent dirigible/sand jeep, but I had failed to take into account Arjun himself, because the boy would not stop moaning about anything and everything.

He complained about not having enough room inside the now-airtight compartment for the both of us.

Then he started griping about how we were traveling at a much slower pace than we had on land; I had chosen to sacrifice speed for survival by converting one of the engine pipes into an air purifier.

Lastly, he said the echoes were horrible; the sound bounced back and forth between the walls of the rig, making even the barest of whispers sound like ringing threats, all made more terrible because Arjun wouldn't *shut up* even knowing that.

And while it was true that I'd had to forgo a bit of comfort to make sure there was enough metal fully encasing us in our little sand bubble, and while it was true that we were not as quick as before in exchange for better defenses against the potential threats that might come after us as we sailed merrily along this Sand Sea, and *while it was also true* that I had failed to take into account the flutter echo from being in so confined a space, it felt like this was far too much criticism for the otherwise reasonable measures I had taken to ensure we would still be alive once we'd reached the other side of this dust-ocean, and I said as much.

He grunted. The sound pinged against the opposite wall and scored a direct hit somewhere within my inner ears. Words followed. "Well, your elbow is *still* currently somewhere inside my left shoulder blade."

"You're a terrible partner," I said, trying my best to wriggle away. I hadn't slept well in the cramped space, but admitting that would mean he'd been right about me being too privileged to rough it for long. Arjun was terrible and those cannibals (cannibals?!) chasing us were terrible and whatever Sand Sea creatures swimming around preparing to eat us were *also* terrible. I just wanted to find a way to repair the world and bring life back to it and not have to deal with all three. "Are we still traveling in the right direction?"

He squinted through the glass. The mirage was still missing. "No idea, but I know we haven't turned around. You were supposed to be keeping a lookout for the specter."

I scowled. "I've been making sure there were no holes for any sand to get through. You're the one driving!"

He harrumphed, then tried to lift himself up for a better view. The rig was half-submerged, in the same manner as a boat might float along an actual sea, so we could still take stock of our surroundings. "I can't tell if there are any more creatures poking out of the sand nearby."

"Well, excuse me for working a miracle in just under three hours." He hadn't even thanked me!

That must have struck his conscience a little, because he winced. "Look, I can turn around. I'll find us some new spot to beach at without any Hellmakers nearby."

"No. There's no time, and you can't guarantee there won't be more cannibals. I don't even *see* any place where we could dock. As for the mirage, I'll chase it to the end of the world if I have to."

"Fantastic."

"I can still drop you off somewhere."

He glared at me. "I'm not going to leave you alone. You'd have been eaten by sandsnakes without me around."

The rig rocked, swaying precariously as something pushed hard at us from outside. I found myself smushed to one side with a startled Arjun practically on top of me. "Get off!" I hissed, shoving at him.

"Sorry," he muttered, trying to right both himself and the vehicle. "What the hell was that?"

I saw a quick flash of a scaled tail lifting up from the sand in front of us before disappearing from view.

"What are you doing?" Arjun yelled when I unlocked the hatch above us.

"Keep your voice down," I snapped, clapping one hand over the ear he'd just roared into. "They're not going to hurt us."

"Not going to hurt us? What are—"

But I'd already pushed the lid away, popping out into the open and breathing in a huge gulp of fresher air. The Sand Sea continued to stretch on for miles around us, with no shore in sight.

Beside the rig, a gray head poked cautiously out of the sand, revealing large, bright golden eyes, a long smooth snout, and furred feathery ears on a head with a texture not unlike a rock's. The snout parted to reveal small, pebblelike teeth, and the creature chittered excitedly at us. Another peered out of the sand-water, and then another, and then more until we were mobbed by a dozen of the critters, all calling out to each other and to us.

"What are those things?" Arjun sputtered.

"Dolugongs!" I said happily, as one of them leaped grace-fully into the air, showing off its coarse, elongated body, two flippers, and a disproportionately large tail, before diving back down into the fine gravel. The others followed its lead, and soon the whole pod was leaping out from the sand.

"What's a dolugong?"

"Well . . . their hides are as hard as stone to help them sur-vive the desert by minimizing their water—"

"In two sentences or less."

"Uh. It's like a giant fish, but not exactly."

"That looks nothing like a fish to me."

"It has some characteristics of one. Big flappy tail, flippers, and gills. But it can also breathe above water—above sand, in this case—"

"How can they breathe sand *and* water?"

"That's going to take more than two sentences, buddy."

Arjun looked unimpressed. "How do you know they won't hurt us?"

"We're not their prey. They feast on smaller worms and bugs that burrow underneath the Sand Sea. They can defend themselves, and they *can* attack if they think we're a threat, so I don't advise throwing things at them."

"Not even thinking about it. Tell them to quit pushing us."

"They were probably just curious." I barked back at the dolugongs, trying to mimic their pitch and sound. One of them chirped back a reply; it brought down its tail, and a small wave of sand spilled into the hatch.

"On second thought, maybe just stop talking," Arjun grumbled, shaking sand out of his hair.

A higher-pitched whine came from another recently arrived dolugong, more frantic than the rest. Three of members of the pod swam ahead to meet the newcomer, who was swimming in small, panicked circles. "Wonder what they're doing," I whispered to Arjun, who grunted again.

The others were now also agitated. They swam rapidly

around us, emitting quick bursts of yelps before dashing off.

"Follow them," I said immediately.

"Like hell I will."

"They're in trouble!"

"You've mastered their language that quickly?"

"I don't need to. I recognize the sounds of creatures in distress." I hated to beg, but he was the one driving. "Please?"

He made a small snort of disgust, but obediently shifted gears so we were following the group.

"Thank you."

"Save your gratitude till we're sure they're not leading us to some kind of trap."

"Have you always been this suspicious? This cynical?"

"Not cynical. Sensible. One of us has to be."

The reason for the dolugongs' anxiety soon became obvious. A baby dolugong had found itself stuck at an outcrop between two large rocks, and despite all its wriggling, it couldn't free itself. A thick mesh was draped over its body, limiting its movements. Another, larger dolugong, possibly its parent, circled the trapped baby, crying. I knew the little calf could die under the baking sun in less than an hour.

"Draw us up as near to it as you're able to," I commanded.

"You're not seriously considering—"

"Do it!" I raised my voice, and Arjun grimaced. The rig veered closer to the struggling baby.

I lifted the hatch and clambered out, ignoring Arjun's outraged squawk. "Hi there," I called out softly to the calf, who

215

looked petrified at the sight of me. Its parent drew closer, ululating threateningly, but one of the other dolugongs yapped at it. "I'm not going to hurt you. I just want to help. Will you let me?"

"It can't understand you, you know," Arjun grumbled behind me.

"It's your turn to shut your rathole."

The baby was too tightly wedged between the rocks for me to extricate it without potentially injuring it, so I concentrated on the boulders pinning it into place. I gated some Air, working at it until it was as thin as a needle and as sharp as a sword, and began chipping away at the left stone's surface.

"You'll take all day." I hadn't even noticed Arjun climbing onto the rig's hood with me.

"It's the safest way," I grunted. "Fire might injure it."

"Not necessarily. Let me try."

I shot him an apprehensive look, but he set his limb against the slab and his eyes blazed red. Smoke curled at the end of his wrist, followed immediately by a bright blue flame that seared through the rock at a much faster rate than I could.

"What's that?" I gasped, fascinated despite myself. I'd never seen fire that color before.

"Dunno." It was burning with knifelike precision, slicing cleanly through the rock without leaving any jagged edges. Any of my mother's sculptors would have killed for such accuracy. "I've always been able to do it. It's hotter than regular fires and eats through things quicker, too."

The rock was loose in no time at all—it toppled off, and we watched it sink down until it disappeared from view. Arjun lifted the heavy net off the squirming baby dolugong as it slipped back into the sand, where it reemerged beside its now-calm mother.

"And you didn't want to follow them," I murmured, out of the need to be contrary but without any of my previous annoyance.

"It's every man for himself out here. Or goddess. Or dolugong."

He glanced at the cluster surrounding the freed dolugong calf and shrugged. "But the last thing I wanna do is separate a kid from its mother."

"Ah. I'm sorry." His clan were mostly orphans, he'd said. I'd never realized that for all my talk about my own mother, he'd never had one himself.

His smile, more genuine now than ever before, warmed me. "Don't be. But what's this mesh doing out here in the middle of nowhere? It's definitely man-made."

I frowned. "I'm not sure, either. Could it have . . . floated here, somehow?"

"Not likely. Things stuck here don't just float to other places. Sand doesn't move like water does, and there aren't any currents here. Can we get back to heading west? The damned mirage is nowhere to be seen and—wait." His voice rose when the dolugongs made an immediate beeline for him. "What are they doing?"

I hid my grin, watching them swarm him. One leaped into the air behind Arjun; a flick of its tail sent him stumbling off the rig and into the center of their herd, where they had gathered together like a breathing, moving mattress. With loud screams of pleasure, they began carrying him, circling around me at a speed that not even the rig could manage. "What does it look like? They're *thanking* you."

A sputtered yelp of outrage was his reply.

"I'm never going to help those damned fish again," Arjun fumed much later, shaking more sand from underneath his collar, and I couldn't stop laughing, even as the rig sped toward the horizon, flanked on all sides by a pod of grateful, happy dolugongs.

We passed strange structures the farther west we drove, the dolugongs occasionally nudging at our vehicle as they swam alongside it. There was debris that could have been buildings once, stone monuments buried and broken. "Well, think about it," Arjun pointed out. "This wouldn't have been all Sand Sea seventeen years ago. Maybe the Sand Sea didn't even exist until the Breaking upended everything. Could have been villages here. Cities."

"Do you think we'll find people?" I asked him. "Surely there were survivors."

"Depends how bad things have gotten in other parts of the world, I guess. We live under extreme weather, but I'd say it grows more temperate the farther out west we go."

The dolugongs kept butting their heads adamantly against the side of the rig for close to an hour before I realized why. "I think they want us to use them," I said to Arjun, "to speed us up."

The boy eyed them warily. "They do swim faster than we can move."

"Let's take them up on their offer and see. If we've got some rope, we could tie it around their fins."

It was Arjun who'd figured out how to keep the knot secure without injuring the dolugongs. I'd pointed out that their rough hides meant they wouldn't be sensitive to rope burns, but he'd growled at me and said we were going to do it the *right* way. I hid my grin. As much as he liked to grouch about the dolugongs, he was even more attentive to their needs than I was.

"Give Parrick the lead," I suggested. "He's the most observant of the bunch."

"You've already started naming them." It wasn't even a question. He was getting to know me well enough.

The dolugongs took off as soon as we gave the signal. They were at least three times faster than the rig, and all we had to do was guide the wheel to mimic their direction, conserving the precious energy it took to funnel Fire gas for emergencies. Every now and then I'd direct a dolugong by tapping it lightly with a pipe, just to make sure we were still on course.

"Guess this isn't too bad," Arjun said reluctantly, never one to admit he was wrong even when he was. Me, I leaned out the rig, threw my arms up, and enjoyed the blasts of air against my face, my short hair whipping about as I laughed into the wind.

"How sure are you?" I asked much, much later. I had no idea how many hours had passed, because the day was just as bright as it ever was, but Arjun seemed fairly certain. "We've been moving for close to ten hours now," he said, pointing up at the sun while he shielded his eyes with an arm. He changed into his Stonebreaker-crafted armor, the faint viridian aura around it giving him a fair amount of protection, even with the hatch open. "Notice anything different?"

I squinted. "Not really."

"You think it's in the same place it used to be when we started traveling?"

"Now that you mention it . . ." It was still bright out, but the sun seemed to have moved just a little bit to the right. It also cast strange, stunted shadows against the sand.

"The sun might not move anymore, but we're moving. So the farther west we go, the farther east it'll shift in the sky. And if we travel far enough, we may not even see it anymore. That's the part of Aeon where the day meets darkness, I guess." He had shut off the engines, allowing the rig to float peacefully along. The other dolugongs had already fallen asleep underneath the sand, dark shapes against the surface.

The rig's hatch was open. Arjun had erected a small tarpaulin over our heads bespelled with Stonebreaker shielding to ward off most of the harmful sunlight. He'd also handed me my food rations for the day: smoked whale meat, a bit of water from one of the heavy canisters he'd brought along, and also a few pieces of dried fish. Without the sand buggy, my own rations wouldn't have lasted me this far. For all his previous protests that I wasn't ready to face the desert alone, he was silent on the matter now, and I was inclined to be nicer to him for it.

"I was wondering if I could ask you a question about your mother," I began tentatively, nibbling on my dried fish because I wasn't ready to eat Betsy-meat just yet, "if it's not too personal. You said you were an orphan, but did anyone tell you about her?"

"Yes, that's a hell of a personal question." Arjun shrugged. "Not much to say. Never knew her. I was raised by Mother Salla all my life, and she told me my mother was the leader of your aunt's Devoted, supposedly. She died at the Breaking."

"I'm sorry. I've good reason to believe my sister died there, too. And my father."

"I think Mother Salla mentioned you having a sister. I didn't know about that until she told me a few days ago."

I sat up straighter, not bothering to hide my eagerness. "She knew? Did she tell you anything else about her?"

He shook his head, and my shoulders slumped. "Sorry. If we ever make it back, that's the first thing I'll ask."

If we ever make it back. I liked his optimism. "And *I'm* sorry if I forced you on this trip." He looked surprised, but I forged ahead. "You're right. I'd have died out here on my own. You brought the rig, the water, everything we needed to survive. Your Mother Salla might not think I'm the enemy, but you weren't under any obligation to help me. So why do it, anyway?"

He ate the last of the jerky, swallowed, then cleared his throat. "It knew my name. The mirage. Said we were both supposed to be at the Abyss. Turns out the mirage might be an old friend of Mother Salla's who didn't survive the Breaking. She's convinced this is important, and I trust her. And besides . . ."

He looked around us, at the sleeping herd that had made us a part of their pack. "It was either live out the rest of my life in some goddess-forsaken desert, trying to eke out an existence with depleting water resources and food—or take a risk and see if you really could bring life back to Aeon. I got brothers and sisters back home, and they deserve a better world than this. And just because the people in charge screwed everything to hell and beyond doesn't mean we can't find a way to take back what we're owed."

I nudged his shoulder with mine, then reached over to give him a hug.

"What was that for?"

"Nothing. Thank you for believing in me." My mother didn't trust me; most of the people in the Golden City didn't want to hear what I had to say. But this nomad from a tribe who called themselves her enemy, who had every right to kill me where I sat, trusted me better than people I'd known all my life. "So you *were* looking for me."

He glared at me again, and I giggled.

"You have no idea . . . how much I needed someone to listen to what I say for once, instead of just what they want me to say." He'd opened up about his past, and I wanted to return the favor. "Mother doesn't know I sneak out of the city, and she hates that I've been hanging out with the other mechanika. She tells me I need to learn how to manage our subjects but rarely gives me anything of importance to do. I'm expected to marry someone of her choosing and sire another daughter."

"Sounds as bad as I expected, then."

"I don't know a lot about what happened between her and my aunt, about how the world broke between them. But I know it's one of the reasons she forbids me from leaving. She's afraid of what I might find out here."

"So she's right pissed now, I reckon."

"Very much so, I'm sure. But I have to do this. There's—I don't know how to explain it, but there's something calling me west. Mother can run the dome without me. But as far as she's concerned, the city is the only world that matters anymore; it's where Aeon begins and ends. I disagree."

"You're risking a lot based on just a gut feeling."

"You're risking a lot based on the same thing."

"Good point. Guess I gotta stick around a little longer, then. You've got the tools and the brains, and I've got the jeep and the self-preservation instinct you obviously don't." He stretched out, ignoring my glare and swinging his leg over my part of the rig. "I'm taking a nap."

"Where am I going to sleep if you're hogging all the space?"

"You should have figured that out when you rebuilt this thing."

I waited until he started snoring, then clambered over to his side. He grunted and shifted to make space by his arm for me, proving he was more of an asshole awake than not, and I settled by his shoulder.

As far as pillows go, he wasn't too bad.

Chapter Thirteen

LAN IN THE MIST

———————————— ☾ ————————————

"MILADY," CATHEI SAID MEEKLY, her face pinched with worry. "Something's been bothering me all day."

"What is it?" I'd spent the greater part of the night among the bright new plants Odessa had coaxed into ripening, lost in my maps. From the campsite I could hear Noelle singing as she cleaned the weapons that had survived the journey. She had a beautiful voice.

"Well, it's the rigging, mainly."

"I'm not very knowledgeable about ships, Cathei."

"Neither am I, milady. That's why—it's all so peculiar. I tried talking to Gracea, but she wouldn't listen. I just thought it odd how she would be outside the ship. It's almost like she did it deliberately."

"Who did what deliberately?"

She faltered. "I—I don't know."

I rubbed my eyes. "Is there a point to this, Cathei?"

"No, I guess not. I'm sorry for taking up your time, Lady Tianlan."

"Wait." I reached out to grasp her arm, healing the bruise there. "Who did this?"

Cathei paled. "It doesn't hurt, milady—"

"Did Gracea do this?"

"I have to go, milady." But the girl's face was still pinched as she walked away, and I set my jaw. Gracea took poorly to stress—but this went beyond proper decency. I made a mental note to announce to the crew later that abuses would not be tolerated on my watch. Lashing out when unable to get her way, it seemed, was a disgusting habit of the Starmaker's. I didn't blame the clerks and the crew members for being afraid to speak out, but I was hoping someone would come forward so I could have a valid reason to relieve her of command.

There was already little love lost between us. My previous argument with Gracea had nearly deteriorated into a screaming match. I had no intention of traveling through the western border, and she was just as equally adamant that we must. Odessa's unexpected harvest had only postponed the fight.

The thought of our planned route made my hands sweat. Sumiko had offered to help again, but I had refused. There was nothing wrong with me, because it wouldn't happen again. I wouldn't let it control me again.

I glanced down at my maps, spread on the ground. The maps of the riverwinds were now useless. Going forward meant traveling through the Spirit Lands, which stretched over half the night side of the planet.

My hands felt clammy. I didn't want to go there. But I couldn't find any other path now that the riverwinds ended prematurely at the Lunar Lakes.

I had to find another way. I had to. I *had* to. I—

I heard voices raised nearby. Odessa was heading toward me, accompanied by Gareen. The goddess looked serene, but the boy was visibly sweating.

"I trust that you'll bring my request to his attention," Odessa said sweetly. "I'd be very much put out if I see no changes by tomorrow."

"I'll let him know r-right away, Your Holiness."

Gareen scurried off, but Odessa continued heading in my direction.

"What was that all about?" I asked, curious.

"It's nothing. Just relaying some orders to Holsett and the others." She hesitated. "Are you still mad at me?"

"Yes. Maybe." I rubbed at my eyes. "It doesn't matter."

"I'm sorry. It was never my intention to mislead you."

It may not have been her intention, but she'd misled me all the same. "Like I said, it doesn't matter."

She offered me a bowl. "I grilled some maize for you. Why eat what's left of the ship's stores, when you can have something hot and fresh?"

"Don't you think there's something strange here, Your Holiness? How did you develop this sudden skill for growing crops?"

"I'm not trying to poison any of you."

"Was it another galla? Did it touch you again?"

"*I* touched it," she corrected me. "Nothing happened. It disappeared, and I could read the patterns around me."

My unease grew. "What patterns?"

"They're unlike any I've seen in Aranth. I felt them flowing through me before I knew it." She raised her arm to encompass the flourishing verdant plants spread across the ground around us. "It was as easy as breathing. And I . . . no longer feel exhausted or weak like I used to. These galla . . . they want to help, Lan. I know it."

She was too trusting. That she wanted to see the best in people was something I loved about her, but these were shadows spawned from the Great Abyss. Her optimism was going to get her killed. "For someone so sure, you can't seem to provide as much information about *them*."

She stamped her foot. "Why must you always be so suspicious?"

"I wouldn't be doing my job if I wasn't, Your Holiness."

"Then it's time for my nightly healing. You've been negligent in that as of late."

That was true, so I set the maps aside. Odessa sat beside me, taking my hand and pressing it against her cheek. My heart slammed against my chest at her sudden closeness.

"Get on with it, then," she said softly.

It was worse than before. The black hole inside of her had spread again. My hopes fell away. *Why couldn't I help her?*

I opened my gate wider, trying in vain to diminish the miasma within by even a millimeter. My head spun slightly from the surplus energy—to wield this much was too dangerous even for the experienced, but I had to try—

"No," Odessa said quietly, taking my hand away, forcing me to suck in air, for the patterns to dissipate harmlessly on their own.

"It isn't enough, Your Holiness." I *wanted* her. I wanted her badly, but this was a mistake. I couldn't be her Catseye if that meant I had to watch her wither away and do *nothing*.

"Again with 'Your Holiness.' I'm sick and tired of 'Your Holiness.' You never used to call me that!"

"No," I said brutally, already hating myself as soon as the words spilled out. "I used to call you Ame."

She froze. "I'll apologize for that every day of my life if I have to. Surely you know how sorry I am for it? Surely you know why I couldn't tell you who I was?"

Before I could say anything, she was on her knees before me, pressing the palm of her hand against my mouth. "And don't you dare say it," she hissed, her beautiful pale eyes all aglow with her fury. "Don't tell me that it doesn't matter anymore, because I know it does, whatever you say. I—" Her voice broke. "I can't do what you can. I can't just turn off my own feelings because there's a job to do. Unless you never took it—took *us* seriously in the first place."

As if stricken dumb by this new revelation, she started to withdraw her hand. "If you thought I was just some fling, some girl you wanted to fool around with to get over your dead lover, then at least have the decency to say it to my face—"

I grabbed her wrist with one hand, grabbed at her riotously colored hair with the other, and kissed her.

She gasped, made a soft little whimper, and for one brief, horrifying second I wondered if I'd read her wrong. But then her arms came up around my neck, and she was kissing me back.

She tasted just like I remembered, in those early days when we had nothing but bookcases and a bookseller willing to give his best customers their privacy. Her lips against mine, sweet and soft and shy at first, before her mouth parted and she was rocking greedily against me, giving as good as I did. Somehow, after I had started and she had permitted, she had found herself on my lap, heels drumming against the small of my back.

She felt like a break in the clouds, how a glimpse of sun might feel. The desires I'd thought to stamp down and bottle up, the desires I was so sure I could master after becoming the Spire's new guardian, after the hurt of Odessa's subterfuge—the continued ferocity of those feelings stunned me.

I should never have accepted this job.

"How did you know," I whispered thickly, finally coming up for air, "about Nuala?"

She blinked down at me, disoriented. "I . . . you looked so sad when you stared at her ranger badge on your wall. . . ."

Ah. "Sometimes people can have a relationship and still have no lasting feelings for each other." It was strange to talk about an ex while your current love was practically molded to your hips, but sweet Mother did I try. "Nuala and I were comrades first and foremost. It never moved beyond anything physical. I grieved for her when she died, like I did the other rangers. But you're different. Did you know what I planned, when I asked you to spend the night?"

She shook her head.

"There's an old custom among my mother's people, one they took seriously." I couldn't stop running my fingers through her hair, entranced by the way the strands shifted from purple to pink to red. Learning these colors was another thing she'd denied me as Ame. "In the old Liangzhu tongue, *yexu* meant 'we might.' Accepting an offer of *yexu* meant the start of a courtship. *Yexia*—'we are'—was a renewal of commitment to the relationship. Ye*zhiyao*—'we always'—was an offer of marriage." I was no innocent—I'd had dalliances in the past, but Odessa was the only one I had ever contemplated this with, this desire to offer something formal and sacred and profound. "I've never offered that kind of commitment to anyone else. You've never been a fling to me. But I shouldn't have asked you to spend the night. We were moving too fast. For all those romance books you love, you've never read one with a Liangzhu theme?"

She shook her head again, still speechless.

I gently disentangled myself from her. "I need to talk with Gracea about tomorrow. Our last conversation didn't end well." I shouldn't have kissed her. Not after learning she was Aranth's goddess; all that was going to leave me was heartbreak. She would get married in time, to someone who could give her children and continue Asteria's line, and already I wanted to kill the man she would have to choose. "It's getting late."

Her fingers grazed my elbow. "Is there still time?"

"Time?"

"To say yes. To your offer of the *yexu* and"—her voice shook, but she controlled it with a soft gulp—"staying the night. I don't want this to be over."

I don't know what I must have looked like when I stared back at her, but from the way her breath quickened and her eyes took on a glazed look, she must have liked what she saw.

You can't, I snarled to myself, even as I leaned toward her.

I saw her eyes flick to my right, saw them widen—and turn into a sudden fury of blazing green. Something vine-like whipped out from behind her, shooting past me to stake a shadow creature through where its heart ought to be. It skittered, squealed, and dissolved.

It had been almost directly behind me.

I whirled around, my broadsword already in my hands just as more shadows staggered out from the darkness. "Intruders!" I yelled, raising my voice loud enough for the others to hear and clamber into defensive positions, then lowering it again for Odessa's benefit. "You said the galla were on your side."

"Only the horned ones, with the blue jewels." The plants curled around Odessa's wrists, seemingly under her control. "The rest don't necessarily want me here."

"And I suppose there was a good reason you didn't mention that." I lunged forward and cleaved through another shadow with a clean stroke of my blade. These shadows appeared vulnerable to Asteria's blessing, which meant they were also vulnerable to our swords. The new creatures were human height, at least, but there were enough of them to cause worry—three dozen, at least.

I took down another silhouette just as Noelle appeared by my side, her halberd already slicing through the air. From behind us, I could feel patterns being forged into weapons as the other Devoted readied themselves, sharp ice and blades of air cutting into the monsters. Odessa's vines were just as effective, boring through those shadows' bodies like rapiers or winding around them, squeezing them dry. I led a charge into the darkness, taking down as many of the creatures as I could, releasing the pent-up fears and anger I'd been holding in these last few weeks. I didn't need magic. All I needed was my sword, and my rage, and my memories of Merritt and Nuala and everyone else to redouble my hunger for vengeance.

It felt great.

By the time we were all done, nothing remained. The shadows left no corpses, no indication that they had even existed. Gracea's lights revealed nothing else lying in wait.

A cry rose from where most of the noncombatants had huddled. "Cathei's gone!"

Gracea turned, incredulous. "Impossible! I just saw her standing—"

"Janella's gone, too!"

The Starmaker looked furious. "Split up into groups.

Holsett, take the lead and head into the north side of camp. Graham, you'll go west—"

"No," I interrupted.

"People on my team are *missing*, Tianlan! Why would you dare—"

"Because that's what got *my* team killed, Gracea." Breathe. *Breathe.* I kept seeing the dead in my mind's eye, the bodies strewn around me when I knew they weren't actually there. I was not going to break down again, and not in front of Gracea of all people, either—but it was getting harder to take in air.

I cleared my throat—several times, but my voice came out hoarse all the same. "Does anyone remember where they were last seen?"

"They were standing right beside me when the attacks started." One of the crew spoke up—Salleemae—gesturing helplessly at the empty space beside her.

"I was standing guard right here," Graham stuttered, his own face gray. "I saw nothing!"

"There are some marks on the ground," Noelle pointed out quietly.

She was right. I knelt down to study them. "It happened the same way all those months ago." My palms felt slick, my breath hitching at an uneven rate. "They're smarter than we give them credit for. They want to divide us up into smaller groups, make it easier to pick us off."

"Then what do we do?"

I wet my lips. "We wait."

"We wait?" Odessa all but shouted. "We can't wait! They could be out there, injured, trying to—"

"We have no other choice. We split off, that's how they find us."

"Are you saying we do nothing?" Gracea demanded.

"You've told *me* enough times that doing the opposite cost me my team."

She glared at me but couldn't find a proper answer.

"You can't," Odessa was nearly sobbing. "You can't just abandon them to whatever is out there!"

"I'm sorry, Odessa."

She took a step away, into the darkness.

"No!" I grabbed her arm, let just enough patterns through to let her know I had no qualms about rendering her unconscious again. She stared back at me, hurt and betrayal in her beautiful pale eyes. Was it only several minutes ago that we'd kissed like nothing else mattered? Her mouth was still swollen.

"I'm not going to stand here and wait like a coward when I know I could help them!" she shot back, and damn if that didn't *hurt*.

"Your duty is to remain with the group," I spat out. "Set out and search for Janella and Cathei, and you'll risk the rest. What do you think is going to happen when you leave? Do you think there's no mind at work here, conspiring to lure you away so it can slaughter the rest of us without your protection?"

Odessa paused, conflicted. The others shifted, discomfited by the thought. "Are you saying there's nothing we can do?"

"I'm saying that there's nothing *you* can do." It took considerable effort to force the next words out. I didn't want to do it. But this was how I'd protect her. *Breathe in, Lan. Breathe out. All good.* "Let me investigate."

"What? No!" It was Odessa's turn to grab me. "You're not going out there alone again!"

"No visions this time, Your Holiness? Nothing for me to use as a guide?"

She hesitated, and for a second I thought she had one. But then she shook her head. "I forbid this."

"They . . . the things out there spared my life before, and I don't know why. Goddess willing, they'll spare it again."

"No!" Her voice rose, shriller. "I—I can't allow—"

"She's right, Your Holiness," Gracea said. "She's the sole ranger here, and the best choice."

"Do you want me to remain and do nothing, Odessa, or do you want me to try and save these two women?" I grabbed my pack, adjusted my sword belt. "You chose to leave the Spire. Did you expect to treat everything else like some game the way you stowed away on the *Brevity*?" I didn't want to act like she had no better motive for escaping in the first place, but it worked.

"You're hateful," she choked out.

"Maybe I just wasn't the person you thought I was." I strode into the darkness, leaving the brightness of the camp behind me. Everyone watched me leave without another word, and I didn't need to look back to know the silent disapproval in Noelle's eyes nor the crushed disappointment in Odessa's.

I must have been half a mile away before I started breaking out into a cold sweat.

It was colder here, without any light to guide me by, even though my eyes had adjusted well enough to the darkness to know my own steps. But I wanted to run back to the safety of the group. I wanted to board the *Brevity* and sail back into Aranth and face the storms and the approaching seas instead of this agonizing silent darkness that had gutted me once before and would do so again. I wanted to run because this was where my nightmares were birthed, where everything I had always thought about myself as a person—strong, brave, fierce, unyielding—had been so easily proven wrong by the swipe of a dark, scaled claw and Nuala's blood on my face.

My legs felt like lead, but I dragged onward. The cloak did nothing to keep me from feeling the cold, which numbed my fingers and bit at my ears. There were more marks on the ground here, more signs of some previous disturbance, and I pushed on.

The shadows took on new forms this time; now that my eyesight had adjusted, I began making out more details. Some swirled into view like fog, taking on vaguely human features that gestured threateningly at me before disappearing again, to be replaced by more of the climbing mist, which drifted in from nowhere and everywhere at once.

Lan.

It was a figment of my imagination. It must be. Because when one of those flimsy shapes twisted and turned in the wind and called out after me, surely it hadn't done so in Nuala's voice.

Lan.

More figures. Ghostlike fingers brushing against my cloak, combing through my hair. Shapes dancing in and out of view, ambiguous enough to be anything but with enough form to imply that I could be mistaken.

No. I was seeing things. *They can't possibly be here. They're dead. There is no way they could be . . .*

Lan.

Clinging hands now, growing rougher. A faint ripping noise as my sleeve gave way to a particularly rough attempt, and I ran.

Lan!

Faces floated before me. Nuala, mouth open and face frozen in a never-ending scream. Merritt, her unblinking gaze focused on mine even while her face remained bloodless. Derel, Madi, Cecily, Aoba—they were all here, gazes accusing because they'd all died on my watch, and I hadn't even given them the respect of doing the same.

Lan! Lan! Lan!

Not real, I gasped out to myself as I stumbled. *Not real, not real, not real—*

I almost didn't see them until I'd heard a horrified, broken sob and nearly tripped over Janella. She was trying to roll herself up into a ball, to make herself invisible.

"Janella!"

She froze for a moment, then all but leaped into my arms.

"You're real!" she wept. "You're not a—you're not a—"

"I'm here," I said hoarsely, my eyes on a figure sprawled on the ground a few feet away. She was staring up at the sky, her eyes wide and a frozen look of despair on her face.

The mist disappeared. Panting, I scrambled to her, felt frantically for a pulse. There was none.

Aoba had been the first to die. I'd come across her body this way, too; stumbling in the dark, terrified of what lurked within it, like a little child who'd grown up on far too many nightmares. Like Cathei, she'd stared up into the starless sky with sunken eyes and mouth agape, and nothing we did could bring her back.

No. No no no no no nonononono—

"Lady Tianlan?" It was Janella's voice that brought me back into the present. I gulped in another mouthful of air, willed myself to stop, *stop, stop it, Lan, stop it, get a damn hold of yourself!*

But Aoba—no, this was *Cathei*—wasn't the only dead body here. Another corpse lay sprawled against a large rock—picked clean and broken in places by the teeth of some creature I would much rather not know about. What little fabric it wore was tattered and falling off in places, but I recognized the partial remains of an insignia that had been sewn into the cloth.

It wasn't any of my rangers. It was *a* ranger, but the corpse was too old; the clothing style different from the one my rangers and I wore. A brooch rusted and tarnished by the elements gaped out at me from in between its ribs: a silver star. I gathered what bones I could, shoved them into a sack I'd brought along.

"I need you to move, darling. Can you do that?"

Janella nodded. The fog was gone, and there were no other

figures twisting in the darkness. At least I could bring Cathei's body back to camp.

Aoba's had been the only body I was able to bury. I choked back a sob. Another death. Another death on me.

A movement to my right. A figure from a distance, shrouded in a cloak of haze, watched us, and I swore it lifted a hand up— as a greeting or as a threat, I was never sure. But when I looked again, the fog had lifted, and it was gone.

Chapter Fourteen

ARJUN, SON OF CLAN ORYX, GOING TO HELL

———————— ☼ ————————

OF COURSE SHE NAMED ALL the dolugongs.

In the space of a dayspan she had transformed the whole pod into pets. They swam before us like one big happy goddess-damned family, and I was annoyed at Haidee for encouraging the facade.

"Don't nudge the side, Anastacia!" she scolded one especially playful dolugong. "You'll tip us over again!"

"How can you even tell them apart?" I grumbled.

"How can you tell other people apart?"

"That's different, and you know it!"

"Not to me. Shepard! Don't stray too far from your mama!" The pup we'd rescued barked out an assent like it actually understood, shooting me an adoring expression. The mama in question scooped her baby up in its squared jaw. "Thank you, Madeline!"

"What are you gonna do when we finally leave the Sand Sea?" I asked her. "I'm not bringing them along."

She shrugged, brushing the details off like she always did until they came right back to bite her in the ass, like this undoubtedly would. "We'll figure something out. Besides, dolugongs are fiercely independent creatures, and highly intelligent. Maybe we can come back to visit, or something?"

"*Visit*? We're not doing this for *fun*."

She hummed, ever the optimist. Her short hair billowed in the wind, blue and purple and white, and I immediately hated myself for the way I stared. "Who knows? I mean, you're here because you think we can save what's left of Aeon, right? Who's to say it won't be better for them, too?"

I huffed my exasperation and reached for one of her tomes.

She'd brought a few books along for the journey (I'd asked if they were for kindling, and she'd threatened castration), and she'd given me permission to look through them under further veiled threats about what would happen if I marred them in any way. I'd obliged, mostly because the sand buggy wasn't getting any bigger, the hours weren't getting any shorter, and her voice wasn't getting any softer. I'd taught her how to handle the rig, and she'd gotten competent enough for us to start taking turns driving.

So far, though, the books seemed nothing short of fantastic to me. Ice-capped mountains? Never-ending storms? Neither of them sounded appealing, but looking out at the sandscape right now made it hard for me to believe they used to exist. I flipped through a few more pages, taking in some illustrations of surrealistic-looking creatures—four-legged beasts with impossibly long necks, flappy-eared giants with tubes for noses, round animals made apparently of nothing but spiny thorns—before spotting a folded letter tucked between two pages.

"Is this a love letter? Did someone write you a love letter?"

She slapped the wheel, irritated. "Of course not, why would—No, it's a letter I believe my father wrote to Mother."

I frowned, silently reading it through. If this was her father, he sure seemed terrified. Sounded like a betrayal in the works—but which goddess, exactly, had done the betraying? "'The magic that place wields can destroy the world as easily as it can revive it.' That's what makes you think there's something at Brighthenge we can use?"

"There has to be. The letter was clearly important enough for Mother to keep it."

"She could have kept it out of sentimentality."

"Mother's never been the type to be sentimental." She paused. "She never told me anything about my father. All I know is that Brighthenge was built atop the entrance to the Cruel Kingdom—Inanna's kingdom—to keep any monsters at bay."

"What are you saying? That we're going to hell? That we're *literally* going to hell? We're going to a *literal* hell that *demons* are escaping out of?"

She scowled at me. "I—look, I don't know what the state of Brighthenge is right now. But from what I can gather, the Great Abyss is where the temple used to be."

"We're going to hell," I groaned.

Haidee huffed at me again. "And there's the mirage. It seems to want us there, too. Mother never told me much about our history. Even some of the nobles know more about it than I do." She sighed. "And I never went to the balls she was fond of hosting, so I never mingled with them long enough to learn. She played me well enough."

"I'm still on the fence about this mirage of ours." I craned my neck. "I haven't sighted it again, by the way. You think it's leading us on a wild-goose chase?"

"I don't know. But it sure is expending a lot of energy for a jest."

"Yeah, well." I rubbed my eyes. "As long as we keep heading west, we'll be heading to Brighthenge. No doubt we'll find the mirage waiting there. May as well see if the temple still exists too, if that will ease your mind. And what's with that 'of course not'?"

"What?"

"When I asked if someone had written you a love letter, you said, 'Of course not' like it was offensive. No one's ever written you one?"

"Hasn't anyone written one to you?" she shot back.

"I live in a hellhole, and the closest neighbors we've got want to eat us." There were definitely a few back in Clan Oryx who were obviously sweet on each other, like Millie and Kad, or Sam and Lybeth, but . . . I personally wasn't interested in bringing kids into this kind of future, or expecting to live long enough to spend it with someone else. "On the other hand, *you* live in a city full of people, and you've mentioned suitors."

She looked away. She didn't seem annoyed anymore, or angry. She seemed . . . sad. "Heavily supervised by my mother, yes. Love letters written to me behind her back would have taken them out of her favor instead of the other way around. It's always about politics in the Golden City." She inclined her head toward me. "You never had someone? You've had more freedom than I do."

I coughed. "I . . . well, there was a girl."

"Oh?"

"Don't make anything out of it. We weren't in a serious relationship. We both ended it when Lisette moved away."

She frowned. "But if you weren't in a serious relationship, then what else would you be doing togeth—*ohhhhh*. Oh. Never mind."

I grinned, watching her face turn red. The goddess was an innocent. It was almost cute.

"I never had anything like that. Not even a letter, or a poem."

"No one you liked?"

She paused. "There is one guy. Vanya Arrenley. He's polite, for a noble."

I snorted. "Dumbest name I've ever heard."

"You've never even met him. He's very kind, and he won't

lie to me just to make himself look good!"

"So marry him already," I snapped back, my irritation growing.

She quieted. "I don't know. He's the only choice I can stomach—but I don't think he'll side with me against Mother, no matter how sympathetic he is."

I grunted. My opinion of Latona had gotten worse the more I heard about her. What mother forced that kind of marriage on her daughter? Haidee could be annoying, but she deserved more than settling for some sycophantic idiot. "Your mother's a real piece of work. Never met her in my life and have no plans to, but seems like you're too compassionate about other people to be anything like her. If I didn't think you were a good person, I wouldn't have tagged along, either."

She shot me a startled glance that barely registered in my head. I was too busy gazing out at the sands, frowning at some specks of black in the distance that hadn't been there before. "And that's odd. . . ."

"What's odd? Oh!" She straightened. "Parrick? What's wrong?"

One of the dolugongs was working itself into a near frenzy, swimming back and forth in panic. The other dolugongs stirred as well.

"I think they're sensing something within the sands," Haidee said. "Do you think it might be a predator?"

I hoisted myself halfway out the hatch and fished out my spyglass. "Tell your friends to get to the other side of the rig.

I'll cut off the ropes to give them room to move. And get ready to run."

There was—movement—to the west. Sand was churning three hundred paces away, in a quasi-whirlpool that was starting to grow in diameter, and anything that could whip it up into that kind of froth would have to be impossibly large, and therefore undoubtedly dangerous. There was even more activity farther off. I squinted through the glass and swore under my breath.

There were rigs out there, four in total. And they were heading our way.

"We've got company!" I snarled down at Haidee. "Gun the engines, we gotta—"

And then I forgot what I was about to say, because some hideous *thing* burst forth from the sand near us, twisting and turning in the air before falling back into the grit-sea. It was a long son of a bitch, sharp and angular in all the worst ways, from the swordlike spikes sticking out along its back to the hollow gaping mass that was its mouth, devoid of any observable teeth but as deep as the ends of the earth and stinking to the highest heavens despite the stretch of sand between us, though that was shrinking fast. It didn't have any eyes that I could see, but somehow that was worse, because I had a sneaking suspicion it could see us anyway.

A heavy grating sound filled the air as our sand buggy lurched to life, barely escaping the sudden tsunami once the monster hit the sand again, its immense weight sending wavelike ripples crashing against our vehicle. The dolugongs were clever enough to get out of the way, and we followed quickly in their wake.

I traded my spyglass for the Howler, set my sights in between the horrific creature and the other sand buggies that were coming our way. They weren't Hellmakers. I didn't recognize these assholes.

They brandished rusting metal hooks, whirling them in the air—and sending them toward the monster.

They were worse than the Hellmakers.

The creature wriggled away from the hooks, slipping back easily beneath the surface, but they tried again when it reemerged, one wrapping around its spiny head.

"Explains the mesh around Shepard," I muttered. Whoever they were, they were used to fishing the Sand Sea for their food, including huge-ass monsters that no one should have any business trying to catch, but I didn't want to stay around long enough to compare hunting methods. Haidee was doing a good job putting distance between us, but a couple of the nomads had already spotted us. They veered around the still-thrashing monster, leaving their comrades to deal with the monstrosity and setting an intercept course toward us.

I opened the hatch. "Faster!" I roared out, letting Fire bounce around my Howler into lethal levels, though I knew trying to outrun them was pointless. The nomads had built their rigs for speed and efficiency and would soon catch up.

Haidee was trying to steer the buggy and yell at the dolugongs at the same time. "Get out of here!" she screeched.

"Leave! Dive down!" But some members of the pod lingered, unwilling to go without us despite their urgency.

I concentrated on the two rigs bearing down on us. Each had a man clinging to its side, sharp harpoons trained in our direction. I had enough firepower to take down one; the guy on the right already had his arm thrown back, a second away from launching his attack.

My aim was true, but the man had done this before; he and his partner dove out seconds before my attack hit, turning their rig into a burning wreck of metal that sank quickly down into the Sand Sea.

A scream, coming from neither of us. The man in the second buggy launched a harpoon through the air with terrible efficiency. One of the dolugongs, Parrick, screamed again, and the others ducked their heads underneath the sands as one and swam for their lives.

An inhuman howl burst from Haidee's lips, and she scrambled onto the rig's hood, pulling at the ropes to bring the injured animal closer to her as I killed the engine. One look, though, told me that there was nothing else we could do.

"Haidee."

She was sobbing, clinging tightly to Parrick, who was now floating belly-up in the sand, bright blood seeping through the wound and staining the sand around us a dirty, muddy scarlet. I could hear cheers rising from the direction of the remaining buggies, and my vision turned red.

I shucked the Howler off my wrist.

Fire burned along the length of my arm, running down into the center of my stump. Without the protection of the barrel, I had to grit my teeth against the heat.

The man chucked another harpoon at me. Streams of fire encased my arm like a sleeve, blazing higher and brighter, sapphire-bright and brilliant, and I flung my arm out in a wide arc, sending those beauties flying, blue wildfire shaped like lightning bolts.

The harpoon melted in midair, the metal liquefying into a useless curled lump as it flopped back onto the sand. The lightning spiraled farther on and struck one of the nomads' sand vehicles. Liquid bubbled up and sizzled as parts of the hull disintegrated, its driver screaming as he jumped off. The harpooner did the same as the rest of my inferno consumed their buggy. When everything settled, soot and ashes clung to the now-unsalvageable wreckage.

I cursed, dropping to my knees. Mother Salla had warned me about the costs of blue fire, of using it too frequently. My forearm felt tender to the touch, small blisters starting to form, but I was lucky—I'd suffered worse than this in the past.

The other rigs avoided the fiery onslaught that had taken out their buddies. The displaced men were still flailing chest-deep in the sands, but more vehicles were speeding our way. I tried to build more Fire to muster a second shot, but I was way too exhausted to channel that intensity again.

Haidee lifted her suddenly red hair, her eyes alight with both anguish and fury. The wind was growing stronger, and it wasn't because we were moving.

"Haidee," I panted, trying to retake the wheel. "I'm sorry about Parrick, but we have to move."

Another small whirlpool had appeared between us and our pursuers, but the monster was no longer its cause. The wind was a hell of a lot fiercer now, and I had to grab at the hatch to retain my balance.

I'd annoyed Haidee on occasion, made her seethe enough to get into dumb arguments with me. But I'd never seen her this furiously, unequivocally, terrifyingly angry, and a part of me was glad I'd never riled her this much.

Haidee screamed.

A sandspout shot out from the sea, wild and spinning, and hell, Haidee wasn't thinking *again* because we were way too damn close to the thing not to get caught up in its deadly spiral. I could actually see fire mixed with lightning shooting in and out of the flying dust, watched it char the surrounding sands in seconds. One of the men shrieked as he was hit, his body pitching forward into the sands while his clothes caught fire.

The rest of the bandits were yelling, swerving away, and it occurred to me that Haidee could no more control the hurricane she had generated than she could control those men. I grabbed hold of the wheel again, grimly twisting it to the side in hopes we could break free.

One of the sand raiders continued the chase, however; he was a fierce-looking man with an eye patch. The tornado swerved his way but he flung an arm out, and a sudden wall of sand lifted out from the ocean, slowing its approach. He leaped out of his rig, and I swear to every goddess that existed he *floated*, using the tornado's own momentum to push himself away from the worst of the winds. Was this fucker part bird?

"Haidee!" I hollered. Despite the tornado around us the girl was deathly still, her eyes trained on the spout, with the fiercest and also the most heartbreaking look on her face. It wrung my own heart dry. "Haidee!" I shouted. "Snap out of it! Damn it, woman, don't make me have to slap you!"

She blinked, and just like that, the sandstorm was gone.

Not so the Sand Sea.

The sudden dissolution of the sandspout didn't stop the large wave that came crashing over us, upending everyone in the process—the men's rigs, ours, me. I plunged headfirst into the thick sand and kept sinking through the grit. My throat clogged up as I gasped for air—I no longer knew which way was up.

I'm not going to die like this! Not breathing in sand like a desert neophyte, just because some damned goddess couldn't manage her—

Something nudged at my side, and I clung to it on instinct. And then I was moving. Fast.

I scrunched my eyes shut and buried my face against the slightly rough texture of whatever it was I had latched on to, which was better than having to keep eating the millions of grains of sand that keep trying to force their way into my windpipe—

I was thrown abruptly out of the Sand Sea and into the blessed burning air, my breaths coming out in wheezes as I landed, sprawled against the edges of the dust-ocean, holding on to the firm ground like it too might disappear on me at a moment's notice.

Firm ground. We'd reached the end of the Sand Sea. Hell.

I devoted a few more minutes to coughing out the rest of my lungs before I mustered enough sense to assess where I was. The sand buggy was gone. So were the men. So was Haidee. Crap.

A chittering sound to my right. I turned and spotted a rock-eye peering hopefully up at me. "Shepard," I muttered. Another pair of eyes popped up beside it. Its mother. "Madeline. Where are we?"

Most of the pod had escaped unscathed, but there were no signs of Haidee or the rig anywhere. I gulped, a sudden heavy lump forming in my throat, replacing all the sand I'd just spewed out. There was no way—Haidee hadn't caused all this trouble only for her to—

If she died, I was going to kill her.

The book.

A swirl of a cloak, inches from my splayed fingers. I looked up.

The mirage stared down at me, closer than it'd let us get, and I instantly regretted trying to before. Its face was still swathed in shadows—until I realized it wasn't.

There was no face underneath that hood.

Chapter Fifteen

ODESSA THE LIFE-GIVER

CATHEI WAS STILL DEAD.

They laid her out on a small stone slab some distance away from camp, as if they were ashamed to look too closely. They'd stretched an old cloak over her body, tucked it around so no stray breeze could shake it loose. But even with her face covered, I fancied she was staring through the cloth and up at me, sad and accusing. *I thought you'd protect me,* I could almost hear her say. *Is this all I get?*

Catseye Sumiko was busy with her examination of the long-dead ranger's bones. "It's difficult to ascertain how she died," she said, "but my best guess would be a stab to the head with some sharp weapon."

"How can you tell?" Gracea had been making a pest of herself, elbowing people aside for a better look.

"The skull remains intact, and there's a lengthwise break

along the side of the temple indicating a knife, or something very similar. It's too clean a wound to have been caused by jagged fangs, and death must have been almost instantaneous."

"We're out in the middle of nowhere," Holsett said. "What was this ranger doing so far from home?"

"The wildlands actually housed flourishing villages and communities before the Breaking, sir," Janella said meekly. "It wasn't the desolation you see today."

"I know that," the Seasinger snapped. "What I would like to know is what she was doing so far away from Asteria's domain then, which would have originally been west of here."

"The corpse has been here sixteen, seventeen years. No more than twenty." Sumiko glanced at Lan for confirmation, and the latter nodded.

"About the same time as the Breaking," I surmised. "Killed by Asteria's sister's faction, probably. Or a traitor."

"No honorable ranger would turn against their own kin." Lan looked shocked by the very thought of it.

"Too many variables to be sure," Gracea said dismissively. "Give it a burial. I'll take the brooch."

"No," I said.

The Starmaker's eyes narrowed. "It's a useless trinket, Your Holiness."

"If it's such a useless trinket, then why insist on having it? This poor corpse once served my mother, and you know it." The rumor in camp was that this had been one of Asteria's Devoted before the Breaking—a colleague of Gracea's. But only I had the guts to say it to her face. "Don't you want to find out who this was? It could have been a friend!"

Gracea plucked the brooch from my grasp. "I am the leader here. I have more experience in my smallest toe than you have in your whole body. Goddess or not, my Devoted will follow my orders, because I follow Asteria's. Your presence here is ample proof that you do not."

She strode away, and the rest of the Devoted followed, looking at me and trading uneasy glances with one another.

I'd always found Gracea overbearing in the past, but only now did I realize just how tyrannical she could be. How had Mother allowed her to get away with so much for this long? *When I assume my throne in Aranth,* I vowed, silently seething, *she'll be the first to go.*

"Odessa," Lan whispered.

"Bury the bones well, Lan." And I too moved away.

Conversation around the fire was muted, sober. I refused the warmth, choosing to stay with Cathei. Gracea and Lan were in another argument. The Starmaker was nearly shrill; Cathei was the first death under her watch, but she was more concerned about who else was to blame.

Janella had been of little help; she remembered nothing before her disappearance, and Gracea would have tried to throttle the answer out of her had it not been for Lan's intervention. The Catseye herself was the complete opposite; grim, angry, terse.

I watched them plan our next move—Lan wanted to return

to Aranth and abandon the mission altogether, a failure Gracea was not willing to accept.

More of the clerks were sporting suspicious bruises and injuries they sought to conceal with their clothes. I remembered Lan announcing days ago that such actions would not be tolerated from the Devoted, but the problem was that Lan was far too nice. She believed calling people out was enough for them to do the right thing on their own.

Maybe I was just as naive, never having thought about the abuse going on because I'd been insulated in the Spire for so long. It took this journey for me to understand just how insidious the Devoted's control was. But you can't have Asteria for a mother without picking up on a few tricks yourself.

Lan was attempting to be diplomatic; I chose bluntness. Earlier on I'd taken Gareen to one side and told him in no uncertain terms that any fresh wounds I saw among the clerks the next day I would return tenfold to their masters starting with Holsett, brushing aside the boy's halfhearted protests at innocence. The Devoted don't know me well enough to be sure whether I'd follow up on that promise, but knowing that *I* knew would make them more cautious. It was the best I could do for now.

I despised Gracea, but I had to be patient. I *had* to be patient. As strong as I was, I could not underestimate the Starmaker, and the other gate-users who would rather fall in line than admit responsibility.

I laid my hand carefully on Cathei's leg. She felt solid

underneath my fingers, but in the darkness I almost expected her to dissolve into smoke.

"I'm sorry," I whispered to her still form, wishing there was some way to turn back time. Lan was right. My visions had told me they would die if I didn't go with them, but they never said that they wouldn't still, if I did.

But I'd seen Lan with the silver brooch, with Janella. Which meant I did have Mother's visions now; they were real. I *was* right to travel with them, even if they were too stubborn to see. It was bitter vindication.

"Your Holiness?" Catseye Sumiko hovered by my shoulder, worried. "Would you like me to heal you today?"

"Lan already did, but thank you."

"I don't mean that, Your Holiness. You've had a trying experience, especially for someone who has not been so long outside the Spire, much less outside the city. There is healing for the body, but there is also healing for the mind. One can be at the peak of health but mentally and emotionally drained, especially in the face of traumatic incidents."

I looked down at Cathei again. The one who'd suffered the most trauma was her, not me, but I nodded all the same.

Sumiko's healing was different from what Lan and other Catseyes have done for me in the past. I would normally feel the warmth along my chest, where they would concentrate their patterns, targeting the black hole above my heart I had long learned to live with, and because of which I had learned to accept that my life would be shorter than most.

But Catseye Sumiko focused somewhere higher, and I felt a lightness gathering around my temple, as if all the worries that had been festering in my mind in the last few weeks had been temporarily expunged from my soul.

"This isn't permanent," Catseye Sumiko warned me, taking her hand away. "It never is. But I've found that this helps in times that demand the most strength from us. If you ever feel the need to bolster your spirits, Your Holiness, please find me again."

"I will." I glanced over to Lan and the others. "Have you offered this to them? They have more burdens on their mind than I do."

"Lady Tianlan, you mean?" Sumiko shook her head sadly. "She turns me down every time, Your Holiness. I wish she wouldn't. Hers is a more serious affliction than most."

"What do you mean?"

"May I sit?" At my nod, Sumiko gathered her skirts and set herself down on a log. "There are physical sicknesses," she said. "Injuries that one can see and observe, such as broken bones and open wounds. But there are other kinds of sicknesses that go beyond visible form, all the more dangerous because they are not so easily detected.

"And sometimes the people who suffer these injuries don't believe they have them, or are unwilling to seek treatment for many reasons. Sometimes it's pride. Sometimes it's a sincere belief that there is nothing wrong. But more often it is because of shame. To accept that they need assistance implies that they are weak, that they cannot take care of themselves."

That sounded a lot like Lan. "I see," I said softly.

"Lady Tianlan . . . is a stubborn woman, and in her line of work that quality works very much in her favor. But her strength cannot always be constant. To protect, she believes that she cannot ever be vulnerable. She is a very proud lady. That is also a disadvantage."

"And that's why she's refused your help? Since returning from the wildlands?"

"She suffers much guilt over the deaths of her comrades."

"But that's ridiculous!" As able a fighter as Lan was, she couldn't have saved everyone. That she had survived was a miracle on its own.

Sumiko shifted. "I must admit that I do have a motive for approaching you in this manner, Your Holiness. I know that Lady Tianlan is your guardian, and that you two are close. She will not listen to me, but I hope that she would listen to someone she trusts more."

I snorted. I was the last person Lan wanted to see right now, especially after our fight.

After our last kiss.

The memory still thrilled me, made my breath catch. I ducked my head down to hide my heated face. "I'll try," I said roughly. "I can't make any promises, though. As you said, Lan can be very stubborn."

Sumiko smiled her relief, rising. "That's all I can hope for, Your Holiness. You have my deepest thanks. If you will excuse me, there are others who also need consoling." She inclined her head respectfully at Cathei, before picking her way to the others.

I wasn't sure how successful I was going to be. But if Sumiko was right and Lan was suffering . . .

Tell her you love her, idiot.

Gracea saw me stand, glared before deliberately turning away. Even now, I thought, anger growing, she was trying to usurp my position. She must have been persuading the other Devoted that I was too young, too impulsive, too reckless. She didn't care about Cathei. She'd denigrated me in front of everyone else, abused her staff, mocked *Lan*. . . .

I wanted to *break* her.

I would have to do something about her soon.

I turned back toward Cathei and stopped.

The body was gone. Where there should have been a definite human shape underneath that faded cloak, there was nothing lying beneath the cover but even ground.

I whirled, about to shout my discovery, but everyone else was gone, too. The small bursts of light that Gracea used for illumination had disappeared. Even the *Brevity*, once a looming silhouette against the silver of the lake, was missing.

"Hello?" I called out, attempting my own flares of light, then dispelling them immediately. The galla wouldn't hurt me, but there were many other demons in the wildlands not as accommodating. As terrifying as the darkness was, any light out here would be a beacon for them to find me.

I knelt and pressed my palms against the soil. The ground was a series of networks that I could access, every pathway of vine and plant a point on an invisible map that I could feel. In my heightened state, I could feel every possible seed and plant nestled beneath, and I let my newfound bond with them draw my mind farther out, using the ground as a map to guide me, to alert me to anything else that moved in this silence.

There was something farther north; not a movement I would define as human, but something that slithered, crawled. The idea chilled me more than the cold winds blowing through the area, but I had no choice. There was nothing else that suggested life here; if I were to escape this nightmare, I had to look for anything that might bring me out of this trap.

I formed sharp vines around my arms and manifested a sliver of light as a makeshift sword, wishing I'd thought to procure one of Noelle's weapons. "I'm a goddess of Aranth," I muttered to myself. "Mother has faced worse. I can survive this. I *will* survive this."

So dark, though. So cold.

The ground broke apart beneath me, and I shrieked, leaping back.

Lan had never told me the particulars of what she'd had to face in her last mission, but I had heard enough of the gossip spread about, even from my lonely perch in the Spire. There'd been shadows the size of rogue waves climbing out from the ground, slicing the men and women into ribbons with their claws and feasting on them with their fangs. This new monstrosity rising before me was one of them.

I attacked first. The vines on my arms uncurled, lengthened, whipped out. They punched a hole right through the giant, but it shrugged off the assault. It reached for me again, and this time I saw that what it lacked in a face, it more than made up for in incisors; black as night, yet still shining, sharp and gleaming and obsidian, in the near night.

I conjured up everything I could think of—blades of air, jagged ice walls to impede its approach, more vines, but it brushed off the blades like they were nothing, tore down the ice walls like they were made of paper, and ripped away the vines. I was running by then but knew it would catch up to me before long.

Inanna's shadow. The thought crossed my mind out of nowhere, born out of fear rather than logic. *This is Inanna's shadowed self, angry that I take the gifts intended for her!*

A spark of light up ahead. The shadow this time was a familiar one; another ox-horned demon, a glittering brooch of sapphires coiled on its breast.

I ran toward it, even as the malignant darkness pursued, the shuddering of the earth a testament to its rage as every step brought it closer. I could feel the tips of its claws grazing my cloak, and I whipped a hand back without thinking, gathering the first patterns I could detect and lobbing them behind me. I heard it yelp in pain for the first time, enough to convince me to look back.

Parts of the creature were on fire. I stumbled, mesmerized

by the sight of flames I had never been able to command in such volume or magnitude. And then my survival instincts kicked in, and I managed the last few feet separating me and the sapphire-studded demon practically on my knees, my fingertips brushing against the shadow's own outstretched hand.

The world disappeared around me again—the flames, the shadow—and I was left in total darkness. *Come,* that now-familiar voice intoned in my head.

I knew what was coming. Another sacrifice, another gift. My fourth galla; the galla of life. How appropriate.

Come.

As always, my mouth formed the same word, took the same risk. *Yes.*

I could feel unseen things brushing against me, jerked at a sudden cold touch across my chest, and it felt like something that had been locked away, a part of me I had always restrained and held back, was finally set free.

And Cathei. Oh heaven and below, *Cathei.*

She stood before me, a formless wisp with features I nonetheless recognized. Poor Cathei, who had been so eager to be part of something greater, beyond the daily drudge of a Devoted's clerkship. Cathei, who had trusted in me, believing I was strong enough to protect her from harm. Nobody paid much attention to Cathei back when she was alive, for all her eagerness to please—I hadn't, and I was sorry for it now.

I reached for that silvery figure. When I touched her cheek, she felt almost warm.

And then she shimmered back into nothingness, and I was alone.

Be satisfied. A divine power of the underworld has been fulfilled. You must not open your mouth against the rites of the underworld.

A delirious sort of freedom swept over me, and then I found myself returned to the wildlands. The galla that had chased me was gone, and so was the hulking giant of a shadow, though the faint smell of char and smoke remained, stealing into the air. I had traveled a considerable distance from the campsite.

I placed my hands on the ground again, was rewarded by irregular beats and patterns of feet on soil, a few hundred yards away; *I made it back,* I realized, relief sweeping through.

"Where have you been?" Lan all but screeched the instant I stepped back into the light. Her face was wan, and I felt terrible.

"I'm sorry," I mumbled, "but it's not my fault."

She had every right to be angry, but the arms that folded around me were gentle, trembling. "Tell me everything."

I tried to be as brief as I could. The other Devoted listened with furrowed brows and worried faces. "That must have been how they took Cathei," Graham finally said. "This is troubling. We could remain within the safety of our circle and they could still pick us off."

No, I thought. *The Galla sought out only me this way, for the gifts they owed me. This is not how Cathei died.*

"Where is Cathei now?" Noelle asked suddenly.

The body was still missing. "If this is a trick—" the Star-maker threatened.

"There is no trick." My palms were drenched in sweat, as I began to shiver. "I—I know where she is."

"Did you hide her body? Your Holiness, this is not a game—"

"Shut up and let her speak, Gracea," Lan snapped.

"I brought her back."

They stared at me, uncomprehending. "What do you mean, 'brought her back'?" Lan finally asked.

A shuffling sound nearby was as sharp as a twig breaking, arresting all our attentions. It reverberated from the opposite side of the camp, away from the ship.

I was not surprised when she slid into view. The horrified gasps around me, though, said otherwise.

Cathei looked nearly the same. Her eyes were still gray and her brown hair had lost none of its luster. But her skin had acquired a glossy sheen that looked almost transparent, and she seemed to slide in and out of the shadows—there one second and then not in the next, but so quickly that you could only observe a strange jittering of her body, the way one's vision blurred in the middle of a heavy rain.

"Cathei?" I heard Janella cry out.

The newly resurrected woman said nothing. Her gaze was a careful blank, as if emotions were a luxury she no longer needed. She turned toward me, inclined her head respectfully as she would have done days before, and stepped back out of the light and into the blackness.

Immediately, Lan dashed forward, stopping at the spot where she had vanished. "Gracea," she barked, and needed no other

266

words as the Starmaker increased the luminosity of her patterns. "She's gone. It's like she was never here. Odessa . . . ?"

It didn't matter. She was here in some form, and that was all that counted. The galla of life, indeed. She was as alive as she could ever be.

"I brought her back," I whispered, terrified and strangely exhilarated. "Oh, Lan. I—I brought her back." And then I threw my head back and laughed wildly at the storm clouds gathering ominously above.

Chapter Sixteen

HAIDEE AND THE PIRATES

I WAS IN BIG TROUBLE.

I knew it from the moment I woke. I could still view the Sand Sea from where I lay, the mounds of fine dirt moving back and forth along the boundary like they were waves crashing against a shore. There was no sign of the other dolugongs.

But Parrick—oh, my beautiful Parrick. The dolugong was clearly dead, hanging from a small scaffold to be butchered for food. I scrambled for him, only to discover that I couldn't move.

I was heavily bound. My arms had been tied behind my back, and for good measure a shackle encircled one of my ankles, its other end chained to a wooden post behind me. Faint laughter from somewhere nearby told me people were present; the sand nomads from before.

They were camped a hundred feet away from the edge of the Sand Sea—the solid construction of the outpost and tents suggested that the encampment was more permanent than I would have expected for nomads in the desert. Most were hauling in the gigantic sand creature we'd encountered, or at least a huge portion of it. They strung up heavy chunks of its body, but the pieces were smaller than the monster I'd seen out there. They'd either left most of it out in the sea to rot, or the rest of the creature had gotten away.

Judging from the preparations around the campfire, I presumed it was supper. They were roasting large slabs of meat, and for a brief moment I panicked, wondering if they were cannibals and if I was next, before spotting a long, skinned tail and realizing it was the rest of the sand creature. I was silently glad they had elected to start with the monster and not with poor Parrick.

One of the men spotted me, made a gesture for the others to be silent before making his way over to where I sat. He was an evil-looking man, heavily muscular, with an eye patch and an overly large beard to compensate for his bald head. He crouched down before me and said something in a language I was unfamiliar with, but with a tone I understood all too well.

I glared at him. "Release me," I snarled, trying to look my most intimidating.

The man shook his head and asked me another question.

"I said release me!" I pulled against my restraints. I tried to gate, reaching out expectantly for the patterns—and found nothing.

A sudden, sickening wave of exhaustion washed over me,

and I collapsed on the ground, my breathing uneven.

The sandstorm I had summoned. I had never channeled that powerful an incanta in my life, or called up something of such immense scale. Even my mother, who had more strength and aptitude than I did, would never have created one on her own; when sandstorms strayed too close to the Golden City, she would recruit me or one of the other Devoted to dispel it with her.

I was utterly drained. I was useless.

I couldn't fight my way out of this.

I was in big trouble.

Eye Patch shook his head and continued to talk, occasionally pointing at what looked to be the hulking remains of one of their sand buggies, no doubt a direct consequence of my experiments with said sandstorm.

I kicked sand in his direction in response. They'd killed Parrick. And Arjun was missing, and I was terrified that something had happened to him, that he was dead somewhere in this camp and they were going to spring that surprise on me to break my spirit.

Because it would.

Don't you dare die on me, you stupid ass. Don't you dare die on me!

Eye Patch pointed at my hair and raised his eyebrows.

"Yes, it's my natural color, you killer," I spat out. "I'm the goddess of the Golden City. The rightful ruler of Aeon. And if you don't let me go, I'll do more than destroy your rides. I'll end your whole tribe, I swear it."

Eye Patch laughed loudly, silver teeth gleaming, then rose to his feet. He said a few more words that sounded more admonition than threat, before departing to help his fellow murderers divide up their monstrous prize.

How was I going to get out of here? I didn't have any of my mechanika equipment. I had no rig, no dolugongs, no Arjun.

Don't you dare die on me, Arjun. If you die and show up as a mirage, I'll chase you as long as I need to so I can strangle you. Because you're not dead. I won't let you be dead!

I glanced back at Parrick and allowed myself a sob. Some savior I turned out to be. I couldn't even save a dolugong.

Once the tears had ebbed, I rattled at my chain. It felt solid enough, and if I'd had enough strength to gate, I could have burned the metal off in a minute. I gave it a good hard yank again, but it refused to give.

I studied the wooden post it was wrapped around. Parts of it had rotted away from insects and old age, and its total diameter couldn't be bigger than two inches. Easier to destroy than the shackle, but I wasn't sure how long it would take without any incanta on hand.

The sun above wasn't as glaring, at least, and I could even feel a cool wind coming in from somewhere. We must have traveled far enough west for the change in climate to become obvious.

I stole another glance back at camp; despite the display of power I'd shown them at the Sand Sea, none of them seemed inclined to station a guard over me, like some girl come whirling

271

out of the desert blasting sandstorms was something they saw on a frequent basis.

They'd have their meal soon enough. When most were asleep would probably be the best time to escape.

But first I had to figure out how.

I struggled to a sitting position, waited until the dizziness had passed. I focused on the part of the wooden post I deemed the flimsiest, a section that looked easiest to snap off.

The blade of Air I conjured was smaller than even a needle, thin because that was all I could manage without throwing up. I let it hover in the air briefly, until the faint vertigo disappeared, then introduced it to the compromised wood. A faint buzzing whirred through the air, too low for the others to hear, and small chips flew out as the Air dug greedily into the surface, slowly but surely whittling it down. I paused to take a breather every few minutes, annoyed by my weakness.

I had finally gotten it down to a point where one hard push against the wood would send the post toppling over, and my shackle to come away, when Eye Patch returned, carrying my meal. He tsk-tsked, then set my plate down beside another wooden post, this one closer to their tents. To my shock, he reached over and gave the post I'd been working on a firm tap. It fell over without further delay.

"Don't even think about it, girl." He grabbed the shackle attached to my leg and used it to drag me to the other post, while I shrieked and scrabbled at the ground in a poor effort to resist, sand digging into my skin. The others watched us with amusement, but eventually turned back to their own food, talk and laughter resuming among them.

Once I was properly leashed again, he untied my hands, prodded the plate at me with his boot. "Eat. There is much to discuss later, Your Holiness."

"You can understand me." He had a strange accent. "And you know who I am. Why pretend?"

His eye closed, then opened again, his version of a wink. "Mainly to mess with you." Then he walked back to his clan mates, me gaping after him.

This wooden post was thicker than the previous one, but knowing I could still gate, even if it was just the barest of patterns, gave me hope. I dutifully ate, one of Eye Patch's men coming to collect my plate and giving a satisfied nod when he saw I'd finished everything. I waited until they had settled back into their own tents or sprawled out on the ground for their naps. A few men continued to patrol the area, and I had to pause in my work, pretending to sleep, every time one of them drew too close.

After what felt like hours, I had sawn my way through the wood, enough to attempt a second escape. I closed my eyes and held my breath when one of the patrolling pirates passed me and disappeared around a corner, and gated as much as I could before pushing the column over. It fell, was buffeted up by a spinning cushion of air before it floated noiselessly to the ground. That caused a few minutes of retching as I doubled over from the nausea, trying to keep my groans down to a minimum.

I still wasn't strong enough to rid myself of the shackle, so I gathered the end of the chain with my hand, hoping it wouldn't clank much while I was on the move. I snuck off quietly to where the body of Parrick remained. Whatever happened, I couldn't stand the thought of the pirates eating him.

The nomads had constructed many small wooden sheds along the Sand Sea's edge, but they didn't have a lot of people patrolling the area. If I was quiet enough not to attract attention—

—but I'd never been that fortunate, as I stepped into a sudden patch of air that quickly rendered me immobile. I floundered, my body rising up unwanted as Eye Patch strolled closer.

He was a Skyrider. That explained his acrobatics back on the Sand Sea, his ability to avoid my sandstorm despite his size.

"I wouldn't have thought someone of your bulk would possess a gate that allowed you to defy gravity," I said evenly, trying not to sound agitated.

He winked again. "I be a man of many talents. I could walk on air again, if you wish."

"I'd rather you let me go."

"You are going to be dying out there," he said, his accent even more prominent now. "There will be the endless walking on the sand, with the impassable Sand Sea at your back, and no other means of transport. You will die baked into the ground, and the sky rocs will peck at your bones."

"I don't care," I snarled, trying to right myself. "You killed my friend!"

"Your friend is gone. Abandoned you—or taken by the Sand Sea, more like, and your transport be gone with him."

They hadn't captured him, at least. "You killed Parrick!"

He frowned. "Parrick—"

"My dolugong!" I tried to spark enough Fire to at least slap his face with it, but he simply brushed away my meager attempt, looking perplexed.

"You are friends with the meat?"

I tried to burn him again.

He waved that away, too. "Very well. I apologize for killing your . . . Parrick."

"Why keep me here? Why not let me go out into the desert and leave me to die?"

"My soul will burn in all the eternities of hell if I allow a goddess to perish on my watch, Your Holiness." He smiled. "This old warrior knew your mother, once. You are too young to be out alone. I know the legends of your ancestors intimately. I was there." An odd note entered his voice, and he ignored the gasp I uttered. "Where are the goddesses now? Asteria?"

"My mother, Latona, didn't come with me. Asteria . . . died at the Breaking."

"Ah." He stilled, and for a moment I thought he'd stopped breathing. And then he was smiling again, though this time it didn't quite reach his eyes. "Yes. She died, I heard. And so you are her twin's daughter."

"Can you please let me down?" I whispered. He complied, and I massaged my temples once I felt the ground underneath

275

me, flinching at the new rush of dizziness.

"I recognized you immediately, back at the Sand Sea," the hulking man said. "No one else has that hair. Some of my men wanted to kill you, goddess or not. We are of the Liangzhu clan, and we do not scare easily—but you are a force to be reckoned with, more dangerous than some of the beasts we hunt. You slew one of my men."

"You slew my friend," I shot back.

He inclined his head. "True, so we be nearly even. But the goddesses—once upon a time, they saved my life. And I saved theirs. It starts a bond that neither one of us could ever break. I swore to defend your aunt Asteria. Forces at work were more powerful than I, but I defended her till the end. And while our true homes have long been gone, we are still of the Liangzhu. Our word will not be broken for anything."

"What kind of person was Asteria?" I asked despite myself. I had been taught to view my aunt as the enemy, as the reason for Aeon's destruction. It was strange to find someone who spoke of her with such reverence.

He grinned. "Stubborn. Used to getting her way. The smartest person I'd ever met." His smile faded. "Never one to settle for second best. I am sorry that you have never met her."

"And you were at the Breaking with her—with them," I stumbled. "What happened there?" Here was someone who had actually survived the encounter, who might have the answers I sought. "Please tell me, Mr. Eye P—ah . . ."

He smiled. "The name is Sonfei. And do you promise, then, not to wander off into the unknown again?"

"I promise not to without ample protection."

His smile widened. "You are just as crafty as your aunt, never one to give herself away for anything."

"Or," said a voice behind him, "maybe she's someone more like her mother, who would burn down the rest of the desert and your little tribe besides if you crossed her wrong."

My knees buckled and I took in a shuddering intake of air, willing myself not to cry, because that would be one more thing for Arjun to poke fun at.

His clothes were ripped, and I could tell from his cuts and bruises that he hadn't come out of the Sand Sea unharmed. He must have hidden in one of the nearby sheds, biding his time. A thin blue flame was blazing at the end of his stump, and that same cobalt fire was now leveled against Eye Patch's throat—far enough away to avoid burning the man, but close enough for him to feel the heat.

"Arjun," I choked out, nearly weeping in my relief. "I could kiss you!"

He reddened but kept his grip. "And I see you've gotten yourself in more trouble. Whatever possessed you to whip up that damned storm? You caused more damage to the rig than they did!"

"The rig's still working?"

"I don't know, I'm not the mechanika. Wouldn't start, though, so I had to keep walking until I came to this—"

"They killed Parrick! What did you think I was going to do?"

"Nothing irresponsible and impetuous, I was hoping, but obviously I'd forgotten who I was talking to!"

"You're an idiot! They would have gotten more dolugongs if I hadn't intervened!"

"It sounds like you both be needing time to reconcile," Eye Patch said amenably. "Should I leave you two alone?"

Arjun's presence hadn't gone unnoticed at the camp. I spotted a couple of women idling along the side, though a faint twitch from Eye Patch indicated they should stand down and wait.

"Don't even think about it. Tell me why I shouldn't gut you where you stand."

"Don't!" I protested, and Arjun transferred his glare from the man to me. "He was there when the Breaking happened! He could give us more information!"

"I bet he'd say his mother was a goddess and be convincing about it, too!"

"Knew one other Firesmoker who could whip out the fires that were as blue as yours," Eye Patch said conversationally. "Fearsome woman, she was. Called herself the leader of the Devoted, under Asteria's command. I didn't quite notice the resemblance between you before, though looking closer now, you look well enough alike."

The flame wavered. "You knew my mother?"

"I knew her sister better. Devika was suspicious of me, always. I was the outsider in their little circle, but Asteria stuck up for me, and your mother had no choice but to acquiesce. Didn't mean she liked me. Took a while to get her on speaking terms, but in the end she knew I'd fight for Asteria even if it killed me." He looked back at me. "So you're little . . . Odessa? Or is it Haidee?"

"Haidee," I whispered, head spinning. He knew about my mother and my aunt and my sister. The letter was genuine; my father had called my sibling Odessa, too. It took effort not to cry. My mother had hidden all these from me.

And surely Sonfei knew about other things too, like the prophecy and Brighthenge and my father—

"If I let you go," Arjun said, "and that's a mighty big *if*— what's stopping one of your men from putting buckshot through my chest for this?"

"I ain't be killing Devika's son." He snorted. "She'd rise back from wherever the dead goes and hunt me down. That's how frightening your mother was, boy."

"You don't know if she really was my mother," Arjun said, but the tremor in his voice was stronger.

"It seems you know enough about your mother to be giving credence to my words. As I said, the Liangzhu take our vows seriously."

Three heartbeats later, the blue fire flickered out and Arjun lowered his arm, a wary gaze still on the loitering women. Eye Patch sighed. "Could use good help around these parts, mind. Blue fire's the hottest thing that burns around here save that blasted sun above, and you'd make a good addition to the camp, if you're both willing."

"I'm afraid not," I said, relaxing a little. "We have to keep moving west, to Brighthenge."

His eyes widened. "Brighthenge? What business have you got in that wasteland, girl? Nothing lives there anymore."

"I think there's a chance we can heal the breach."

"I didn't know your mother as well as I knew Asteria, but Latona would never be the type to send you two off alone for this mission."

I shifted my foot. "She didn't."

A pause. "Ah," Eye Patch said, and then exhaled. "Ah. I see where the land lies. Well, there's some truth to what you say, but I had thought it impossible, believing both goddesses had perished. I remembered only chaos at the Abyss—I was barred from entering their temple and knew little of what happened until the ground shook and the monsters overran Brighthenge. I was convinced no one could have lived through that terrible Breaking. To find that Latona is still alive . . . I am glad, at least, that you have not grown up bereft of a mother. My first look at you, out in that Sand Sea—so certain I was that you be Asteria's mirage. Gave me the shock of my life."

"Who told you that fixing the breach was possible?"

"A few things your aunt told me. I was never smart enough to understand. But I keep a book she left behind still."

My pulse quickened. "A book?"

"It's survived the years. Your aunt wrote it. I'll let you read, and we can accompany you to the edges of our territory if you still want to push on. But in exchange, there's some chores I want done as payment."

That sounded like a reasonable deal, and Arjun's reluctant

nod sealed it for me. "Thank you," I said. "But I would also like to make another request."

"And what would that be, Your Holiness?"

We buried Parrick's body along the edges of the Sand Sea. It wasn't much, but it was the only thing left I could do for him. From farther out into the sand-water I could see curious heads poking out, watching us.

"Haidee," Arjun said, but I was already shedding my cloak to wade out into the thick sea, until the sand swirled around my waist. Madeline swam forward to meet me, and the other dolugongs followed suit.

"I'm sorry," I whispered, and wrapped my arms around her fin, hugging her tightly. She cawed soothingly, like she was the one offering me comfort. Dolugongs had rough lives out here in the desert. Hardship and death would have been no strangers to their little pod, but I felt like I should have done more. "I'm sorry," I said again, sobbing, and was forgiven once more as the dolugongs encircled me, snouts pressed against my back and sides.

"Ah, hell," I heard from behind me. And then Arjun was there, and the dolugongs took turns pressing up against him, bidding him goodbye. "I'll come back," I whispered fiercely against Shepard's hide. "And when I do, I'll change the world for the better. I'll make it up to you guys, I promise."

They sang their agreement, slowly moved away. I watched them dive out of view until the rest of the sands swallowed them up, Shepard taking a second or so to stay behind and watch us before flicking his tail and plunging back down into the deep.

"You idiot," Arjun muttered hoarsely. "I thought I'd lost you."

"I know," I whispered. I wanted to touch him again, make sure he was really alive. I didn't.

"I thought you'd drowned with the buggy."

"I know."

"What am I going to do with you, Haidee?"

My heart spiked at the rough emotion in his voice. He looked a mess, just like I did. He still had sand in his clothes and in what black hair was escaping from his *hezabi*, and more than a few scrapes on his arms and face, shallow cuts across his brown skin. He had every right to be mad at me, but he wasn't. If anything, the expression on his face was . . . gentle.

"I don't know. I'm still too exhausted to gate. If those pirates had been anything like the cannibals chasing after you, I would have been dead by now."

"But you're not," he pointed out. "We made it this far. Let's see it through. If Baldy's got information, then let's see what he has to say."

I risked his wrath and hugged him. He made a small sound of surprise but didn't push me away. "Thank you," I said softly. "I'm glad you're not dead."

His arms dropped away, and he said nothing for a while, his dark eyes still on mine. "Yeah," he said, voice gruffer than before, and an unexpected thrill went through me. "I'm glad I'm not dead, too.

"Let's go back and see what the old man wants, so we can get out of here."

I pressed my hand down against the sand, bidding Parrick one last goodbye, and stood. *I'll fix this,* I vowed silently. *I'll fix this somehow.*

Chapter Seventeen

LAN UNDERWATER

———————————— ☾ ————————————

CATHEI'S FORM HAUNTED THE OUTER limits of the camp while we packed up, always shimmying out of view whenever anyone thought to draw too close. Her presence troubled me; there was no indication that she would turn violent, but there was no evidence she wouldn't, either. She was simply there, for no apparent reason other than to remind us that she was. Odessa had brought her back, but that didn't mean she was alive.

Nobody talked about sending the goddess back to Aranth anymore.

"The patterns in the wildlands are different in intensity from the ones in Aranth, and growing, we believe, the closer we get to the Abyss," I overheard Jeenia, one of the clerks, say in a hurried, impromptu lecture to the others as they took down their tents. "That's why Her Holiness Odessa can perform the spells she's been doing. The rest of us can't change our gates. I have an air-gate, for instance, and can only detect Water patterns, which makes me an Icewright. But Her Holiness can alter her gates whenever she needs to, so she can be an Icewright or a Skyrider or even a Firesmoker."

"But they said she's never done them in Aranth before?" Andre asked.

The Icewright sighed. "Because Aranth has a lot of Water and Air patterns, but not much of the rest. You can't channel Fire patterns if there aren't many of them to draw from. Starmaker Gracea is one of the rarer ones, able to manipulate Air even with a fire-gate. That's why she's got a lot of standing with Asteria.

"But here in the wildlands there's a lot more Earth, more Fire patterns. That's how Her Holiness can make use of more gates and patterns than she had back home."

"But how can the goddesses keep using different gates even when they don't got the practice for them?" Slyp wanted to know.

"That's what separates goddesses like Her Holiness Asteria from the rest of us. They're tied to the land. As long as Aeon's got Fire and Earth and everything else, so will they. Even after the world's gone and broken itself. That good enough an explanation for you?"

It was a good explanation, and it mollified the crew, but I remained disquieted. More patterns or not, these abilities didn't come out from nowhere. There was something Odessa wasn't telling us.

We'd decided to circle the lakes and strike out for the Spirit Lands despite my fears. I was not hypocritical enough to deny that Odessa was a deciding factor here; if she could beat back any more of the shadows that prowled the area, then we had a fighting chance—more than I ever did with my rangers. But her safety remained my priority. We couldn't risk any detours into the unknown.

But I didn't want to go back out there. Cowardly as that made me, I didn't want to see the blood-soaked ground that had haunted me for months, to see any evidence of the team I had left behind. I had no choice.

At this point I believed the gateless crew preferred Odessa's leadership over Gracea's, as did most of the clerks. I suspected some of the Devoted thought the same, but their vows bound them to Asteria and therefore Gracea, too. I couldn't blame them.

But some of the other Devoted did resent those shifts in loyalty, adding to a tension already at a breaking point. Sumiko had informed me that Jeenia had a bruised arm but wouldn't admit to how. She'd found another, Salleemae, crying some ways from camp, because Holsett had been verbally abusive, yelling at her for packing his things the wrong way.

"Was I away for too long?" I asked Noe at one point.

She raised an eyebrow. "What do you mean?"

The last three months had been the longest I'd spent in the company of the other Devoted. Was this how they always treated their subordinates? Why hadn't Asteria stopped this?

And despite the time I spent away—why hadn't I noticed?

That's how the game is played. Pitting them against each other means they'll be too busy to plot against me. Hadn't Asteria told me that? Did she deliberately allow this simply so they'd be too busy fighting to plot against her?

Odessa would never have done this. Though she had been acting odd as of late . . .

"Never mind." No one had reported anything to me, and I realized that my mistake was assuming they would. The Devoted's hold on these people was stronger than the clerks' fear.

Still, the guilt remained—how many of these instances had I been witness to in the past, in Aranth, and how many had I ignored?

I sought the goddess out while the final preparations were underway and found her hidden behind more of the fresh new vegetation she had grown for the forthcoming journey. Her eyes were closed, her fingers tracing the ground.

"I can feel another one," she said, without opening her eyes. "Another galla. Toward the lakes."

"What is your relation with these galla, Odessa? Neither you nor Asteria has ever deigned to go into details." I'd been doing so many things wrong on this expedition, and my mistake with Odessa was treating her like she knew nothing. Because I'd thought her mother knew best.

She smiled archly at me. "If I tell you more, will you finally listen?"

"I will."

"I knew you wouldn't approve, just as I knew I couldn't refuse. In Mother's day, goddesses performed many rituals. Rituals to protect the world, rituals to grant us more powers to do just that. But since the Breaking, Mother thought they no longer worked. One in particular called Inanna's Song states that in my seventeenth year seven galla would come to me bearing gifts—radiances, they called them. For every radiance I accept, I must also accept a terror—a sacrifice. Something about myself that I must give up. Four galla have already offered their gifts."

"And what happens if you *don't* accept?"

She made a halfhearted gesture, at everything around us.

I clutched her shoulders. "Was this how the world broke, Odessa? Did Asteria refuse any of their gifts?" Hadn't the goddess hinted as much before? The idea that Asteria hadn't been as forthcoming to me as I'd thought—that I was just another piece to manipulate in her games of politics—was like a stab to the heart. She'd taken me off the streets, and I owed her. But she had no right to fool me like this, either.

"What sacrifice did you offer in exchange for their gifts?" I wasn't sure I wanted to know, but—I had to.

"I don't know. I don't feel like anything's changed. But I feel stronger, more confident in myself. I've never been that back at the Spire." She shifted languidly, and her dress slipped slightly, exposing a slim, pale shoulder. "I don't know what they took from me, but it was well worth the rest. I can sense them now, you know? This is the real reason Mother wouldn't let me out of Aranth. How ridiculous. The first galla caught me right in the city, where she thought I would be most protected. They'll follow me wherever I go. Mother simply refuses to accept the inevitable."

"Odessa—"

"Am I still infected, Lan? Is there a darkness inside me still?" She took my hand and pressed it against the curve of her neck. "Have I been healed?"

I let my gate flare and probed at the darkness inside her. It had not increased in size, but neither had it diminished from my last healing. I started to withdraw, but she pressed my hand more firmly against her. The collar of her dress slipped down just an inch more.

"Your Holiness—"

"You only call me that when you feel trapped," she whispered. "When you need the distance to remind yourself that I am your goddess. You used to call me Ame, and I wish with all my heart that I was still the merchant's daughter I pretended to be, because when I was with you, I was better at being Ame than I ever was being Odessa." Still with a tight grip on my hand, she pushed my fingers lower.

"I'm not frightened anymore," she purred, her eyes glowing. "I have no regrets. Anything that could make me live my life a little fuller, that could make me serve my people better, would be better than the safe prison of the Spire. We're not going to die. The galla wouldn't have sought me out only for me to die, right?"

"Odessa . . ."

"I love you," she said, and my whole being centered on those words, at the sudden wild rush of euphoria they inflamed in me. "And I know that as Odessa I can't," she murmured, and I'd realized belatedly that she had somehow wormed her way into my lap again. If anyone could see us, it would have been a scandalous sight; her atop me, my hand down her dress. "But as Ame, I want to. I need to."

"Ode—"

"Call me Ame." Her mouth caressed my neck, and I bit back a groan. "Is that what you really want, Lan? Will we survive these wildlands only to return home and have my mother marry me off to some man? Will you still stand guard over my room every night of my married life, hearing *him* behind my door? I was raised to know my duty, my love. I'll welcome his attentions and bear his children, but I'll close my eyes and think of you every time. But not if you say no. Not if you'll tell me you'll defy my mother and claim me for your own."

"Odessa—I—"

"But you can't. And you won't. And I understand why you won't. We're all broken in some way, but the fracture is deeper in you. You don't think you're good enough for me. You thought Ame was good enough—so why not Odessa, too?" She smiled. "Catseye Sumiko told me you'd been refusing her treatment. I need you to be in the best shape to protect me, Lan, and this isn't that. You have a duty to me, and to the people here, and to yourself most of all, to accept her help. Please."

"Odessa—I—"

She nipped at my throat. "If you pledge to talk to Catseye

290

Sumiko, right here, right now," she murmured throatily, teasingly, her hand stroking the back of mine, "I'll let you do more than touch." I could feel her take hold of my other hand, slowly sliding it up her leg, underneath her skirts.

And like a besotted fool, I was letting her.

"You feel so far away sometimes. Sometimes I see your gaze turn inward, and I wonder if you think about her. Your Nuala. You tell me there was nothing serious between you, and perhaps the love between you was not as strong as ours, but I think you lie. You care about people you involve yourself with. That's how compassionate a person you are.

"But I—I am beginning to find that I am not so good a person after all. Sometimes I grow so very jealous. Sometimes I let darker thoughts take over, and imagine Gracea cowering on her knees before me as I finally take command of these Devoted who mistreat their subordinates and treat me like a child still. Some nights I—I'm even glad that your Nuala is dead."

"Odessa—!"

She stopped, her beautiful eyes flying open. Quickly she was off me and smoothing back her hair, like we had done nothing at all, just as Noelle and Salleemae came stepping through the small thicket. "We're ready to leave, Your Holiness," Noe reported.

But Odessa's eyes were already trained on the horizon, toward the Lunar Lakes behind us. "No, we will not," she said softly. "Tell the others that we're to head back to the lakes."

"Your Holiness," Noelle began uncertainly, "I don't think we have enough time to—"

"That's an order, Noelle!" Odessa snapped. "Be ready to move in five minutes, if you'd rather not be left behind." She stole a quick glance at me, and her mouth curved up. "We'll talk again," she whispered, before walking back to the camp.

"She grows more like her mother every day," Noelle murmured.

I didn't answer. Around us, the greenery Odessa had summoned swayed in the wind.

"Bright Lady." Salleemae had lingered behind, her earnest face confused. "Something has been puzzling me."

"What is it?"

"She was wrong, milady. About Cathei."

I lifted my head. Salleemae was chewing her lip and staring off into nothing. "What do you mean?" I pressed.

She started. "What she said about Cathei, milady. It wasn't right. How she went off like that."

No, it wasn't right for Odessa to be off chasing shadows and raising people from the dead. Everyone but Odessa knew that by now. "What do you expect me to do about that, though? She's practically in charge now."

She gazed at me in awe. "You're right," she said. "She is. Even despite Gracea."

I was growing impatient. "You'd best start preparing, too."

"Yes, milady."

Once she had left, I pushed back an overly large stalk and spotted unhealthy black rot along the ground. The same rot had gotten to the roots of many of the other plants; it was already turning the once-green stalks a withered shade of yellow.

Odessa was barking orders to the rest of the group, a faint ethereal glow cast over her lovely face.

I paused, looking at the ground again one last time, and stepped away.

There was something about the glittering surfaces of the Lunar Lakes that made me think of things unseen lurking underneath, despite their placid appearance. What short time I'd spent here had told me that the most innocent terrain often held the worst dangers. A breeze wafted out at us from their direction, almost as cold as those back in Aranth. Save for Gracea's and Odessa's channelings, there were no other visible lights.

"I see nothing of note here." Gracea was already eager to be off.

Graham strayed closer to the lake, his eyes flaring blue. "There don't seem to be any . . . creatures around here."

"Are you sure this is where you wish to stop, Your Holiness?" Janella asked nervously. Ever since Cathei's death, the young clerk had been staying closer and closer to Odessa's side.

Odessa nodded confidently. "I'm sure." And then, to my horror, she started to strip.

"What are you doing, Your Holiness?" A conniption did not sound too far off in the Starmaker's future.

"I need to reach the center of the lake," the goddess said matter-of-factly. "I can't have my clothes getting wet, and we'll need to move quickly afterward." She grinned coyly at me.

"Will you keep me company, Catseye?"

"Not like this, Your Holiness!" She frowned at the title, but I pushed on. "We're not going to swim out into a lake several thousand feet deep and possibly filled with creatures that could kill us!"

She giggled. "Spoilsport." The ground around her began to shift, plants sprouting and growing and twisting until several oak trees stood before us. "Perhaps we can fashion a raft from all these lovely trees?"

"We are wasting time here!" Gracea seethed.

"I will do whatever I want," Odessa said coldly, "and you won't stop me."

"We are leaving! The danger grows every moment we linger here. You may have been a spoiled little brat in the Spire, child, but your insolence will not be tolerated while I'm in cha—"

Odessa punched her.

Stunned, we watched her fall, crumple to the ground.

"Ow," Odessa said mildly, and rubbed her knuckles.

"Odessa," Holsett said, wavering. "You can't—Gracea is—"

"Sumiko, attend to Gracea once we've gotten a raft ready. Inform her that my 'insolence' is all that keeps her and the rest of you from falling prey to the beasts that roam these parts, and she would do well to remember it." The goddess spun around in a circle. The air changed, and I thought I saw strange shadows gathering around her, like the wildlands themselves were ready to stand with her against the rest of us. "Does anyone else have a problem?"

No one spoke.

"Good. Now let's get to those trees."

Several more gates and half an hour later we'd lashed a few logs together for a sturdy-looking raft. Odessa and I were aboard, as were Graham, Noelle, Miel, Janella, and some crew members—Graham and Miel to channel their Seasinging, the others to help steer the raft. The rest of the Devoted remained ashore, watching over their still-unconscious leader.

"She won't forget this, Odessa," I warned her.

She shrugged. "A worry for another day. For now, the galla."

We pushed off. Noelle sat down on the side of the raft with her beloved halberd and stared stonily down at the water, like the force of her gaze alone would prevent anything from surfacing.

"This is ridiculous," Graham muttered, but unlike his leader, kept the words mostly to himself.

"Are there any markers that would tell us we're getting closer?" Noelle asked.

"I'll know it when I see it," Odessa said tersely. Underneath her calm, she was just as worried as the rest of us. "Graham, scan the area."

"Your Holiness . . . this is a most unusual—"

"Are you questioning me?"

Graham sighed, resigned.

"There are many legends about this place," Janella informed us quietly. "Some say that a siren lurks within one of the underground caves, luring men to their deaths with song. We do know there were a substantial number of unexplained deaths from the communities that used to live around the area."

"I'm not sure this is the best time to be talking about unnatural deaths, Janella," Noelle pointed out quietly.

The clerk flushed. "I didn't mean to. My apologies."

"It's still too quiet," muttered one of the crewmen, a young man named Bergen. He shivered. "And too dark. I didn't think I'd miss the roar of the storms and the waves back in Aranth, but this is harder on my nerves."

"Mind your tasks, lad," said Slyp. "We got enough on our plates. Don't add inattention to it."

"Thank you for accompanying us, milords," Odessa said to them.

It was the older man's turn to redden. "Our pleasure, Your Holiness. After everything you've done—we don't get to see much of you or your mother back in the city, and sometimes we forget. But in the last few days you've put the faith back in us. We'll follow you to the ends of the earth if need be."

"Better hope it doesn't come to that," I muttered.

With Graham and Miel's Seasinging coaxing us along, we reached the middle of the lake without incident.

"I'm sure of it," Odessa insisted. "I can feel it." She began to strip again. "It's directly below us."

"You're not going down there!" I exploded.

Janella was already expecting the worst and had lain flat against the raft with her hands clenched.

"What exactly are we looking for?" Noelle asked.

Odessa braced her hands on the edge of the raft and peered down at the water, glaring at her own blurred reflection. I placed my hand against her elbow. "There's something here," she muttered. "I know it's here. I just need—"

A pair of dark arms rose from the water without warning, shadowy hands planting themselves on both sides of Odessa's startled face, and then pulled her underneath the surface.

"Odessa!" Ignoring Janella's startled gasp and Graham's swearing, I kicked off my boots and cloak, and plunged into the lake after her, desperate. The water was clear, but the lake was deep enough that I could see no bottom. Still, I spotted the trail of bubbles drifting up in Odessa's wake and followed it grimly down, moving as fast as I could.

Twenty seconds in, I saw Odessa's hair floating like colored smoke, saw her struggling against a strange creature. It was not a shadow, but something close to it; long, dark green hair and thin, almost bony arms, scaled and midnight black. Its lidless eyes bled a stark red. It appeared anchored to one spot; a wealth of roots climbed down from its waist and onto a large boulder that overlooked a deeper trench, the mass of tangles spreading around the bedrock like a broken spiderweb. A bright, peculiar light surrounded the monster; it seemed to emanate from within the stones piled around the creature's territory.

I dashed to her side and found her arm. With my other hand, I grabbed at one of the tree roots wrapped around the goddess, realizing they must be an extension of the monster's body, and allowed my gates to flare gold and silver.

What I felt sickened me. The creature itself was personified sickness, a never-ending whirlpool of miasma and hate; attempting to cleanse it would be like bailing water out of an ocean, and attempting to add more maladies would make no difference.

It grabbed for me.

Lan.

All of a sudden I was surrounded by drowned specters, all of them wearing my dead rangers' faces. They stretched their hands out to me, imploring, pleading. *You left us,* they mouthed as they floated closer, and though I'd been holding my breath I swore I could smell their stench, the decay that accompanied bloated corpses. *You left us.*

Every part of me wanted to swim away, to make for the surface and forget I'd ever come here. The Good Mother knew how close I came to doing exactly that—until I saw Odessa. Her face was pale, her struggles weaker by the second.

I forgot all about the dead rangers, the sea creature. All that mattered in that moment was Odessa; that in my panic I had nearly abandoned her. *She's drowning,* my mind screamed. *She's drowning, and you have to get to her now!*

I shook the undead free, latched onto the creature again. I shifted tactics. My attack shoved itself into its inky bloodstream, snaking past its diseased organs and something that might have passed for a heart, and slammed up into its eyes, corrupting the nerves there so that its sight was lost. It screeched, the sound loud despite being underwater, and its grip on Odessa slackened.

I moved toward its arms, paralyzing as much of its root system as I could reach. The monster hissed, let go.

I made a grab for Odessa.

And then I was no longer underneath the lake, but in some dark, haunted place where I could see nothing but a faint blur I recognized as Odessa because of the colors in her hair. She stared back at a gigantic shadow, with flickers of strange blue lights sparking around it and a pair of cruel prongs on its head. A voice that was not a voice echoed through my mind.

Be satisfied. A divine power of the underworld has been fulfilled. You must not open your mouth against the rites of the underworld.

And then I was back in the water holding on to Odessa, the lack of air straining my lungs. A halberd sailed past me and cleaved one of the root-monster's arms. The limb drifted away, spurting black bile, and its hold on the goddess slipped completely. I grabbed at Odessa and kicked my feet, pushing us both back toward the surface, with Noelle following behind.

I burst onto the surface, gasping, hoisting Odessa's body onto the raft before scrambling up myself. All three of us lay sprawled against the bottom of the raft, gulping in air.

"Damn it, Noe," I croaked out, gulping. "Who told you to follow me?"

"You gave no orders to remain on the raft, milady."

"I nearly breathed in water when I saw that damned halberd swoop past my head." I looked at Odessa, who was sitting up groggily. "Your Holiness?"

She shivered. I grabbed the cloak I'd discarded and wrapped it around her shoulders. "That was a scylla," she whispered. "Not a siren. I've read about it in one of Mother's books. It consumes drowning sailors, eats ships. I'm glad we didn't bring the *Brevity* here. It could have been much worse for the rest of the crew."

"Damn your mother's books and the *Brevity*," I said roughly. There was the scylla, but there had also been something else, the shadow I saw as soon as I grabbed Odessa.

"'You must not open your mouth against the rites of the underworld,'" I muttered. What did that even mean?

She stared at me. "You heard it. You saw it. When you touched me."

"What happened?" Noelle asked sharply.

It took a moment to realize that Graham was no longer on the raft. Miel and the other men were on one end of the raft, staring at Janella, who sat serenely on the other side.

"She pushed Graham over!" Slyp yelped.

"I did," Janella said.

"What happened?" I demanded, rounding on Janella. "What have you done?"

"She *pushed* him," Miel wailed, wringing her hands.

"I had to," the clerk said. "Merika can't stand it anymore. You think Gracea is cruel, Lan, but Graham is the worst of them all. He hurts Merika, and so many other clerks, and the Devoted look the other way. He was ready to leave you both here, if I hadn't intervened; I could see it in his eyes. I didn't even have to do much. Something in the water took him away."

I swore. I believed Janella—but regardless of what he'd done, saving Graham was still the priority, even if I had to kill him myself afterward. "Miel, do *not* do anything to Janella unless she attacks again. I'll be very much put out if something else happens while we're gone."

"I'll make sure of that," Odessa said, voice hard as steel.

Miel gulped. "Yes, Your Holiness, Bright Lady."

"I won't do anything else," Janella said cheerfully.

We continued searching for over an hour, but the Seasinger was long gone, Miel still weeping, and Janella extraordinarily calm.

We returned to shore, and the rest of the group soon took up the search, the stronger swimmers taking turns diving, the others setting out on the raft to expand the scope of their hunt. I sat and watched them, too exhausted to move. I gripped Odessa's hand tightly, refusing to let go. "I nearly—" If I'd been a few seconds later . . . if I'd allowed my fear to take over, Odessa would have . . .

She squeezed my fingers. She was taking this better than I was. "I'm all right," she whispered.

In the end, we had to give up. Graham was gone.

"I'll kill you!" Gracea shrieked, rounding on Janella.

"No," Odessa said.

"She murdered my second-in-command!"

"What did Graham do to Merika?" Odessa asked softly. The girl in question shrunk back. I'd seen her face when we came bearing the news—her tears were not from sorrow, but from relief and joy.

"He did nothing! These lying, scheming women seek to undermine my—"

"Shut up, Gracea." Air wrapped around the Starmaker's form and she froze, suddenly immobile. Odessa turned to the other Devoted, many of whom had trouble meeting her gaze. "What did he do?" she repeated.

Poor Merika was trembling, but it was another clerk who stepped forward. "Merika wasn't the only one," she whispered. "The Seasinger preyed on the others, too. I—he cornered me and—with other women he was also—"

"More lies!" Gracea screamed.

"Miladies," Holsett quavered, his face the color of ash. "We are not alone, miladies!"

Cathei's specter was back. She stood on the edge of the lake, staring placidly back out at us, waiting. She was looking right at Odessa.

"Did he hurt you, too?" Odessa addressed the ghost.

A pause. A nod.

The goddess knelt upon the shore. Her eyes were closed, her breath coming in quick bursts, and her hands were pressed against the ground.

I sank to my knees beside her. "Odessa." She'd nearly died. I felt nauseous, knowing how close I'd come to losing her. Stricken by the guilt, I almost didn't realize what she was doing, until a strange sound made me look back up.

"Let us ask him," the goddess said, without opening her eyes.

Out on the lake, ripples spiraled out from its center, like a disturbed mirror. The small waves grew larger, drew closer to where we stood watching.

A head lifted itself out of the water. We saw the top of Graham's head, and then his eyes and his face and his shoulders, until he was now waist-deep, stepping slowly out of the lake to join Cathei.

But his eyes were blank and his face was pale, and the slight transparency of his form told us that he, too, had suffered Cathei's fate. There were no traces of regret or anger in his expression; only a quiet, unforgiving hollowness.

"Graham," Odessa said pleasantly. "These girls accuse you of unspeakable acts. Do you deny them?"

The ghost didn't move. Slowly, it shook its head.

"That will do, then," Odessa murmured, and under the moonlight her skin too, for a moment, took on the ghosts' grayish cast.

I found Sumiko much later, sitting by the campfire with a bowl of tea in her hands. She looked up as I approached, startled by whatever it was she saw in my face.

"Help me." Odessa had nearly drowned today, because I was too busy fighting my own demons. My hands still shook. If I'd taken longer . . . if I'd swum to the surface in my fright and had forgotten about her entirely . . . .

There was something wrong with me.

I sank to my knees before the Catseye. "Please," I begged. "Help me."

Chapter Eighteen

ARJUN, WORM-MILKER

───────────────── ☀ ─────────────────

AS FAR AS BOOKS WENT, it wasn't all that impressive.

It was a dirty, ratty thing, some of the pages torn and dog-eared, a far cry from any of the pristine tomes Haidee had lugged around for most of our journey. The goddess, however, looked at it like it was Inanna herself come to life.

"May I bring this with me?" Haidee asked.

"I have little in the way of possessions, but this I intend to keep, girl. Without that book, all I have are the memories, and they fade quick enough with age. But you be welcome to read and copy what you will from it."

"Thank you!" Haidee said happily, flopping down onto the ground.

I moved to join her, but Sonfei laid a friendly, firm hand on my shoulder. "You and me, boy, we got business elsewhere."

"What about her?" I protested.

"The girl's been through enough. She wore herself out back at the Sand Sea with that impressive stunt of hers, and it'll take time to get her full strength back. But I'm sure this is something right up your alley. Easy to do, for men like us."

"Sure," I said sourly, already dreading it. If it was as easy as he was promising, the liar wouldn't have used it as leverage for both the book *and* escorting us for part of our journey.

"Arjun?" Haidee asked, as we were leaving.

"Yeah?"

"I really—I'm glad you're here. I thought I was going to— that I might have—" She paused, eyes shiny.

"I'm still here," I said, trying not to sound too gruff. "Damned if I let some half-assed pirates kill me." Sonfei chuckled. "And Haidee . . ."

"Yes?"

But I'd hesitated already, not sure how to tell her, and gave in to cowardice. "It's nothing. I'll see you later."

"Every twenty-eight days, we be hunting for water," Sonfei said, as we stepped out of the tent. "As you see, the great dying ocean to the east's too far away to take our fill, and we can take nothing out of the Sand Sea but food. So we need alternatives, see?"

"If you say so," I said, still apprehensive.

"We set up camp in this area for a very good reason. Close to the harvest of the Sand Sea, yes, but also because a few thousand paces to the east is the breeding ground for deathworms."

"Not sure I want to know where this is going."

"The deathworms do not often stray from their territory, which is good for us. They also be having the unique ability to take the scant moisture from both the air and the ground and transform it into water. They store it inside one of five large sacs in their bodies."

"So you kill deathworms for their water."

"Well, 'kill' is not being the right word, exactly. Death-worms live for hundreds of years, and the older they get, the larger the sacs. But deathworms do not breed frequently. To kill one would be a waste. The younglings do not hold as much in their sacs as their elders."

"So. What exactly do you . . ."

"We milk them."

"What?"

"We milk them." He sounded *pleased*. "With the right kind of incision, we extract the water without harming them."

"And you . . . want *me* . . . to *milk* them. . . ."

Sonfei waved a beefy hand at me. "The procedure requires an experienced touch, a deft hand. But the deathworms, you see, are very drawn to fire. Like moths to a flame, as an old saying once went. But we do not have many Firesmokers among my men. Certainly no one who could breathe blue fire."

I'd gone very still. "You want to use me to lure in your deathworms?!"

He beamed. "Now you get it."

"How big are these creatures, exactly?"

"The average we see is maybe fifty, fifty-five feet long."

He should have led with that! "You're not making me do this. I'm not going to be bait to a fifty-five-foot-long *worm* just so you can all milk its pee or—"

"No milking, then you and your goddess walk the rest of the way without help from us. No rigs to borrow. No provisions. I offered the pretty goddess an early chance at my book as a token of good faith, but now I will have to go back and tell her the deal is over, and you will have to manage not just the hot sun and no food for your trip, but also her ire."

I gritted my teeth. It occurred to me that perhaps we should have asked about the chore he'd proposed *before* accepting the deal. "How dangerous are we talking here?"

"Almost no danger at all. My men are very rarely fatally wounded."

"That's very comforting to hear."

"It is," the man said happily, ignoring my sarcasm. "The deathworms spend two days at their breeding grounds before they set off again, so we are on a very strict schedule."

"Everybody owes me everything from now on," I growled, stomping off after him.

He had to be shitting me.

"You've got to be shitting me." I stared at the extremely large, extremely wriggly worms frolicking in and out of the sand hundreds of feet away. They had no eyes and they were grossly corpulent, each looking like it was about to burst out of its thin, slightly transparent skin. Grotesque ringlike constrictions ranged down their lengths, making them resemble a piece of mechanika screw, if mechanika screws were alive and disgusting.

They did have a mouth; small in proportion to the rest of them, but filled with circular rows of sawlike teeth. They paid no attention to us, more concerned with breeding and laying eggs or whatever the hell things called deathworms were wont to do out here. I watched one lazily bury half a dozen eggs in the sand and shuddered, trying not to imagine what their babies looked like.

"Gorgeous, aren't they?" Sonfei asked me proudly, like some doting father.

"Veritable beauties, one and all."

"We'll be focusing on this one." He jabbed a thumb at the largest deathworm, flopped on its side and enjoying the hot bake of the sun on its flesh. "This one, we never been able to milk before. Even the strongest of our Firesmokers couldn't attract its attention. But with your blue fire, I have much hope. Imagine how much water it be accumulating by now."

"You guys willingly drink whatever comes out of *that*?"

"It is clean water, and our Mudforgers do good work taking out any impurities." He grinned. "Afraid?"

"Quaking in my boots, but what choice do I have? What do I gotta do? Wave till it sees me?"

"You must travel out into the sand and give it a friendly poke with that blue fire of yours. The hotter the flame, the more in love they be. How fast are you at running?"

I stared at him. He broke into loud, boisterous laughter, and the men and women around him followed suit.

"I kid. I be accompanying you on one of our little boats, and help lure it back onto more solid ground, where it cannot slide around as easily. My men will take care of the rest from there. Wave your blue fire around to attract its attention as I drive."

That didn't sound *too* hard. "Fine. Let's get this over with before I change my mind."

The other deathworms paid no attention to us as Sonfei drove his rig over to the creature, still lolling about in the quicksand-like ground. He drifted the vehicle closer to its side, and I smelled the faint stench of bracken and salt that I had often associated with the retreating Salt Sea.

"We are ready," the man said, revving the engine experimentally. "Smoke it in. Wave the fire around. It will see you soon enough."

Grumbling, I concentrated, willing the Fire patterns around me as hot as I could make them, and raised my arm. Blue flames flared out from the end of my wrist like a torch.

The deathworm did nothing at first, only made a noise that sounded suspiciously like a sniff. And then a curious, tiny cheeping sound not in keeping with its large frame. Then more snuffling.

It moved fast, too ridiculously fast for its bulk. One minute I was standing with my arm raised, feeling like the biggest idiot in the desert; in the next it had inclined its round fat head and had made a beeline for my stump, its circular saw-shaped teeth gunning for my outstretched limb. I had the presence of mind to snap my arm back before it could take the whole of it off.

Sonfei hit the pedal and sped away the next instant, but the deathworm was having none of that. It barreled after us, with no sign of its previous lazy dawdling, and was actually *gaining on us.*

How the hell could something without legs or feet move so goddessdamned *fast*?

"Its body is made to glide effortlessly through the sands," Sonfei shouted over the wind back at me, and I realized I'd screamed the question aloud. "Quite a masterful inventor, Mother Nature is. Keep those blue fires aloft, boy, or it'll lose interest and we'll have to do this all over again!"

"I'm not doing this all over again!" I shouted back, clinging to the edges of his boat as I watched the deathworm behind us gain momentum. To my mounting horror, I watched those rows of teeth expand and warp, the mouth now large enough to swallow a person whole. "Are you sure your boat can outrun it?"

"I am eighty percent confident!"

"All I'm hearing is you're twenty percent sure we could die!" The monster was drawing closer and closer. I swore I could smell its fetid breath, could see the hideous rasping of its sagging folds over the sand as it squirmed nearer—

The boat hit the bank of the shore hard, sending the whole thing plus us flying through the air. I called out every curse I knew and invented some new ones in the process, while the madman behind the wheel let out a joyous froth of laughter and revved the engines in response. "Hold on!" he yelled back at me, but I had already sunk down to the rig's floor, blue flames gone, and was just clinging on with all my might.

We landed with a bone-rattling thump maybe fifty feet from where we'd lifted off, and continued with a series of progressively softer and less noisy thumps until we finally shuddered to a standstill. I'd slammed my jaw against the side of the boat at that first thud, and the stars hadn't completely left my vision when I heard the other men let out cheers.

I staggered up and saw that the deathworm had been swimming too fast to stop itself from hitting the sand embankment as well and was lying halfway out of the Sand Sea, its tail swishing as it tried to find its way back in. The solid ground had rendered it immobile, though, and the other Liangzhu had already surrounded it.

One of their rare Firesmokers was feeding short tendrils of fire directly into that horrifying mouth, which seemed to help calm it down. As it lapped up the flames, a woman was already by it, making short incisions in its side while others hurried forward to fill barrels and buckets with water.

"Never seen a deathworm move that fast!" Sonfei chortled, as I somersaulted over the railing and landed with a heavy *oof* on the ground. "They must like your blue fires very much, my lad. For a moment, I wasn't even sure we were going to make it!"

"That's fine," I mumbled into the sand.

Still chuckling, the Liangzhu man helped me stand. "We'll

push the deathworm back into the Sand Sea once we're done, and it'll be off on its merry way without much fuss. It's a shame you're not planning on staying—you'd make our milking faster this way. But I'm as good as my word. We'll bring you to the woods at the edge of our territory and give you supplies besides, since you've lost most of yours to the sea."

"How kind of you," I said weakly, watching as the first of the barrels was filled with the surprisingly clear water. The deathworm inclined its head, it seemed, in my direction, gave a small grunt, and returned to greedily consuming more fire.

One of the women approached with a bowl of water in her hands. "It's clean," she told me, not unkindly, and demonstrated when her patterns of Earth combed through the bowl and found no dirt or mud to squeeze out.

I took a small sip. It might have been the thirst I'd worked up after the horrible ride, but it was cool and delicious, much better than what we could usually get from the retreating sea back east, and it tasted good going down my throat.

Sonfei sat beside me with his own bowl, and we watched the Liangzhu fill the rest of their containers with the lifesaving liquid.

"As positively *enjoyable* as it was driving for our lives through the Sand Sea while a deathworm the size of a small army chased after me," I began, voice still scratchy, "we're still getting more out of this deal than you are. You're letting Haidee have a crack at a book you've been hoarding for years, you're giving us supplies, and you're taking us closer to the Breaking, away from your own territory and into danger. Why so generous?"

Sonfei lifted his bowl and drank noisily, the knob in his throat bobbing up and down. Then he smacked his lips noisily and wiped at his mouth.

"You be right and wrong," he said. "This is not a place for kindness, this new Aeon. To be kind means to give up resources that could mean your life or your death, and I like life a little too much still. But I understand the importance of your enterprise, and what that might mean if you are successful. I remember the world back when it was soft and good, where I could watch the sun set before stars graced the sky with their shine. Do you know what I would give to see a sunset again, lad?

"I was there when everything died. Have you ever seen a goddess disappear into eternity in a flash of light? Watched her be sucked into a mountain? To see your dreams crumble and die along with her? Ah, Asteria. She was not always a good woman, but I was not always a good man, either. Neither was I the smartest of men, and that was perhaps why I could never get her interest for long. I am not intelligent enough to understand much of what happened at the Breaking, boy, just that the world broke. I kept the book solely because it was hers."

He sighed. "What your little goddess says gives me hope. If they can destroy the world, then perhaps they have the secrets to patching it back together."

"You've only just met us," I grumbled.

"I already see some similarities between us, boy. Not so long ago, I was that same besotted fool with hearts in my eyes, following Asteria around and hoping I could save her from the evils to come."

"I am *not* a besotted—"

"You come from the desert. You have that hard, lean look that tells me cities hold no meaning in your blood. And the nomads have long resented the goddesses for sending us the eternal sun. So tell me—why follow her? There is nothing about her you find compelling? Or attractive? Was her conviction that she alone can save the world enough to convince you, or are you more afraid that she would not survive alone, even if her dreams are false?"

I opened my mouth. I shut it again.

That was what I couldn't tell Haidee earlier. How the mirage had leaned down with its ratty cloak and its robe with that damn silver brooch pinned to its lifeless chest, how underneath that hood its headless neck bored holes through me with its not-eyes. It had taken me a while to understand that it had used up the last of its energies to haul me out of the depths of the Sand Sea to keep me breathing.

The Liangzhu's book, it had whispered, and then also **You will die for her one day**, and I couldn't even muster up the right kind of anger for its presumption, because it had sounded so *damned* sad in the process, **and you will do so willingly**. And then it disappeared, the cloak and the corpse gone like it had never happened.

I wanted to live just as much as Sonfei did. But.

"I know the signs, boy. I thought it best to give you warning.

I wish someone had done the same for me, back in the day." And then he grinned and slapped me hard on the back. "And the milking was good bonding for us, eh? Certainly, where would my manners be if I didn't introduce you to what the Liangzhu consider a fun time?"

"Where've you been?" Haidee asked, barely looking up from the book as I trudged back in. She was looking slightly pale, her voice strangely wooden.

"Glad to see you too," I grumbled, resisting the urge to crawl under a blanket and wait for the world to stop spinning.

Haidee peered curiously up at me. "Are you okay? You've got sand in your hair."

"I always have damned sand in my hair."

"Are we good with Sonfei?"

"I've satisfied the minimum requirements for his help, yeah." I flopped down beside her. Whatever was in that book, it had better be worth the deathworm-milking I'd had to go through. Haidee looked flustered, though, and I frowned. "Something wrong?"

"There were always two goddesses born in every genera-tion after Inanna," she whispered. "Twins. I never knew that. Every history book I've read only ever talked about one goddess ruling in every generation. And now it's saying that Mother having a sister wasn't unusual—that it was the norm. That meant the sister mentioned in my father's letter—she was *my* twin. And—" She paused, then shook her head as if to clear it.

"Soon after their birth, the goddesses are kept away from each other, to be raised separately. In their seventeenth year, they then go through a Brighthenge ritual."

"What ritual?"

"It doesn't give any details, only that it's the custom. Next, it says one of the goddesses would be 'chosen.' Again, it doesn't explain how, but it does say what happens after." Her voice shook. "Oh, Arjun. It's terrible. Part of the ritual involves killing one of the twins."

"What?"

"I think that, politically speaking, separate factions could rise around each twin and cause unrest. But this is more than just keeping them from squabbling over who gets to rule. The chosen twin will be received by seven galla—demons—with seven radiances as gifts, but with consequences for every one. One radiance, for example, could grant the ability to control plants and make things grow, ensuring bountiful harvests for all. But in exchange, it would corrupt the soil, preventing anything from growing there ever again. How well do you know the legends surrounding Inanna?"

"Like I said before, just the standard mythology."

"Twin goddesses reflect Inanna's dual nature, according to Sonfei's book. That's what the ritual is about. The legend of Inanna isn't complete if both her dual natures remain *aboveground*, here in Aeon. Half her soul has to enter this—this Cruel Kingdom, while the other half remains behind to rule."

"You mean the ritual is about killing one of the twins—thus

fulfilling the whole 'go down to the underworld' part—while the other twin is kept alive? And when she has twins of her own, they have to go through the process all over again?"

"Was it me?" Haidee's voice was so small. "My aunt Asteria and my twin sister are both dead. That would have satisfied the requirements, right? But the Breaking happened anyway. Was it because the wrong goddess was chosen? Was my mother the one supposed to be sacrificed? I've always thought Mother selfish for the decisions she made for the city. But what if—what if she tried to save either my sister or me, and that's what caused the Breaking? Am I even supposed to be alive?"

"Stop thinking about that," I said sharply. "You don't know what happened."

"Remember the letter my father left Mother? He said they would kill *her* instead of my aunt Asteria. Was that what happened? I can't blame Mother for not wanting to die. I can't blame her if she tried to save me. Save *us*. But if she was to die, then that means we *were* responsible for the Breaking. Not Asteria."

"Stop!" I commanded, lifting her chin up to face me. She was trying to rein in her tears, but they were spilling out of the corners of her wonderful eyes all the same.

"Look," I began again, moderating my voice. "Remember all the things you've been annoying me with on the way here? About how it's not fair for me to hate you, because you weren't even a year old when everything went to hell and back, so it didn't seem right that people were blaming you for things you had no control over?"

"I wasn't annoying you," she whispered.

"Agree to disagree. Well, I'm throwing those words back in your face. It's not your fault. We're going to Brighthenge, and we'll figure things out once we get there. And if there's nothing to be done?" I shrugged. "Then we lose nothing. I'm sure Sonfei won't mind letting us hitch a ride across the sea."

I'd made my choice, hadn't I?

She smiled at me, her stupid little face so wonderfully bright and lovely. "Thank you," she whispered, and scooted closer to give me another long, tight hug, because apparently we were doing more of this now. I let her. "I just wish I could see Mother right now. I don't think we ever really understood each other. There's so much I want to talk to her about, especially now that I know . . ." She sighed. "You must really think I'm an idiot."

Yeah, I thought, *but I guess I'm attracted to idiocy now.*

Chapter Nineteen

ODESSA THE GATEBRINGER

$$\mathbb{C}$$

I'D BEEN HAVING THE STRANGEST dreams.

I kept seeing two mountains in them, though there was something odd about their shapes that sent me bolting out of sleep, something so disturbing and unnatural that I had to force myself awake. Sometimes I dreamt of the Great Abyss spread before me, knowing that I must look down into its depths to find the answers I sought, but there too, I would come awake before I could finish the attempt. One night found me clinging to the hand of yet another corpse, another member of our team I would be unable to save, though I woke before I could take a good look at their face.

Other nights I had only dim recollections of something writhing and wriggling in the darkness, but it was nothing I could give any form or shape to, and when I woke, that vague unease lingered even as we resumed our journey. Like every bush and rock had eyes watching my back.

Maybe they did. I don't know. I would much rather keep awake.

I took out my anxieties on Graham. With Cathei's ghost I was polite, wanting to give her freer rein despite her condition. With the Seasinger I showed no such concern.

"Odessa," Lan murmured, face pale, as the third nightspan we spent in the wildlands drew to a close. This was not the first time she'd made this appeal. "Please stop."

I surveyed Graham's bloodied form before me. I was pleased to learn that even in this aspect, the man could still bleed. That he exhibited no signs of pain or agony took some of the fun out of it.

"Stop what?" I asked, and delivered a quick flash of ice straight to his gullet, and left it sticking out. "Not all the girls were willing to provide testimony, but I've heard enough. You heard it too, Lan. Tell me why *this* should be spared." I was disgusted—at Gracea, at the other Devoted's willingness to look away. Had Mother known about his cruelty and ignored it, too? Unlike some of the other Devoted, Graham had always seemed polite to everyone, including the clerks. That deception infuriated me.

"This will do nothing but incite Gracea's ire further. I don't think you want her as an enemy so far from Aranth."

"I disagree. She would become even more impertinent in Aranth, with Mother's support." The Starmaker was quiet; I knew her unexpected docility was a disguise for some new scheme.

The Devoted were all against me. They'd kept that disgusting man within their ranks. Even now they still defended Gracea.

They were *all* plotting against me. I couldn't sleep, knowing they would stab me in the heart, if not for my loyal crew standing guard. I had to be vigilant.

I was tempted—so *tempted*—to have it out with the Starmaker once and for all. But dealing with her alone was one thing—while those who loved me were greater in number, all unflinchingly loyal as they should be, it was Gracea's Devoted who possessed most of the gates.

I had to be cautious. Always cautious; biding, waiting for a better time to strike.

I had separated Janella from the others in case Gracea and her ilk planned to retaliate, bade her stay beside me most days. She was silent but obviously grateful, and the other gateless looked at her with something nearing reverence, for her bravery. Only Janella could be trusted now. And Lan.

My Catseye sighed, retreated to confer with Noelle. Lan had been spending more time with her these last few days. Was my steward plotting with the Devoted, too? Were they seeking to corrupt Lan against me?

I'd kill them all if they did.

We had finally reached the borders of the Spirit Lands, but Lan had been delaying our entry. I suspected that she was still uneasy, that her previous trauma was one of the causes for her hesitation, though it warmed my heart when I learned she had approached Catseye Sumiko that night at the Lunar Lakes, after I had shown the world that dying didn't mean Graham could escape his due punishment.

Still, the changes in the wildlands grew more remarkable as time wore on. The sky was several shades lighter, enough that I could make out a scattering of twinkling lights above us, the stars finally making their appearance. And if I squinted far enough into the horizon, I could even catch a glimpse of a steadier, more permanent light beckoning to us farther east—proof we were drawing closer to our goal.

Cathei still followed stealthily after us. She wasn't dead; she simply existed in some space allotted between the living and the dead, and if I could do that much for her, then perhaps I could find out how to truly bring her back to life before our journey's end.

I couldn't explain my confidence. I only knew that it was possible, clung to the idea because if I could perform so many other new wonders, why not that as well? Old Odessa would never have dared to presume, but I liked the feel of new Odessa better, her skin a more comfortable fit against me.

I had received a fifth gift from the galla in that lake, but I didn't realize what it was, or to what extent those abilities would go, until that third night.

It had started softly, with small trickles of floating light; I assumed they were Gracea's. But soon I realized that only I could see them, saw them drifting around certain people in the group rather than expanding their reach into the night the way the Starmaker preferred.

They settled first on Janella, dancing around her hair like she wore rushlights on her dark locks, the brightness taking on a reddish hue. Then I saw more emerging around Bergen, his dark skin a stark contrast to those fluttering green glows. Tiny flares started behind Jeenia, a blushing pink this time, and took further shape around Slyp, winding around his patchy skin like a rope. None of them took notice of this strange phenomenon. Instinct told me this was not a threat, but something much more profound.

"Stop."

"Odessa?" Lan trotted quickly over to me, her beautiful face worried.

"Can't you see them? The lights?"

Blank faces stared back at me, some wary. I had to stay on my guard. They could so easily turn this against me, proclaim me unstable, especially after the scylla and Graham.

"Lan, I see patterns here, behaving erratically."

"Erratically?"

"Around Slyp. And Jeenia, Aleron, Tracei, Janella, Lorila."

Slyp gulped. "Is someone targeting us?"

"No." The patterns ebbed green and red instead of the whites and blues I was used to seeing, abundant here where they'd always been scarce before. "Aranth mostly has Stormbringers, Seasingers, Windshifters, and Icewrights—people who possess water- and air-gates."

Well, there were exceptions. Powerful Firesmokers could generate their own flames, and Starmakers and Mudforgers could draw plentiful Air or Water patterns through their gates instead of Fire or Earth. Those were rare, though.

"But we're not in Aranth anymore, are we?" I mused. "The weather here is more temperate. There are no harsh winds or constant storms, but the reason we haven't made this our home is that the constant monsoons and the occasional kraken were a better trade-off than the monsters that grow in abundance here. Without the ice and storms constantly sapping both Earth and Fire patterns, they have the chance to flourish here."

"You're right," Lan said, surprised. "I never thought about that. People with recessive gates could channel them here, couldn't they? But most people wouldn't be able to now, not if they've gone for years without ever using a gate."

"Unless—unless I can somehow jump-start their abilities?"

"How?"

"I would need a volunteer."

There was silence. Then Janella stepped forward, trusting. "What do you wish me to do, Your Holiness?"

"I want you to hold still."

The lights swirled around her body; had patterns a sentience, I would have said they looked eager to start, like they knew she was ripe to channel.

There was a spot above Janella's heart that *felt* softer for entry than anywhere else—the same spot where the darkness festered within my own chest. That was either a strange coincidence, or . . .

And in that moment, I knew. The lingering sickness in my chest served as an entry point for the galla to activate my abilities, in the same way I was activating Janella's. I could not receive their gifts without it.

I guided the patterns through there, painstakingly chipping away at the barrier and pushing them into Janella in gradual waves. The barricade broke; light shone through.

Janella's eyes widened, and she let out an odd, choking gasp, like she'd just taken in breath for the first time in her life. She stared down at her hands, and then back up at me.

"What did you do?" she asked wonderingly, before her eyes shifted color and her gate opened, a startlingly bright red.

Flames flickered to life, licked at the top of her fingers. With a squeal, Janella dropped her arms, extinguishing them immediately, wringing her hands like she'd been scorched.

Lan was already by Janella's side, taking her hands and examining them carefully. "She's not hurt. But it almost feels like . . . Janella, you have an active fire-gate."

The young girl stared at her, disbelieving. Then she trembled. She covered her face with her hands and quietly began to weep.

I saw more green sparks ricocheting off Slyp, and my fingers curled into fists. Janella's unexpected joy, her tears—I felt like I was leeching off her emotions, making me feel powerful, useful. Wanted.

Having a gate meant a rise in rank, more prestige. The gated were allowed more opportunities for higher wages and a better quality of life—even a crack at joining the Devoted if they were powerful enough. They might lose their gates again once we returned to Aranth, but here in the wildlands, being able to weave Fire and Earth made them valuable.

"Who's next?" I asked, and everyone in the group with recessive gates dashed forward.

Lan had been insistent that she and Catseye Sumiko treat everyone to daily rounds of healing as a means to help cope with their newfound gates. Most of the others took easily to their new abilities, and my smugness increased at seeing Gracea so distraught. It would be harder for her to heap abuse on the rest of the crew when they could now retaliate in kind.

I'd encouraged them to use Graham for target practice, and many of his victims had been eager to take up my invitation. Merika, in particular, had rained down acid again and again onto the Seasinger's withered form, screaming obscenities into his face until she'd finally collapsed, exhausted. "It's a normal reaction," Sumiko told me. "It's not good to keep her emotions bottled up."

"Did you know? About Graham?"

The gentle Catseye stared me in the face without guilt. "I wish I had, Your Holiness. Not all the Devoted knew. Gracea should not have let this happen."

Gracea. All my problems always led back to Gracea, and Asteria herself. *If Mother knew everything, as she likes to claim, then she must have known this,* I thought, and my resentment grew.

Lan's poise lasted until the next day, when we finally spotted spiraling twin peaks from a distance, signaling our entry into the Spirit Lands. Those mountains were still too far away, but it wasn't just the sight of them that unnerved us; it was the ground underneath our feet. To my eyes the plains looked too flat for nature to allow, and something about the evenness of the land disturbed me. At least back at the Lunar Lakes there were bumps and ridges to disrupt the monotony of the horizon. Here, it was as if some celestial creator had reached out and smoothed away the blemishes on the soil, leaving something unnatural in its wake.

Lan, who had been leading the pack, halted. The line behind her faltered.

"Do you need some time?" Noelle spoke up, approaching the Catseye and laying a hand on her shoulder, and I cursed myself for not having thought of doing that first, forced down the sudden surge of jealousy. "We can take a break before we—"

"No." Lan squared her shoulders. "The sooner we're done, the sooner we return to Aranth. Stay alert. Follow no other path but the one I take. If you see anything out of the ordinary, sound a cry to the rest of us."

And with that grim notice we officially entered the Spirit Lands.

The silence here was intimidating. There were no winds or rain, not even a suggestion of clouds in the sky. All we had was a gaping black emptiness that made up the heavens above us, and the flat plains that went on for miles. It felt like the ground was made of finely meshed soil, almost velvety beneath me. Despite the lack of a breeze the air remained cold, frozen into the stillness, and I huddled inside my cloak. How courageous had Lan and the other rangers been, to enter this horrific twilight? The weather was clear, but I preferred storm-swept Aranth to this.

There were no animals, not even so much as an insect, but I couldn't shake off the feeling that we were being watched.

"This is creepy," I heard Bergen say, and he was immediately shushed by one of the other men. In the eerie silence, making too much noise seemed an open invitation to the unseen things watching our every move.

Lan stopped. "Wait." Her voice came out no louder than a rasp, but we all heard her in the quiet. "There's something— moving—up ahead." The words came out choked. "Prepare yourselves. Form a circle, facing outward. Noelle, distribute what weapons you can among those without gates. I want you all lined up, with at least one gated in between those who aren't. Do not step out of the circle. This is important. *Do not step out from the circle.* Fight where you stand, make sure the person on either side of you doesn't stumble out, either. Do you understand?"

There were a few murmurs of assent.

"There are creatures here. I've encountered them before. I don't know what to call them, but they resemble winged birds with humanlike faces."

Merika whimpered.

"They'll try to attack from above, so you'll need to keep your weapons in the air and attack their undersides. It'll take a few hits to knock them down, but once they fall, very few get back up. Eyes always on the sky. Odessa, I want you standing inside the circle."

"I can fight!" I protested.

"Yes, and that's what you'll do. You'll see the attacks from all angles, and I want you to prop up the places where the rest might be getting overwhelmed. Got that?" At my nod, Lan's expression softened. She bent down toward me, and for a moment I thought she might actually kiss me in front of everyone. But then she blinked and straightened again. "There's a lot at stake here, people, and for the love of the goddess keep an ear out and follow any further orders from me!"

We hurriedly took formation, with Lan and me in the middle. Weapons were lifted and readied, all of us staring into a darkness we knew would fight back.

It happened quickly. I heard a steady rush of wings from somewhere in the distance, growing louder with every passing second, until *something* that looked like a bird but wasn't at all came soaring out from the blackness, bearing down on us with sharpened talons and a low, inhuman howl bursting from its mouth.

Fire sizzled through the air, and the bird-creature burst into flames. Its body burning, the monster plunged to the ground, writhing. I looked to my right and saw Janella flexing her fingers, the look of shock on her face slowly turning into one of glee, then of determination.

More rushed out from the darkness, carrying with them the

stench of death. They were terrifying chimera; a cross between a hawk, a lion, and a scorpion, but with faces and hair that could pass for human, if a human face could be distorted in such a manner. They swooped over our heads, raking us with bone-like claws, but spears and halberds and swords struck back from below. All the weapons Noelle had distributed had been blessed by Mother, and where they struck, they struck with deadly results. The bird-creatures veered away, bleeding heavily, and were taken down by lightning, fire, sharp ice knives, and water blades—every shape of pattern we could throw at them.

"Keep up the pressure!" Lan called out. She was darting in between the spaces that separated each armed person and gate user, her hands just as deadly as her sword. Each bird-creature she could snatch at came away with black bile pulsing out of its wings, in the grip of some sudden disease it had no defenses for. Many fell as the poisons did their work, froth bubbling from their mouths as they shuddered and finally lay still.

I extended my range, throwing my arms up to the sky and sending a storm of sharpened hail raining beyond the circle protecting me, toward the monsters still not within weapons' reach. I hoped to slow down the numbers meeting my vanguard. Several I pinned to the ground, staked through with heavy icicles; for those avoiding my storm I simply summoned sharp stalagmites, stabbing them through from underneath.

Fresh screaming cut through the air. I saw blurred forms striking at the birds, saw many of them drop, dead before they even hit the ground. I caught brief glimpses of faces—Cathei,

Graham—before they disappeared into mist again, leaving more dead monsters behind as they did.

My newly gated warriors fought admirably. I could see more streams of Fire as Janella took down the harpies with near precision. I watched Lorila summon Earth from the ground to encompass us like a Stonebreaker shield. Even old Slyp was brilliant, shooting Earth-arrows like he'd been born for this.

The attacks slowly trickled to a stop. We waited, panting and wild-eyed, while Lan tested the ground again for more threats. "Stand down," the Catseye finally said, her voice weary. "That's the last of them."

A soft cry wafted up from one of the circle. Salleemae was on the ground, bleeding from the stomach. Sumiko hurried forward, pressing her fingers to a spot beside the wound. "She needs emergency care immediately," she said, voice terse.

There were other injuries, but none as life-threatening, and the rest of the uninjured got to work hastily setting up a makeshift camp so that Salleemae could be tended to. A fire blazed to life nearby, without the benefit of logs or twigs; Janella had started it.

"Don't show off, Janella," Noelle barked at her, tossing a few pieces of kindling into the flames so it could keep burning on its own. "Using your gates without proper training will exhaust you."

"Yes, milady," Janella said, but once the steward's back was turned, the flames burned even higher, and she smiled in satisfaction.

I gave the orders to spend the nightspan here to rest, with three people on watch at every shift. Gracea made no protest; I suspect she was still figuring out how to wrest back her position, and I knew, despite my own orders, that I would not have much sleep tonight.

Salleemae's teeth were chattering, her face turning pale; I knew it wasn't a good sign, from the way Lan and Sumiko kept looking at each other.

"I don't know if she'll make it through the night," Lan told me wearily when I came to her, offering a small bowl of hot porridge for supper. "I don't understand how she was hurt. Slyp was standing beside her; he swore that he hadn't seen any of those creatures so much as touch her."

"It's not your fault, and you know that," I soothed.

"I know." She stared hard into the fire. "But I could have done better, all the same."

I hugged her waist on impulse. It was so typical of Lan to take every injury on her conscience, but that was what I loved about her. "I'm going to stay with Salleemae for a little bit," I whispered. "You and Sumiko should get some rest."

She smiled wanly at me and squeezed my hand. "I'll do that."

The small tent we'd set up was warmer than it was outside, but Salleemae wouldn't stop shivering. She was swathed heavily in bandages, but even those weren't enough; I could see faint tinges of red underneath the linen and knew they hadn't been able to completely stop the bleeding. Sumiko rose to her feet when she saw me, but I waved her back down. "I just want to stay with her for a while," I said apologetically.

The Catseye smiled at me, but like Lan's, it was a sad one. "I think she will like that, Your Holiness."

I settled down beside her patient, taking Sumiko's seat while she moved to busy herself with the ointments. Salleemae's eyes flew open almost immediately. "Your Holiness?" she whispered.

"I'm here." Not sure where to touch for fear of hurting her worse, I settled for the tips of her fingers, which were clammy. "How are you feeling?"

"Like I've been split open," she said, and laughed softly. "I don't feel much of the pain, though."

"It's the medicine. I want you to sleep. We'll wait for as long as necessary for you to heal."

"I don't understand," Salleemae whispered. "Why did she do it?"

Did she mean Lan? The assault had happened too quickly, but she had instructed us as best as she could. "I'm sorry, Salleemae. Lan tried to—"

"No. Not Lan. I—" She broke into a fit of coughing. "I just wondered—she said that she would look out for my left, but . . ." Her voice trailed off.

"I forbid you to take the blame for something you had no—"

"Your Holiness." The fingers I held clung tighter. "Please give me another chance to be useful. Let me watch over you like Cathei. If my body is too weak, then let me be strong some other way."

How could I answer that? My own face was already streaked with tears. "I promise," I said hoarsely, since she so desperately wanted me to say the words, "but I would much rather you heal on your own."

Salleemae smiled and nodded.

But it wasn't to be. She died four hours later, her hand still wrapped tightly around mine.

Chapter Twenty

HAIDEE OF THE SACRED SPRING

———————— ✸ ————————

"THIS ISN'T A FOREST," Arjun said, staring. "Aren't forests supposed to have trees or shit like that?"

Arjun was rarely right, but he had a point. I'd been imagining towering oaks with an abundance of foliage and branches, so tall that they blocked out the sunlight as you strolled underneath them. I'd seen enough of those in illustrations to know how they should look. But all we saw were strange wooden bumps sticking out of the ground for miles, like ridges grown too big for the soil.

Sonfei shrugged. "I didn't make the forest, boy. I'm only bringing you to what's left of one. Used to have scores of those big green fuckers as far as the eye could see, before the world went to rot. Don't be touching any of those stumps, girl. They've got two decades' worth of poison in them."

I shouldn't have been disappointed. The sun might not have burned as fiercely in these parts, but journeying farther west didn't always mean more from the old world had survived. The Breaking had left no part of Aeon unharmed.

"And this be where I leave you two," the Liangzhu man continued. "We don't stray too far from our territory, and even dead forests hold dangers, peaceful as they might look. Strange creatures move beyond these parts." He looked at us. "I lost more men exploring out here than I've ever lost patrolling the Sand Sea."

"What strange creatures, exactly?" There didn't appear to be any wild predators afoot; any prey that would have called these woods their home was gone. In fact, I doubted that there was anything alive in here at all.

Arjun, too, was unconvinced. "So, like the ghosts of former trees trying to beat you to death with their branches or what?"

"Mock all you want, boy, but at the end of the day it still be you walking this cursed forest. Many of my best men I've sent in to explore never returned, and I've soon learned it's better to leave this place be." He stared at the nearby trunks, an odd look of longing in his eyes. "This was a beautiful place, once," he said quietly. "The wind . . . it had its own song. Good spirits made their homes here. But now they are gone, and there is something in the lifelessness of this place that eats at my gut, makes my knees shake. No, I will take all the risks and the creatures that the Sand Sea can throw at me rather than risk the quiet beyond these dying woods. Will you both reconsider?"

"You won't stop us if we turn you down, will you?" I asked.

He shook his head. "Not in the habit of forcing people—I

learned that dealing with your mother and her twin. But you have both survived crossing the Sand Sea. It is a feat my own men would struggle with. And if you are meant to help Aeon as you and I believe you will, then perhaps you will carry through when lowly men such as I cannot."

"I have to, Sonfei." As much as the thought of staying with him and the safety his clan promised was tempting, I knew I had to continue. "I owe it to the rest of Aeon to do what I can."

Sonfei glanced over at Arjun, who scowled.

"I'm not milking any more of your damn worms."

"Here is a map you may wish to follow. We escaped from Brighthenge through this route." Sonfei bowed, more formal now than he had ever been. Behind him, his men did the same. "We will toast to your success, and hope to whatever god or goddess is still listening that you will return victorious. Should you ever find your way back, know there will always be a place for you at camp." He grinned at Arjun. "And more deathworms waiting for your blue fires."

He patted one of the rigs. "Consider this a gift from the Liangzhu to you. Good speed, Haidee, Arjun. Should the stars align, perhaps one day we can meet again."

Waving, we watched them take their leave, their rigs speeding away until they were gone from our sight. "Milking worms?" I finally asked, once we were alone. "What was he talking about?"

He told me, and the silence of that clearing was broken by the sounds of my laughter, and his indignant sputtering.

337

Much of my mirth, however, faded as we stepped into the forest-that-was-not-quite-a-forest. From what I could see of the narrow trails ahead, the rig should be able to fit through them.

Sonfei's statement that the woods were still was not entirely accurate. The first sudden, unexpected crack had me jumping into the air in my shock. It sounded like it had come from everywhere at once, and my first instinct was to assume aggression.

Arjun had come to the same conclusion, already readying his Howler; I could see the faint glow of its barrel as he repeatedly slammed more Fire into it. "Is this a trap? Is something attacking us?"

But as the sounds continued, I relaxed. "I think it's coming from the forest itself. I read about something like this once. Stop for a minute."

"What are you doing?" Arjun asked, as I headed for one of the withered tree trunks that squatted on the ground. I knelt down, careful not to touch it, and whipped up a fresh froth of Air, so I could amplify the sounds emanating from within. I didn't have to wait long.

Another rattling noise, even louder this time, sent Arjun jumping.

"Remember that time in our old buggy when you complained about our voices being too loud for the small space?" I pointed at the trunk. "I amplified the sounds from inside it in a similar way."

"That's what made that sound? It's alive?"

"No. The exact opposite, actually." I sighed. "My mother had books about the world as it used to be. Sometimes when trees die, they make odd popping and cracking sounds. Desiccation, I think it's called. And it looks like these trees have been dying for a long time."

"You mean . . . can they feel pain?"

"I don't really know. Maybe."

Arjun crouched down beside me, looking awkward. "Is there anything we can do for them? I mean, I know crapsack about trees, but . . ."

I felt a sudden rush of warm affection for him. Weeks ago, he'd been complaining about having to take care of a pod of dolugongs, and now he was worried about how a forest might be feeling. "There's not much we can do. There's been far too many years of drought for us to solve things in just one day. We'll just have to push on."

"I don't like this place," he muttered, rising to his feet. "Maybe ol' Baldy had something there. Let's get back on the rig and not stop until we've found somewhere safe."

We rode on, past more tree carcasses and shrubs dead and dying. Sonfei's buggies were true works of art. They were fast without rattling so much you felt like the whole rig could fall apart, and sturdy enough for the demands of the weather. This one was worth far more than what we had offered in exchange, which was mainly just Arjun being chased by giant worms.

"He believes in you," Arjun grunted, over the wind. "He

thinks there's something to your conviction that Aeon can be healed, and it's a small investment compared to what could happen if you actually pull it off."

"You're different," I told him, and to my surprise he froze, his brows drawn together. Why would that anger him? "That's not an insult. It's just that you haven't told me I was an idiot for a while now."

A ghost of a grin appeared on his face. "Would you like me to call you that every now and then, just for old times' sake, princess?"

I rolled my eyes. "Forget I said anything. We need to figure out if we're still heading the right way. We haven't seen the mirage since the Liangzhu tribe dug me out of the Sand Sea, and I'm worried we might have veered off course somehow."

He hesitated again. "I don't think the mirage is going to come back, Haidee."

"Why do you say that?"

"Just call it a feeling. I don't think anything can expend this much energy traveling halfway around the world from the Breaking to flag us down and then race back there again. Besides, I think it completed what it set out to do."

I raised an eyebrow. "Is there something you're not telling me?"

"Of course not." Arjun stared straight ahead, his hand gripping the wheel tightly. "Well, just one thing I forgot to tell you. I saw the mirage again when I was dragging my ass out of the Sand Sea. It said something about the Liangzhu's book, then disappeared. I think it was leading us to Sonfei and his clan all along—if Sonfei knew your mother and her twin, then the mirage would have known who he was, too."

"That does make sense." In the wide expanse of the Sand Sea, stumbling on the one person who possessed the information we needed had to be more than just a coincidence. "Why didn't you tell me this earlier?"

"Must have slipped my mind, what with almost dying," came the testy reply. "We don't need the mirage to get to Brighthenge. I trust the sun. As long as we're heading directly away from it, we should be good. According to the map Sonfei drew, the Great Abyss is long enough that you can't miss it wherever you're traveling from."

"That's true."

"Your dolugong friends were a big help—they dragged us faster through the Sand Sea than we would have gone on our own, and no one's been able to document just how big that is. If even Sonfei's surprised to see anyone make it across from the other side—and given how far away the sun is now from the center of the sky—then I'd say we're far closer to this Brighthenge than we are to your own Golden City."

"So we're really getting closer?" Dread and eagerness warred for supremacy inside my stomach, uncertainty gaining traction. What if this was all for nothing? What if I was wrong, if I'd misinterpreted my father's letter and the mirage's words, and there was nothing we could do for Aeon after all?

Spotting the look on my face, Arjun patted me awkwardly

341

on the hand. "Best we can do for everyone is see this through to the end."

I smiled gratefully at him. He'd changed a lot. Or maybe he hadn't, and he was just opening up to me a little more than he had before.

That feeling of camaraderie went away very quickly as soon as we spotted the spring.

It shouldn't have existed. I didn't know much about nature as it was supposed to be before the Breaking, but I felt like I'd read enough to know what should exist and what shouldn't, and I was certain that this hot spring, in the face of our endless drought, among the thousands of dead trees we must have passed by now, shouldn't be able to survive in all its hot, soothing glory.

The only indication that the spring was more than what it appeared was a forlorn, weather-beaten statue beside it, a woman whose features had long since been obscured by time.

But neither of us were thinking. Arjun immediately killed the engine, and we both scrambled out of the rig in a mad dash toward those beautiful waters. Arjun had already shed his boots and I was in the process of tugging my shirt off before we both froze and stared at one another.

We hadn't had a bath in weeks. Not the decent ones I could still have back at the Golden City, the privilege I enjoyed of washing in small buckets of water where many others had to make do with a washcloth over a basin. This was a pool I could actually *soak* in, something I had never been able to do before.

"Look," Arjun said, trying to sound sensible even though he was not. "We can't both get in there at once. One of us should stand guard."

"I agree," I said, my tone every bit as polite as his was. "So I should go first."

He glared. "I'm not going to wait my turn. You look like the type who'd spend days up to your ears in this if you had your way."

"So would you."

"Maybe there's some creature lurking at the bottom. Maybe it's got a hidden whirlpool. I can't ask you to take the risks, Your Holiness."

Of course the first time he'd use my title was when he could use it against me. "I can take care of myself. I can gate Water, now that there's an abundance of it. I'll find out if there are other things lurking inside the spring faster than you could by splashing around."

"Then gate some. Outside of it."

I glowered, but the threat of some hidden monster lying in wait finally reached the part of my brain that was still logical, so I flared my gates blue and probed the water before he could react, trying to find anything alive in there. A faint tremor of exhaustion ran through me; I was slowly getting my strength back, but gating enough water for what should have been a mundane chore still tired me out.

Still I found nothing. The hot spring was just that: a hot spring. "See? It's safe."

"If you're going in," Arjun threatened, once I had also tugged my boots off, "I'm going in, too."

He was impossible. "Fine," I snapped, trying to will my cheeks not to color. The spring was wide enough that we weren't going to be accidentally bumping into each other. "But you get even *remotely* near my side, and all you'll find is a knee to the groin."

"We've been sharing space a lot smaller than this one for the last few weeks. If I wanted to go even remotely near you, you'd have known by now."

That stung. "Fine!" I snapped again, briefly switching my incanta to a Mistshaper's. The water sizzled briefly at the dead center of the spring, and a fine spray of steam rose up, serving as an effective enough screen to offer a generous amount of privacy between us. "You stay over there, and I'll stay here."

"As you wish, Your Holiness." Arjun was already climbing out of his own clothes in his eagerness to get to the water, and I flushed, turning around and hurrying over to my side of the steam-wall so I could do the same.

The softest of groans escaped my lips the instant my toe made first contact with the water. The warmth immediately seeped into the rest of my body, filling me in the most satisfying way. It was hotter than I'd expected, but I soon grew used to the temperature without further complaint. I felt like I could stay in here forever.

A pained grunt on the other side of the screen told me that Arjun was not as quick to grow accustomed to the spring's heat, but even he settled down. I could still make out a vague outline of his figure through the steam; not enough to give me clearer details, but enough to spot generalities without the specifics—and maybe a shade more of the latter, if you looked close enough.

Not that I *wanted* to look closer, of course.

It was just that he was a little more muscular than I thought he would be. I knew that he was strong and that he worked hard; when we'd had no choice but to sleep side by side inside the buggy while the dolugongs pulled us along, he'd hogged enough of the space that I couldn't help but feel muscle through his clothes.

Not that I *was* looking. Or *feeling*.

The spring was large enough to accommodate us both—maybe eight or ten feet at its widest—but not so large that I couldn't reach through the screen and touch him if I wanted to. And without the mist I'd set up, I would see *everything* of him.

And he'd see me.

I shifted uneasily, not sure I liked where my thoughts were going. He was silent on his end, too—no doubt wishing he'd let me bathe first, like any decent man would have. Vanya would have been enough of a gentleman to have done that.

But Vanya wouldn't have bailed me out of half the messes I'd gotten into since leaving the Golden City. I hadn't even thought about the man in weeks; Arjun was bothersome enough that he didn't leave much room in my head for anyone else.

"Like what you see?" I wasn't sure, but I thought Arjun was

studying me through the fog-curtain, though he didn't sound as derisive or mocking as usual. But his voice was low, scratchy in its sudden hoarseness, and despite being neck-deep in a hot spring, I couldn't hold back a shiver.

I sank down until the waters were up to my chin. Could he see more of me than I could of him? Would he try to look? Shouldn't I be angrier at the thought?

"Don't even think about it," I grumbled halfheartedly.

I didn't think he'd heard, but his response came swiftly, an unexpectedly soft growl. "Last thing on my mind."

I turned away and spotted the statue again, several feet from where I basked in the water. I frowned, studying it closely. "Inanna."

"What?"

"I think this was once a statue of Inanna. The spring might have been consecrated to her in the past. It could explain its presence here now. Her benediction is strong enough to survive centuries, I'm told."

"Huh. Good for her."

I scowled. So much for attempting small talk.

We sat in near-awkward silence for several minutes more, and then he ruined it by talking again.

"About the mirage," he mumbled, and a faint splash in the water told me he was shifting position. Something touched my bare calf, and I squeaked, nearly shooting out of the water.

Whatever it was immediately retreated. "Sorry," I heard him mutter, his embarrassment filtering through the steam. "Just wanted to stretch my legs."

"Stretch them on your side!" Realizing I was naked and halfway out of the water, I sat back down. Surely I couldn't stay this panicky, because something was going to break. Some*one* was going to break.

"Sorry," he said again. "Just wanted to—urgh." It wasn't quite a groan of pain, but something was obviously distressing him.

"Are you hurt?"

"No. It's just—in between the traveling and the Sand Sea and then those damned worms—I haven't had time to tend to my arm in a while. Aches every now and then if I don't take the time to rest."

My ire disappeared. "Are you okay?"

"Yeah, just—just having some difficulty trying to tend to this on my own. Normally Mother Salla or Millie would be around to help."

Who was Millie? "Do you . . . want me to help?"

A pause. "I don't want to impose." His voice sounded wary, but he wasn't turning down my offer outright like I thought he would. He must really be in pain to even be considering me.

"What would I need to do?"

"Just—I've got some ointment for it in my pack."

He'd left it on his side of the spring, but I coaxed Air to make it float over to mine. I rummaged through it briefly, then held up a small tube. "This one?"

"Yeah. Hold on." He lifted himself partway out of the water, and I looked away, blushing. "Just need to pat it dry first."

"Hold it out this way."

"I don't want to impose—"

"We've been imposing on each other from the moment we met, so let's not break the habit now. Hold out your arm."

Another pause, and then he stuck his arm out through the steam-screen. I took it and, after puzzling out where to let it rest without using any body part I didn't want involved, finally settled it on a smooth rock surface beside me.

My fingers closed over the stump; it was the first time he'd even allowed me to touch it. It was a mass of scars and discolorations at the base, like it had been infected and healed and then reinfected again over the years. He said nothing else, so I squeezed out some of the ointment and slowly rubbed it in.

"Thanks," he said, the words sounding like they were forced out through gritted teeth.

"Does it hurt?"

"Yeah. Like something's pinching from the inside. Can't usually concentrate hard enough to do this myself."

"Is it okay for me to ask? About how . . ."

"I was ten. Chased by a pack of nomads. Didn't even know I had a gate." He sighed. "I'd already been restless all that day. Had my whole body shaking without knowing why. I had a friend—Jerbie. They shot him right in the head and I just snapped."

"I'm so sorry." Ten years old, and already being hunted down. At ten, the worst problem I'd had was Mother forbidding me mechanika lessons with Yeong-ho. Most Firesmokers didn't survive, post-Breaking. Without proper training, they could too easily combust when their abilities manifested for the first time—especially out in the desert, where Fire was too strong for most bodies to withstand.

"I felt like I was burning. I just let loose this inhuman howl, turned to the men, and raised my hand." There was no emotion in Arjun's voice. He could have been talking about the weather. "I set them all on fire. Watched them turn to ashes in front of me. I didn't even know my own hand was aflame until Mother Salla started screaming.

"They couldn't save it, and I was in agony for days—they had to amputate, too charred for them to do much about it. Had enough medicine to save the rest of me, but not much for the pain, if you didn't count the whiskey they forced down my throat to keep me drugged."

The stump underneath my hand shifted. "Was worth the hand," he added quietly. "I got those bastards who got Jerbie. Lucky I'd directed the flames with the tip of my finger rather than just letting them loose uncontrolled. There wouldn't have been anything left of me to bury."

"I'm so very sorry." It was easy enough to take Arjun's snark at face value. He wasn't the type to let people pity him, and I knew he wouldn't want that from me. "I wish you hadn't had to go through that."

"Past is past. Just because I'm down a hand doesn't mean I don't carry my weight like someone who's got two."

"You do more than that. Thank you." Despite my exhaustion, I couldn't help myself; I gated Aether and let its warmth seep into his skin, into the aches and pains where not even the hot springs could reach. I wasn't very good at healing, but at least I could offer this.

He made a strange, gasping sound. "That feels good," he said thickly.

I explored the stump gently, where his wrist would have been. "I'm glad you didn't die," I whispered.

He stopped. I stopped. I knew that he was staring at me through the steam, and I could hear his harsh breathing. I felt his pulse underneath my fingers, speeding up. "Haidee," he said.

What was I doing?

"I'm done," I stammered, placing his arm on the stone beside me. "The spring's all yours." I waded out of the pool and grabbed my clothes, hoping that he would remain and not do something stupidly Arjun-ish, like run after me and demand an explanation, because I had none to give.

He didn't and, disappointed, I fled.

Chapter Twenty-One

LAN AND THE SIXTH GALLA

☽

THEY FOLLOWED US LIKE PERSONAL demons: Cathei, Graham, and now Salleemae, glittering in the mist.

We did our best to ignore them, but their presence loomed over us, greater than the shadows that stole across the sky despite the absence of clouds; their ghosts seemed to us like some signal of doom, like we were helpless to do anything but wait for the inevitable.

Odessa flogged Graham only occasionally now, but she delighted in torturing Gracea with his specter. The presence of all three was a testament to her new gifts, an intimation that she could protect us from creatures we had no inkling of.

But they weren't the worst of it. As much horror as their ghostly company triggered in us, they were our constant reminder that we hadn't been able to save them, that there were more terrifying things waiting for us in the near darkness. Just because they hadn't attacked us again since we lost Salleemae didn't mean that they weren't out there, curled up in the shadows of these twilight lands, biding their time.

We had been traveling the plains for close to four nightspans, and the constant fear of an attack did nothing for anyone's health. The sky had lightened considerably, but that realization came with more inexplicable noises around us, and more nightmares of creatures hiding, biding their time. We increased our watch, but in the wildlands, everything played havoc on our nerves. More than once we'd come stumbling out of our tents, wide-eyed and close to panic, to find it had been a false alarm, some trick of the shadows that caused our sleep-deprived guards to sound an unnecessary alert. After that first disastrous watch, I'd instructed both Catseyes to clear everyone's minds before they took up their posts. It helped, if only a little, but we needed every advantage we could muster to survive.

Whenever everyone else had settled into sleep, I would sit with Sumiko and she would ask me to talk. About my friendship with the rangers in that last expedition, about the decisions I'd made leading up to that final, fateful encounter that I still couldn't remember. I rarely mentioned Nuala's or the others' names aloud, and it took effort to whisper them now, out here in the open so close to where they'd died.

"And are you afraid now, Lady Lan?" Sumiko asked me gently. "Surely this lies very heavily on your mind today."

"Not a lady. And aren't *you* afraid?" Sumiko had always been unflappable. I couldn't help but envy her strength. If I hadn't been to previous sessions with her, I might have gotten angry at her composure, because *how dare she throw another one of my failures back in my face?*

She nodded. "Of course. If I had my way, I would have very much preferred to remain behind in Aranth. But I have a duty to both my goddesses, the same as you. I will not shirk from my responsibilities, and if I can bring any small comfort to this expedition, I shall do so gladly. But this session is about you, and how you think we will fare on this journey."

I leaned forward, hands against my knees, and stared into the fire. "I think we're all going to die," I said, about as candid as I allowed myself to be, keeping my voice low because the last thing everyone around here needed was my personal, expert opinion on how we were all doomed. "But I am also fighting it every step of the way. I have a duty to keep Odessa alive, and the more of us I can keep that way, then the better the chances my prediction comes to naught. You see them?" I didn't need to move my arms to point, because of course she could see the three ghosts, always hovering on the edges of our vision, like they were waiting for an acknowledgment none of us were prepared to give.

"It chills my blood to look at them, but in some small way I'm actually glad they're there. It means if I die out here, if another one of the monsters lurking out here puts me out of my misery, then I can still protect Odessa in some way. That's all I ever wanted to do."

"Do you still believe that you're not worth saving, then?

That you should have died out here with the rest of your rangers, Lady Lan?"

"Not a lady."

"That is another topic I wanted to broach with you. You never rejected being called 'lady' until after your return to Aranth. Do you feel like you no longer deserve the title?"

I stared at the ground. "Yes," I admitted quietly, and the tears fell, just like that. "There should be honor in serving with the Devoted. There's honor in being called a lady. But I can't lay claim to that right. Not after surviving when I had no right to, when they didn't.

"And it's not just them. I realize now that the clerks have been abused and mistreated in Aranth for a long time. I was so caught up in my own spat with Gracea and my own stubbornness that I couldn't see it before." The clerk who had tripped over Holsett's trunk back in Aranth—I'd touched him then and felt the bruises from a previous beating.

I should have done more. Why hadn't I known about Graham? At the Lunar Lakes, seeing how Merika had reacted to him on the ship—I'd *known* something was wrong, but I had shrugged it off. None of those Devoted deserved their titles— neither did I. And Asteria was just as guilty.

Sumiko leaned over and touched the back of my hand reassuringly, letting me sob my way through, until I'd quieted. "You cannot be expected to fix everything. A part of learning to forgive yourself is acknowledging that you still deserve to be called 'Lady Tianlan.' Let me rephrase: Do you believe you're worth saving?"

A part of me still didn't believe that, and I don't think that part of me was ever going to change its mind. "I'm glad I'm still alive," I said roughly. "I'm glad that I survived, because I wouldn't have met Odessa if I hadn't. I've served Asteria for most of my life, and my duty comes first. But Odessa . . . she gives me more reasons to keep going."

"Is Odessa aware of the depth of your feelings for her?"

I looked up, but all I saw in Sumiko's gaze was understanding. She had assured me countless times before that her sessions were strictly confidential. "She's all too aware of them, believe me."

"And you have no intention of acting on those feelings?"

"She's the goddess, Sumiko. I mean . . . damn it, you know as well as I do that fraternizing isn't allowed, and with her least of all. This isn't Gareen and one of his flunkies gullible enough to think he's monogamous." Asteria had gone to the trouble of informing herself about our affair for a reason. She'd placed me as Odessa's guard to ensure that I wouldn't step out of bounds. She'd insisted that joining the expedition was voluntary, but she'd forced me all the same.

I could understand Asteria's need to protect herself, sometimes even from her own Devoted, but her actions had forever soured our relationship, and I wasn't sure if it would ever get back to the friendship we had, if it had ever been that.

"I know," the Catseye said reassuringly. "But our talks aren't to discuss what we should and shouldn't do as members of Asteria's Devoted. These sessions are to explore your own feelings. Any resentment and emotions that you might not have the opportunity to express in your day-to-day life, you are free to air now. There is no scrutiny here, nor will there be judgment."

"I don't know. To be honest, I'm not thinking of any future beyond surviving our present." I closed my eyes. "But you're right. Sometimes I don't think I deserve to be alive. And I know what you're gonna say—that it's natural to think that, right?"

"Quite so. As well as believing that you don't deserve any happiness that comes your way."

"Are you seriously telling me to forsake my duties and go after Asteria's daughter?"

"As you're a member of the goddess's Devoted, it would be frowned upon. But as your counselor, whose main priority is to help you heal, to put you in the best physical and mental condition possible; and because you and Her Holiness are the keys to the rest of us surviving this trip . . . I would say that the goddess's daughter knows her own mind, as do you."

A faint rustling sound made me open my eyes again.

Odessa had left her tent. Now she stood several feet away, pink-cheeked in the twilight, her cloak wrapped around her. "Sorry."

Sumiko rose to her feet, graceful as always. "Let us end our session for tonight," she said easily. "I am pleased by our progress, Lan. Perhaps we can schedule another soon. Your Holiness." She bowed low to Odessa and moved off in the direction of her own tent.

Odessa still made no move to leave. How much of my conversation with Sumiko had she overheard?

"Not much," she muttered, when I asked. "Just the part where—where you said you don't think you deserve any happiness?" There was a question in her eyes, and I knew what she really meant.

"My responsibility is to get us all out of this alive. I can't let anything else distract me."

"And afterward?"

I took a deep breath, giving in to the idea of a future. "And afterward—there's a lot we can discuss."

She glided closer. "Can't we talk about them tonight? When the whole world and their dead are sleeping?"

This was a new kind of Odessa. While I had loved the soft, shy girl I had first met at Wallof's bookstore, I couldn't deny that this new, more confident goddess also held some attraction. I took a step back on impulse, because to hell with Sumiko's suggestion about giving in. That didn't stop her from drifting nearer.

Her fingers brushed against my collar, tugging lightly at it. "But not tonight?" she whispered. "Not now, even if only for a little while? I'm sorry, but—I just want something good to hold on to while we're out here. Something good to remember."

"Odessa. I can't."

This time it was her turn to step back. "You don't want me, even after all you said to Sumiko?" she whispered.

So she'd been listening longer than she'd claimed, but I was in no shape to be mad. "You have no idea how much I want you." Her eyes widened. "But I can't let anything distract me from getting us to Brighthenge, Odessa. Not even you."

"But I just want—just for a moment—"

I saw it the instant she did. Something passed through her—some dark wind, or perhaps the faintest flutter of a silhouette. It touched her briefly at the spot where the infection bloomed closest to her heart, and then it was gone.

I saw a brief vision—a lone light, shining out of the black, hovering around a gray giant hidden within the shadows. Almost at the same time I felt pain within my chest, almost at the exact same spot. I staggered back but refused to relinquish her hand. "What . . . ?"

"You saw it?" Odessa's eyes were wide, her hand pressed against the rise of her breasts.

"I saw *something*." The pain was disappearing almost as quickly as it had struck, but damn if it hadn't *hurt* all the same. "Another galla . . . ?"

"How did you see it?"

I stared at our joined hands. Hadn't I seen Asteria's vision like this, too? "An unexpected side effect of a Catseye's gift, apparently. Just like with the scylla."

"She fooled us, Lan." It was barely a whisper. "As soon as she saw that galla out at the Aranth port, she *knew* that I was supposed to accompany you here."

"That's impossible. Asteria would never put you in danger like this."

"I was never going to be in danger. The galla aren't my enemies, they're my servants. She knew that. As I said before, there's a ritual every goddess is meant to go through, and this is it. Only the true goddess, the one chosen to rule, goes through these rites. It used to be done at Brighthenge. But with the shrine gone, the galla sought me out instead."

My mind reeled. "And Asteria knew this?"

"I don't think she realized the rituals would still continue until that first galla arrived. That's how she knew I would be protected.

"But she also knew I would disobey her. When I snuck aboard the *Brevity*, I was so shocked to realize that I'd gotten away. I thought Mother wasn't as good at keeping an eye out for me now that I was older. I thought I'd gotten smarter." She laughed bitterly. "I was wrong."

It might not appear that way now, her mother had told me, *but there is no one else I would trust on this journey than you.* She had known Odessa would disobey her. She had known about our previous trysts. I shouldn't have been surprised that she'd been two steps ahead of us this whole time.

"Your mother fooled everyone," I said, not completely in anger. She hadn't stopped Odessa from sneaking aboard the *Brevity*; she had let her go. She'd allowed our clandestine meetings to continue so she could appoint me Odessa's guard and tie me closer to her. Asteria was a manipulative bitch, but in her position it was a commendable trait, even an admirable one. "Then why did she forbid you to leave the Spire in the first place?" I remembered Asteria by the window, staring at the shadows that dared come to her territory, saw the unnatural slope of her shoulders as she relaxed in relief, a smile on her face. I should have suspected it then.

She frowned. "I don't know. Perhaps she really was being overprotective at first. Perhaps it was when the galla arrived that she knew I would be safe."

"How many of these galla have come for you?"

She paused. "Five."

Five. Two more nightmares to wait for. "And what do you give them in return?"

"I'm not sure. It feels like I lose a little piece of myself each time. I know that Cathei and Graham and Salleemae are dead, but I don't feel grief like I'm supposed to. I don't feel . . . other emotions like I should. I can't explain it."

That was worrying. "And now? That . . . shadow I felt? What does that mean?"

"There's a sixth galla nearby."

My grip tightened. "Surely you can't do this again."

"I have to, Lan." Odessa's voice was tinged with desperation. "Once you start the ritual, you have to go through with it till the very end. Refusing might bring about another Breaking. I think that's what happened with Mother. She failed her ritual. That must be the reason why the world broke."

"The last thing I want is to see you suffering." Belay that; I *was* angry at Asteria. For letting her daughter go off to face these demons all on her own, paying for the crimes her mother had committed. *She* deserved to face the consequences, not Odessa. "What happens after you accept all seven gifts?"

"The books were never clear on that, but I believe it gives me the authority to rule Aeon in Mother's place, to wrest it from her if I have to. I'll stop being beholden to her, Lan. I can forge my own path from now on." A look of wonder crossed her face, her eyes coming alive with a strange light. "I could *rule*, Lan. I won't have to hide anymore. I could do what I see fit, protect the lands as I should." Her fists unfurled, clenched, unfurled again. "Think of the *power* I could wield. So many things in these wildlands already bow down to me. Imagine my full potential. I could tame these creatures, bind them to my will instead. I could be ruler to more than just the city of Aranth. I could stake my claim here, turn these empty waste-lands into fields of green and gold. We could rule happily like this, you and I."

"Odessa. Not everyone wants to live here. There are far too many—"

"I'll *make* them change their minds." There was a harshness to her now that I'd never seen before, the words grating against the soundless air. Her eyes blazed as hard as agates. She could be like Asteria sometimes, I realized. Asteria, who could be terrible and cold. "And they will love me for it."

I pressed two fingers against her wrist, feeling the jittering rhythm of her pulse underneath mine, and felt her relax. "And where is the sixth galla now?"

She made a gesture out toward the plains. "It's not so far away that I can't walk."

"Then I'll go with you." I silenced the beginnings of her

protest with another look. "There's a reason I'm here, and that's to protect you. Take me to wherever the galla waits for you. Let me see it with my own eyes."

Noelle was on watch, and she quirked an eyebrow at us when we approached. "We won't be gone long," I told her, hoping that truly was the case. "Keep an eye out. If we don't return in—" I paused, looking at Odessa.

"An hour," she supplied.

"—an hour, send out a search for us."

Noelle rose to her feet. "Sounds like I should be accompanying you both."

"No," the goddess said.

"This is dangerous, Your Holiness. Surely you and Lan could stand to have more—"

"I said *no*, Noelle," Odessa said coldly. "Are you disobeying a direct order? You've always been keen to ignore them when it suits you. I did not condone Gracea's use of force on Janella, but perhaps we need one more example to discourage disobedience wherever it festers."

I was shocked. Noelle froze in a half-standing, half-sitting position, her mouth hanging open. "I mean no disrespect, Your Holiness. I only offered backup should it be necessary."

"You will not be necessary, Noelle. Keep watch, and leave us be. I know many ways to remind you that I am in charge, all of them painful."

"Odessa," I whispered, as we headed out into the plains, the Spire's steward staring after us. "What has gotten into you?"

"People need to know their place, Lan. I'm their goddess. It's about time Noelle stopped treating me like a child."

I said nothing, though my heart was heavy. I was wrong. This was not the Odessa I wanted. How could the girl I loved have changed so much since leaving Aranth?

We walked in silence for several minutes until Odessa stopped, her eyes trained on a point in the distance, though I saw nothing. "It's coming. The galla of rulership."

I took her hand again and concentrated. I felt a trickle of energy flow between us, and my vision seemed to shift until I saw something approaching out of the twilight. Its shape was unfocused, like it was trying desperately hard to be solid, though nothing about it was real. "Is that it?" I asked, already knowing the answer.

Odessa said nothing, only waited.

The being had a band of blue jewels surrounding what should have been its finger, but the rest of its features were shrouded in an inky blackness. Despite Odessa's assurances, I braced myself, guarding against a possible attack, but Odessa was languid, almost welcoming, like it was an old friend. She extended her hand when it drew near enough, and I couldn't hold back my shudder.

It was not of this world. Nothing about it should exist.

The darkness shifted, and something that should have been an arm, a hand, reached out to take Odessa's own.

I thought I knew what to expect from my experiences with the galla at the Lunar Lakes. I was wrong.

I was staring into an abyss, an unending spiral into unfathomable depths. I could hear myself in my own head; screaming, begging me to look away before I lost my mind completely, and with great effort I did.

Odessa stood serenely by as, once again, the horrifying figure inclined its great and misshapen head, the jewels it wore the only source of light in this hellscape.

Be satisfied, a voice sounded, hanging over us like some great and terrible judgment. *A divine power of the underworld has been fulfilled. You must not open your mouth against the rites of the underworld.*

I saw it, then. Beasts of horrifying visages, of twisted bones and facades of flesh came tearing out of the Abyss, full of wings and brittle teeth and sharp edges. We were outnumbered, and nothing we could do would stop them from tearing us limb from limb, just like . . .

Come, Odessa called, and like obedient children, they drew closer. As one, they fell on the hollows of their bodies that passed for knees, prostrated themselves on the ground, and cried out their exultations, in a grating, gnashing language unsuited for human tongues.

They are calling to her, I realized, and the horror of it gripped me worse than when I thought they were going to rip us apart. *They are calling her their queen.*

But a contrary rush of pleasure soared through my veins, overcoming my terror. Lust hit me like a sword through my gut, filling me up so quickly, and in that sudden shock I let go of Odessa's hand.

The Abyss disappeared and the flat plains returned, leaving me on my hands and knees, choking on air as sanity returned in short bursts, the world restoring itself to normalcy. Odessa remained where she stood, staring up at the night sky, ecstasy still stamped across her features. Her beautiful hair shifted in the wind, and as always I couldn't look away.

"Odessa." Desire was still swimming through me, and it took everything I had to remain still. *I want her,* I thought ferociously, unable to stop the lurid thoughts, my own inner beast coming to life. *I want to strip her naked. I want to take her hard on the ground until I'm all she can feel. I want—*

I couldn't. I couldn't—

She made the mistake of looking back at me then, and I saw her lust mirroring my own.

She flung herself at me, and my defenses fell. She kissed me, tongue demanding within my mouth, body squirming urgently against mine.

Frenzied, out of my mind with hunger, I tore at her clothes, shoved her skirts up. She spread her legs, panting, eyes glazed. "Yes," she breathed. "Oh *yes*, Lan . . ." She was attempting to tug off the light armor I still wore, complicated when compared to my easier access to the rest of her, but I was too impatient, still too caught up in this inexplicable curse to need anything else but her, her, *her.*

I was rough, rougher than I should have been. Her head rolled back, her hands gripping my fingers as I kissed her neck, her breasts, her stomach, plotting a new map along her hips, between her thighs. She bucked her hips desperately, mewling for more. I withdrew, pressed harder.

Beautiful Mother of mercy, I could drink her till the end of time.

She thrashed, wailing up into the heavens as pleasure seized her, but I kept my mouth on hers, greedy and thirsty, drinking her in. When she finally stopped, spent and breathless, I lifted my head.

"We're not done yet, Your Holiness," I hissed, still desperate for more, and she moaned her assent.

"What are you doing?"

Odessa reared up, alarm replacing her passion. I sat back, breathing hard, already knowing there was nothing we could do to hide.

Gracea stood with several other Devoted in tow, and behind them a pained-looking Noelle. The look of pure horror on the Starmaker's face, I thought, as I still fought the fading pangs of pleasure, was almost worth the discovery.

Almost.

Gracea pointed at me, triumph shining in her eyes. "Arrest her!"

But Odessa was the first to recover, and the first to react.

Something dark and clawed ripped through Gracea's shoulder, and she fell screaming. The others turned to find an army of shadows, just beyond the group, waiting. Odessa was already standing before the fallen Starmaker, hand pressed against the other woman's forehead. Gracea's eyes widened, staring off at something the rest of us couldn't see, and she screamed. She thrashed in apparent pain, squirming in agony on the ground until the goddess finally took her hand away.

"Well," Odessa murmured, in a lighthearted tone that nonetheless chilled my blood in its bright cheer. "The galla of beginnings and endings. I should have known. If its gift meant I was capable of granting gates to those loyal to me, then it follows that it also grants me the skill to take them away."

"Your Holiness," Gracea stuttered. "I cannot let her—she took advantage of—"

"*I* seduced her, Starmaker," the goddess said with a laugh, ignoring the gasps of the others. "I encouraged her in every way. She was hesitant, thinking my rank made our relationship inappropriate, but I insisted. I chased her almost every step of the way, even when she endeavored to keep me at arm's length. If there's anyone here who should be sanctioned for unwanted overtures, it should be me."

Smiling, Odessa moved toward the dark shadows that towered over the whimpering Gracea, reaching out and patting one head like she would a treasured pet.

"It's over," she said. "I've won."

Chapter Twenty-Two

ARJUN, THE PREY

———————————— ☼ ————————————

SHE HADN'T SAID A WORD since yesterday.

I should have been delighted.

I wasn't.

We passed more dead trees as I drove; hundreds and hundreds more decaying stumps, their roots and twigs crunching underneath the wheels as we tore on ahead, hoping to leave this never-ending forest for another place where some semblance of life could actually flourish.

She stared out the window as was her habit, but instead of the usual barrage of irrelevant chatter that I had been growing used to in the last several weeks, she contributed nothing but a silence I found worse than her constant chatter.

"Well?" I found myself demanding, irritated that I'd caved in first.

"Hmm?"

"You said you were going to tell me more about that book from Sonfei you've read. Stuff that would help us figure out what to expect at Brighthenge."

She made a vague gesture toward one of our packs stored in the back seat, still not looking at me. "I made some notes. You're free to read them."

"I'm driving, if you haven't noticed."

"I can take over."

"Haidee . . . !"

"Hmm?"

Look at me, I wanted to shout. *I felt it. I sure as hell know you felt it, too. Are we gonna talk about what happened at the spring or are we never to talk about it again? Because "never" might not be that long, considering the undoubtedly shitty places we still have to bull our way through. But if you're not interested in me the same way I am in you, at least have the decency to tell me straight to my face!*

But I couldn't say that, either. I didn't want to know her answer.

"You take over, then." Trying to make sense of Brighthenge ought to be better than staring at this barren landscape. "Gonna need to check our engine, too. Might have gotten a few dead leaves and twigs stuck to the wheels." I'd taken to sleeping outside instead of beside her in the rig, giving her all the space she wanted, because I knew I could do something stupid with her so close. It had been hard enough the other mornings, back when I hadn't even realized I loved her.

She nodded, her eyes downcast. I found a larger clearing to

stop at, cast a nervous glance around to see if we had attracted the attention of some other creature that might have made this place home. The unexpected advantage of a dead forest was that when the trees were gone, you could see an ambush coming from miles away. The sun didn't burn through skin in these parts the way it liked to melt bones back east, but I pulled my head scarf over my eyes and checked to see if my Stonebreaker armor was still as strong as ever. As much as Sonfei and his merry band of worm-gutting Liangzhu annoyed the hell out of me, they'd at least offered safety in numbers.

Their rig, too, was a work of art. The Liangzhu were able to use Sand Sea scraps to build better vehicles, without needing to fight other clans over resources.

Very few things could outrun us in this. Even the mirage wouldn't have stood a—

You will die for her one day.

I sat back abruptly, scowling. The Liangzhu rig required Air to keep the engines running. Sonfei had explained to us how they filled the tank up with sand, then used some sort of combustion engine underneath to swirl the sand like it was water, making the wheels move in the process. They'd improved the technique enough that it could spin almost four hundred cycles a minute and not overheat. Occasionally a Windshifter or a Fire-smoker had to be on hand to churn the sand again, if it clumped up. Popping the tank open, I could see that that was the case.

I rolled up my sleeve. A faint blue sliver flickered into life at the end of my wrist.

"Let me do it." Haidee spoke up unexpectedly, stammering. "You—yesterday—if your wrist is still hurting—you shouldn't overuse it and—"

"I'll be fine." It would normally have taken a few more days before the last of the pain left, but thanks to the hot springs and—well, whatever the hell she'd done to me to soothe the stump—I felt better. "It helped. Yesterday."

She jammed her hands onto the sides of her breeches and stared at me for the first time in nine hours. "Let me do it," she repeated stubbornly.

I was tempted to start an argument with her just for old times' sake, but I didn't want to fight, either. So I shrugged and let her take over, hoisting myself back into the rig while she gated some Air. I slung myself onto the back of the buggy and fished out her notebook from one of her sacks.

Haidee's handwriting was neat and evenly looped, which made for easier reading. From what I'd gathered so far, every pair of twin goddesses was separated at birth, each to be raised by a different group of Devoted who attended to their needs. Each girl had a specific role to play in protecting Aeon, and it was believed that feelings of kinship would make them derelict in their duties.

One of the twins would eventually wed, to sire a new generation of twin goddesses. The other would be privy to some sort of ritual that amplified her abilities instead. Nonetheless, both goddesses were free to enjoy their share of consorts at their discretion—

Haidee had underlined the sentence for emphasis.

I buried my face inside the book, hiding the sudden flush I was certain reached all the way up to my eyebrows.

Consorts. Sweet Mother Aeon.

I turned the page; to my relief, there was nothing else but an outline of a brief history of Inanna, which I already knew about. Imperfect creations, ran into hell to save her beloved, blah blah blah. I was sure Haidee knew this already, but I suspected she was this meticulous about everything.

I heard her climb inside the rig with me, taking charge of the wheel, but I was too engrossed to notice beyond hearing the engine flare back to life and feeling the rig move forward again.

Some tidbits about Brighthenge now. Haidee's earlier theory had been accurate—Brighthenge had been built atop the alleged entrance to the underworld. Since it was a holy place, wards and magic spells were woven into it to prevent unwanted creatures from escaping and tormenting Aeon. It was hoped that regularly consecrating Brighthenge would keep it that way. Some success that turned out to be.

I turned another page, found myself staring at something unexpected:

Key Features of the Brighthenge Ritual, Haidee had scrawled.

After her seventeenth birthday, the goddess shall be presented with seven galla, all of which she is to accept before she turns eighteen.

There was a small note in parentheses underneath—Haidee's personal opinions on the matter: *(But what are the consequences of*

rejecting these gates? Did Mother and my aunt do so, resulting in the
Breaking??)

Seven galla—underworld demons historically nicer to goddesses than the average fiend. The galla were discernible by their lapis lazuli, a mark of their high rank.

I read on.

For every gift bestowed by the high galla, an equivalent sacrifice is required:

1. The Clarity: a galla with a beard of lapis lazuli. Bestows the gift of limited prophecy in exchange for foresight.

2. The Courage: a galla with a turban. Enhances one's ability in the gates in exchange for caution.

3. The Abundance: a galla with egg beads. Bestows the gift of harvest but permanently poisons the soil against future crops.

4. The Life: a galla with a sapphire brooch. Brings the dead back into a half-life, but requires mercy in exchange.

5. The Beginnings and the Endings: a galla with a measuring rod of lapis lazuli. Gains the ability to take away and bestow gates, in exchange for one's modesty.

6. The Rulership: a galla with a jeweled ring. Controls the creatures of the dark, but requires self-control in exchange.

7. The Mother: a galla with glittering jewels for eyes. Seals the ritual and guarantees the protection of Aeon, but requires a beloved life in exchange.

"This is ridiculous."

"What?" Haidee craned her neck toward me. I didn't realize I'd said it aloud.

"The notes on ol' Sonfei's book. This part doesn't make a whit of sense." I tapped the page. "We've encountered nearly every sort of monster on our way here that could possibly crave human flesh, but I don't think any of them fit these descriptions."

She turned back toward the dashboard, shrugging. "I don't know. Mother never thought to enlighten me. I figured I ought to take notes on what they looked like, just in case. This was Asteria's journal, so I assume her experiences differed from Mother's, if they were raised separately. Besides, those jewels they wear should make for good identification, when we encounter one."

"*When* we encounter one, and not *if.* I like your optimism." She didn't rise to the bait, though, so I persisted. "And what about these gifts? How exactly does an exchange like this happen? How exactly do you give up 'self-control' or 'modesty'?"

For some reason she blushed. "The book didn't say."

"You haven't encountered anyone wearing strange jewelry who wants you to bring back the dead in exchange for your soul, by any chance? While I wasn't looking?"

"Don't be ridiculous." Talking about the book was getting her to talk to me again, at least. "No, I haven't met any galla. I haven't exactly displayed any new skills since we started. But I suspect that this ritual forces one of the goddesses to become some monster in exchange for the gifts, from the sound of it. It could explain my father's letter warning Mother that she would be killed. Asteria must have undergone the ritual."

374

"What's the murder of a goddess gonna solve?"

"I don't know." Haidee stared straight ahead, her knuckles white from squeezing the wheel too hard. "I reread those passages in the book several times just to make sure that I was understanding it right. Sonfei was no help—he has the book, but he holds on to it for sentimental value more than anything else. But I think the last Brighthenge ritual was the reason the Breaking happened. Maybe her twin tried to kill her, but Mother wound up killing her instead. But how could any goddess choose to *murder* her own sibling?"

Her voice broke. "I don't think I would be able to do it. Mother can be power-mad sometimes—but I don't know if this was something she would do, either. How can so many of my ancestors before me have made such a decision?"

"You're saying every goddess who came before you killed her twin?"

"That's what's odd. It says nothing about what became of the other goddess once the ritual was over. I've read a couple of tomes that documented the lives of some of my ancestors, but none of them mention twins. There aren't any references to them in *A History of Aeon*, and most of our scholars swear by that book. That's why I always thought Mother and my aunt were anomalies, the only twin goddesses in a long line of lone daughters."

I glanced back down at her notes. "Wasn't that one of the gifts offered by these high galla for the Brighthenge ritual? Resurrecting the dead in exchange for taking away her mercy?"

She nodded. "But Nyx wasn't a tyrant. All the history books spoke of her in glowing terms. Even in her own personal journal, her writings were sane and empathetic."

"Some people are pretty good at masking their insanity, Haidee."

"Maybe the books that do talk about both twins were burned after the Breaking. I don't know. I . . . it's almost my eighteenth birthday. I've yet to encounter any galla. Does this mean that I'll be the one stricken from the history books?"

"Of course not!" I growled, angry that she was even considering this. "Your aunt and your twin sister are dead. You and your mother are the only goddesses left in the world. I'd say that the ritual no longer works after the Breaking, and that's why there aren't any galla wandering about. No sense making wild guesses about something you don't have any proof of."

She threw a startled glance back at me, started to smile—then caught herself, reddened, and looked away. "I suppose."

I wanted to throttle her. A part of me wanted to yell, *If you don't like me, then tell me here and now, I can take it,* and another part of me was whispering, *No, you can't, you dumb bastard, and if she's got any sympathy in her, she's gonna tell you after you've lived through Brighthenge, when she won't have to travel beside you and you won't be reminded of her rejection every time you see her ridiculous, infuriating, wonderful face.* I didn't want to be like Sonfei, pining away for a woman who didn't want him back.

I didn't have a chance to tell her any of those things, because she'd gone deadly silent in her seat. I followed her shocked gaze out into what looked like the entrance to hell itself.

We'd long since left the dead forest and its decaying tree stumps behind. I'd been too busy looking at Haidee's notes to pay attention. Instead, what we saw were literal holes in the ground; in many, fountains of hissing, steaming, boiling water were shooting up noisily. The humidity clawed at my skin, and the faint rumblings of the ground underneath us indicated that this area had been spitting out steam for a long time.

"Geysers," Haidee whispered. "That explains the presence of the sacred spring from a while back. They're hot enough to boil the skin of your back if you get caught in the spray."

That was a comforting thought. "Any chance we can turn around and find another way through?"

She nodded. "I think that's for the best. We can drive the rig north and see if there's someplace where these aren't as abundant. It might mess up our engines if we attempt to push our way through here."

I had no arguments there, and soon she'd shifted gears so that we were running parallel to the angry geysers in a tract of land as vast and as abundant as the forest had been.

"You think this was where some of Sonfei's men were killed?" I asked Haidee nervously, keeping a wary eye around us, in case there was something else lying in wait.

"If he just sent them to scout around their camp, I don't know if they made it this far out."

Lucky us. "What if there are geysers all over? What if there isn't a way around?"

"You're the one telling me I shouldn't be formulating any wild guesses when there's no proof, right?"

For close to two hours we headed north, the deadly fountains going on for miles with no end in sight. I wondered briefly if these had existed long before the Breaking, or if it was that cataclysm that had destroyed this landscape, too. I suspected the latter.

I was about to suggest trading places to let Haidee rest when she let out a loud whoop of joy. We had reached a stretch of land where nothing was angrily spewing forth water hot enough to kill. It was an odd plain where even a small bump would look out of place—it was far too even, far too unnaturally symmetrical. I caught a glimpse of shapes in the distance, which Haidee said were mountains.

"I'll take over," I offered.

"I can keep going," she insisted. "Just stay alert." She summoned a wave of Air, passing out of the rig and stirring up a faint breeze around us, before rippling out to survey the sky. "The air's too thick here, and I'm not able to gate as far as I'm used to," she said, her voice strained.

"You need rest."

"I'm fine."

"Stop the bullshit." I couldn't help it; the bitterness managed to seep out into words, after all. "You're stuck with me until we get to Brighthenge, whether you want me here or not, so at least let me be useful."

She looked down, biting her lip. "Arjun, that's not why I . . ."

I said nothing, realized belatedly that I was holding my breath.

She exhaled. "I'm sorry about the spring. I didn't run away because I was mad. I just didn't know what to say without . . ."

My spirits sank. "Can we talk about it after we get through this place in one piece?"

"Okay," she whispered.

"Let me drive."

She nodded again, the fight gone from her.

Our precautions made our travel slower, at a far lesser speed than we had gone through the forest. Every half hour or so Haidee made a perfunctory stop so she could reassess the wind, figure out if we were sharing space with something with enough sentience to kill us. There wasn't much time to rest in between but we didn't have much choice, and the look on her face told me she wasn't interested in another argument.

I scanned the area, but found nothing. The ground sank a little underneath us as we drove, not quite sand but still not completely solid. We didn't talk much for the rest of the ride, either. Haidee looked embarrassed, maybe a little ashamed, but I was trying my best not to feel anything, like she'd never spoken up.

We'd made about five or six of those stops when Haidee froze. "Wait," she said, her lips barely working. "Don't move. Don't say anything."

I didn't see anything amiss, if you considered the silent plains to be nothing amiss.

Haidee frowned. "There's movement in the wind—

something abnormally large, it feels like—and it's not coming from this rig or from either of us."

"Is it heading our way?"

"I'm trying to figure that out. It almost feels like it's coming in from all direc—" Her eyes widened. "Arjun, get us out of here. Get us out of here. Get us out of HERE—"

I'd already hit the gas before she'd finished the second sentence, and just in time. The rig lurched forward, just as a long, spiny, and heavily segmented tail burst out of the ground beneath us and lashed at the empty air where we should have been. I kept my eyes in front of me, turning my head briefly when I heard Haidee cry out in fear. It was only a glimpse, but it was enough for me to whip my head back around and slam my foot down, urging us faster.

It was an abomination. I'd seen my share of small scorpions out in the desert; chop off their poison-filled tails and what remained were tasty snacks, if grilled just right.

This scorpion, however, was exactly how nightmares were born. It was easily four times the size of the rig, and its pincers were more than enough to swallow either of us whole. Its deadly looking tail arched high over its head, and it lunged again, meeting empty ground as I swung us out of its way.

A fireball left Haidee's hands, hitting its side like a small explosion. It chittered, worrying at its injury as we placed more distance between us.

"What the hell," I panted. "How did it—"

There was another explosion, but this time it was us sailing through the air, and I had no idea what had made us airborne in the first place. I twisted the wheel hard to the right, felt Haidee frantically gating Air to push us back upright, and we managed to land back on the ground with us still on board. The left wheel on the back of the rig paid for our flight, though; I could feel it come off, making control tenuous.

Another scorpion had appeared right underneath us, even larger than its friend. By some stroke of luck we had avoided its tail when it sent us flying, but with one wheel down to scraps, there was no way we were going to be able to outrun two of them. I swore.

Both scorpions made for us, only to be hit full in the face by two separate blasts of my Howler. They veered away, the things I was optimistically calling their faces burning, and stumbled away. For a moment, I thought we would actually make it—and then saw more of those crawlers scuttling out of the sand behind them. By the dozens.

We'd tripped over their lair.

Haidee stood, eyes bright and pale.

"You're not healed yet!" I shouted. She hadn't attempted anything harder than steam since leaving the Liangzhu.

"Of course I am! You're the better driver—keep us out of their claws!"

I fired my Howler one last time, then complied, driving as fast as the rig allowed while blazing patterns shot through the air above me, aimed at the cadre of scorpions literally crawling out of the sandwork. I turned my head long enough to see Haidee shoot down one of the nearest scorpions with an impressive display of lightning she'd somehow summoned from the sky, frying the creature until it was a steaming pile of shell and carcass. That did nothing to deter the others, who continued to press on toward us.

For several minutes we stayed ahead, me making sure we didn't fuck up the rig any more than we already had, and Haidee concentrating on shooting down any scorpion that got too close. But soon I heard her gasp, felt the patterns wilting in the air before they made impact, and I knew she was weakening again.

"Haidee, take over." There must have been at least two dozen of those bastards after us now. Already one was lumbering up beside us, pincers snapping dangerously near our heads.

"Arjun, no . . . !"

"It won't take long." Grimly, I set my sights at the center of the writhing mob, allowing the patterns to fill up my Howler, waiting until it hit maximum capacity, and then taking in even more. "Ram its ugly ass."

"Arjun . . . !"

"Ram it!"

The scorpion lunged for us, and Haidee swerved hard to the right, ramming against its midsection. It squealed and fell away, but not before its tail swung down and stung me on the hip. Pain exploded—it felt even worse than when I'd lost my hand.

"Arjun!" Haidee was screaming.

Through the blinding agony, I could feel the spells swirling around us, gathering at the back of my neck—a danger signal telling me I'd filled the Howler too much, too fast, too close.

But there was no other choice.

I pulled the trigger.

And everything exploded.

Chapter Twenty-Three

ODESSA THE GATEBREAKER

☾

DURING QUIETER MOMENTS I RELIVED Gracea's downfall over and over again in my head—I had not known how pleasurable it could be, to take everything from the person you despised most.

I remembered the little croak she made when I took her vaunted gate. I could feel my shadow-warrior's teeth like they were my own, tearing into her flesh, and I swore I could taste her blood then, as sweet as the finest wine. My fingers flexed from the memory, as if they, too, were claws.

A pity. I should have done more damage, drawn it out a little more—but I had been too invested in her humiliation to risk her death.

There would be more opportunities to play later.

Gracea still screamed even after they bound her. Spat all manner of curses our way as she struggled and strained to break free. But the clerks had endured similar treatment before, from petty passive-aggressiveness to outright harassment. They were used to it; if I had my way, this would be the last time.

Because without her ability to channel, Gracea was powerless.

The rest of the Devoted were not as combative and acquiesced easily enough, sensing that the tide had turned in my favor. One by one, I took away their gates, and it was *so easy.* So easy to take something someone else had built their whole life around.

I had to. This wasn't politics anymore. This was justice.

It felt right.

I had won.

It was a logistical nightmare, traveling with a string of prisoners trailing in our wake, though we managed. The ship's crew were used to dealing with rowdy subordinates, and the occasional cuff on the back of the neck was enough to quiet most of the Devoted. Unlike the Starmaker, who had threatened to leave Lan out in the wildlands for nothing more than an insult—but I refused to stoop to her level. Goddesses ought to have standards.

She'd threatened Lan. Everyone else had stood aside and let her. They *would* pay, but in the time and manner of my choosing.

The goddess Asteria didn't have much in the way of standards, though.

Mother had lied to me.

Mother had manipulated me.

I was just as much her pawn as I was her daughter.

How much of my illness had been real, and how much of it a ploy to keep me close to her until the time came to wield me like a weapon?

How much of her concern about Lan and me was manufactured?

The rage grew.

I pushed it away, for now. Mother was in Aranth, and my anger was impotent here.

I cautioned my own people from taking too much of their frustration out on the Devoted, though I didn't reproach them *too* stringently when they disobeyed. It was easy to see which clerk had suffered their abuse under which particular Devoted. Lorila took particular glee in tripping over Filia's food rations, forcing her to scavenge for scraps in the dirt. Tracei kneed Gareen twice in the groin without ever pretending that it wasn't deliberate, and Miel had been shoved into some spiny bushes when my back was turned.

Janella had not been the only assistant Gracea had taken her frustrations out on, and many of the clerks handled the woman more roughly than was necessary, as did some of the ship's crew. Apparently, the Starmaker had wasted no time inflicting her own notions of discipline on the men and women she had hired for the *Brevity*.

"Filia liked to slap Lorila around," Janella murmured quietly to me one nightspan, as we ate our meal. "Literally. She was brutal a few nights before we left for this expedition—accused Lorila of stealing one of her brooches. Gareen wasn't the horrible lecher that Graham had been by comparison, but that's not saying much. He was the old man's protégé and had learned several of his perversions from him. You'd think he would have been satisfied by the female Devoted willing enough to give him their attention. Talk to the rest, and you'll find similar stories about the others."

"And no one thought to tell my mother?"

The girl bowed her head. "We tried, Your Holiness. But Asteria did little in the way of punishment, and they took it out on us worse when they found out."

I closed my eyes. Mother had known all along. "I will not make the same mistakes, Janella."

"It's why the others love you, Your Holiness. You have no idea how hard a life the gateless lead. We have always been treated as something less, and yet are expected to be grateful. Many would die for you if you'd asked."

"I hope it would never come down to that," I murmured, hiding my pleasure at her remark. This was how true Devoted should act.

I conducted my own experiment that night and ordered Sumiko over. I had made the decision not to strip her of her gates, unwilling to burden Lan with the role of our only healer. I had decided to spare Noelle as well. Still, I made sure to separate them from the rest of the prisoners. Noelle and Sumiko might not have been part of the Devoted's inner circle, but they might entertain some foolish honorable notion to free them, for Asteria's sake if nothing else.

I didn't want that. I didn't want to have to punish either Sumiko or Noelle.

Slyp had volunteered as a test subject, his trust in me absolute. He made no sound when I gently took away his gate again, closing his accessibility to the patterns that floated around him. "I am not sure what this is about, Your Holiness," the Catseye said nervously, watching the proceedings.

"Heal him, Sumiko."

"Pardon me?"

"Bring back his gate, allow him use of his patterns again. I would like to know the extent of a Catseye's healing."

The dark-haired girl obeyed. Her gold-and-silver eyes glowed, and I watched as the patterns stole back into Slyp, his eyes regaining their green aura. I nodded, satisfied. The Catseye could reverse my sanctions, bring Gracea and her ilk back their abilities.

All the more reason to kill Sumiko where she stood, before anyone else found out.

No. Lan could not do this on her own. Separating the Catseye from the prisoners should not be too difficult a task.

"I trust that you will tell no one about this, Sumiko. Or there will be repercussions."

She gulped. "Understood, Your Holiness."

Oh, Lan. The risks I take for you.

We resumed our trek toward the mountains. The skies had

lightened even further, now with an odd infusion of color beyond just blacks and grays. Depriving Gracea of her gate had come at a fortuitous time; we no longer needed her light to see around us.

Those twin peaks puzzled me at first; compared to the unnatural symmetry of the region, their odd, lopsided features with their awkward slopes stood out like sores. Their mismatched sides broke the monotonous perfection of the wildlands.

A long, terrible cry rang out, and it came from Lan's throat. She collapsed, shaking, and I dashed to her side immediately, Noelle not far behind. "They were there," Lan wept, clinging to my robes. "They were *dying* . . . !"

"Sumiko!" I called, and the other Catseye was beside me, hand raised. My love no longer thrashed but was breathing heavily, her eyes distant.

"She's remembering," Sumiko said soberly. "We need to give her time."

"Strike up camp here," I ordered. "Give her time to recover."

"It's not two mountains, is it?" Nebly whispered, stunned by the discovery. "It's one mountain split into two."

I didn't know what kind of abomination existed with the power to cleave nature down to its very foundations like that. The idea that we might encounter that very being once we reached that fearsome mountain had put everyone on edge.

But the worst of it was the darkness *that we could see emanating from* the mountain, even this far away.

The miasma around it was like a fog, thick and opaque,

hiding what I know we'd find—a gaping hole in the ground that stretched for thousands of miles on either side. It was said that the pit was endless, spiraling into the center of the world, where horrible things dwelled and shifted—some said straight down into the Cruel Kingdom itself.

Here lay the breach; the Great Abyss. This was what we had sacrificed so much to find.

"Surely you cannot think to enter that accursed place, Your Holiness," old Slyp uttered. Traveling to the breach sounded like an adventure until you finally saw the extent of the Abyss with your own eyes. We would not reach it for several more days, but I could practically feel the courage leaching away from my followers.

"That is my destiny, Slyp, and not one I would force on anyone else. We will figure out a more cohesive plan tomorrow. In the meantime, I require rest for everyone. The next nightspans will be our hardest."

Easier said than done. The Abyss cast a pall over the camp. I had not left Lan's side; the Catseye appeared to be in a catatonic state, and once my tent had been set up, I ordered Nebly and Sumiko to bring her there, intending to nurse her back to health myself. I no longer needed to order people to stand guard; my loyal shadows were more than competent for the task, and it was their presence that prevented Gracea and her ilk from protesting their imprisonment too much.

Once Sumiko was assured that Lan was as comfortable as we could make her, the others took their leave. Only Noelle remained behind. "Surely you won't let her travel to the breach with you in this condition?"

"I would never force her." I hadn't wanted to bring her anywhere near the Abyss, to be honest, but my hackles were raised around Noelle as of late. I didn't like that she was so close to Lan. So protective. I didn't like that she was more concerned for her safety when she should be prioritizing mine, as her job required. How well did they know each other? Had Lan shared the same relationship with Noelle as she had with her ranger lover?

The thought infuriated me. "Is there anything else?"

Noelle didn't budge. "If there's anything I can do to help—"

"I am more than capable of taking care of Lan on my own. I'll let you know when I require any more assistance."

It was an obvious dismissal, and yet Noelle lingered briefly, uncertain. I wanted to—

Kill her.

It was a quiet thought, but it was loud in the silence of my mind. It would be so easy. Take out the competition. Noelle had served the Devoted, and she could be a spy. She would do anything to hurt me, even if it meant harming Lan.

Killing her was the right choice.

Killing her would be so easy.

Killing her would mean that Lan never looked at anyone else but me.

"Very well, Your Holiness," Noelle finally said, unknowingly saving her own life. She glanced at the inert Lan, bowed, and took her leave, ducking out of the tent. I sank down beside my Catseye.

Had I really considered that? Killing my own steward? Lan would have never forgiven me. I couldn't have—

No. I'm the goddess. I could do anything I want, and no one would dare disobey me. It's only right to suspect Noelle. It's only right to suspect everyone.

I turned my attention to Lan, who was asleep. Remembering Sumiko's instructions, I tried to keep her comfortable with what meager blankets we had—we'd already stripped her of her light armor, leaving only her robes and breeches. I crawled onto the makeshift cot with her, finding comfort in her warmth. "Please," I whispered, though I wasn't sure if it was to her I was making the entreaty, or to something else on her behalf.

The nightmares came later. I found myself constantly jolting out of sleep, assailed by strange images of claws and lurking figures in the dark, but remembering little beyond the foul taste they left behind when I woke. Were these visions, too? Lan slumbered peacefully beside me, and I hoped none of the vague horrors that plagued me had found their way to her.

I got out and idled by the entrance of my tent, looking up at the stars. The sky over Aranth had always been nothing but a blanket of darkness, the constant storms too dark for those pinpricks of light to break through. My eyes traveled past them, into the dark fog on the horizon, that impenetrable mist. Something lay in wait for me there, but I was uncertain whether it would be another enemy—or a means to an end.

The seventh galla would be there. I knew it.

A demoness is what men call a goddess they cannot control. No truth was better spoken. Gracea and the Devoted had sought to bind me with tradition and authority, attempting to make me less than what I was. I had proved to them that I was so much more.

I looked around the camp, reassured by the quiet. None of the Devoted were misbehaving tonight. Deprived of their privileges, they huddled near the campfire, their hands temporarily freed though their feet remained bound. Surrounded by my people, they had nowhere to flee to.

Kill them anyway.

I had no reason to keep them alive—their attachment to my mother meant they would be more hindrance than advantage from here on out, destined to make trouble for me whenever the chance arose. It was a new order now. It was time to rid Aranth of Mother's machinations, and that started with her most trusted—

I raised my hands to my temples, fought to stop the thoughts from spinning, boring, tempting. What was wrong with me?

"Odessa."

Lan was awake, pale-faced and trembling but completely, utterly sane, and relief rose in me. "You worried me," I whispered.

"I worried myself." She stared at the ground, then back at me. "I remember," she said softly.

She let me bring her in, let me wrap my arms around her as

she sat, shivering on the cot, and I waited for her to form the words, though they took a long time to come.

"We were in the thick of that fog," she finally said. "The winds came at us from all sides, sometimes shifting direction mid-gust. I wanted to retreat. We had little visibility beyond a few feet, and I was worried we might stumble up against the Abyss and fall in. The others thought we should push on ahead, relied on me to make sure we wouldn't get lost.

"And I did. I led us right to the edge of that cliff. There was a strange stone there—a statue of sorts, except it had been split in half like the mountain had been. Yarrow was the bravest. He forged on ahead, tried to look into the—"

She stopped, and she began to weep. I held her, helpless and unable to think of anything else I could do to offer comfort, except wait for her crying to cease.

"They got him first. Ripped him up from throat to groin. He died instantly, toppling over into the chasm without another word. And then more of *them* crawled out. They weren't anything. They were shadows, but solid as you and me. Nothing we did stopped them. They murdered my team, until there were only three of us left—Merritt, Nuala, and me.

"There was one demon there. Taller than the others, with a crown on its head—or something that glittered like it. It stared at us for a long, long time. 'It is you who brings her to us,' it finally said, though I don't remember that it had a voice. It laid a hand on the broken statue, and it glowed. 'Choose your sacrifice,' it said then, and I realized it was asking me to *choose* between Merritt and . . ."

She trailed off, nails digging into her palms.

"I didn't," she finally confessed. "In the end, I didn't. I couldn't. But they did it, anyway. I couldn't choose, so they butchered them both. The statue worked as some kind of blood sacrifice. I tried to—Nuala was the closest, and I tried to—" Her voice broke, and she covered her face with her hands.

I rocked her slowly, murmuring soft sounds in her ear, wishing I could absorb her pain, her loss. "I'm so sorry, Lan."

"The statue—glowed. There was a flash of bright light. And then the Abyss was gone."

"And you found yourself on the outskirts of Aranth," I finished. A portal of sorts? Was it a coincidence that Mother had founded Aranth near where Lan had been found? Or had she unintentionally—or deliberately—used such magic herself, to escape the breach when the Breaking happened, as everything around her was being destroyed?

"Let's return to Aranth, Odessa," Lan begged. "I can't go through that again. I don't want to see the same thing happen to them that happened to my rangers."

I shook her head. "It will be different this time."

"No, it won't! Those monsters *want* you there!"

"Yes they do, and they knew sparing your life would convince me to go. They would not have gone through all this trouble only to kill me. I will finish this journey, but under no circumstances are you allowed to enter the chasm for any reason. Even if I have to bind you as I did the Devoted." I knew her soul, knew it during those precious minutes alone out there in the wildlands, when she had just been as eager for me as I had been for her, the both of us for once completely honest with the other. She loved me. But her past was caught up in these mountains, and it pulled at her like an invisible string.

"I cannot allow—"

"It's my decision, Lan. In the end, not even Mother knew what was best for me." *And perhaps Mother didn't want me to accept the galla's gifts after all,* I thought, and my fury grew hotter. She had been a coward who had failed her own ritual. Now it was my turn, and I refused to be beholden to anyone else. Not anymore.

A commotion outside shook me out of my thoughts—a wild scream. I dashed out of the tent, fearing the worst.

Holsett stood over Nebly, who lay unmoving on the ground, blood seeping into the soil from an injury on his head. A bloodied stone lay on Holsett's hand. "I didn't mean it," the Seasinger said dumbly. "He got in the way, and I wasn't . . ."

Sumiko was already there. She sank to her knees before the fallen boy, searching for a pulse, before giving up and sadly shaking her head at me.

I saw red. "What did you do?" Nebly had been nearly my age. All he had wanted to do was sail on a ship. So young, with his whole life ahead of him, like Cathei and Salleemae had been . . .

Holsett staggered back. "It was an accident, Your Holiness! I didn't mean for—"

"And yet you killed him all the same." I could make a guess. Holsett had found a way to cut himself free from his bonds, and he had been in the process of doing the same for Miel when Nebly had happened upon them.

It was easy to see what had happened. In a panic, realizing he had been caught, Holsett had struck him down without thinking.

He deserved no mercy.

Punishment was swift and deadly. It required no more than a thought, a wordless decision, and the shadows moved, descending on the Seasinger before anyone else could react.

Oh, the sudden strength that coursed through me, at the power I wielded! I could feel the shadows in my head, in my blood, braying for more pain, for more vengeance. In no other instant had I felt more alive.

There was very little noise, and that was almost a disappointment. Holsett was overwhelmed far too quickly to even cry out. In the end, a crimson stain on the ground was all that was left of him, and it occurred to me that in my pleasure I had neglected to urge restraint on my pets. Miel had fainted, a white figure on the ground, and many of the crew had doubled over, retching. Even serene Sumiko was trembling, her eyes wild.

A pity that it had been over so soon.

I crouched beside Nebly. I would raise him again in a few hours, once I had gotten my much-needed sleep. He would be the same Nebly as always, my trustworthy helmsman. I would give him a different kind of life now. "Holsett was lucky—he died quickly, with little chance to feel pain. A second attempt from anyone else, and it will take longer."

"What have you done, Odessa?" Lan whispered.

"Asserted my authority in a way they can finally understand, as I should have long ago."

"This is wrong."

I knelt down beside her. In full view of the others, I drew her close and kissed her hard on the mouth. "On the contrary," I purred. "I was born for this."

I turned toward the remaining Devoted. "You are not my enemies," I informed them coldly. "But I will kill each and every one of you if need be. Holsett's actions have shown me you can be traitors. Remember that."

I expected no protests, but it was Lan who spoke again. "Odessa. You can't!"

"They were rebelling against us. He killed Nebly. I had to put him down."

"But not like this. Odessa—"

My anger grew. "I *saved* you. They could have chosen to send you out into the wildlands as punishment. Gracea would have murdered you if she could, and found a way to excuse herself before my mother. I was being magnanimous, allowing them to remain my prisoners without any further sanctions. They broke my trust." Why couldn't she see that everything I did was for her sake?

But she shook her head. "Asteria would never have gone this far."

"She would have! Do you not see what these people are capable of? What *she* is capable of? I've been sick for almost all my life with an illness she *cultivated*! She knew that bonding with the galla would make me stronger! Instead, she hid them from me, allowed me to suffer, made me believe that Aranth's storms and the never-ending darkness were responsible for my condition!" I had realized this the instant I opened Janella's gate for the first time, saw how the trigger was at the same place the dark spot in my heart lingered. I wasn't sick at all—it was a requirement for the ritual.

"This isn't you, Odessa. It's those galla. Those gifts that they give you—they're what's warping your mind, making you do things you never would have on your own. You have to stop accepting them. What they take from you—it's far too high a price to pay for—"

"No!" I shouted. We would never have survived this long if it wasn't for those galla. I couldn't have brought Cathei and Graham and Salleemae back. I couldn't have kept the crew fed and alive without their offerings. I couldn't have gifted my people with their gates and punished the Devoted by taking away theirs. I wouldn't have had all these beautiful creatures under my command. "If you're not with me, Lan, then you're against me."

"Your Holiness!" Noe had stepped forward, blocking my path. "Your Holiness, you cannot possibly do this."

Patterns whipped around my hand and I thrust my arm out, but Lan shoved the steward away, exposing herself to my fury.

I stopped just in time. She stared at me, pained, but didn't back down.

I moved closer. I could take away her abilities as a Catseye in the space of a heartbeat. Of all the Devoted here, it was Lan who was the most dangerous, I knew. To remove her powers would have been the wisest course of action, no matter my feelings for her.

And still I hesitated. I lowered my hand.

"Slyp." At my command, the man stepped forward, surrounded by the rest of the crew members. They were still clearly frightened, and I knew I had to take back control of the situation, to assert my authority before they could think to follow Lan's lead. "See to it that they're comfortable, but don't let either Lan or Noelle out of your sight. Should Lan make an attempt to immobilize any of you with her Catseye abilities, I give you permission to incapacitate her without killing her."

"Odessa!" Noelle blurted out, trying to wrestle herself free from the others. Lan said nothing, but something in her expressionless face only made me angrier.

"Don't hurt her, though!" I added harshly. "Injure her, and you all will answer to me."

My people, at least, knew the wisdom of my words, nodding in agreement. They wouldn't dare disobey. I was their leader. I knew what was best for them.

I turned away, ignoring Noelle's pleas for me to listen as the rest of my followers led them away. Lan said nothing.

Only when I was finally, truly alone, tucked outside the

camp and surrounded by the shadows that continued to watch me without words, with nothing but loving obedience, did I collapse and weep.

I loved Lan. I truly did. But if I had to forsake her love to finish this ritual and get us all out alive, then I would. *I will.*

Chapter Twenty-Four

HAIDEE THE LIFE-GIVER

◯

HE WASN'T BREATHING.

As pristine as the plains had been before our intrusion, we had left them a smoldering heap of fire and frenzy. If any of those strange scorpions had survived my wrath, they were nowhere to be seen. Nothing twitched in the aftermath; only their twisted carcasses remained, bodies still jerking spasmodically even in death, tails swaying lifelessly in the eerie silence.

I didn't care. I would have slaughtered each and every one of them a thousand times over if it meant saving Arjun.

But he wasn't breathing.

"Don't you dare do this to me, you asshole!" Gating had sapped most of the strength I'd conserved after the Sand Sea, and it took the rest to drag him off somewhere the ground wasn't burning, nearer to the scorched but still-functioning sand rig. There, I fell to my knees and pressed my mouth against the wound on his side. Scorpions were toxic vermin, and the more poison I could draw out of him, the better his chances. When I thought I'd gotten all that I could, I sat up, wiping my mouth.

He still wasn't breathing.

I was no Catseye, but I'd seen Franck employ manual resuscitation techniques for some of his direr cases, and he'd demonstrated them enough times for me to remember how.

I wadded up some clothes and pressed them against his side, where the scorpion's tail had done the most damage. The bleeding wasn't as profuse as I initially thought, trickling out of two puncture marks on his waist where the pincers had struck deep, but not deep enough to be fatal. It shouldn't have been enough to kill him. He shouldn't be dead. The fight at the Sand Sea had knocked him around harder than this.

I rolled him over to his back, and pushed down hard against his chest with the flat of my palms, starting a rhythm and counting quietly in my head. One one-thousand, two one-thousand, three one-thousand, four. A pause while I held his nose and blew air noisily into his mouth, then repeated the whole process again. "Come on," I pleaded. "Please don't die on me here. You can't. You can't. Please!"

His eyes looked right past me, half-lidded and glazed, staring into an eternity of nothing. I redoubled my efforts, waiting for his chest to rise on its own, for him to blink back up at me, to recognize me and call me a fool for being so reckless. But there was nothing.

"Please, Arjun!" I was crying. Big fat drops of tears splashed onto his pale cheeks. I summoned all the patterns I could, gated them all into him. Nyx had performed the Gate of Life on her dead bird. I could do it, too. I could. I could. . . .

How long had I been working on him? A few minutes? More? Sometimes Franck could bring back a patient after as long as five minutes, but sometimes he would stop and shake his head and say there was nothing more he could do. . . .

I refused to give up. I worked on him frantically, even as the minutes ticked by and stretched into what must have been an hour, and then another. Somewhere in my grieving mind, I must have thought that if I kept it up no matter how long it took, there was a chance he would survive. It took a long time for that derangement to fade, and my faith along with it.

I punched his chest, almost believing he would sit up and yell at me for the temerity. His body jerked up slightly from the force, then settled back down.

"You can't," I whimpered, burying my head against his bloodied shirt. He was dead. He'd been raised to hate me, but somehow I'd talked him into giving his life for me all the same. "Don't leave me alone. You said you're here to make sure I don't trip into some damned hole or let some monster rip me to shreds, remember? You said I wasn't going to survive on my own, and you were right! And now you're going to leave me to fend for myself without you? You're going to make me fall for you, and then pull this on me?" Another fresh wave of tears. I crawled up his body, cupped his face with my hands.

"Please," I begged, pressing a kiss against his cheek. "Please look at me. Look at me when I tell you I'm in love with you.

Yell at me for as long as you like, call me an idiot from here to Brighthenge and back. Just . . . let me tell you that I love you. Tell me you know that. Please."

But there was nothing. And I knew then, in that bleak, horrifying moment, that he was gone.

I reached up and gently closed his eyes. Then I settled myself against his side, in much the same way I'd tucked myself against him for so many days as we crossed the desert, and cried until I had nothing left.

I must have fallen asleep at some point, because when I woke the skies were darker than I first remembered. I was confused for a moment, staring straight up from my position on the ground. I had never been able to look right up into the sun before; it had hurt too much, and those who were both stubborn and reckless enough to persist irrevocably ruined their eyesight and eventually went blind.

Except the sun here wasn't as hot as it was out east. I was used to it being in the center of the heavens, but the farther west we traveled, the lower it had descended behind us instead of hanging directly over our heads. A gradual darkness loomed up from the opposite direction, a faint suggestion of gray and black hues that told me somewhere farther toward the horizon was that phenomenon called night.

I could see faint wisps of smoke—clouds?—dragging through the air, drifting in the direction of the mountain.

I turned my head to look back at Arjun. Still caught in the fog before fully waking up, my first thought was that he was still asleep. He was still so warm to the touch. Then reality hit me, and a tight, horrible pain gripped my chest.

"We're almost there, Arjun," I whispered to him, gently pushing back some of the long hair that had fallen over his face. So close; we'd been so close to making it.

But I was still too tired. An attempt to summon a whisper of Air failed, and even that small act of gating made my head spin. Somewhere in the back of my mind I knew I had to make a choice. I had to bury Arjun somewhere, or perhaps cremate him, or find some way to bring him along for the rest of the journey.

But the thought of giving him back to the earth, of allowing buzzards and insects to consume the rest of him, brought another fresh wave of hurt. I was not yet strong enough to offer him the dignity of a quick burning, and it said much about my agonized mind that the third option sounded the most appealing, that bringing a corpse along with me actually sounded like the sanest, most sensible course of action.

A corpse. I began to cry again.

I hoisted his body back inside the rig and drove aimlessly for the next two hours, away from the stink of the dead scorpions, until I was too tired to drive any farther.

I was feeling cramped, so I dragged Arjun back out again, huddling with him against a large boulder. With nothing better to do, I watched the sky, taking in more peculiar features I'd never noticed before; the dark streaks of ash that stretched out in the horizon before us, a stark difference from the lighter tints of silver overhead. There I could make out the faint outlines of another shape that was as round as the sun, but with none of its heat.

"I've seen that before," I whispered to Arjun, "in books. They called it a moon, and it acts like a light when the days are dark, to keep the world from complete blackness. The world no longer turns, but they say the moon still exists, although the sun's too bright for us to see it in our part of the world. I would prefer the sun to its absence. Did anyone survive in this part of the world, I wonder? If we could live through the worst of the sun, I think some people must have survived the worst of the darkness, too. I would have gone out of my mind, living without light."

I kissed his cheek again; his skin was cool, but it wasn't as cold as I expected, and it made it easier to pretend. We'd replenished our water at the spring, so I dampened a fresh cloth and started to clean his face. I couldn't stand for him to look so dirty.

"I think I love you," I said again; if I said it enough times, perhaps somewhere out there his soul could hear me. "I can't place exactly when or where it happened, but it crept up on me, the way I might read a book and know within the first few chapters I would fall in love with it before I'd reached the very end. Was it across the Sand Sea, when you were such a grouch to the dolugongs even when it became clear to me that you couldn't stand to see them hurt? Or was it much later, when we were burying Parrick and you looked at me like . . . Or was it even earlier, when you found me sitting on the aspidochelone?

When you told me you were going to kill me, but didn't? I liked the look of you even then, and I was so mad when all you cared about was shooting me."

I pressed another small kiss to the corner of his mouth, his death making me bolder, then drew away. "I'm sorry," I whispered. "I didn't know how to ask. You never seemed like you were interested, except maybe that day we buried Parrick, or at the hot spring, when you . . ." A sob found its way out of my throat as I moved the cloth down to his neck, pushing back his collar to clean as much of his skin as I could.

"I *liked* how you looked at me then. Like maybe you weren't immune to me, either."

I moved over him and pressed against his injured side again, wiping away what I could of the blood. "I would have liked to keep touching you," I whispered, finally admitting out loud the one thing I'd refused to acknowledge that day. "And I think that's why I ran. I didn't want things to be weird between us, especially if I'd guessed wrong and you were never interested. But if I'd had more courage that day . . . I would have let you . . ."

A sudden rattling sound filled the air, and I leaped back in alarm. My first thought was that some new creature had stumbled into our makeshift camp. It had come from somewhere much closer—

From Arjun?

Still wary, I pressed my fingers tentatively against his chest. Was it my imagination, or could I feel, just barely, the very faintest of a heartbeat?

"Arjun?"

That odd deathlike rattle again. I was sure this time it had come from his mouth. I straddled him quickly, pressing my ear against his heart, battling a sudden surge of hope.

"Hai-dee." It was my name, a barely understandable whisper. The muscles underneath me shifted, and Arjun grimaced twice before his eyes opened.

I couldn't speak. We stared at each other for several long moments while my mind worked to produce thought. I opened my mouth.

I burst into tears.

"Idiot." His voice was more croak than words, sandpapery to the ears. But he was talking, and he was breathing, and he was living, and oh sweet Mother, Arjun!

I fell on top of him, unintelligible sounds bursting from me as I babbled past my tears to try and form more coherent sentences.

He calmly waited until I was done and then spoke again, sounding stronger. "I heard you."

No. That was impossible. I hadn't thought about the whys and hows of his surviving just yet, but he'd had no heartbeat, and he hadn't been breathing.

"Paralyzed," he growled. "Damn scorpion . . ."

Oh. I'd read about animals who used paralyzing agents. I'd assumed poison but hadn't thought about this possibility.

"Faded in and out," he mumbled, "but heard you most of the time."

And then I realized what it was exactly that he had heard,

and I turned beet red.

I felt him shift, his legs moving slightly and showing he was gaining back his mobility, though he was still sluggish. "Stop trying to get up!" I barked, struggling to hide my humiliation. He wasn't supposed to know. There was no possible way he could have told me before now that he could hear me, but I felt betrayed all the same.

I stalked toward the rig and retrieved a small canteen full of water, returning and forcing him to drink some. "And stop talking." I was embarrassed, but the last thing I wanted to do after his horrific ordeal was yell. "And stop squirming around."

"No."

My irritation grew. I welcomed the familiarity of it, the unexpected relief fighting him gave me. "As far as I'm concerned, you've just returned from the dead, and I've got no patience for—"

His arms circled my waist, pressing me down against him. "I thought"—Arjun's voice was deeper, a new raw timbre, but even that paled in comparison to the heat in his eyes as he looked up at me—"that you wanted to keep touching me."

He'd never sounded like that before. Possessive and hoarse and wanting, and a million dark promises in those brown eyes. "Yes," I whispered. It would have been pointless to deny it.

"Should've splayed you underneath me in the hot spring like I wanted, then."

It was my turn to stop breathing.

His lips curved. With a strength I didn't know he still had, he pulled me closer until his body covered mine, and then kissed me—fully, hungrily, roughly.

I gasped into his mouth, but it was like his near death had unleashed a hunger in Arjun I couldn't comprehend. His hand roamed up my back, and his knee came up, carefully nudging my legs apart, so he could press himself more fully against me. A fresh jolt of excitement fizzled through my body, and I stifled another gasp.

"Yes, you sweet idiot." He broke the kiss long enough to growl the words out at me. "Couldn't move my blasted limbs, but there was one part of me that had no damn trouble this whole time." His hands found my hair, fingers winding through the locks. "And your damn hair, you know that? Ruined me the first time I laid eyes on it."

"I'm s-sorry," I stammered, not sure what I was apologizing for.

He shifted me higher so he could start on my neck. "Gotten used to it. Waking up to see you curled beside me left me a mess most mornings anyway."

"You mean—is that why you started sleeping outside the rig—"

"Why else? I thought I'd been rejected." A new note entered his voice, quiet and teasing. "I even prayed to your damned mother while I was paralyzed, you know. I was so desperate that I prayed to your mother, and to you, that you wouldn't bury me or set me on fire while I was still alive and helpless in my own body to stop it. And if I heard you right, you were more than willing to touch me more if I'd made my move back then. You gonna back down from those words, Your Holiness?"

A part of me wanted to, the part that was used to our constant fights and belittling, the part of me that had grown to enjoy our constant needling of each other. But I remembered the horror and the anguish of the last several hours, and while there was a lilting, cajoling cadence to his words, some of the wariness had returned to his eyes, like he wasn't ready to believe I could announce this so easily to his face now that I knew he was alive.

"No, you idiot," I breathed, and bent down to kiss him just as roughly as he had kissed me.

It took several minutes for the adrenaline to wear off and for Arjun's strength to leave him again. "Damn it," he snarled miserably, trying to move and only managing to lift his arms and legs an inch off the ground. "This isn't funny."

"It's a little funny." I wasn't quite at peak health either, but I managed to dump his sorry ass in the back seat of the rig, where he could lounge around the larger space, with the bags that had survived our journey as his makeshift cushions. "Comfy?"

Arjun responded with a grunt, and some faint rustling as he struggled to find a better position. "We can start driving tomorrow," he said roughly. "Come here."

Obediently, I crawled over to him, snuggled against his uninjured side. Arjun hadn't wanted anything for his wound, but I'd wrapped a fresh piece of cloth over it anyway, so as not to risk any infections. I'd also taken a look at his chest, worried that I'd gone overboard with my attempts to resuscitate him, but beyond his complaints of a faint soreness, nothing seemed to be broken.

He kissed me again. "It was the damned whale," he said quietly. "I think I wanted you almost from the moment you looked down your nose at me from atop that aspidochelone of yours, with those stunning bright eyes. It made me angry."

"As early as that?"

He shrugged. "You were right. I had no reason to follow you out here. I could explain away the mirage if I really wanted to, and Mother Salla wouldn't have forced me to go. But I couldn't walk away and see you hurt. And I knew for a fact you had no head for danger or anything remotely sensible—"

I punched him lightly on the arm. "I wasn't that naive."

"Naive enough that I wanted to protect you anyway." He looked away. "Kept pushing it aside until the Liangzhu," he admitted roughly. "When I thought you'd died at the Sand Sea—I thought I was going to lose my mind. When I saw that Sonfei had saved you, I wanted to kiss him for it and at the same time punch him because I thought he was going to keep you prisoner."

"I'll be sure to tell him that if we ever meet again," I teased lightly, and he shot me a sour look. "I . . . I thought you'd rejected me."

He laughed dryly. "I'd thought you'd rejected *me*. You ran like you couldn't wait to be as far away from me as possible."

I blushed. "I was seeing more of you than I knew I should.

413

A lot more. I didn't know how to react."

He snaked an arm around me. "Was that . . . did you ever, uh, kiss anyone before . . . ?"

I flushed harder. "You know I didn't. But I know you did."

A pause. "Yeah," he admitted quietly. "As I said, nothing serious. I liked Lisette well enough, but we never wanted something permanent."

"Why did she move away?"

He sighed. "Hellmakers raided their camp. Wiped out half of them; she was one of the few to get out. They had to leave for somewhere safer, but we never heard from them again after that." He didn't say anything more, and I understood, leaning my head against him. It explained why his hatred for the Hellmakers extended beyond their just being cannibals.

"I suppose," he said finally, "that once you get back to the city, your mother's going to want to foist one of those lordlings on you."

"I have a choice."

"Somehow, I don't think a desert boy's gonna make it through the official selection process."

"I don't care. I'm not interested in anyone else."

"Not even your Vanya?"

"Are you jealous?"

He scowled. Sweet Mother, he *was*.

I couldn't stop grinning. "He's nice, but too *refined* for my tastes. I like rude guys."

He snorted. "You know we're gonna have to deal with it sooner or later."

"I know. I don't want to deal with it now, though."

"Fair enough."

"But if Mother knows that—that I like someone else, she might . . ."

His laughter grew louder. "She'd have my head on a stake is the more likely possibility."

"I won't return until she accepts you. Your clan will have to take me in."

"They'll be more welcoming of you than your mother will be of me, at least." He stroked my hair. "Are you sure, Haidee? I can't offer much. You deserve better things."

"I've had better things, and I don't want them. I want to—" It was clear that neither of us were in any shape for anything, but I turned red all the same.

"You deserve more than a fumble in the back of a rig, Haidee. You deserve a real bed, at least, and a good several hours for me to explore you proper. Or maybe we ought to head back to that hot spring and do it right this time. Unconsecrate the waters." He grinned cockily. "Blushing again?"

"Go to sleep!" I shot back, trying to ignore the lightning bolt that had fizzled through my core at his words, and tapped him on the head with a book for good measure. He laughed and kissed me some more, but exhaustion was quick to take over and soon he was fast asleep. It took me longer to follow suit.

Things changed in the days that followed. I fixed the wheel with some metal scraps and we resumed our trek heading west, but now that there were no more secrets between us, we were prone to touching each other, and kissing often. Most of the paralyzing poison was out of Arjun's body by the next day, and his staggered steps and clumsy movements evened out the day after that, until he could walk and drive the rig like he used to. I insisted on doing most of the driving, because his hands still spasmed every now and then and his grip trembled when he tried to line up a shot, to gauge his accuracy.

Without the barrier of secrets between us, I was surprised and thrilled by how affectionate Arjun truly was. Every now and then he would throw looks my way when he thought I wouldn't see, making me ache with strange sensations. We hadn't talked about the spring since he'd woken, and there was an unspoken agreement between us that it would be a matter to deal with after we'd reached Brighthenge.

There was . . . a *lot* of kissing. Making out. Hours when we should be sleeping, instead of stretching out side by side, my insides turning to mush wherever his fingers trailed.

I couldn't stop touching him.

But despite his suggestive promises, Arjun was going slowly, a source of both gratitude and frustration for me. Did I want him to go further? I didn't want to rush things. I knew he was right. But sometimes logic fell to the wayside whenever he was within lip distance.

By the fifth day we had reached the end of those endless plains.

It was Arjun who was driving, and he halted the rig, standing to get a better look. He whistled softly. "Look at that."

Puzzled, I stood up beside him. Not far from where we stood was a series of small dwellings scattered haphazardly before us.

"A village." Arjun was stunned. "It's a village."

But something else took my breath away entirely. "Look beyond them," I whispered, pointing at the two mountains looming above us—no, *one* mountain, I realized, split down its very middle to become two. The dark clouds spiraled in between those peaks, funneling down into a strange break in the ground—a wide canyon that went on for thousands of miles on either side, encased in heavy smoke and a thick fog of darkness.

"The Great Abyss, Arjun. We're finally here."

Chapter Twenty-Five

LAN THE CAPTIVE

———————— ☾ ————————

"WE NEED TO DO SOMETHING," Noelle said quietly, without moving her lips enough to attract attention from our jailers.

I'd worked and fought alongside her long enough to know what *something* meant: overwhelm Odessa's followers, knock out their leaders, take back control of the expedition. Strategy-wise, it was a viable plan. It would take years for the newly gated to gain the experience necessary to defeat us, even out-numbered as we were.

I shook my head slightly, and Noelle's frown grew.

"I know you don't want to go against Odessa, Lan, but we can't let her continue. She's just as inexperienced as the rest of them."

"You forget we're talking about more than just a mutiny." I stared pointedly down at the ground. Odessa had grown more crops to feast on, and they'd ripened in the space of a few hours, without the need for sunlight or water to flourish. What the rest failed to see was the slowly rotting ground underneath the harvest, partly covered by the newly sprung grass.

"Odessa is"—the words stuttered in my throat, but I swallowed hard, again and again, until I mustered enough strength to form the words through my grief—"dangerous. The galla have warped her mind. And then there are the shadow creatures to worry about. To go against her is to go against them, and I'm not sure we can fight them all off." I could overpower Odessa the same way I had in the past—by using my ability to render her unconscious. But I had no way of knowing if her control over the shadows would waver. Without her influence, they could attack the camp, and I couldn't risk that.

"So we do nothing?"

"We do nothing for now. Odessa shows no inclination to do the other Devoted any injury. Let's not give her more reasons to."

"No talking!" Bergen said sharply, poking at my side with a stick.

We were moving again. The shades of Cathei, Graham, Salleemae, and Nebly continued to follow quietly in our wake, but accompanying them were the strange creatures of the wildlands, shadows that shifted in and out of vision. Odessa's new Devoted were no longer afraid; they treated these monsters as proof that she was their true leader. I couldn't blame them. Their survival was now tied to Odessa's ability to carry them through the wildlands safely; it was in their best interest to believe.

No other beasts had confronted us on our journey so far,

and it looked like we were reaching the end. The changes were gradual, but I noticed soon enough that the sky was beginning to lighten, color leaching through the clouds more vividly than I had ever seen before. The endless plains ended at the foot of the broken mountain, its peaks shrouded in even more darkness and fog as a stark contrast to the heavens' now-softer hues.

I started to shake without realizing it, until Noelle placed her hand on my shoulder and slowly squeezed.

My fellow rangers had died under the mountain's shadow.

"We'll make camp for now," Odessa said, apparently unimpressed by the sight. "And enter the mountain in the nightspan after next."

After what had happened to Holsett, the Devoted were watched at all times. Their hands were still bound, though they could walk on their own. Janella had assumed leadership of the Devoted and responsibility for the prisoners, with Odessa's approval. Asteria's followers talked very little, though Gracea's cajoling and threats more than made up for their silence, quieting down only after Andre cuffed her on the back of the head hard enough to draw blood. As odious as Gracea had been to me in the last few weeks, I saw no difference between their treatment of her and her previous treatment of them.

I was treated far better than the rest of the Devoted, though I was closely watched when Odessa wasn't around. The goddess frequently insisted that I be invited to her tent for company, and she would keep up constant chatter about our journey and speculation about what we might see upon reaching Brighthenge.

The conversations were not always pleasant. Every nightspan found her in worse shape than the one before, and it became clear that she wasn't sleeping. Dark circles formed under her eyes, and her behavior grew even more erratic. That someone from within the camp might come along and usurp her authority became a growing obsession she felt she needed to defend against; sometimes she would accuse me of preparing to betray her, only to become apologetic and tearful a few seconds later, begging forgiveness for ever doubting me.

She said nothing about Holsett's death, acted like nothing had changed between us. She talked about finding a way to change her mother's mind, finding a way to continue our relationship without interference. I said relatively little, allowed her the fantasy. Whatever her mood, she made no move to touch me like she had in the past.

The galla had corrupted her. I repeated that over and over in the solace of my mind. The galla had corrupted her, and Odessa wasn't herself. I was afraid of what might happen when we finally reached the Abyss—what would the galla demand of her there? What more could they ask of her?

And the closer we drew to the Abyss, the more effort I had to exert to keep myself from falling apart. As destructive as our relationship was becoming, at least her nearness chased away the nightmares that threatened to overwhelm me.

She sent for me again the next nightspan, another invitation to have dinner with her, and as always I obeyed without protest.

"We're close," she told me, smiling, pushing her fresh

vegetables around in her bowl. "So close I can practically feel the energies spilling out of the chasm. Don't you feel it? So much power, running through the breach? Will I see the seventh and final galla there, do you think? What will it offer me this time around? Surely there is a reason they allow me this much strength, this much control over their creatures."

I said nothing.

"I'm sorry I have to keep you under watch until then," she continued like I had spoken. "I have to look impartial. You're a Devoted in name only, but the rest of my followers don't make that distinction." She smiled sympathetically at me. "I know this is the most difficult leg of the journey for you. I wish I knew how to make this easier for you."

Reject that last galla, I thought. *Give up all the powers you've accumulated, and return to being the Odessa I know and love.* "You can't, Your Holiness."

She frowned. "My name is Odessa. Must we go back to being so formal? Tomorrow will be the most difficult, I think. I may wield an army of galla, but there could be other surprises waiting here. I'd like to figure out more about this mysterious portal that allowed you to return to Aranth. Janella and the others had been concocting theories, and some sound unbelievable, but after everything I've seen out here, anything seems possible."

She abandoned her bowl to pace the length of the tent. "I've stopped sleeping altogether, you know," she admitted softly. "Every time I try to close my eyes, something tells me to remain awake, to be vigilant. I'm not foolish enough to trust the galla just because they've given me power. I don't need to sleep to have waking nightmares. Nightmares where the shadows will attack if I allow my control to slip just a little. Nightmares where they consume the whole camp. I don't want that to happen. I refuse to let you witness another massacre when I know I can make a difference. When everyone else is counting on me.

"I tried to grow more food earlier today, for everyone. But the ground refused. It told me I could only poison it the once." She laughed, a curiously high-pitched sound. "In every land I will ever walk, the harvests shall grow for me once, and then never again. Do you know how I suffer, knowing that the Earth rejects me even when I strive to save it? No, it is not the galla's fault. No, not their fault. It is the rules of the ritual, is all. Only the rules.

"You understand that, don't you?" she asked, turning to me in appeal. "I work so hard to make sure no one else has to die out here. I failed Cathei and Salleemae and Nebly, though not completely. They're still with us. All I need is something to bring them back completely; then I won't have failed at all. You understand that, right?"

"Yes," I said, shaken, for lack of anything better to say, watching with horror as Odessa slowly came undone before my eyes.

"Mother never thought I would be competent enough. That's why she imprisoned me in the Spire all this time, and never gave me a chance to prove my worth. She only thought me important when the time came to complete the Banishing. How foolish I've been, to believe her! Mother couldn't do it on her own. She needed my strength, my skill. I could have completed the Banishing all on my own, but for years she had me believe that I was weaker than her. That I wasn't as important!" Her hand whipped through the air, and her bowl broke. I started, but she didn't even notice.

"I'll make her see," she seethed, staring at nothing, her hands balled with patterns of Air still spinning around her fists, seeking out another target. "I'll show her, and I'll show everyone. I'll undo the Breaking and turn everything back to the way it was. To the way it should be."

I wet my lips, trying to find words to pacify her, and momentarily coming up with nothing. "Your Holiness . . ."

"It's Odessa!" she shouted. The whole tent shuddered. "Why won't you call me by my name?!"

"Odessa," I responded quickly. "My love." She calmed down visibly, a small smile on her face at the endearment, and my heart hurt. The girl before me wasn't the Odessa I loved. How could I bring that Odessa back? "I believe you'll find a way to heal the world. I have no doubts about that. But even goddesses need sleep. Or you'll be in no shape to enter Brighthenge tomorrow."

She shook her head. "I can't. Every time I try, I know they'll find a way to break free. They're always whispering, taunting me in my mind, telling me that I am not strong enough. They all wait, you know. Just waiting for me to make a mistake so

424

they can attack. The galla wait for me to weaken, to lose my grip on them. Gracea waits too, watching for a weakness in my armor so she can take back leadership. Mother waits, because she always waits."

"Gracea knows she's been defeated, Your Ho—Odessa. She won't escape."

"It doesn't matter," she said bleakly. "How far can I trust my own faithful, Lan? They may not have sworn to serve Mother with the same fervor as the Devoted have, but they turned against her all the same. If I could lure them away with honeyed words, then what would stop them from turning against me, toward someone who carries speech more sugared than mine? Even Noelle, who I thought served me out of friendship and respect, thought it would be easy to rise against me."

Her eyes softened when she gazed back at me. "You're the only one I can trust," she confided, settling down beside me. "You knew me when I wasn't a goddess, when I was just that odd girl who read romances. Do you remember? You thought I was a merchant's girl, a girl who never carried the weight of the world on her shoulders, but you loved me all the same. There is no one else here who could say that—that they thought I was unimportant, and loved me in spite of it."

"Odessa."

"Maybe you should call me Ame. It reminds me of better times. Oh sweet Mother, Lan. I wish we could go back to those days."

"Odessa, please. Get some rest." Sometimes I wished we

could go back, too. But I didn't want someone that Odessa pretended to be; I just wanted Odessa. But not like this, either.

Her expression changed, grew frightening. It was almost like a devil looked out from behind her eyes. "Why? So you can ally them against me, to destroy me when I'm at my most vulnerable? Is that what you really want to do, Lan? Play with my feelings only to betray me in the end? Is that what they're telling you to do? Is that what Gracea ordered you to do?"

"Odessa!" It was so hard to do this—to beg her every night, trying to find the girl behind the growing madness. "Odessa, please! You know I would never do that!"

Her eyes filled with tears. "I'm so sorry. Why did I say that? You have no idea how hard it is for me, Lan. If I could find someone else to take this away from me, I would. But there isn't anyone. I can protect everyone. But I'm so tired . . ." She trailed off, her eyes on the broken wooden bowl on the ground, where the rest of her dinner lay. "Please, go away," she said sharply. "I don't want you to see me like this."

"Odessa."

"Just go." Already she had drawn back the tent flaps, summoning Slyp to take me back, and I knew there was nothing more I could do tonight.

"There is a sickness in her mind, I believe," Sumiko told me quietly, as we resumed our trek the next nightspan toward the foot of the mountain. "It's a strange disease that isn't easy to diagnose and heal."

"I've touched her many times, and found nothing," I protested. "If her mind is ill, why can't my touch affect it?"

"Some sicknesses not even a Catseye can heal. For now, the strange blackness around her heart is contained, but I believe it is her mind and not her body that is being attacked."

"By the galla?"

Sumiko shrugged helplessly. "Certainly her condition has been exacerbated since she first came into contact with those galla, but her symptoms are very similar to some I've encountered in the past. Impossible mood swings, unexplained shifts in her emotions, uncontrollable anger at times . . . does she still display sexual aggression toward you?"

I turned red. "She isn't letting me touch her, if that's what you mean."

"That means she still has some control." Sumiko pursed her lips. "I would need more time to analyze her further—she isn't allowing the Devoted much contact with her, so it's difficult to know for certain without your observations."

"I don't think we have much time for that."

"I know." She looked at me. "And how are you faring?"

I knew what she meant. As we approached the mountain, I kept my eyes on the ground, holding my breath every time some unusual rock formation or strange shrub graced our path and releasing it once I realized that it wasn't a corpse. "I'm good."

"No, you're not. Would you like to talk about it?"

"Not right now, no."

"Over there!" came a cry from the front. Odessa gestured

at her faithful to fall back while she hurried forward, her eyes eager.

A thick, impenetrable-looking fog surrounded the Abyss, so that much of the wide expanse was still hidden from view. The sky was light now, but there was a peculiar, dead emptiness that surrounded the chasm, cloaked in its own black miasma that no natural phenomenon could breach.

"We're here," Odessa whispered, eyes aglow. "We're finally here."

"Is this what you saw before?" Noelle whispered to me.

"Yes," I said, my voice dull.

"Stay back," the goddess commanded.

"That's not what Asteria commanded us to do, Your Holiness," Gracea implored her. "Our mission was to find a way to access the breach, and return to report our findings to—"

"Janella," Odessa said calmly, interrupting her.

Without pause, the other girl lifted her hand and casually backhanded the Starmaker across the face, sending her crashing onto the ground. "You were warned not to speak unless you were spoken to," she snapped.

Odessa turned to me. "Where were you attacked again?"

"Along the edge," I whispered.

"And did you find the remains of any temple?"

"No. We had little time to explore the area before we were ambushed."

Odessa paused, studying the Abyss carefully. "I shall investigate it up close."

"Your Holiness!" Noelle, Janella, and even Gracea all voiced their protests at once.

"I have the best chance of surviving whatever lies beyond that canyon. You are all in enough danger by just being here."

"Your Holiness," Windshifter Halida gasped out. "If we were all armed with our gates, we would stand a better chance of surviving."

"Prisoners have no privileges," Slyp barked.

"This is a death sentence for us!" Gracea shrilled.

The old man shrugged. "Then I would advise staying close. If necessary, you will be provided weapons, but that is the extent of Her Holiness's generosity."

"This is a dangerous task," Odessa informed her followers quietly. "And I will not force you to volunteer. But I shall enter the Abyss. If you are willing to take a chance with me, come forward."

For a moment, no one moved. Then Janella did, her eyes fervent, and soon Lorila, and then Andre followed suit.

"The rest of you, be on guard," Odessa told the others. "And I want a force ready to come at the first sign of trouble."

"I'll go with you," I said.

"No."

"Odessa—!"

"I won't put you through that again, Lan." Odessa crooked a finger, and the shadows materialized around her, eager to do her bidding. "I will not go unprepared. You have nothing to worry about."

"You're not going to do this without me! I'm coming with you!"

She approached me then, smiling gently and looking so much like the old Odessa that my heart ached. "Lan, my love," she said, laying a hand on my cheek. "I'm sorry, but you will not."

And then I blacked out.

"About time you woke up," Noelle said dryly, as I struggled to sit up. "Though you didn't miss much."

"Don't move so quickly," Sumiko cautioned, placing a hand on my shoulder.

"What happened?" We were still there by the foot of the mountain, and the crew still stood guard over us and the other Devoted, but the goddess herself was gone.

"Couldn't stop her," Noelle said, nodding toward the Abyss. "I don't think anyone could have."

She'd taken me out the same way I'd taken her out on the *Brevity*. I shook my head, trying to clear the cobwebs from my mind. "How long was I out?"

"No more than an hour."

"And why aren't we going after her?"

"She left behind enough of her people to make fighting our way through rather difficult." The steward sounded calm as always, but there was no mistaking the edge to her voice. "Our best bet would be to wait and see if anyone sends back word." She glanced at me. "But I don't think that's something you're interested in doing."

"Hells, no," I growled. They might be at an advantage, but I wasn't going to be stopped by some inexperienced chits still learning to gate. Janella was the most dangerous of them all, but she'd left for the Abyss with Odessa. One less threat to worry about.

Of the ones who remained behind, I'd singled out Slyp as having the best mastery of his gates. They'd been smart enough to separate most of the Devoted from each other, to stop them from scheming when their backs were turned, but if I played it right, then I wouldn't need many to overpower them all. Much to my relief, the undead Devoted and the shadows that hovered just beyond our camp were gone as well.

"I don't know if Her Holiness intended it," Noelle whispered, "but all the shadows and the undead Devoted went with her."

That was the goddess's first mistake. Another was allowing Sumiko to speak to me. I focused on the other Catseye. "You know that Odessa's going to be in danger at the breach, right?"

Sumiko nodded, looking worried. "I know what you intend. But I cannot recommend you entering the Abyss, Lady Tian-lan."

"Not a—" I paused, took a breath. "You know I have to."

"Then what do you propose?"

It all worked rather well, if I may say so myself.

"Stay away from me, you liar!" Miel screamed, shoving Gareen away with a knee and attracting the attention of everyone in camp.

431

"What did I do?" The poor Mistshaper sounded sincerely confused.

"I'm sick and tired of you messing with the other girls!" the girl shouted. "You pay me compliments like you care about me and say we could be more, but now I learn you said the exact same things to Halida and Filia. And you have the absolute gall to say you love only me?"

The normally confident Gareen was stumbling, "I—of course I meant it, I would never have—"

"What?" Filia shouted, struggling to her feet despite her bound hands. "You told me that I was the only one you ever loved!"

"You damned liar!" Halida screeched. "You told me you would propose when we return to Aranth!"

Most of Odessa's loyal Devoted had moved toward the fighters, and I saw Sumiko scamper nimbly to Gracea's side amid the commotion. It took a good amount of effort to pull the girls away from Gareen, and despite knowing what was going to happen, I couldn't help but feel amused at the sight, even as I inched closer to Aleron.

It was Slyp who first noticed Sumiko missing, and his eyes narrowed when he saw her attending to the Starmaker. "What are you doing?" he demanded threateningly, and the gate in his eyes opened—

—and he immediately dropped to the ground, Noelle looking ruefully down at his crumpled form. "Sorry," she muttered.

The others turned, but were immediately bowled over by

the unexpected bright light singing from Gracea as the Devoted channeled her powers to their fullest extent. I'd turned my head away just in time, finishing up my healing of Aleron. The Icewright sprang into action, partly encasing the other guards in ice to immobilize them, even as Sumiko and I moved to the next imprisoned Devoted, working swiftly to heal their gates.

The tides turned quickly at that point, and now it was the Devoted who stood guard. "That was a good distraction," I complimented Sumiko. "I'm surprised they even agreed to do this."

Sumiko coughed. "It wasn't scripted. It was Noelle who told Miel, making sure the others were close enough to hear."

"And they . . . had no idea Gareen had been cheating on all of them?"

"I suppose love can be blind in a lot of ways."

"They're no danger now," Gracea reported tersely, coming up behind us.

"Bind them. Aleron, remove the ice before they develop hypothermia."

"It's no more than they deserve," the Starmaker retorted.

"My orders, Gracea. Keep the Icewrights surrounding them in case they attempt anything else, but no one is to be harmed."

We stared warily at each other for a few seconds. "Odessa's safety is paramount," I finally said. "I want a vow from you this instant, a promise not to harm her or her followers until we return to Aranth, where any punishment will be decided by Asteria herself."

Gracea's lips twisted, but she nodded. "I promise. Though the idea sorely tries my patience."

"I intend to make for the Abyss and find Odessa."

"You'll need someone to light the way."

I wasn't expecting her to volunteer. "No. You're needed here."

"I'm coming, too," Noelle said quietly.

I knew better now than to argue. "I can't guarantee what might happen inside that chasm. Or what might come out of it."

"We know our duties." Gracea extended her arm and sparks of light illuminated the plains. "We will see to them. I'll light as much of the path leading in as I can."

"Let's go, then," I said, trying not to think about the last time I found myself near these mountains, and stepped toward the chasm, into the horrors that I could only imagine waited for me there.

Chapter Twenty-Six

ARJUN THE DOMESTIC

———————— ✦ ————————

THE HUTS WERE EMPTY. It didn't look like anyone had made this place home for a long time, no doubt because of their nightmarish neighbors next door. So near to the Abyss, who knew what atrocities had come climbing out to visit?

"They were close enough to see the earth split when it did," Haidee said, hugging herself. "They saw the world break."

"I guess we're the only idiots to choose to get closer instead of running away. We're going to have to risk whatever spirits are still lingering in this place and rest up in one of those huts, though. Maybe we'll learn more."

The house we finally picked was a solid stone affair, with the roof still intact, at the center of the village. I guessed it was the head chief's house, being larger than the others. There was a collection of wooden and metal instruments in one of the rooms, and I puzzled over their use until Haidee laughingly informed me they were cooking utensils.

"Hell of a lot of doohickeys just for food." The only things we had back in the desert were a large pot, a spoon big enough to stir the stew, and a small spit for meat to roast over a fire.

"The cooks used similar things back in the Golden City. I don't have as much experience with cooking, but I can try."

Her eyes wandered to something behind me, her cheeks coloring, and I turned to look. There was a large cot taking up half of the room, its size clearly a sign of luxury in these parts. The fabric had rotted and fallen in, but the wood itself looked stable even after years of neglect. We could get one of the canvases from the rig and stretch it over the frame for a comfortable dayspan's sleep. It was even large enough to accommodate my height.

It would be large enough to accommodate the both of us, actually.

I felt my own face heat up. "Ah," I stumbled, "I'll find another place."

"No!" she nearly shouted, and then blushed again. "It's the only bed here, and I'd rather we didn't have to split up into separate houses to sleep. We need to stay together in case something happens."

Something sure as hell was going to happen if we slept on the same cot together, but I hadn't worked up the nerve to say that to her face yet. "I'm going to see if we can start a fire," I said, deciding that sleeping accommodations were future Arjun's problem. "And I'll bring the tarp in and see if we can fix the bed with it."

"I'll see if there's anything edible outside," she offered shyly, then eyed the bed again tentatively. The weather here was almost pleasantly temperate, but I found myself sweating all the same.

It took nearly half an hour to stretch the tarp out over the bed—it was still lumpy in some places, but infinitely more comfortable than being cooped up in the rig. I kicked away as much of the debris as I could into the corners before venturing out to see where Haidee was.

I found her at the edge of the village, closer to the mountain, with a bundle of greens gathered in her hands. She was staring out into the Abyss that loomed just beyond, a strange look on her face. "Do you see that?" she whispered.

"What?"

She pointed with one of the leafy plants. I screwed up my eyes and peered out—within that dark fog, half-hidden by the darkness, was what looked to be the remains of a structure, large enough to be visible at this distance, albeit clearly in ruins.

"Brighthenge." She took a step forward, like she wanted to keep marching on until she'd reached it.

"You're not up to strength yet," I warned her. "And neither am I."

She paused and nodded reluctantly. "I'm getting better, though."

"Better isn't good enough. We won't waste much time if we spend another dayspan resting. We're here already, and neither the chasm nor the mountain's going to run away if we wait a few more hours."

"I suppose. I just—it's *here*. Brighthenge is right in front of me. I'm so close to finding out if there's anything worth discovering inside it—or if it's all been for nothing. I don't know what I'm afraid of more—whether I'm going to be proven wrong, or right." She looked down at the plants in her hands. "I'll go prepare these."

Haidee was good at figuring out edible plants, but she was hopeless when it came to making food. So while she tried to make our temporary living space just a little more livable, I went back to our stores and added to the pot some pieces of Betsy's meat that had survived our journey, muttering a brief apology to the damn whale's spirit as I did, because Haidee was a bad influence on me.

It took a while to finish the stew, but it wasn't like we had anywhere else to be. "All set," I called out, and turned—and saw her standing by the doorway, clad in nothing but one of my shirts, her hair a soft shade of rosy pink and wet and sticking to her neck. *Burn me.*

"I found a tub," she whispered. "At least, I *think* it could be a tub. There's a stream nearby, and I gated some water into it for a good scrub. It was only big enough for one person to fit—but I heated some more water for you, if you'd like?"

Goddess burn *me.* "Meal's ready," I muttered, suddenly aware that my tongue was halfway out my mouth. "I'll, uh—I'll go and find that spring—I mean that tub—and I'll just—I mean—yeah, I'll go."

I've never washed myself so quickly in my life, and there was still steam curling up from our bowls by the time I'd returned, hers still untouched. "I wanted to wait for you," she offered, but she was shaking slightly, and it wasn't because of the cold.

I closed my eyes, not sure whether I was going to regret this. "Haidee. I meant it last time." I sat myself gingerly on the edge of the bed. "I'm not—I don't want to impose anything on you."

"Impose?" she whispered.

"It isn't just because this place is a damn shithole and you deserve better for your first . . . uh, for any experience, really. We've gone through a lot the last few days, and if we both want to take a step back and breathe for a moment instead of rushing into things . . ."

I'd guessed right; I saw the brief flash of relief on her face, though it was swiftly replaced by worry. "I'm sorry," she muttered, pulling her legs up to her chest. "I really did want to . . ." She blushed. "I'd almost lost you. And I started thinking about all the what-ifs. What if I never have another moment with you like this? What if we never have a next time?"

"Hey," I whispered, tugging her closer, and waited until she was settled against me. "You know that I, um . . ." Trying to explain the importance of my relationship with her by talking about a previous relationship was probably not going to be the best course of action, but I knew I had to make a point. "Was with someone before. In the past, long before I'd even met—"

I received a poke in the side for my efforts. "I know you've had a lover, you idiot." Her face was buried against my chest, but I swore I could feel her rolling her eyes. "I get it. You don't need to trip over yourself trying to make me feel better."

I harrumphed. "And like I said, we weren't serious. I liked her, but if I had to be blunt about it, I'd admit maybe we both just wanted a distraction from everything else going on. You and I"—and I started stumbling again—"it's the opposite. We don't need to do anything else for me to know that I care about you. I'm not concerned about the what-ifs. Spending time with you—that's all I need."

She pressed her mouth against my chest, and I knew she could feel my heart racing through the thin fabric. The bowls were still untouched on the table, but I wasn't hungry. "You surprise me sometimes. Thank you. For giving me that choice."

I looked down at her head, at the rippling colors of pink and red and purple suffusing her locks. "You shouldn't thank me for something you're supposed to have anyway," I said gruffly.

I don't how that functioned as some kind of come-on, but she was all over me in an instant. Her mouth was hot and sweet against mine, and it was she who forced my head back, demanding. I groaned, threading my hands through her riotous hair.

"Can we—just—do this?" she asked breathlessly in between kisses. "Nothing complicated, but—just like this?"

"Shut up, Haidee," I growled, meaning every word, and tipped her backward onto the bed.

It might have all been her idea, but she wouldn't stop blushing even several hours later, frequently casting looks my way that were a cross between dazed and aroused, and it took everything in me not to break my promise and do more. It had been pleasant to wake and find her sprawled atop me, though the faint spasm in my back informed me the bed had not been as comfortable as we had both let ourselves believe.

Worth it, though.

Occasionally, she would look at my hands and give an alluring little shudder, and I remembered all too clearly where they'd wandered, the soft places on her body they'd explored—and the strangled, pleasured sounds that left her throat when, on a stroke of sudden genius, my mouth had moved farther down.

"Did you like it?" I drawled. She'd practically passed out afterward, so I knew just exactly how much she'd liked it, but my male pride required that I hear it from her all the same.

She gave another delightful little shiver and turned away. "Shut up," she muttered.

I grinned at her back. Damn if I didn't love this girl.

Focus. Not the best time for romancing when you're heading into hell.

Sobering enough to remember, the closer we got to the Abyss. The hours had done little to lessen the strange fog surrounding Brighthenge; every now and then we caught glimpses of a broken pillar or a row of shattered columns before the dark mist returned to sweep them back out of sight. Beyond that ruin, the chasm beckoned, a black maw on the ground that stretched on into nothing.

"You think there'll be more demons there?" I asked aloud, wanting to float that idea in case she had suggestions, or perhaps some alternate route in mind.

"According to the stories, all manners of horror came crawling out of that pit when the world broke," she said tersely, paler now. "It explains the abundance of strange creatures roaming the lands, but . . . I would imagine quite a few of them still make this place their home."

"Well, we survived everything the dregs of the world had to throw at us, so no reason to think we won't do the same here, right?" I gave her hand a reassuring squeeze. "You're gonna tell me you plan on backing out now?"

"No. I'm just scared about what we might find." She set her shoulders. "All right. Let's go."

The cold wind gripped us on all sides as we approached the remains of Brighthenge. It reminded me of the crumbling old structures I sometimes saw out in the desert after a sandstorm had done its number on them, leaving nothing in their wake but broken hulls of what must have been flourishing civilizations.

Considering its location teetering practically over the edge of the Abyss, the shrine was in better shape than I first thought. Much of the structure had fallen in on itself, but the main roof was intact, which suggested that anything housed within could have possibly survived, if the years and the dirt hadn't gotten to it first.

Beyond the temple was the awfulness that was the Abyss—the bane of all our existence, the physical manifestation of the world's breaking. The dark fog obscured the rest of that gaping chasm, preventing me from seeing how wide the fissure went, but I wasn't brave enough yet to look out over the edge to see what lay beyond it—or within it.

I paused to stare at a large statue outside of the temple. Like the mountain, it had been split in half. It also bore similar features to the statue at the hot springs consecrated to Inanna. Its ruined face gazed back down at me.

There was an inscription carved on a plaque by its feet: *A life for the west. A life for the east. Immortality below.*

"What's wrong?" Arjun asked.

I couldn't place it into words, but something about the statue made me uneasy. I turned away. "Nothing. Let's go."

By some unspoken agreement, we made for the broken temple instead. It looked sound enough to enter, though I was understandably reluctant—just because something had survived seventeen years in ruins didn't mean it was going to survive another day more, given my luck. "Don't touch anything," I warned Haidee, "and I'm going in first."

She glared at me. "This is my shrine."

"A shrine you've never even set foot in."

She didn't have a good answer, so she rewarded me with yet another glare.

Brighthenge's architecture was straightforward enough; it was a long hallway marked by statues on either sides, leading into a large altar on a circular disc. The roof above it opened up into the heavens, though the impression was marred by unplanned holes in other parts of the ceiling. It was a testament to the temple's builders that many of the pillars remained upright. Clouds of dust rose up wherever we walked; we must have been the first living things to enter these once-sacred halls since the Breaking.

At first glance, it didn't look like there was anything that could be saved. What I could only surmise were priceless vases littered the ground, broken and forgotten and covered in thick layers of dust. Intricate tapestries had been torn off the walls by some unimaginable force, many ripped to shreds. Haidee crouched down beside one that had remained mostly intact, studying it carefully. "It portrays Inanna's descent into the underworld, I think," she said sadly. "How many more priceless artifacts had been destroyed here?"

"Well, there's a few things here stronger than vases and tapestries." I studied the plaques chiseled into the stone walls, bearing strange text.

Haidee drew in a quick breath. "There are names inscribed before every tablet."

She was right. Many of the names had been rubbed out and distorted, but a few of them were still distinct: Alathea. Camrin. Sovvya. Nyx.

"These are the names of the goddesses that came before me," Haidee whispered. "Look, here's Mother's name—Latona— and beside hers is Asteria. Every plaque bears the names of both twins, but talk only about the surviving sister. This one is Sovvya—her achievements are well documented here, but there's nothing else regarding her twin, Salaka, beyond her name. The same goes for the rest: Alathea and a twin named Argenta. And Camrin and Perth, Phoebe and Thalia, and so on. None of the books I've read ever mentioned their sisters' names—no, wait. Nyx and Hemera. When Nyx wrote about raising a bird back from the dead, she named it Hemera. Her *twin's* name."

"They're really pushing that 'only one goddess existed' lie, aren't they?" I broke my own rule and brushed away some dirt with the base of my hand so I could read some of the words better. "None of these make any sense to me. Listen to this one: 'Where the waters recede will the city flourish, and when the dead open their eyes and sing with their throats shall the harvest continue.'" I turned and saw the look of growing horror on Haidee's face. "Hey, what's wrong?"

"That was from Nyx's time," Haidee whispered. "There was a terrible flood that wiped out many villages and cities. The drowned made—gurgling—noises in their mouths even after they'd perished, once their bodies were recovered from the water. It was well documented by historians."

"Well, why not just say that instead of sounding so mysterious?"

"These aren't historical documents, Arjun. They're prophecies. Predictions of what each goddess might do in their lifetimes. Every goddess has some prophecy in her name. So what went wrong?"

"Haidee—"

But she was already dashing off, her eyes locking on every plaque on the walls she passed, stopping every now and then to skim through a few passages. "We're starting on the wrong end," she breathed. "What I need to find isn't any of the other goddesses' prophecies, but Inanna's."

"Inanna has her own prophecies?"

"She has to. She's the greatest goddess of us all. Oh . . ." She ran toward the altar, ignoring the debris in her path. I swore and followed after her.

She skidded to a stop and stared at the wall behind the altar, at a set of two plaques more impressive than the others, carved side by side. I could dimly make out the faint image of a woman stooping behind them both, her sculpted hands lying atop them as if offering both her benediction.

"It says *Inanna's Song*," Haidee whispered. "These must be the incantations that were used for the ritual."

Time had rubbed out some of the lettering, but most of the strange ode remained intact:

> *A demoness*
> *Is what men call*
> *A goddess they cannot control.*

> *There is no shame*
> *In goddesses falling*
> *Into the Abyss*
> *Where they find new purpose*
> *As darkness.*

> *Praise the women who fly*
> *And fail and succumb to*
> *Night;*
> *Death sustains Inanna,*
> *Who is One and Whole,*
> *Who sacrifices her life into the Below*

To save her life in the Above
Who is the sacrificed and the sacrificer,

The demoness and the goddess
Rule the heavens
And the Cruel Kingdom
As two, but One.

As the enduring Above,
So shall the Great Below.

"That makes even less sense," I complained.

"Inanna enters hell to rescue her beloved from the Cruel Kingdom, only to find that this is an impossible feat, even for her," Haidee breathed. "The twin goddesses are considered part of her dual nature. But if one is destined to rule the Above—here, in this world—then the other, doomed to rule the Great Below, must be the twin to be sacrificed." She was pale now, shaking.

"Haidee—"

"Who tells us these prophecies?" she yelled at the altar, at the plaques, at the faint suggestion of the goddess behind them all. Bits of plaster and stone crumbled down from the ceiling, but she gave them no notice. "What priestess wrote them down? How does she predict these destinies, foretell who is to die and who is to live? Does she claim they come from the mouth of Inanna herself? I want to know!" She whirled around, her panicked eyes searching the rest of the walls. "They say the prophecies are created when the next generation of twins are born," she croaked. "Where are my prophecies, then? And my twin's? Who foretold our futures? Which of us is to die, and who gets to live?"

I couldn't stop her. She tore through the hallways like a madwoman, flitting from one written destiny to the next, trying to ascertain her own. Finally, she fell to her knees before one of the walls that had partly given way to rot and erosion, sobbing. "No," she whispered. "No."

The world torn asunder, I read silently from the plaque she had stopped at,

Night and day rule from their two thrones,

Where the darkest hour and the brightest light meet
the Hellmouth shall be crossed
by she strengthened under the gift of day,
by she liberated with the gift of night.
And the world is whole again.

But the Cruel Kingdom hungers for a sacrifice.
Sacrifice overthrows chaos.
Sacrifice is necessary
for what was two to become one.

Test your worth; offer
to her, Inanna's immortality.
She will grieve endlessly for the sister

who slumbers in the house of the dead,
but her tears will save us all.

And until the Gates of Death and Life intertwine,
Love continues to be the toll.
And she will pay.
She will pay.

But the upper parts of the plaque had not survived, leaving gaping holes in their wake.

"Is it my name that's written there?" Haidee wept. "Or is it my sister's? Will I be the one sacrificed?"

"Haidee!" Feeling helpless, not sure how to comfort her, I hugged her tightly, burying my face in her hair. "Haidee, you're the only surviving twin, remember? Your sister is dead."

"I know," she breathed. "Did they sacrifice her by mistake? Oh, sweet Mother. I had a *sister*. Did she die so I could live? I could have had a *sister*! My sister! Did they kill my father as well? Oh, Arjun—would all this never have happened if it had been me? Am I living the life my sister should have? Poor Odessa . . ."

A loud crack sounded from outside the temple. We both jumped.

A long, sonorous howling rippled through the air and sent fear down my bones.

Haidee pushed me gently away, now almost inhumanly calm, and stood.

"Haidee, you're not seriously considering—"

She pointed. Through the openings in the wall I could make out the beginnings of some hideous maelstrom, whipping through the sky and sending frenzied froths of lightning-kissed air spinning forth from the edges of the Abyss. This was bad.

"You've said it yourself," Haidee said. "We've come this far. If there's something out there that's taking umbrage at my being here, then I'm going to see what it wants from me."

This woman had nerves of steel.

Damn if I didn't love her.

"Let's see what it wants, then," I said, bracing myself for whatever the hell was waiting for us outside, and together, we stepped back out into the light.

Chapter Twenty-Seven

THE TWINS AT THE ABYSS

——————— ☾ ———————

IT WAS STRANGE TO BE in the middle of this foul fog, with the stench of brimstone and burning wood surrounding me on all sides, and yet to be so calm.

I could hear my faithful followers struggling behind me, coughing and trying to keep pace, but I ignored them and forged on ahead, not wanting to wait. They were staunch companions and, I was sure, willing to risk their lives for my cause, but this was something I had to do on my own, and their help, earnest as it was, amounted to little in this place.

The Abyss gaped before me, yawning open like the jaws of some toothless beast that sputtered fire and damnation back into the sky in defiance of nature. I knew that I should be frightened. Every horrible creature we'd encountered had been spawned from these depths, and the blame for every death we'd suffered could be laid on their account. But I was strangely at peace.

However this might end, at least there would be an ending.

The galla that accompanied me didn't bother to keep their distance; they fanned out behind me, acting as my guards, and it felt right.

I could no longer hear my companions.

I stopped at the edge of the Abyss and waited. Nothing crawled out from those bottomless depths, or moved to attack. I felt the wind pick up, as if some unseen spell ran through the air. It crackled at my skin, charging the air with terrific energy. But I remained still, waiting. I had, after all, one more galla to greet, to complete the ritual.

And when it finally arrived, it was a tiny, unimpressive thing, nothing at all like its brethren. It had the features and size of a small child, squat and slightly deformed and no taller than my waist. It tottered toward me with its not-legs, its eyes like bright sapphires. It extended a hand, its not-fist clenched.

One more gift to take for my own, and I could face anything that sloped out of that chasm to challenge me.

The little waiflike creature stared at me without eyes and showed me what it wanted.

Its fist unfurled.

It was a small, beating heart.

No.

Not just any heart.

I knew without knowing how.

It required the heart of one whom I loved best.

The world shuddered and stopped.

Lan's heart.

No. Anything but that.

"You can't," I snarled, anger and fear spiking together into one emotion. "Take anything you want from me. Whatever I can give you, I will give freely. But not that. Anything but that . . ."

You must not open your mouth against the rites of the underworld.

"Yes, I will!" I screamed. "I defy you now! I'll give you everything you want but Lan! I forbid it! I refuse your gift!"

Something in the galla twisted in on itself. *Submit.*

I raised my hand, but it was neither in acceptance nor surrender.

Ice tore into the galla, picking it apart like a beast might tear into its helpless prey. I strengthened my will and sent Air to shatter it into a million pieces, Fire to burn the remains of its corpse down to its bitter ashes. I attacked the ground it stood on, desperate to eradicate every iota of its being from this world. *You will not have her. You will not have her. You will not have her!*

"Odessa!"

And then Lan was there. I sobbed, clinging to her, desperate for her touch and sorry for everything I had done to us. "It's my fault," I warbled. To refuse one gift was to reject them all, and the wave of lucidity that sang through me as I reclaimed my sanity hit me like a punch, the guilt too great to ignore. "It's all my fault!"

"Shh," the Catseye soothed, stroking my hair. "Everything's going to be okay, Odessa."

"No, it won't." What had I done? I had taken most of the Devoted prisoner, elevated my inexperienced followers into positions they were not ready for because of my pride, brought them into this fog of death with no thought of their safety. . . . "Lan, we must get away from this place. We have to return to Aranth now, find some other way to restore the world. I can't do it, not like this. I'm not going to lose you."

"Sweet child," Lan murmured. "You've already lost me."

I pushed her away, shocked. The thing before me wore Lan's face, her smile. Until the shadows behind her lengthened, and she was no longer Lan.

I screamed.

It was the scream that terrified me, because it sounded so human. I'd thrown all caution to the winds and raced toward the Abyss with Arjun hot on my heels, shouting words at me that didn't quite reach. "Hello?" I called out into the mist, hoping to receive a response and at the same time hoping I wouldn't.

"You damn idiot!" Arjun shouted, finally catching up. "Whatever possessed you to run into this accursed fog without thinking through—"

"There's someone else here." That cry had triggered something in me, had made my chest hurt with the terror in it.

"It could be some kind of ruse—"

"No. It didn't come from the chasm." I peered desperately into the fog, trying to find anything that would back up my claim. Gating Air, I tried to funnel the current into a straight line, pushing what mist that I could out of the way. It was like struggling with quicksand, a dense soup that was quick to flow back into the empty spaces I had carved out.

Arjun scanned the area I had cleared. "I think I see something," he murmured, frowning. "There's a girl."

Then his eyes widened, and he glanced at me, and then back out at the fog, and then back again.

"What?"

"Either that's a mirage, or it's another you I'm seeing out there."

"What?" I squinted into the mist, trying to make sense of the faint figure I could see from a distance, fading in and out of view as the fog fought to obscure the pathway I had worked so hard to clear.

I saw a glimpse of hair, the colors standing out against the faint light. I watched the way it shifted from brown to blue and then yellow. "That's my hair," I choked out, disbelieving. But while mine was short, hers was long, nearly past her waist.

The girl herself was cowering on the ground, hands raised to protect her head. Looming over her was some strange beast, a hulking figure that stood on two legs. But any similarities to humanity ended there; dark fangs stood out against what must be its mouth, and one of its clawed hands was raised, as if to attack.

I didn't even think. I sent an arc of lightning spinning across the chasm, striking the creature's chest dead center. It hollered and stumbled back, but Arjun was already kneeling beside me with his Howler out and one of its sights against his eye. He squeezed the trigger, and a blazing blue light shot across the Great Abyss that stood between us and the girl, and enveloped the monster in flames.

The other girl stumbled back, gasping, and the monster teetered precariously over the edge. I gated more Air, wrapped it like a lasso around the beast's midsection, and gave a hard tug. It toppled over, its animal-like screams fading soon enough as it dropped deeper into that endless Abyss.

"Odessa!" I heard distantly, as two more girls appeared out of the fog, dashing toward the other stricken girl—one with black hair, and the other a redhead. The dark-haired girl's lips moved, and my doppelgänger let out a huge sob, enveloping her in a tight hug.

"What happened?" The brunette's words drifted out to us from across the divide, the silence amplifying her voice. Her long hair was knotted in braids much like the Liangzhu women I'd seen at Sonfei's camp. Her mouth fell open. "Who are you?" she roared from across the crevice. "Answer me, demons!"

Of course, it was Arjun who took offense. "Watch who you're calling demons, demon!" he yelled back. "And stop wearing Haidee's face!"

"Haidee's face?" came the angry response. "*She's* wearing *Odessa's* face!"

"Odessa?" I rose, hurried as close to the edge of the Abyss as I dared. "Your name is Odessa?" I shouted.

The other woman with the same color-shifting hair as mine copied my movements, scrambling nearer to the precipice. "Yes," she called out, her voice shaking. "Who are you?"

I stared at her, and she stared back. *She has my face,* I thought, stunned. *She looks almost exactly like me.* "My name's Haidee."

A harsh, garbled noise rose between us, from somewhere within the depths of the ravine. My gaze drifted below.

Until that point, I had refused to look straight into the Abyss, out of fear at what I might find. But now I couldn't look away. As I watched, horrified, a strange frothing mass rose from that endless hole, its spindly, shrunken movements too cracked and twisted to be of any sane shape.

"It's all my fault," I heard the other girl—Odessa?—cry out. "I refused the last galla, Lan. I refused it and rejected all the other gifts, and now it—it's coming for me. . . ."

That didn't sound good. I scrambled back. "Get ready," I told Arjun, trying not to let the fear show in my voice. "Something's coming."

To his credit, Arjun spared only a glance for the Abyss, and then righted his Howler. "You think?"

"It's my fault," I wept. Already my shadows had turned traitor, melting back into the Abyss—no doubt to join their inhuman brethren ascending from the hole.

"What's done is done." By all accounts, Lan should hate me. I had betrayed her, had nearly given her up. My one saving grace was to spare her from entering the mist that had massacred her rangers. She was here solely because I was, and I wanted to cry all over again. "We need to get away from here, Odessa."

I saw more figures swimming in through the mist, and spotted Janella making her way toward us. The Firesmoker stopped when she saw Lan. "What's she doing here?" she demanded.

"I want her to stay," I told her, gathering as much calm about me as I could. "Where are the others?"

Janella shook her head. "All this fog. I couldn't find them." She blinked. "Is there another you at the other side of the chasm?"

"My twin." I felt . . . shocked. Stunned. Happy. My sister was alive. My sister was alive!

"There's no time, then," Janella said calmly. "You must accept the final galla's offering, Odessa. Inanna will accept you as the sole ruler of Aeon. Only then will she claim the other false goddess for sacrifice."

No. We stared at her—at mousy Janella, with her scarlet robes and her bright knowledge and her eager devotion. "How did you know about the galla and the rituals?" I whispered.

"Accept the galla's gifts, Odessa. Assume your place as the next goddess of Aeon, and your mother's true heir."

"Asteria sent you, didn't she?" Lan said slowly, staring at the clerk. "Asteria knew Odessa would sneak onto the *Brevity*. My role here was not to help lead the expedition, but to protect her—it was you she sent to broker a pact with these galla."

"Salleemae said it before she died," I breathed, understanding coming in waves. "She said something strange—wondered about someone who'd promised to look out for her left. I thought they were the ramblings of a dying woman—but you stood to her left when we fought those demon birds, didn't you? You let her die. Just like you let Graham die."

Janella shrugged. "There's no point in keeping it a secret anymore. Graham threatened the whole mission—he was always a coward at heart. To save his life, he thought to sacrifice yours and leave. I had to push him, and counted on your mercy to save me."

"But what did Salleemae ever do to you?"

"She said something," Lan said unexpectedly. "Salleemae approached me once. 'What she said about Cathei, milady. It wasn't right.' I thought she was referring to Odessa, but she was referring to you. Somehow Cathei had discovered you weren't who you said you were, and Salleemae caught on to that." Her eyes widened. "The ship. Cathei approached me once, puzzled, asking about the *Brevity*'s rigging. She thought there was something wrong with it."

Janella laughed. "I damaged the ship and hoped it would be blamed on our descent to the lakes. I knew she tried to tell you. The unexpected attack by those shadows was a blessing. Easy enough to loiter at the back of the camp and drag her away, then pretend some supernatural force had done it."

"You took a great risk."

"I was put on this mission to take risks. I read your report, Tianlan. Something similar happened to your team last time, and I knew you wouldn't question it happening again."

"What are you people going on about?" I heard the boy accompanying my twin yell out at us.

"And Salleemae?" I demanded.

"I knew Cathei had told her. I overheard them talking. Salleemae just wasn't smart enough to figure out how to use it against me before I got my hands on her."

"But why?" Noelle cried out. "Why would you do this?"

"My goal was for you to reach the Abyss. Damaging the ship ensured that Gracea's plan to bring you back to Aranth would fail even if we found another riverwind back. Cathei and Salleemae were collateral damage. Graham . . ." She grinned. "Graham was just a sweet bonus."

"You've been posing as the shy, insipid clerk all this time," Lan accused.

"I was Asteria's spy. She knew the galla would come. She hoped that the previous gifts would change you enough that you would be willing to overcome what the last asks of you."

"The seventh galla asked me to sacrifice Lan," I said dully. It was Lan's turn to freeze. "Mother really expected me to give her up?"

Janella shrugged again. "It was the best outcome for everyone involved. She needed heirs, and Lan would not be the person to give you any. You would mourn her loss, of course, but in time, you would move on."

My fists clenched. "She knew about my trysts with Lan. She appointed her my guard to encourage our relationship, rather than try to hinder it. But she never thought I was as serious about Lan as she was about me, right?" Soft-spoken Janella, gentle Janella. Janella, shrinking away from Gracea's abuse, her helplessness—all an act.

The Firesmoker shrugged again. "She knew Lan was serious, and she knew you had refused. I suppose she thought your feelings weren't as strong."

"Why tell me now?"

"Asteria took a risk, and misjudged your affection for Lan. You won't accept the seventh gift—not like this, anyway. And besides." She extended her hand, fire brewing at its center. "*This* was unexpected. I felt that I owed you something. I've had to pretend to simper and fawn over Gracea for years. The temptation to slit her throat was great, but I had little choice. It was my job." She smiled. "But to wield Fire? Oh, Odessa. This is the best reward you could ever bestow upon me, and I shall always love you for it. I thought it fair that you learn the truth in exchange. Unlike Gracea and her ilk, I am truly devoted to both you and your mother."

"If you ask me to give up Lan, then you are no friend of mine."

"If you refuse Inanna's shadow, then she might claim you both."

She broke off when another inhuman cry sang through the air, sounding closer this time. "What was that?" Noelle demanded.

"Something's coming out of the Abyss," Lan said tersely.

Janella laughed. "You'd best get ready then, and make your decision quickly. It's here."

A claw rose out from the darkness and landed on the ground

nearby, and we all scrambled back as one. The creature that slowly pulled itself up from that Abyss was an unfinished abstract; it was a mass of twisted contours and a tangle of limbs, like it wasn't done forming itself into a shape meant for human eyes just yet.

With horror, I realized why; all the other galla that I had once controlled were attaching and melding gradually into its form, resulting in a larger, more grotesque creature with each fusion. The monster's features warped, twisted, and then reassembled themselves. The figure of a woman now stared back at me; its eyes glowed and the shadows of its hair moved and slithered like live snakes. It wore a strange crown upon its brow, crafted from the blue stones I had long grown familiar with. But now that it had taken on a face, its expression was strangely benevolent as it turned to me.

Was this Inanna's spirit?

"It's her," Lan whispered.

Odessa, it crooned. *We are one. We sleep with our loves in the houses Below. We are purpose; our rewards, sublime. Help us find peace, Odessa. Accept our gifts. There will be no suffering. You are welcomed here.*

Despite my fear, I had no recollection of taking a step forward until I felt Lan's arms around me, dragging me back. "No! They'll kill you!"

"But I—" I looked down, straight into the Abyss. Another step and I would have gone right over the edge.

A sudden burst of fire from behind the demon took out its

shoulder. The monster hissed, the darkened flesh re-forming on its own, sinew and meat and skin flexing together until not a scar remained. The boy on the other side of the ravine had aimed his weapon at it, smoke steaming out from one end. The other girl with him—the one who looked so painfully like me—had cupped her hands around her mouth and was shouting something at us.

But for some reason, the possibility that I was the one to be sacrificed comforted me. Had the world collapsed because it was I who was meant to die? If I accepted this creature-goddess's hand, would it right the world, return it to the way it once was? After all the mistakes I had made, wasn't this the best course of action, the ultimate penance for my sins? I moved forward again, but Lan was too strong.

"If you think I'm going to let you do that," she yelled in my ear, "then you never knew me at all!"

The shadow-ghoul had already turned, a new target in mind. It clawed through the air toward the other girl and the boy, who showed no signs of fleeing. The girl raised her hands and sent a torrent of fire toward the creature, bravely standing her ground.

Another barrage of ice stopped the demon in its tracks, as I brutally punched a hole through what should be its sternum. It wheeled about, now forced to wage a battle from both sides.

"I will refuse her, and she will claim nothing from me," I said through gritted teeth. "Mother rejected her before. Surely there must be another way to do so again without causing another Breaking."

~

"We are so damn screwed," Arjun said, staring at the hideous creature making its way toward us.

"You're an optimist, you know that?" The people on the other side of the chasm appeared to be immersed in some argument among themselves, momentarily forgetting the demon in the space between our camps, or that it was angling for us. "You remember seeing anything in Brighthenge about repelling monsters like these?"

"I was too busy chasing after you when you'd lost your mind."

"I didn't lose my—! Look, this is not the time to be arguing—"

Shards of ice left a gaping hole in the center of the woman-creature's stomach, and they weren't from me. The other girl sent another flurry of sharp knives into the monster's head, catching it exactly in the center of the forehead and taking out some of the blue stones there. Black steam rose from the demon, and for the first time I saw it wavering.

"Take out all its jewels!" the girl yelled out at us.

That was easier said than done, because the monster's head was practically covered in them. But we redoubled our efforts all the same.

Desperately, we waged a two-pronged battle from either side, trying to break down the demon's strength before it could sap us of our own. The other goddess sent more patterns its way, ripping through the stones on its crown, while the red-haired girl had traded in her spear for a bow and fired arrows at the monster, though they served more to distract than to actually wound. The Catseye had her hand on the goddess's shoulder, and from her shining eyes I knew she was wiping away the other girl's fatigue. I wished there was someone on our side to do the same.

It was Arjun who finally delivered the killing blow; he'd built the patterns inside his Howler to another frenzy, and I knew from the waves of heat off the barrel alone that this was his most powerful shot yet. "You'd better stay away," he muttered, wincing, "because I'm not holding back this time."

I didn't even bother with a quip; I ducked out of the way as soon as he squinted through the sights.

The biggest ball of blue flame I'd ever seen, practically the size of the demoness's jeweled head, sang out from his rifle. Arjun's aim was impeccable; his shot blew out everything atop the creature's neck, and the now-headless monster toppled wordlessly back down into the Abyss it had crawled up from. With relief, I watched its form disappear into the seething mass of that black hole.

But it was Arjun's turn to waver, and I just managed to catch him before he could stumble forward into the chasm himself. "You idiot," I muttered, but with none of my usual annoyance. He was beyond exhausted, but his steady heartbeat told me he was going to be all right.

He grinned weakly. "The things I do for love."

With the enemy gone, I turned to the other side—and found the other girl staring at me again.

Her hair had the same impossible colors and fluctuations. I

watched as they turned an opaque silver, then red, then blue, and knew instinctively that my own hair was involuntarily matching hers in hue. Her face was the same one I'd seen in my mirror countless times; pale eyes and a small mouth, her skin perhaps a few shades lighter than mine; a testament no doubt to the colder climate she lived in. She wore long robes that nearly hid her form, and I wore a worker's outfit and the muddy boots to match, but the aesthetics of our clothes didn't matter.

My twin. This was my twin. *Odessa*: the daughter my mother had hidden for so long.

"Odessa." I called her name across the chasm, wanting to be sure that she was real, and not some mirage of a dead sister back to taunt me.

The response came, soft and clear. "Haidee."

"How do we make it across?" one of her companions called out. "There's nothing here to help bridge this gap."

"I'm not sure I want to walk across that hellish Abyss, Noelle," the Catseye said tartly. "Where did Janella go?"

The other girl in their party was missing. The Catseye swore. "What the hell is she planning now?"

The rest of the conversation flowed around us, mere noises at this point. A sudden burst of longing rose within me. I reached out a hand toward her, knowing that it was a futile gesture.

Almost at the same time, her own hand rose, as if straining to meet mine.

And then, as one, the whole world shifted.

Chapter Twenty-Eight

THE TWINS OF THE BREAKING

—————————— ☼ ——————————

EVEN DYING, THE WORLD HEARD us, and responded.

A great heaving ricocheted through the ground, the growing tremors felt by every mountain and surviving treetop, from the clanking and whirring towers of the Golden City to the raging storms and seas that savaged Aranth. Something heavier than air and stronger than lightning lanced between me and my twin; light crackled between our outstretched fingers, validating and confirming something we never knew, and yet must have known all along.

And between us the gaping stretch of the chasm, impassable and treacherous and untenable, did the impossible.

With a heavy shudder the world performed a miracle, and the ground lurched underneath our feet. The heavy rock twisted forward, pebbles crumbling over the edges, but we both stood secure, knowing we were safe. The ground heaved again, and then again, each groaning shift propelling the cliffs forward, narrowing the gap of the chasm and propelling us both toward each other, to a point where our hands could meet and I could finally touch my sister for the first time.

My sister.

This was my *sister.*

I could hear our companions on both sides, the panic in their voices at the onset of this new cataclysm, the fear that this was another Breaking in the process. But I was calm.

My sister was alive.

My sister is alive!

Not every part of the ravine obeyed our thoughts; sections of the Abyss still stood thousands of miles wide, and not even this newfound bond could overcome the realities of nature. But our patch of ground, a hundred feet wide, bowed to our whims and continued that maddening drive forward; inch by reluctant inch it pushed us farther, until we fell into each other's weeping arms, and could finally feel the truth.

I had a *sister*!

For a moment, I had a flash of strange sagacity coupled with a peculiar notion of otherness; it was like something inside of me was finally complete upon that first instance of my twin's touch, like destiny was forcing new prophecies into being, offering a happier fate now that we stood together instead of separately, after seventeen years and more.

We held each other; our emotions gave way to sobs. And in that instant, I was uncertain as to which of us was which goddess.

But even as we clung, I was aware of a strange shadow that rose behind us, a suggestion that the forces Below were not ready to relinquish their hold. We turned as one but were too late to stop the assault, as a large claw came down onto us, over the cries of horror from our companions.

We moved.

It tore through one of our shoulders, and as one we felt and cried out from the pain. But the lightning crackled in our joined hands, and beyond the hurt our fury sparked and burned, even greater than the agony. Inanna sought to divide us. We would not surrender. The Great Below would not take either of us.

The energy we released was an explosion that lit up Aeon, a sound I knew would be heard by all who still lived here. It would send Latona up from her bed, screaming obscenities, and it would send Asteria dashing to her tower window to view this newfound threat to her claim for control. We poured our heart and soul and strength into that spell, gating every element we could reach.

Inanna's shape contracted and expanded and contracted again, until, with a mighty cry, it collapsed into itself, shadows and dust drifting back into the Abyss, her soul splintered and sent screaming back to the Great Below.

Once the silence descended, we collapsed.

And with a harsh, grating sound, for the first time in seventeen years, the world began to turn.

Chapter Twenty-Nine

THE TWINS IN THE AFTERMATH

──────────── ☾ ────────────

"I'M FINE," I SAID, COUGHING weakly as Lan fussed over my wound. I'd taken a heavy swipe of the Shadow-Inanna's claws; although the Catseye had found my injuries not to be life-threatening, and the healing had been swift and not as painful as I had feared, she would not stop berating me.

"You fool," she whispered, her beautiful face haggard. "What possessed you to do that? That shadow could have . . . !" She buried her face in my hair, words failing her. "You're truly going to kill me one of these days," she finally whispered.

"I'm so sorry." I had so much penance to do, so much forgiveness to ask for. Haidee—my long-lost twin, Haidee!—still had a deadly grip on one hand, so I used the other to tug Lan closer. "I should never have allowed the galla to consume me," I sobbed. "I thought I could control it. I thought I could temper the shadows and save us all—"

"Shh," she soothed. "You rejected them. That's all that matters." She lifted her head to stare warily at Haidee. "You're not supposed to be alive," she finally said.

"I was told the same thing about her," the girl said softly. "But if you must know, I am so glad that you are. Mother was not as good at keeping secrets as she would like to believe."

"Why are you here at Brighthenge?" I asked her, squeezing Lan's fingers tightly, though she made no sound of protest at my tight grip.

"For the same reason you are, I suspect—to find a way to heal the world, to see if there was a way to overcome the Breaking." She smiled sheepishly. "You had more companions for this journey than I had, though."

I glanced over at her friend, a tall dark-skinned man with a thick cloth wrapped around his head like a scarf, and a gun in place of a hand.

Oddly enough, she blushed. "He was the only one willing to see this through with me," she muttered. "I still can't believe we made it."

"I'll say," the boy rumbled. "She'd be damn lost without me." But for all his bravado, his eyes were very soft when he looked at Haidee, a small affectionate smile I doubt he was aware of playing on the sides of his mouth.

"They mentioned," I said, more shakily this time, "that one of the goddesses was supposed to die, so that the other could rule Aeon unopposed."

Haidee nodded. "That's what I gathered too, from what

we've discovered on our way here."

"But—both our mothers are alive. Do you think that's what caused the Breaking?"

"I don't know for certain. But we need answers from them both as soon as possible."

"Haidee . . . who *is* our real mother?" Mother had concealed so many things from me, but I'd always believed that I was her daughter. That I might not be even be her child—that she might have lied—hurt.

Haidee's face mirrored my distress. "I don't know. I don't even know why they seem to hate each other so much."

"And what does that say about the two of us? Have they permanently disrupted the ritual? Or—in order to bring the world back to what it once was, does it mean that *we* have to . . ."

Haidee's face changed; angry and anguished all at once. "I really don't want to think about that. We're in unexplored territory. Maybe it's not an issue anymore. The world is turning again. Didn't you feel it? Surely there'll be no need for a sacrifice."

"But what if—"

"I'm going on the belief," she insisted firmly, "that if we need another way to cure the world, we're going to find it together, without anyone else suffering for it."

She looked so much like me, but we had our differences, too. She had more courage than I ever had, a courage I could only achieve through my pact with the galla. Now, without it, I felt more at a loss than ever. "All right." I rose to my feet despite

Lan's protests. "Show me Brighthenge," I proposed, hoping the confidence in my voice matched hers. "If we want answers, I suppose it's best that we start there."

"I remember now," Lady Lan said, staring at a large statue before the temple. She raised her hand, intending to touch the stone surface, but let her arm drop at the last minute. "This was the portal the shadow sent me through. I . . ." Her gaze drifted to the empty ground before it, and her hands shook. "They should be here. Their—bodies. Where did they—"

"It's all right," Odessa said sharply, rushing to her side. She glanced at me and I knew, without her needing to put the thought into words, that she wanted Arjun and me to go on ahead. Clearly the Catseye knew something about this place that we didn't, but I didn't want to pry at this point. Not yet.

We set to work. By the time we were done with Brighthenge, I'd taken copious notes of every prophecy marked on the walls. We'd explored it from top to bottom and sideways, gleaning all the information we could. The prophecies were still a mystery, but I was confident that we could break the riddles soon enough. "We might be able to find some clues back at the Golden City," I told my twin when they rejoined us, with Lady Lan noticeably calmer. "I know someone who might have access to some rare books. If he can find some about the goddesses, then we can see if any of the prophecies match up with their lives."

"I'm not sure Latona would be happy to accommodate you, Haidee," Arjun said pointedly.

"I'll find a way. We could stay with your clan instead. If you have enough room for us," I added, blushing.

He arched an eyebrow. "Are you trying to figure out if I have a room to myself back home? Because the answer is no."

"Of course not!"

"But there are—other ways to get privacy, if you know where to look." He paused, sent me a quick, searing look that told me he had no intention of backing down since his confession at the abandoned village. "And I do."

I flushed harder. "That would be . . . nice."

Arjun turned to Lady Lan, who was side-eyeing us with a faint grin on her face. "I suppose you're a Catseye," he said with a short grunt, extending his arm. "Haven't introduced myself yet. Name's Arjun. Lady Lan, right?"

"Not a—uh, yes, and nice to meet you." The girl reached forward. Her fingers brushed against his stump, and she blinked down. Arjun, the asshole, just grinned. "Kidding," he said, offering his intact hand. But the Catseye had gotten hold of his stump anyway, her eyes glowing, and the man froze. "You're not taking as much care of this as you should," the woman said matter-of-factly. "It feels like you've had a rash of infections every few months because you've been hoarding your medicine. It will blister soon enough if you don't take care."

Whatever the Catseye was doing worked; Arjun's shoulders sank down as the tension melted away, though that didn't stop him from letting out a snippy, if grudging, "I've lived my whole life in a desert. We're not exactly swimming in water and ointments."

"I still can't believe it." My twin—Odessa—clung to me often, and I to her, like letting go meant something worse was about to happen. "Mother said that you died at the Breaking. That you and my aunt Latona perished, and that we were the only two goddesses left."

"My mother refused to tell me anything about you," I countered, happiness and anger quick to trade places. We'd both been lied to. In the heady hour that had passed after we had done the unthinkable and bridged the gap across the Great Abyss, we talked and laughed and hugged like we had known each other all our lives. And we bore the same growing grudge against the parents who had raised us without knowledge of the other. "She would only say that she killed Asteria in self-defense."

Odessa shook her head. "My mother said the same, but with their roles reversed. And—they both claim we're their daughters. Who's telling the truth? What would either of them stand to gain with these lies?"

"Janella would know more about this." The other warrior— Noelle, I believed—had emerged back from the fog, glowering. "She's not at camp. They're all gone."

"Who is she?" I asked her.

Lady Lan straightened up. "A spy for Asteria. She knows more about the goddess's motives than any of us, and no doubt she's off to report her failure as we speak."

"But how does she intend to return to your city alone, without aid?"

"There's—" Lan's fists clenched, relaxed. "There may be a way to return without having to travel that distance. I've been here before. It's that statue outside the temple. I might have—triggered—a portal within it that could transport us. Perhaps both Asteria and Latona chose to build their respective cities where they were not by choice, but because that was where they were brought after the world broke."

"A portal, then? How do we activate it?"

Lan let out a strange, gulping sound. "Through sacrifice, last time I checked. That was how . . . I made it back."

"We're not seriously doing the same, are we?"

"No, but Janella might." Lan rose to her feet. "The others might be in trouble. We have to make sure she hasn't attacked any more people."

"'The world torn asunder. Night and day rule from their two thrones,'" Odessa said softly. She had come to a stop at the very same plaque that had horrified me so, the plaque that should have one of our names inscribed there but was missing. Her finger trailed down to the end of the prophecy. "'She will grieve endlessly for the sister who slumbers in the house of the dead, but her tears will save us all.' Who are they referring to here? Was it me, or you?"

"I don't know," I said honestly. "But I hope it no longer matters." The world was spinning again. In time, water would return to the desert, and the changing weather would offer more temperate, livable conditions across the world. The prophecies no longer meant anything. Why should they?

"There are no healing springs here," Odessa said quietly. "No restoratives or elixirs like what my mother was led to believe. This is a library, not an apothecary."

I remembered that Odessa and Lan had initially gone to Brighthenge seeking a cure for Odessa's strange disease. Lan had examined me earlier, and found none of my twin's illness in me. We had searched the ruins, hoping for a clue to some remedy, to no avail. I tried to swallow the lump in my throat. "I'm so sorry." I did not want to lose her so soon after finding her. There *had* to be another way. . . .

Odessa smiled briefly. "It's all right. I should have known it wouldn't be this easy. But I don't know if I can save the world when I'm not even sure I can save myself." She turned toward Inanna's Song, toward the strange silhouette of the goddess forever etched on the stone, surveying the ruins of her once-thriving empire. "'Love continues to be the toll,'" she quoted its final stanza, "'and she will pay.' I want to believe that there's some other way to save Aeon, Haidee—but I'm still very much afraid there won't be."

"Odessa!" Lan yelled from somewhere outside. "Haidee! We've got a problem!"

"Do we have everything we need here?" Odessa asked me.

I checked my notes one last time; they included a rough map of the temple, and some scribbled notes of anything else I felt had stood out or appeared unusual. "I think so," I said. "Let's go see what your Catseye has found."

What the Catseye had found, as it turned out, were two very dead bodies. They were lying before the broken statue. The left half of it was glowing, and something swirled beside it, like a bright hole had been suspended in the air. Odessa gasped, her hand over her mouth. "Andre," she choked out, "and Lorila."

"Janella murdered them." Lady Lan turned one of the bodies over. Smoke wafted from the lifeless form, and I spotted two holes in the center of his chest. "Firesmoke." She checked the other body. "Same method."

"But why?" I cried out.

"Why else? To activate the portal back to Aranth." She gestured at the right half of the statue. Unlike its left counterpart, the energy around it had faded. "Some spell within this statue brought me back to Aranth last time. I'm sure of it. When the shadows—" She stopped, visibly pained. "Janella's returned to report to Asteria, and made sure that we couldn't follow."

The other half of the statue was still bright, light spinning around the hole in the air as it shifted in and out of view, almost transparent. I could almost, very dimly, look past it and see the familiar shimmering of the desert sands within its center. "She did it deliberately—a parting gift, maybe. Janella's been proving to be far more dangerous than she's ever let on."

"So we have no choice but to use the other portal?"

"The rest of our group is gone as well," Noelle reported. "There's nothing left but the remains of the camp. Did she convince Gracea and the others to follow after her?"

"We'll worry about that later," Lady Lan said bleakly. "Right now, we don't have much choice. I guess the desert will be a nice change of pace from the constant rain and floods."

"It's really not," Arjun muttered.

A strange, unexpected shaking sent us all flat on our backs. I had already conjured a spinning shelf of Air before I was even

478

back on my feet, and realized that Odessa had done the same. Arjun's Howler was wild with Fire, and he looked itching to point it at someone.

"There!" Lady Lan pointed at the Abyss. To my horror, I saw that more fog was rising from inside of it. It curled into the air, and shadowed beings slowly began lifting themselves out of the gap, red eyes trained in our direction.

"But that's impossible!" I stuttered. "The world's moving! We succeeded!"

"The Abyss has not yet been closed," Odessa whispered. "We haven't killed the shadows yet. Whatever we've done, it's not enough. They want more from us. It's not over."

"Looks like the choice is out of our hands." Lady Lan gestured at the rock. "Inside, all of you! We can figure out how to fix this later—for now, we jump!"

EPILOGUE

THE WORLD SPINS, BUT WITH its churning more demons rise.

A demoness is what men call a goddess they cannot control, it is said. And we cannot control Inanna.

A great shape filled the air, towering larger than any of the hellspawn that had come birthing out of this brimstone canal. It had no eyes, but it saw us. It had no mouth but it smiled. It had no face, but its expression shifted. It had not yet completely reconstituted itself, but we knew it would soon be ready to attack again, like it had before.

Daughters, it crooned.

The portal before us sputtered, offering us the sanctuary of the desert.

It wasn't over. Inanna still hungered. Inanna still wanted her pounds of flesh. There was still some ritual yet to be completed, and what it would demand of us we didn't know, and feared.

It wasn't over, but this had to end, even if it had to end with us.

I took my twin sister's hand, and she tightened her grip in mine.

And together, we jumped.

ACKNOWLEDGMENTS

As always, to my agent, Rebecca Podos, for being my constant support and for never wavering in her belief that I am somehow a competent writer.

To the fantastic team over at HarperTeen, without which all of this would not have been possible: my editor, Stephanie Stein, who has an amazing eye for making stories shine, and who for some reason believes in this odd little book; Louisa Currigan, Jessica Berg, and Valerie Shea, who have all been painstakingly patient over my thousand and one fret-induced changes; Molly Fehr, Allison Brown, Michael D'Angelo, and Kristopher Kam for all their amazing work; and Florian Cohen for this absolutely stunning cover.

All my gratitude especially to the brilliant Jocelyn Davies, without whom this idea would not have even been possible.

Thank you also to Shealea Jenice Iral, who has been such an amazing cheerleader for this book and for everything else, and

I am so very grateful. Also to Gail Villanueva, Kara Bodegon, Isabelle Adrid, Hazel Ureta, Stef Tran, and Kate Evangelista for being my constants throughout this series. Writing had always been a solo affair for me, but thank you for taking me in. Also to Myrth Alegado and Kate Heceta, for being absolute champions!

I was old enough to remember the 1990 earthquake that hit Luzon and killed over a thousand people; decades later, I can still recall the abject terror we felt then, seeing cabinets fall over and glass break. Old enough to remember Mt. Pinatubo erupting a year earlier, the ashfall great enough to blanket places as far away as Manila, where I lived, in gray soot.

I was definitely old enough in 2006 to remember Typhoon Milenyo, known internationally as Typhoon Xangsane, which caused massive flooding, landslides, and power outages. I remember being stuck in traffic for nearly five hours when the worst of the storm hit, the call to suspend work too late for us to leave earlier, all my coworkers desperate to get away but not knowing where to go. I watched a billboard crash down along the highway, fortunately missing cars. My boyfriend's place was flooded up to the waist in rat-and-roach-infested water. Even then, he was luckier; others had to flee to their rooftops because their homes were fully submerged; they had to wait hours for help to arrive.

The Philippines is very much like Aranth. We're a country constantly beset by monsoons, and Filipinos learn early in life about tragedy through the riverwinds that flow above us, marking the path of incoming typhoons. We never know how bad it's going to get until it hits. We don't know how many of us are going to be washed away by the water until the storm passes.

I also remember other things. People returning to rescue children and pets who'd been unable to escape their houses when the waters rose without warning, as they often did. Long lines at supermarkets where people emptied the shelves of cans of food, blankets, medicine, milk formulas, and other essentials—not to hoard, but to donate to the numerous relief groups that often sprout up independently to assist victims. People using makeshift items—basins, homemade canoes, airbeds—to ferry other people to safety, sometimes at great cost. A young boy, Muelmar Magallanes, rescued his family and close to thirty people when floods overcame his village, only to be swept away and drown.

There are many other stories like these, of many other people whose names have since been lost. And when I first sat down to write this story, the idea that the country I grew up in might be so irrevocably changed—or may not even exist—in mere decades, was the incanta in my head that inspired this book and its forthcoming sequel. So many humanitarian crises are due to climate change. If you'd like to help, please do check out https://www.care.org/country/philippines to learn more.

Lastly, thank you to known environmental advocate and occasional actor Mark Alan Ruffalo, because he is an amazing person and because I can.

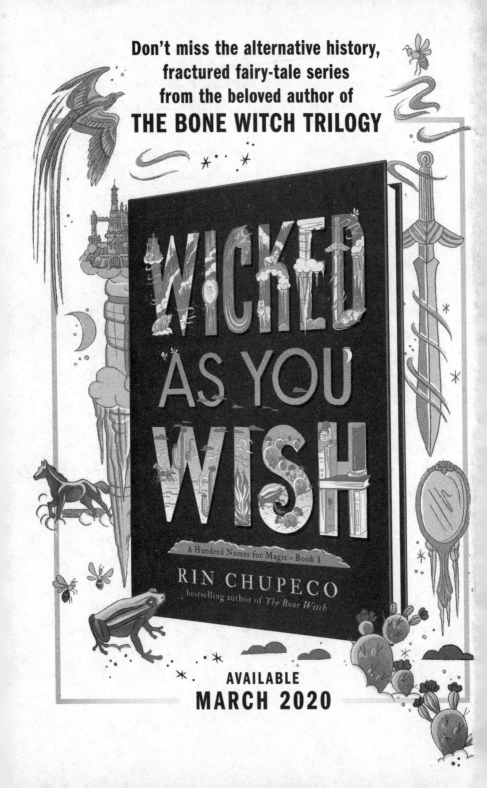